THE WHISPERING PASS
JAY OLSEN-THRIFT

NA'ROG OF NORTH

BALACH YOR

ELIMERE

PROMTHUS

THE IMALAR
WOODS

ELIMAINE

MOONYSWYN

KHERIZHAN

DAARIA

PROLOGUE

Rain fell steadily from the sky, and the ale came even steadier. Tonight was an ideal night for contracts and silent work among the gangs of Auora. Weary travelers huddled in every corner of the Pike and Pint, easy victims for a simple pickpocketing. The tavern wenches ran between the kegs and tables, filling and refilling mugs as they went.

"Are any of you lot brave enough to travel east to the lost ruins of Kherizhan to claim treasures and riches beyond your wildest imagination?" a gravelly rasp called across the tavern. The voice belonged to a man with pointed ears who stood near the fireplace. His clothes were sturdy and well-worn, the sign of a man who lived on the roads. Jette watched him from her table, nursing a mug of dark ale.

Pity we can't make any quick coin tonight, Jette thought. *But we should make a cozy bit from this job.*

"Come now. I see some able-bodied men out there! Don't you want your chance at eternal wealth?" the man continued to prattle, looking around at the rest of the patrons.

Tonight, only a small number of people in the tavern were native to the lands of Promthus, from either the city-island of Auora or the farmlands surrounding the Hourglass Lakes. Many had varying features of the other races: long pointed eared Elviri, short legged and shorter stature Imalarii, mottled skin and large fanged Barauder. Auora was a friendly enough city with its massive bridges on either side of the island, and the city's inns shared the same policies. This particular tavern usually saw more of the natives of Promthus, but that didn't mean foreigners were scarce. Jette, a middle-aged Proma herself, sat in the corner of the tavern at the same table that she usually occupied and watched the crowds as they shifted around the room, drinking and eating and generally making noise.

The patron who made the loudest noise, though, was a pointy-eared fellow spewing out one repeated line after another about Kherizhan, eternal wealth, and adventure. *Why's an Elviri so worked up over these mountains?* Jette couldn't remember when he first arrived in the inn; he seemed to just kind of spring up from the floorboards, bellowing out nonsense about some ruins hidden away in the distant southeast mountains. Lately he was in the inn almost every day trying to recruit some sorry men to go off on an "adventure" with him. *What do far away mountain ruins have to do with the city-island of Auora? Nothing at all.* Jette grimaced.

"Surely one of you wants to embark on a quest that the bards will sing of for ages."

No one seemed to care for what he was saying anyway. Most of the patrons ignored him and his ramblings. There was always one or two interested in what he was going on about, though. He would give them a rather hefty coin purse and an old map, and they would be off that very night. Days later there would be reports throughout the city of that person missing with no sign of them passing through any of the city gates or leaving from the docks. Plenty of people suspected the noisy man of being behind these disappearances, but no one had been able to prove it yet. The city watch had put out a reward for finding either the missing persons or who was behind the kidnappings. The larger gangs hadn't even pinned down where the man was from. If the Walkers or Hawks couldn't do it, then he practically had free reign over the city.

Although maybe the larger gangs don't care about this man the way the city watch does.

Jette waved down one of the serving girls and raised her mug to get a refill before standing up and raising it toward the pointy-eared fellow. *Time to get to work.* "I'll hear you out, good man."

The man turned to face Jette's direction, a satisfied grin on his face. "You want your chance at riches beyond your wildest dreams, d'you now, lass?"

The fake smile slid onto her face easily enough. "Aye. Come, join me at my table and we'll discuss this adventure."

Jette took her seat again as the man crossed the tavern floor and sat down in the chair across from her. A few patrons let out groans of relief. Out of the corner of her eye, Jette saw a small man jump out of his seat and move away from his table, laughing and raising his mug to the other fellows still seated. He stood no taller than the table itself and his mug was as large as his head. Near the front door, a hulking, hooded figure began to make its way back toward Jette's table, staying close to the wall.

My mates are moving into place. Good.

"Have you heard much about the ruins of Kherizhan?" the man asked her, folding his hands on the table. He was dressed plainly enough, but there were a few telltale signs of wealth. His belt was brand new leather dyed a dark green to match his eyes. A few ornamental beads hung in his hair, typical of an Elviri from Lithalyon. His jaw was too broad to be an Elviri, though. And his ears didn't stretch as far out as a normal Elviri's. He was mixed blood.

Curious that he's allowed in the city. Does the city watch know this man is a Provira? Jette thought. "A couple of stories. Something about moving stones and loads of gems that could make a girl rich," she said and took a sip from her mug, giving him her complete attention. Though she intended to play the man like a fiddle, she was honest about her knowledge of Kherizhan. It was a land of myth, often discussed as if it were unreachable. Unobtainable.

He chuckled and nodded, pulling out a rolled-up piece of wrinkled parchment. "Loads of gems indeed. And wouldn't it be a waste for all those gems to just lie around underground with no one to claim them?"

"Such a waste." Her eyes wandered to his hands as he unrolled the parchment to reveal a map that looked ancient. *Older than my thirty years, no doubt.* Arrows and lines were drawn on the map, all pointing to the massive gathering of mountains in the southeast corner.

"There are several different ways to get to Kherizhan, but that's not the difficult part of the journey. What's difficult is getting underground and to those gems." He traced a couple of the lines, which were pretty straightforward with their routes. "Most of the routes pass through friendly cities in either Imalar or Lithalyon where you can stock up on supplies."

Jette nodded. A few of the routes passed right by the mountains that served as a border between Promthus and Moonyswyn. That was dangerous territory to cross through with the war between the Proma, Elviri, and Provira. Beyond the recurring Provira raids into the farmlands of southern Promthus, the lands down there were full of bandits and thieves.

Only someone who was desperate or who had a death wish would travel through those lands.

"Don't fret about traveling alone, lass. One of my trusted partners will be waiting on the southwestern shores of the Hourglass Lakes, in the town of Merrioff. From there, he'll lead you the rest of the way." The man flashed a grin.

Jette nodded politely and returned the smile. The hooded figure practically hovered over the large-eared man. Nearby, the short man made his way toward her table.

"I wouldn't be going alone, sir. I have my own partners, and they would very much like to accompany me on this trip." Jette gestured to the hooded figure behind him, and to the short man who took the seat to her left.

The Provira turned to look behind his seat and jumped a little bit. "You keep strange company, lass."

"Ya'nah has been in my company for many good years. Tomlin, too. Where I go, they follow."

The small man, Tomlin, raised his mug and grinned. Tomlin was an Imalarii, as short as they came. When standing he came up to Jette's hip, which made him ideal for robberies and sleight of hand. He had thick brown hair and a hearty laugh that could fill a room. Ya'nah removed her hood and sat down to Jette's right, scowling. She was a Barauder with murky green skin and stringy black hair. Fangs jutted out from her lower jaw, curving upward along her lips. She growled quietly, watching the mixed-blood man closely behind narrowed eyes.

"You and your...company could leave on the morrow," the Provira said calmly despite his small scare with Ya'nah moments earlier. "I'll give you enough gold to get you to Merrioff in one piece. From there, you'll have to make do on your own."

Jette exchanged looks with Ya'nah and Tomlin and received nods from them both. Tomlin was quick and eager with his, while Ya'nah made a show of taking her time with her decision. Ultimately, the small team ended up with a rather plump coin purse and a map.

The Provira stood up and bowed, grinning. "Thank you for your business. I look forward to welcoming you adventurers back once you return from your expedition," he said.

Tomlin and Jette returned the smile. Jette and her partners had been planning the little scheme for a few days. It would be an excellent way of figuring out what had happened to all those missing people, as well as making some coin on the side.

Get the map, trail the man, find out if he's the one making people disappear. Not too often that my crew and I assist the fellows wearing chainmail and bearing the king's name, but if it helps the people of the streets, then it ain't a bad job. The city guard may even be generous with their reward, Jette thought as the Provira departed from their table, melting away into the crowd. *No need to tail that one for now. We'll see him again soon enough.*

Ya'nah finished off her tankard, placing it on the table none too gently. Tomlin snickered, doing the same.

"Tomorrow morning we'll set off for this Kherizhan place," Jette said, inspecting the purse. She opened it with deft hands and eyed the generous sum of gold inside.

Ya'nah growled quiet enough that only Tomlin and Jette could hear her. "I don't like this idea, Jette. We don't know what we'll be facing."

"Isn't that half the fun?" Tomlin retorted, a cheeky grin plastered on his face. The Barauder rolled her eyes and scowled and grumbled something under her breath in a language only the creatures from the Black Lakes would understand.

"Have I ever led our little pack astray?" Jette asked, her eyes shifting between the two of them. Neither of them made any comment to disagree, so she nodded and continued. "We'll leave tomorrow morning then. It's settled."

CHAPTER 1: MUNNE

The suns began to set, and the townsfolk were already releasing their floating lanterns. Tonight, they would be flying dark blue and white for the return of the Elviri army. Munne Vere'cha, Warlord of the Elviri, led her troops into the valley of Elimere on the back of her gray mare. Dark circles clung underneath her eyes, a sharp contrast to her pale skin and bright blue eyes. Her black hair was pulled back and tied to keep it out of her face. A few strands of hair fell across her cheeks. As she and her soldiers entered the town, their eyes grew brighter, and they began to smile and cheer.

Munne's latest campaign had taken longer than initially planned after two ambushes near the south edge of the Hourglass Lakes. Their supplies took the brunt of the first attack, almost as if the Provira were trying to cripple them instead of outright killing them. This set her return to Elimere back by at least two weeks. She had to gather more supplies from the Proma to the north before she could even think about crossing the Telatorr Mountains back into Elviri territory. The second ambush, though, claimed several lives of her soldiers, and Munne had to cede the supplies and land to the Provira's forces to escape safely. They were lucky to return home before the oncoming winter.

The valley of Elimere was the capital seat of the Elviri. Nestled between three towering peaks, the valley offered a plethora of natural defenses. Its large river that poured in from the north could be traced all the way to the icy bay near Rymo-tehp, serving as a link between the Elviri of today and their gods of the Eldest Days.

Tonight, the valley would be filled with celebration and remembrance. Her troops who hadn't made it back alive would be honored in the dining halls that night. Their bodies would be taken to the Hall of the Dead, where loved ones would be able to adorn them with flowers and gifts. In the morning, the disciples of Azrael would take their bodies to the forest and lay them to rest. For those who were still alive, there would be feasting, dancing, and drinking. Munne planned to escort the deceased to the Hall of the Dead, and then join the rest of her men at the main plaza where her fellow nobles had no doubt put together a magnificent event.

And I hope to miss most of it by staying at the Hall of the Dead, Munne thought as her troops passed underneath the main arch—the gateway to Elimere. The arch was really two towering trees that had been standing since the Eldest Days, their branches curved inward toward one another. Runes and protection wards had been carved into their bark over time. With winter fast approaching, gold and brown leaves fell like rain upon the road below.

The city of Elimere was the oldest city in all of Daaria. While not as large as the other cities within Elviri lands like Lithalyon or Elyr Tym, it was still beautiful and hosted many visitors during the warmer seasons. The older buildings were made from stone dating back to the Eldest Days, while the newer buildings were a blend of stone and wood. The wood, various cuts of timber and white cedar, offered contrast to the dark stone. Some of the wooden structures had been painted, to distinguish one from the other. Many of the shops and stores were painted with murals representing their crafts and trades. Elimere and Elifyn shared this tradition, while the towns in Elimaine chose to remain stark and unpainted.

Within the city the troops were greeted with clapping and cheering from the townspeople, which drowned out the rhythmic march that had kept her company for hours in the mountains. Streetlamps glowed softly all around, casting the wooden and stone buildings in warm light. Further inside the city Munne paused at a crossroads. One road led to the main plaza, and the other to the Hall of the Dead. She breathed in deeply and then led her horse to the left, stepping out of formation. Behind her were the other two members of her triple who would lead the living to the celebrations. The two Elviri urged their horses forward and the troops continued without her. From a distance, the sounds of flutes, harps, and drums drifted from the party. Munne smiled as she listened to the cheers and whoops of her troops. The walk to the Hall of the Dead would not be so boisterous.

As the last of the men and women left the crossroads toward the party, the deceased came carried in wagons led by priests of Azrael. The wagons were only present when returning home after a campaign. Scouts had been sent ahead to Elimere to let the priests of Azrael know how many caskets to prepare. They then escorted the priests to the edge of the Telatorr Mountains to meet with the troops and prepare the bodies of the dead for travel. When the troops entered the valley of Elimere, the dead had marched one last time with their brothers and sisters-in-arms.

The Hall of the Dead loomed ahead, its dark stones towering over all the other buildings in the city. The families of the deceased lined the streets, their reactions mixed. Some families were happy and prideful of their loved one's service while others wept quietly. A few men and women sang softly to themselves while others laid down flowers and branches on the road. Munne was so familiar with the landscape before her that she could paint it with her eyes closed, down to the silhouettes of the mourners lining the streets. It did nothing to quell the storm brewing within her.

As the assembly approached the sacred structure, Munne spotted her mentor and the previous Warlord, Cesa, standing amidst the crowd. Streaks of gray ran through his dark auburn hair. He wore dark blue robes tied with a crimson sash. The emblem of the army was emblazoned on the back of his robes—a barren oak tree standing before the full moon. Although it had been a long time since he served as Warlord, he still wore the garb of the Elviri army. He was much older than Munne's father, approaching his seven hundredth birthday. Cesa was the one who had taught Munne and her father everything they knew about strategy and the military. He had selected Munne to fill the role of Warlord when he stepped down close to fifty years ago. That had surprised Munne, as well as the other soldiers in her triple. Not that she lacked skill or ability, but there was much controversy behind the decision since Munne was the only child of the *Se'vi*. She was expected to take the Hunting Throne and rule over all the Elviri one day, and she would no longer be able to serve as the Warlord. Traditionally, an Elviri didn't take on multiple ranks.

The assembly reached the Hall of the Dead. The structure had been erected during the Eldest Days when the gods still roamed the land. It belonged to

Azrael, the god of war and death. Dark stones from the shores of western Eli-maine had been used in its construction, giving the Hall its solemn aura. The foyer stood tall enough that Azrael could enter in his cosmic form, nearly six stories high. It had been thousands of centuries since Azrael walked among the Elviri, but the Hall continued to awe and inspire.

Munne's horse ascended the stairs in front of the Hall of the Dead, and she was pulled out of her thoughts. Outside the Hall's doors were several priests and acolytes ready to receive the caskets of the dead. It took the strength of four priests to open each door, revealing the foyer within. It was a plain room with sparse furnishings besides the hundreds of lit candles. Their glow filled the room with light, which spilled onto the stairs outside.

Azrael's light washes over me, Munne thought with the smallest of smiles. Her mare let out a quiet snort—perhaps her own form of prayer.

A man dressed in black hooded robes emerged from within the Hall and approached Munne and her mare. He bowed his head and spread his arms.

"Welcome, Vere'cha. Today you bring the fallen ones of your army," he said.

Munne bowed her head in turn and extended her hand down to the high priest, Valanir. "Today they will meet Azrael and walk through his quiet fields. They will rest."

The high priest took her hand and gripped it tightly. His skin felt like warm leather beneath her touch. It brought her some small comfort. After a mo-ment, he released her hand and said, "Today begins their final watch. Their loved ones will say their final goodbyes while you and yours stand vigil."

Munne turned her mare around. The wagons had stopped at the base of the stairs, where they would be unloaded by the priests and carried inside. Within the Hall, the acolytes would lead the preparations for the bodies. They would place a candle and smoothstone on each casket, so that tomorrow the families of the deceased could paint their family sigils on the smoothstones. The stones would be placed on the ground above the caskets in the forest when they were laid for their final rest.

There were thirty-six caskets tonight.

A small gust of wind blew across the stairs as Munne gazed upon the caskets before her. Each of these Elviri gave their lives to her campaign in the war against the Provira. They were good Elviri who had hundreds of years left in their lives—hundreds of years to experience love and joy and be with their families. The bloody war had cost them their lives, and sorrow for so many others. Munne gritted her teeth, her hand tightening on the reins of her mare. There were thirty-six bodies before her, and yet the war with the Provira was no closer to ending.

How many more had to die before those cursed half-breeds would stop?

"Tonight, they begin their final watch." the high priest called out to the assembly, his deep voice carrying on the wind.

The acolytes and priests echoed his words. "Tonight, they begin their final watch." Slowly, quietly, they lifted the caskets and carried them up the stairs and into the Hall.

Munne swallowed, finding the action difficult, and she gently urged her mare to the side. Each of the thirty-six deceased Elviri passed by her and the high priest. Her gaze lingered on each casket, the knot in her throat tightening. This ceremony never got easier. She only hoped she wouldn't attend another one any time soon.

After the last casket passed through the threshold, the doors were pulled shut with a quiet *boom*. The steps darkened and Munne felt the loss of the candlelight. The dead would need their preparations before their loved ones could see them. The priests would instruct the acolytes on how to prepare the bodies when their caskets would be opened to their families. Depending on the injuries, the bodies would be covered in a silk fabric. Perfumes and burial paint would be applied. All thirty-six Elviri had died a warrior's death, so they would be marked with the traditional dark blue paint on their lips and the white stripes across their cheeks.

"Warlord Vere'cha, may I please accompany you to the stables?" Cesa's raspy voice cut through Munne's thoughts like a knife.

She turned her head to look at him, unaware that he had walked up the stairs to stand beside her. The streets of the town had emptied out as people headed toward the main plaza to celebrate with the living.

"Of course, please," Munne murmured.

Cesa patted her mare's neck gently, and then the two set off, his smooth oak cane tapping the ground with each step. He had sustained a grievous leg wound toward the end of his tenure as Warlord and now relied on his cane. Munne ensured her pace was slow enough to not strain Cesa too much.

"You kept your armor on for the parade?" Cesa asked, looking Munne over. "I would have thought you'd want to be out of that the minute you reached the valley."

"It wouldn't have been good form to dress down for the ceremony of the dead," Munne answered, suddenly feeling self-conscious. She looked down at her steel blue and silver armor. Although it wasn't fresh, there were bloodstains spattered across the breastplate and greaves.

Perhaps it would have been better to change into some dress robes. That would have required time away from the parade and her men, though, and Munne wasn't comfortable with that. She didn't want to drag the ceremony on.

Cesa said nothing in response. They continued to walk in silence, and Munne was more than comfortable with that. Cesa might have been the only person who didn't expect her to speak tonight. She would miss that when she joined the rest of her men at the plaza.

"How were things here while we were gone?" It was Munne's turn to ask questions. She was supposed to have returned three weeks prior and had been without communications until a couple of days before she arrived at the valley.

"Your father continues to keep the peace," Cesa said thoughtfully. Munne knew he wasn't telling the full story, but it would be difficult to do so in such an open place. "As you should be doing tonight. Enjoy the peace."

Munne laughed. "Tactful as ever, *sa'vani*. Will you be joining us in the celebration tonight?"

"I could be convinced to have a glass of wine or two," Cesa muttered, smiling.

She laughed as they approached the stables closest to the Hall of the Dead. Munne dismounted from her horse and handed the reins to one of the stable hands, a young woman.

"Then let us have that glass of wine, or two... or three..." Munne grinned and came around to Cesa's left side, locking arms with him. The two laughed together and walked back toward the main plaza.

Night had fallen on the valley in earnest, and the homes and businesses were lit up in warm torchlight. Mimicking the three mountain peaks that surrounded Elimere, there were three structures that towered over the rest of the town—the Hall of the Dead, the Meeting Spire, and the Manor of the *Se'vi*. The Hall stood behind them, and ahead to the southeast was the Meeting Spire. It stood like a shadowed giant on the horizon and blended in with the night sky, the light of the town unable to touch its higher floors. To the northwest was the manor, Munne's home. Even from a distance she could see lights from all four floors. Unlike the other two imposing structures, the manor was built from pale wood much like the rest of the valley. It was flanked by two waterfalls, where the river split and tumbled into the valley. The main plaza where all festivities and celebrations occurred was near the center of Elimere, in between the three peaks and three towers.

As Munne and Cesa approached the main plaza, music filled the air. Members of the professional orchestra played joyous songs to welcome their troops home. Several Elviri danced, bringing much cheer to those seated at the feast tables. Blue and white flowers were strung up along the outer pillars, and lanterns hung in between. Tables lined the outer edges of the plaza on three sides with the orchestra taking up the fourth edge. Platters and jugs of food and drink filled the tables. Munne easily picked her soldiers out of the crowd because of their armor, and she saw that they were all full of joy and excitement. Every homecoming was like this, and she was glad for it. Her soldiers deserved moments of happiness amidst the war.

"Come, I think I see a couple of spaces we could sit at." Cesa led Munne toward two empty chairs at a table further away from the orchestra. They would be able to hear each other speaking while sitting there.

Munne pulled one of the chairs back for Cesa before sitting down in her own chair. Cesa placed his cane against the table and reached for one of the decanters of wine. As he poured into a nearby glass, he nodded appreciatively, watching the golden liquid fill the glass.

"Ah, good. I'm glad they brought out the gold from Elifyn. It's always a joyous celebration when they do." Cesa put the decanter down and drank deep from the glass. Munne laughed and poured herself a glass of the golden wine as well. She raised the cup to Cesa who laughed in turn, and they clinked their glasses together.

"To another homecoming," Munne said proudly.

"Aye, to another homecoming," Cesa replied.

They both drank from their cups, and then assembled small plates of food. Munne was starving. Her trip to the valley had taken up much of the day, which only left time for small provisions on the trails. She had been looking forward to the return party all day, for she knew there would be ample amounts of flavorful food—a *much* better alternative to trail provisions. Munne plucked a handful of sliced fruits, tore off a section of warm bread, and managed to get some roasted meats on her plate as well. She ate, savoring every bite. It was good to be home.

"Welcome home, Lady Vere'cha!" someone cried out from a nearby table.

Munne looked up from her food and raised her glass, a smile on her face. She made eye contact with a young Elviri man at the next table over. He didn't have a suit of armor on, which meant he was one of the townsfolk. Seated next to him was an archer, a large smile plastered all over her face. Munne did not recognize her immediately; she must have been from Elifyn. Was she reuniting with a brother, or possibly a lover?

"It is good to be back, as I'm sure your companion knows!" Munne called back, taking another sip from her cup. She needed to go slower with her wine; she had many more welcomes and cheers to exchange before the night was through.

She scanned the crowd, looking for some more familiar faces. Sitting near the orchestra on the left were members of the royal court. She spotted her friend Gilareana, a brown-haired blue-eyed beauty, sharing her cups with some scribes and noblemen. The men hung on her every word and scrambled to pour her some more wine when she finished with her glass.

Ah, the telltale signs of suitors. Perhaps Gilareana will make a match tonight? Munne knew that her friend loved to play the game, but wasn't so sure she was ready to pick just yet. Being the daughter of one of the oldest families in Elimere, there was no end of proposals and gifts from other noble houses. Gilareana had relished every moment of it for the past fifty or so years. She would be expected to make a match before her three hundredth birthday.

Munne hoped that she would find similar joy in courting when she stopped to take the time for it.

Seated by the end of Gilareana's suitors was Elvarin, the Lorelord of the Elviri. Elvarin and Munne were close in age, and they were both appointed to their respective seats around the same time which formed a tight bond between the two. Elvarin's position didn't carry as much gossip or turmoil though since his ascension had been completely expected. The Lorelord over-saw the preservation of the godsites, and the continued improvements of the Elviri studies. Elvarin's parents were some of the most elite scribes in Elimere, so he was raised as a potential replacement for Lorelord from birth. The previ-ous Lorelord, Sariel Umenta, ultimately picked Elvarin after rigorous testing and competing with other young scribes and archivists.

Elvarin was trying to reach over one of Gilareana's suitors and place some sliced fruit on his plate. The suitor threw his head back in laughter and nearly knocked skulls with Elvarin. The Lorelord had noticed just a split moment before the collision and was able to adjust himself to avoid the collision. Munne thought about going over to rescue him when two people approached her table—her mother and father. Her father, Huntaran, was a scribe before he became *Se'vi*, and he was humble about his position despite being the most powerful Elviri in all the land. Even though her father wasn't a tall man, Munne felt like he was a statue towering over her as he stood beside the table. She met his eyes and forced a polite smile, thankful that she'd been able to get some drink in her before their meeting.

Huntaran's lips curled upward in return. "Welcome home, daughter."

"Thank you, Father. Your army was successful in their latest campaign. We have successfully kept the southern border of Promthus secured for the Proma." It was customary for the Warlord to deliver a report to the *Se'vi* upon returning home. Usually that custom occurred the morning after the celebration.

"Thank you for overseeing their safe return. I will leave you to your cele-bration. We will discuss this more in the morning." He was content with her return, but Munne knew her father had more to say. She would have to wait until morning to learn what it was he had to say.

"We're glad that you've returned home safely, Munne," Munne's mother, Telhira, said firmly, a genuine smile on her face. "We hope you enjoy the celebration tonight. You and your troops have earned it."

Telhira was a beauty, even in her older years, with her raven black hair and bright gray eyes. Her mother was a painter and sculptor, originally hailing from Lithalyon to the south. She had brought warmth and mirth to the valley of Elimere when she married Huntaran.

"Thank you, Mother." Munne reached out and grasped Telhira's hand. The two stayed like that for a moment before Huntaran locked arms with Munne's mother.

He nodded to Munne a curt goodbye before turning to address Cesa. "Cesa, it's good to see you. Hopefully, you're finding the celebration to be enjoyable."

Cesa raised his glass to Huntaran. "Aye, all can see that lady Telhira and the other noblewomen poured their love and kindness in the preparations of this celebration. The troops look pleased with this warm reception."

Huntaran nodded to Cesa as well before escorting Telhira away. Munne looked at Cesa, waiting for him to give a subtle nod that her parents had left.

As soon as they were out of earshot, Munne let out an exasperated sigh. "Why must he address me like that here?"

"What, like you're the overseer of the entire Elviri army?" Cesa raised an eyebrow, amused.

"Like I'm still a child." Munne took another sip of her wine. The blend of grapes and spices invigorated her. "He never addressed you like that at these celebrations."

"We were fortunate enough to not need these kinds of celebrations so often." Cesa's words darkened as he drank from his own glass.

Munne held her glass in front of her mouth so that the others couldn't see her grimace. Cesa's tenure as Warlord had been quiet. There had never more than a border scuffle. Munne often went back and forth thinking that the Provira *conflict*, as the Proma lords call it, was chalked up to her failure to hold the borders. Cesa had reassured her that it wasn't her fault. The Provira had always been the rowdy type, but it wasn't until Munne became Warlord that the Provira became bloodthirsty. They began attacking towns on the borders between Moonyswyn and the rest of the realm. Several years prior, they had been exiled to the rainforest of Moonyswyn after the Proma couldn't tolerate their behavior any longer. Munne thought the Proma would have realized that sooner after the Elviri had banished the Provira from their lands.

The Provira were half-breeds. One parent was Proma, the other Elviri. Most of the unions between races happened in Elifyn to the south. Elifyn shared no borders with Elimaine or the rest of the Elviri lands, so it only made sense that they became close with their Proma neighbors. The Provira didn't take on the grace and sensibilities of their Elviri heritage. Instead, they favored the chaotic nature of the Proma. Munne's father had been the one to issue the decree that the Provira couldn't live in Elviri lands anymore. They had caused much destruction to the forests of Elifyn, and that couldn't be tolerated. They fled to Promthus to the city-island of Auora. Twenty-eight years later, the Proma issued their own decree that the Provira were no longer welcome in their lands. They left for Moonyswyn, the rainforests of the south. Shortly after that, the Provira *conflict* began.

"You look like you could use some fresher air, Vere'cha," a new voice said, drawing Munne back to the plaza and the surrounding celebrations.

In front of her, a handsome Elviri man smirked at her. His dark brown hair was braided, and his gray eyes glowed with affection. He was a welcome sight after the earlier ceremonies and her father's visit. She felt her dour mood lifting, the warmth in her stomach spreading throughout the rest of her body.

"What air could be fresher than sitting outside in good company?" Cesa remarked, leaning back in his chair.

The warmth reached Munne's cheeks. "I always liked standing near the fountains," she said quietly, placing her wine glass on the table.

"Shall we, then?" The handsome Elviri walked around the table to stand by Munne's side.

"Laralos, you know your Warlord should be present at this celebration with her soldiers," Cesa chided the man and turned to face him.

"*Sa'vani*, surely I can slip away unnoticed for a few minutes?" Munne asked sweetly, placing her hand on Cesa's knee. "To get some fresher air?"

Cesa looked her over and tightened his lips before smiling. "I should be able to keep you unnoticed for a few minutes. But nothing longer."

Munne grinned and practically leapt to her feet. She grabbed Laralos's hand and snuck down one of the roads away from the main plaza.

"I'm sorry I couldn't rescue you sooner," Laralos whispered, mindful of the people making their way toward the festivities. "I had to wait until after your father saw you. He would have been displeased otherwise."

Munne laughed, guiding Laralos toward one of the smaller plazas. A tall fountain carved in the likeness of the goddess Belleol stood in the middle of the plaza. Her hands were open as if reading a book, water pouring from them into the pool below. The sound of splashing echoed throughout the plaza. A pleasant breeze blew through the plaza, carrying the mild scent of spilling water by Munne. She had missed Laralos dearly and was happy to have a few moments alone with her friend.

"How have you been, *ebilin*?" Laralos murmured, taking Munne's other hand. He tenderly squeezed her hands, and stepped closer, his head on level with hers. Laralos was only slightly taller than Munne, but when she wore her boots, they were the same height.

Many years ago, her stomach would have pleasantly twisted at hearing him call her *ebilin*. Tonight, she felt uncomfortable at hearing that term of endearment. He still clung to their past when they had been sweethearts. Munne and Laralos had grown up together at court in Elimere. Both served their required time in the Elviri army during their lifepath rotations when they were young. Their paths diverged when Munne enlisted as a regular soldier in the army, and Laralos opted to remain with his parents in the forests of Elimaine. Their paths only crossed when she was at home, and he was visiting the valley. Munne knew the distance and years did little to quell Laralos's feelings for her, but she couldn't say the same. Her rise in rank had made it difficult for her to adapt to "peaceful life" as Cesa had phrased it. It didn't help that she experienced nightmares during her latest campaign in Promthus.

"I've made worse journeys before." she replied and feigned a smile. Her pleasant mood had vanished, but she didn't want to offend her friend. "The weather hasn't begun to turn yet, so we were fortunate enough to pass through the mountains without snow."

"Aside from the return journey, Vere'cha." The smile fell from Laralos's face. The tenderness in his voice had been replaced with concern.

Munne couldn't keep her smile either. Her grip on his hands slackened, and she avoided meeting his gaze. She wondered when the Hall of the Dead would be reopened, and she would be able to stand vigil over her dead soldiers, avoiding questions she didn't want to answer would be a lot easier when she wasn't allowed to speak.

"I'm home for now. With winter approaching soon, I'll need to decide who will be stationed at the foot of the mountains, and who will spend the season with the Proma," Munne said. She was suddenly cold, despite her armor being padded for the oncoming winter.

Munne felt Laralos looking her over. "Are you thinking about joining one of those divisions?" His voice was soft but distant.

"I'll go wherever I'm needed." She chose her words carefully, intentionally keeping them vague.

"I hope you will take some time for yourself in these coming weeks." Laralos squeezed her hands again, drawing her attention back to him. "You need rest, especially if you don't know where your path will take you."

Munne offered him another smile, but it didn't reach her eyes. She brought his hands up to her lips and kissed them. "Come on. I don't want Cesa taking the blame for my disappearance." She turned and started walking back toward the main plaza, Laralos's hands entwined with hers.

"Maybe next time you'll stay with me a bit longer?" Laralos asked, but his voice was little more than an echo in her ears.

As they returned to the plaza, Munne saw the high priest approach from the opposite side. He waited for the orchestra to finish playing their song. She glanced at Laralos before pulling her hands away and returning to her seat next to Cesa. Her mentor's cheeks were rosy underneath the light of the lanterns, and he had a grin on his face. Munne placed a hand on his shoulder and squeezed, a silent notice that she had returned. He jolted backward, his drink sloshing around in his hand.

"The other members of your triple were looking for you." Cesa attempted to whisper, but the drink made his voice louder than he intended. "I told them you'd be with the priests after the doors opened."

"Thank you, *sa'vani*, I'll be sure to find them later," Munne replied, taking a seat next to him. She grabbed a golden apple slice and nibbled on it.

As the orchestra finished playing, the high priest walked to the middle of the plaza. The dancers moved toward the edge of the pavilion, and the crowd quieted. Munne's father and three other Elviri followed the high priest. She recognized them as the other chieftains of the Elviri lands. To the left of Huntaran was the chieftain of Elimaine, Kieron. He stood taller than her father, his light brown hair tied in a simple braid. He wore a dark blue robe that matched Cesa's with the oak-and-moon emblem on the back, the silver sash across his shoulder indicating his senior rank. Kieron held the third highest rank in the army just after Munne and her father. She alternated leading campaigns with him and a few other high-ranking generals. Kieron and her father were close, and he acted like a second father to her.

The other two Elviri were the twin chieftains of Elifyn, Caedwyn and Fael-wyn. The twins had pale blond hair and stood at the same height as Huntaran. Caedwyn, the female twin, wore a blue silk dress with silver trimming and detail. Faelwyn complemented his sister, wearing a silver robe with blue trimming and detail. The twins appeared much younger than their actual age. Most Elviri who spent their days in Elifyn appeared younger than their age. Munne had spent a fair amount of time with the twin chieftains in Elifyn during her lifepath rotation. They taught her much about the arts, something Munne found very peculiar and fascinating. She enjoyed the murals of the gods that were housed in one of the museums in Elifyn.

The three Elviri provinces were vastly different in their professions. Elimere was both the capital of the Elviri lands and its own province, serving as the trading hub and political center for the Elviri. To the west and south of Elimere were the expansive forests of Elimaine. Loggers and hunters popu-lated many of its villages, with its main city, Elyr Tym, serving as the head-quarters for the army. Many godsites were in Elimaine, so the Paladins of the Gods, a sect of the army, were charged with preserving and maintaining them. Elifyn, the third province, was the center of art and beauty. During the Eldest Days, the goddess Lithua chose Lithalyon, the capital city of Elifyn, as her seat, and it was there that she taught the mortal Elviri how to paint and sing.

It was not uncommon for all the chieftains to be in Elimere at the same time, but the purpose for their current visit set Munne on edge. They had gathered to aid in the preparations for Huntaran's descension next year. That meant they would be spending more time with her, ensuring she was prepared to become—

"Elviri of all provinces, I welcome you home," the high priest said loudly to all present. Silence filled the plaza. All attention was on the high priest and the four chieftains standing behind him. "Tonight, we mourn the loss of our brethren. They watched over us in life, and so they shall in death. Please join me tonight in celebrating their time with us on the mortal plane and prepare them for continuing their lives on the other side."

He lifted his left hand in the air and raised two fingers to point toward the moonlit sky. The four chieftains followed suit. Munne stood and repeated the familiar gesture. Soon, all the Elviri at the plaza were standing and raising their left hands in the air. The sign was symbolic of pointing the way to the other side where the deceased would walk with the gods.

The orchestra started playing a new song, this one somber and melancholic. Munne lowered her hand. Her feet carried her around the table and toward the high priest. Any warmth or cloudy vision she may have had from her drink cleared up almost immediately. As she approached, he lowered his own hand and turned his gaze toward her. Munne felt the attention shifting to her. She bowed before the high priest and the chieftains and extended a hand to the priest. He took her hand, and the two walked toward the edge of the plaza in the direction of the Hall of the Dead. The chieftains followed, and Munne was sure most of the party would follow as well. It was customary for everyone to flood the Hall when the doors first opened to pay their respects and show their support for the families of the deceased.

The walk to the Hall of the Dead felt very much like the first, except the people followed behind her now.

Slowly, now. Don't rush.

One of the first times she led this kind of parade, she had walked too fast, and Cesa wouldn't let her hear the end of it the next day. Ever since, Munne took every care to set a slow pace. She found that it gave her time to reflect on the events leading up to the parade and figure out what to say to the families of the deceased. Cesa set the standard for all Warlords to come to speak to each family the morning after the preparations. He had provided the families with words of reassurance and comfort. Cesa was different from previous Warlords in that he cared for each individual soldier. He took the time to meet each one, and spent a little bit of time personally training each of them when they were first recruited. He even acquainted himself with the youngest Elviri as they underwent their lifepath rotations. It was because of Cesa's time with her that Munne decided she wanted to join the army.

The doors to the Hall were already open. Light spilled out from within. There seemed to be more candles than before. Munne and the high priest climbed the stairs, hands still clasped together. They passed through the doors and stopped before the main chamber. One of the priests handed the high priest a large lit candle. He let go of Munne's hand to receive it before turning and passing it to her. With this candle, it was her duty as Warlord to light the candles at each casket, to guide their spirits to the next life.

Munne took the time to look at each casket before she lit the candle. The candles were mixed with dark blue dye, reserved for deceased soldiers and paladins. All the caskets were open now and the bodies of the dead decorated for the afterlife. Munne recognized every body. Each face she looked at had the traditional warrior's makeup applied. Their lips were painted a deep blue, and a white stripe crossed their cheeks. Gray smoothstones had been placed on their chests, awaiting decoration.

She knelt before the candle and lowered hers to the wick. Flames crept from one wick to the other, and the blue candle was alight. She kissed her two fingers and gently pressed them against the casket. "I'm sorry, Kerireth."

She climbed back to her feet, gripping the candle with both hands again. Thirty-five more to go.

When she left Elimaine, she had left with close to one hundred soldiers. This specific campaign was supposed to be simple reinforcements, and to ensure the Proma had secured their southern border. It wasn't supposed to be a bloody campaign. Munne hadn't anticipated the ambush on their supply train, or the battle at the border. Her troops had been split up, and that was their downfall. Before they could regroup and figure out where the Provira had attacked from, the damage had already been done. They only attacked to destroy the supplies. Munne was forced to return north and gather more. Their second trip was successful, but upon returning they learned that one of the three outposts had been entirely overrun. In the ensuing battle, thirty-six of Munne's soldiers lost their lives, and she was forced to leave. They didn't even have a battle priest with them.

Munne apologized to each body. If she had thought things through, perhaps left a portion of her forces at the outposts, they wouldn't have lost. Or perhaps they wouldn't have lost as many. But that was in the past, and all Munne could do was apologize. Apologize, and avenge them.

As Munne finished with the last body and candle, she walked to the end of the Hall and then turned to face her fallen troops. Her grip on the candle had tightened, and her knuckles were whitened.

"High Priest Valanir, I'm ready to begin the vigil," Munne murmured. "The families may enter."

The high priest nodded and walked to the doors, leaving Munne to stand at the head of her troops. From afar, Munne saw the high priest welcoming people in. Slowly, the crowds filled the Hall, standing over the caskets. Men and women wept over the bodies, whispering goodbye to their friends, loved ones, and children. Elviri from all three provinces were in the Hall tonight. Those from Elimere and Elifyn were dressed in beautiful mourning gowns and robes, embroidered with family crests. Those from Elimaine wore dark tunics and dresses. The Elifyn folk were placing various finery in the caskets like swatches of silk, musical instruments, or small paintings. Caskets belonging to Elimaine were filled with beautiful animal hides, short bows, and other arms. Some of the poorer families had nothing to place in their loved ones' caskets, and so they sang quiet hymns and painted beautiful runes on their smoothstones.

Munne allowed her own tears to fall. Her heart ached for every person in the Hall that evening. She silently vowed to do whatever it took to end this war with the Provira. Her vigil had begun. She would stand in the Hall for a few hours before the next person to stand vigil would replace her. She suspected that Kieron may be one of those people since many of the deceased were from Elimaine. He would stand over them as both general and chieftain.

After her vigil, she would retire to her suite in her father's manor, which housed the *Se'vi,* his family, and other families of the royal court.

Munne allowed herself to look elsewhere in the Hall. She visited the Hall of the Dead too often, but it always humbled her to look upon the statues of the gods. Behind her was the statue of Azrael, whom she knew very intimately. As the god of death and war, most of her prayers went to him. She didn't turn around to look upon him, but she did whisper a quiet prayer to him. His statue emulated his mortal form and towered over her, as did all the other statues. He held a claymore in his hands, the tip touching the ground between his feet. In this Hall, his likeness wore a simple robe and no shoes to symbolize his humbleness of escorting the dead to the afterlife. The claymore had runes carved into it that Munne had memorized the translation of. *Rest with ease in this Hall, for the hardship of mortality is temporary, and I am eternal.* All Elviri were guided to the afterlife by Azrael, even if they didn't live a warrior's life.

To the left of Azrael was his wife, Aeona, the goddess of life. Her eyes were closed, and her hands were held out, palms open. The Elviri prayed to her for good health and long life.

Next to her was Karonos, the god of justice. He held a scale with both hands, his gaze firm and decisive. Karonos had been the first Writlord of the Elviri, the figurehead of law and justice in their society. Munne had a strained relationship with Karonos. She tried to humble herself, but she often felt that he didn't hear her prayers when she asked for justice in this war.

Beside him was Belleol, goddess of knowledge. Like the fountain statue, she stood with her hands cupped, as if holding a book. It was commonly believed that Belleol had the gift of foresight in addition to her thirst for knowledge. Munne knew of small communities in Elifyn who worshiped Belleol in that aspect and performed divinations in her name. She always wondered if she should reach out to these communities and see if any would be willing to assist her with the war but worried if Azrael would disapprove of that idea.

At the end of the left side was the statue of Lithua, goddess of love. Her arms were crossed over her chest, hands resting on her shoulders. Lithua was often described as the most mortal of the gods. She would regularly commune with mortals and celebrate different occasions with them. It was her festival of love, Ebala, that was celebrated by other races, not just the Elviri.

On Azrael's right stood Ceyo, the ruler of the gods. Normally she was at the head of all portraits or statues of the gods if they were all present. In buildings that were devoted to one specific god, she always stood on their right, as was the case in the Hall of the Dead. Ceyo had a longsword in her right hand pointed to the ground. She held up her left hand level with her head, pointing two fingers toward the ceiling. Munne prayed to Ceyo for guidance almost as often as she did to Azrael. Ceyo had been the reluctant leader of the gods, and Munne sympathized with that in a way that scared her. She feared becoming the next *Se'vi* because she felt that she hadn't earned it. Sometimes it seemed that only Ceyo understood how she felt, so Munne would often make the pilgrimage to Ceyo's godsite on the edge of the valley. Perhaps she would make that pilgrimage again before winter's first frost set in.

To the right of Ceyo was Nole, the messenger god, holding a lantern. Munne couldn't remember if she had prayed to him before taking the first round of supplies to those outposts. She cursed herself regardless, feeling as though she failed one of her sacred duties as a Warlord. She wouldn't make that mistake again.

Next to Nole was a statue of Vyn, the god of change. He wore a simple garb, which was often the depiction of him. Vyn was the least regal of the gods, and he was also the last one to walk on the mortal plane. It was when Vyn disappeared from the world that the beginning of the second era, Second Sun, began. It was a common belief among the Elviri that Vyn became the second sun in the sky, giving the second era of time its name. Everyone had their own beliefs on what caused the second sun to rise in the sky. Munne wasn't certain what she believed in after spending much time with diplomats from the other races. She took comfort in the idea that one of her gods was still so close to her, though, so she never put much thought into it.

The last statue on the right was of Eloe, goddess of the harvest. She was the twin sister of Nole. She stood shorter than the other gods and was often depicted as younger than them as well. She fell in love with the second son of the first *Se'vi*, Huntlé. When they wed, Ceyo allowed Huntlé to ascend to godhood, and he became the god of the hunt. The Hall of the Dead was one of the oldest structures in Elimere, and it predated the ascension of Huntlé. He didn't have a statue in this building, so people would stand before Eloe's statue when praying to him. Munne often wondered if Huntlé was always destined to ascend to godhood, or if it was an act of spontaneity like the Elviri-Asaszi wars had been.

Munne looked down at the candle, beads of wax slowly rolling down its length. She swore to herself that she would visit the nearby godsites within the week. She had much reflection to do, and the time away from others would help ease her mind.

The townspeople began slipping out of the Hall and returned to the celebration. Several families stayed, not yet finished with their goodbyes. Some people entered the Hall for the first time that evening and waited for the crowds to pass before giving their goodbyes. Munne watched them all come and go for three hours. No one approached her, as was customary. Those who stood vigil didn't speak with the families that night. That would happen in the morning, during the ceremony where the priests left the valley to lay the deceased to rest in the forests of Elimaine.

A man named Saendys relieved Munne at the end of her vigil. He had been one of the higher-ranking soldiers in the latest campaign and oversaw most of the soldiers who lost their lives. Munne offered her hand to him, and they grabbed hold of each other's arms in mutual respect. She passed him the candle with her other hand, and he took it. He nodded, and they switched spots. Saendys let go of her arm, but she grabbed his hand before it fell to his side. She squeezed gently, looking him in the eye—a silent promise that all would be well. She knew he felt as though he were responsible for the number of caskets in the Hall. They had argued at length over whose fault it had been, but neither was willing to blame the other. They ultimately decided to share their guilt, and Munne had promised Saendys a trip to one of the local taverns after their return.

Munne walked down the Hall, no longer bound by any ceremonial obligations. The tearstains on her cheeks had dried, but her eyes felt weary and in need of rest. She looked into every casket now filled with gifts and treasures from loved ones. The smoothstones had been painted with many different colors and symbols. No one stopped her during her walk, and for that she was thankful. Cesa may have been a master at comforting words, but she wasn't. She needed more time to muster the courage to talk to the families. She wanted to apologize to them all, but she knew she would break down if she did. They didn't need a weak Warlord; they needed a strong Warlord who would guide them through this turmoil.

Outside the Hall of the Dead, the celebration continued. Music echoed throughout the streets. People were dancing and laughing, enjoying time with one another. Munne avoided the main plaza and took the quieter roads back to her father's manor. She hoped the exhaustion from returning home would keep the nightmares at bay tonight.

CHAPTER 11: RAY

Running the streets was like a game. Rule number one was to never get caught. There were two players in this game—"eyes" and "hands". For the hands that did the work, it was difficult to stay hidden without looking too suspicious. Fights happened on the regular, either to acquire goods or defend territory from rival gangs. Hands that got dirty tended to stay dirty, and that was a crime on this little island of a city. These were the lessons instilled upon Ray by the lieutenants.

It was easier for the "eyes" to get lost in a crowd. They were supposed to simply watch for any change in behavior, any disruption in the pattern. As long as the eyes weren't caught staring for too long, it was much easier to stay hidden than the hands.

That evening, Ray was searching the marketplace for any sort of shift in the day-to-day occurrences of the merchants. Whispers were stirring in the streets that there was a new seller of athra, whose strain was more effective than what was currently circulating through the city. Of course, with stronger effects came a more lethal outcome. If those whispers got louder, the city guards might pick up on it, and then there would be more trouble on everyone's. It was Ray's job to find the whisperers and then relay their messages back to Naro, so he could handle it before anything escalated.

Naro was the leader of her gang, the Syrael Walkers. He looked out for the people of the streets, protecting them from any harm, be it the city guards or a deadly strain of athra. The crown hunted for Naro's head, accusing him of being a gang lord, murdering several members of the city guard, and trafficking drugs throughout the city. No one could track him down, however. By the time the guardsmen caught word of his whereabouts and raided the place, there was no trace of Naro to be found. He could make anyone disappear, including himself, never to be found again.

Ray wandered around the marketplace, observing the various stalls and watching the merchants interact with the passing crowds. The two suns crawled lower into the sky, casting long golden rays of light onto the streets. Some vendors began packing up their belongings and close their stalls for the evening, while others continued to push their products on passers-by, desperate to make those last few coins for the night. Nothing seemed out of the ordinary tonight. At least, not out on the streets.

She decided to walk over to the Silken Mask, a nearby brothel She intended on meeting Laurel, one of the girls there, and find out if she knew anything about the new strand of athra. Laurel was the one who tipped Naro off about the athra in the first place, so it was possible she had gathered some new information in the past couple of days. She had taken a personal interest in this latest find with the athra, because one of the other girls in the brothel had fallen victim to the drug barely a fortnight ago. It had been easy enough for her to lie to her boss and dispose of the bodies, but it left her wounded and grieving for one of her own. Laurel was very persuasive with her talents, and she kept secrets better than anyone else in Auora. Better than most, anyway. Only a handful of people knew that she was connected to Naro, and those people were sworn to secrecy under threat of a punishment far worse than death.

Ray passed by the entrance to the brothel and instead turned down an alley that was connected to the many backways and exits from several other buildings nearby. It was a way for the men and women who visited the brothel to escape into the night without being caught by peeping neighbors or jealous troublemakers.

Laurel's room was on the second story of the brothel with a window facing the alley. It was relatively easy to climb up the wall now that the two suns were down. Ray's dark cloak concealed her against the stone wall to any wanderers below. The soles of her leather boots gripped the various holes and bumps in the stonework, allowing for her to climb up with relative ease. She pulled her body up high enough for her knuckles to rap against the glass window, the dark red curtains obstructing her view into the room. She quickly lowered herself back down, her gloved fingers gripping onto the windowsill. She quieted her breathing and waited for a response.

Her arms began to tremble after a few moments. She heard the sounds of the streets in the distance, which made it hard to determine what was happening in Laurel's room.

Probably too busy with a client, Ray thought.

She inhaled sharply and climbed back down into the alley. Naro and Laurel had an agreement that one of the Walkers could visit her once per week, and Ray had already visited three days ago. Perhaps it was for the best that Laurel hadn't come to the window. She shook her arms and left the alley. It was time for her to return to one of the Walkers' safehouses down in the Docks District.

Auora was a city on an island as old as time itself, and it was precariously built around the stone hill in the center. The castle where the royal family lived was on a smaller island adjacent to the city-island with a bridge connecting the two. The city was arranged in tiers, starting from the Docks District on the very bottom and rising all the way up to what the citizens called the Sky District where the wealthy and elite made their homes and went about their lives choosing to know nothing about what was below. Many buildings were carved into the stone itself. Others were stacked on top of each other to make the best use of space.

Her destination was a warehouse, one of the oldest buildings on the eastern edge of the island, that looked out to the Telatorr Mountains and Castle Auora. The Walkers had owned the building for close to nine years at this point—one of their oldest hideouts in the city. Their hideouts were always moving, always changing, to avoid detection. There was also no telling which Walker would be staying at a given hideout much to Ray's disappointment. Sometimes she chose to wander the streets and try to find a quiet alcove or empty cellar where she could sleep for a few hours, just to get some peace away from her fellow Walkers. With *that* came the risk of running across other gang members. The Walkers weren't the only gang in the Auora, nor did they come close to being the most bloodthirsty. The Walkers had a certain reputation among the other gangs, and Naro had reinforced that reputation over the years. He had made many enemies, and they would almost certainly jump at any opportunity to strike a blow against him.

The descent from the Market District to the Docks District was swift and uneventful. The city guards never harassed anyone going down the Golden Path, only those going up. They had to protect their rich benefactors in the upper districts. Those down below didn't warrant the same amount of protection. In the lower districts, the gangs served as the muscle for the people.

Outside the main door of the warehouse sat a bored-looking boy of about sixteen. She couldn't recall his name, but she recognized him from training. In one hand he held a dagger and a half-carved piece of wood in the other. As she approached the warehouse, he straightened and got to his feet, setting the carving down on the chair behind him. He held the knife close to his hip. She knew that he was not the only guard on duty that night. Others were undoubtedly stationed on the rooftops surrounding them. Perhaps one or two even had arrows notched and aimed at her.

"Who's there?" he called out.

She took her hood off and raised her hand in greeting. "It's Ray, I just want to get some sleep," she replied.

The boy visibly relaxed once he recognized her face. "Should be an extra bed or two tonight. Place is a little crowded." He opened the door behind him, stepping aside to let her in.

As she passed him, she tilted her head to the side to catch a glimpse at his carving. "What're you working on?"

He shrugged. "Just a boat. Travelers like them."

She let out a grunt of agreement and headed inside. Travelers did indeed like to purchase little trinkets from the markets in Auora. Some of the Walkers made honest coin on the side, if they found time to craft little oddities like that boy and his wooden boats.

She passed through a small entryway and headed up a flight of stairs to the second floor. The main area of the warehouse was dedicated to storing goods that moved through the city. Upstairs was the living quarters. The boy out front was right, there were several other Walkers there that evening. Most of them were boys gathered around a large table. Their guffaws and cackling could be heard from the lower level.

"Did she really say that to him?"

"Honest!"

More cackling.

Ray grimaced and stepped onto the landing. The boys ranged in age from no older than children to several years her elders. The younger ones were moving tankards of ale between the table and some nearby kegs, intent on keeping their elders' thirst sated. Ray had done this plenty of times growing up. It was an effective way to get stories from others, which is exactly what these boys were doing.

"And he *still* convinced her to go into the barn with him!" one of the older boys—really more of a young man—hollered before he raised a tankard to his lips and took a lengthy swig. The others whooped and hollered in response.

"Can't believe Ajak would do that!" a younger boy shrieked with laughter.

Ray felt her stomach tie itself into a knot. Of course they were talking about Ajak. He had made quite a name for himself throughout the Walkers. He had recently turned twenty-three and was five years older than her. They shared similar backstories—born in the slums, parents died, and the Walkers picked him up. They differed in that Ajak was a natural rogue. Whatever task Naro and the other lieutenants gave him, he completed with ease. Many of the younger Walkers, Ray included, wanted to be like Ajak. It felt more obtainable than being like Naro. Ajak was also very popular with women both within the Walkers and in the city. And that's exactly what these boys were discussing that evening.

Maybe I'd be better off sleeping on the streets tonight, she thought.

She didn't want to listen to stories of Ajak's conquests. The thought made her heart hurt. It wasn't that she was trying to get his attention—far from it. She had been on the receiving end of his attentions for the past couple of years, as had several other young women in the Walkers. But she despised the idea of being another conquest. She had never tried convincing him to change his ways because what was so special about her? He had seduced women from the Sky District. If they couldn't keep his attention, there was no way she would be able to. The knot in her stomach twisted tighter.

She corrected her course and instead walked over to where they stored their food. Someone had brought back a few loaves of bread earlier in the day, which had already been torn into. Ray grabbed a couple of slices. Bread and preserved goods were the best she could expect from this warehouse. There was no oven, and they couldn't risk a firepit anywhere near the building. It wasn't like some of the other safehouses that had decent kitchens in them. She took a bite of the bread and then headed back toward the stairs, trying her best to ignore the boys' comments. She heard her name mentioned once or twice but couldn't be bothered to listen and respond.

"Not staying the night?" the boy out front asked her as she exited the warehouse.

"Naw, it's too loud in there," she mumbled, taking another bite of bread. Pungent cheese and garlic flavor filled her mouth, and she savored the bite.

The boy shrugged before returning to his carving.

As she wandered the streets, her thoughts eventually turned to Laurel and her dead friend. Their brothel was in the more extravagant part of the Market District, which was several levels above where the drug trade usually commenced. Ray couldn't help but wonder how that athra had made its way so high up in Auora without either her gang or the guards hearing about it. Typically, any drug that made it so high up was less dangerous and sold exclusively to the wealthy by means of the Red Court gang. The Red Court was almost as old as the Walkers, and they had lasted that long because they were made up of nobles and rich folk who very much enjoyed their illicit activities. And the city guards would turn their heads because, after all, they couldn't be going around arresting the people who paid for their services. It was a nice little arrangement most of the time.

Except for now. This strain of athra was deadly, and that crossed a line with both the wealthy and the guards. It would be the gangs who paid the price for its presence, so it was imperative that Ray learn more information about where it was coming from.

She sighed, letting the pressure of her responsibilities push the air from her lungs. Although she had been with the Walkers for the past five years, she had never faced a situation quite like this. Naro had impressed upon her and the others that this athra strain could be the end of the Walkers if they did not snuff it out in time. She wanted nothing more than to solve this problem for her gang and for Naro.

She wanted to laugh but settled for a smile and quiet snort. It seemed that her thoughts often turned to Naro late at night. The man had become like a father to her after her own father abandoned her and her mother. She owed everything she had, everything she had become, to Naro. He had trained her in the art of stealth, thievery, and trickery. He had also wrapped his arms around her in a comforting hug when she awoke from her nightmares. He would sing softly to her and lull her back to sleep just like her mother used to do. At that moment she craved nothing more than a reassuring squeeze from him. She decided to take her chances and climb up to the Crafting District where one of the nicer safehouses was located. Naro had made that safehouse his primary residence, but he traveled often. Perhaps she would get lucky, and he would be there that night.

The streets were quiet. At this hour, the only other people out were the guards and stragglers heading home from the taverns. Most weren't going to be climbing through the districts of the city. Fortunately, she didn't have to be on the streets for very long. Up ahead was an alley she would disappear down where there were ladders and scaffolding that led directly up into the Crafting District, past the layer of barracks and housing where the soldiers slept and kept watch on the two districts below. If it were any other time of day, Ray would have backtracked to the Docks District and then climbed the Golden Path with the crowds. There was little movement on the Golden Path after dark, however, and the guards were almost certain to stop anyone trying to climb higher into the city at night. Ray needed to stay hidden, so the alleys and ladders in the Gutters would suffice.

The guards of the city never ventured too far into the Gutters, although they knew there were secret routes into the Crafting District hidden within. The main paths were patrolled often enough, but the alleys were sufficiently hidden beneath the cliffside. The Gutters was truly a feat of crafting mastery. Shanties and shacks were stacked on top of each other with interconnected bridges and walkways. There were several homes carved into the cliffside. There was one particular structure that Ray moved toward—a small storehouse that had long since been abandoned.

Over the course of time, a couple of gangs had fought to control the storehouse because of the tunnel in the back that led directly to the Market District. No one knew who had originally carved the vertical pathway, but Ray was sure Naro knew. Despite that, the Walkers had never contested for ownership of the storehouse. If there was one place the guards were willing to go to in the Gutters, it was this storehouse. They had tried sealing the tunnels in the past, but someone always managed to break through. They couldn't risk destroying it lest they bring down parts of the city above. Most of the time they just left well enough alone, but Naro was wary. He didn't want to risk his people getting caught and arrested, so he stayed out of the ownership feuds.

That didn't mean that the Walkers never used the tunnel. Ray always tried to avoid using it unless she knew who was in possession of the storehouse. She was fairly certain that it was currently unoccupied. The last news she had heard was that the Iron Hawks and The Disciples had fought over it and faced more casualties than either side cared to lose. That meant the place was truly abandoned while they licked their wounds. The smaller gangs wouldn't dare risk occupying the space one of the main four had their eyes on.

The storehouse was at the back of a particularly dark alley. It was in one of the older districts of the Gutters where most of the buildings were carved directly into the island rock. The main sound she heard was her footsteps. Sometimes a dog barked, or a couple yelled loud enough to be heard through the stone walls. Ray paid none of these noises any attention. She was on the lookout for any signs of patrols. It was common for one of the gangs to assign a couple of members to guard the perimeter of the storehouse, but they were either exceptional at hiding, or there was no one out there tonight. Ray didn't allow herself to relax. She still had to get inside and make the climb up three districts.

The front door was visible by the entire alley. Anyone could even see it when they first turned down the alley. The only lights nearby were the candles in the windows of homes many stories above the street. She could just barely make out the door frame and handle. Still, no one around. Although she didn't reach for them, she made sure she could feel exactly where the sheathed daggers were at her hips.

As Ray reached the door, she slowed, trying to muffle any extra noise her boots or equipment were making. There was only one window across all the walls of the storehouse, and it was to the right of the front door. A rough sheet had been hung up on the inside, but she could see the faint glow of light surrounding its edges.

Is there someone inside after all?

She must have missed some telltale sign of a sentry on her way down the alley, although she had been *sure* she looked. She had reached the front door without an arrow being shot through her chest, so maybe they were waiting to see what her intentions were.

She swallowed nervously. With a deft hand, she withdrew her left hand into her cloak and pulled out the third dagger that was sheathed right above the small of her back. At the same time, she raised her right hand to knock on the front door. It wouldn't do her any good to try to sneak inside now.

The knock was quiet, barely perceptible. The old wood of the door absorbed most of the sounds. But she knew that if anyone were inside, they would have heard. She held her breath and waited, listening attentively for any sign of movement from within.

When Ray reached her limit and had to exhale, she took one step back and surveyed the door and window again. The glow behind the sheet was steady, as if multiple candles had been lit. She couldn't see around the sheet, so she had no clue if there was a guard stationed inside or not. From previous experiences, if there was a light coming from the window, there was almost certainly a guard waiting on the other side with a crossbow or sword at the ready.

There were no other sounds on the street besides her own very faint breathing. She cast a glance around her once more. No odd silhouettes or movement from the windows and balconies on either side of the alley. She looked directly above the door at the sheer surface of the cliff just out of habit. Nothing was above the door, but she always made sure to check to see if anyone had made any alterations to the cliffside and had carved out a small peeping window or ledge to push something off of. But there was nothing.

She grimaced and reached out to open the door. She twisted the knob and pushed it in, her grip on her dagger tightening. She didn't move forward lest she be caught by a guard on the inside.

Surprisingly, the door swung open, and no one came charging out. It hit the wall of the entryway with a *thud* and stayed open, allowing her to see inside from the threshold. There was no one in the entryway, which was just a small square room with a chair, table, and several lit candles. From the entryway, there was only one other direction to go and that was further into the storehouse opposite the front entrance. It was another door that was also closed. She looked over every inch of the room until she was certain there was no elaborate trap waiting for her. Ray stepped into the entryway and quickly closed the door behind her, her grip never loosening on her dagger.

She held her ear up to the wood of the next door, listening for signs of life on the other side. Again, there was nothing.

What's going on? Uneasiness set in, and her stomach tightened. *This isn't normal. Why are there lights on in the storehouse if it's abandoned?* She wondered what would be on the other side of the door. *Is someone waiting for me? There's no way anyone would've known I'd make the climb. I didn't even know I'd come this way. So, what's the point of having candles burning in the night? Is this a trap set up by a rival gang trying to bring the Walkers down a peg, one kill at a time?*

None of this makes any sense.

She held her breath and opened the door, preparing to strike with the dagger. The next room was the storehouse proper, filled end to end with rows of empty shelves. All the chandeliers were glowing brightly with fresh candles. From where she was standing, she could see the whole floor and the complete absence of people or things. Her heart pounded in her chest, and it was all she could hear. The storehouse was deathly silent. Silent and yet alive with lights.

She exhaled and stepped forward, closing the door behind her. There was one other room in the storehouse that she needed to get through—the back room. At one point it had been another storage room, but a long time ago some gang had turned it into living quarters for those who guarded the storehouse and the tunnel. The entrance to the tunnel was in those living quarters, so that's where she had to go. Her legs were heavy, and she wasn't sure she would be able to cross the room. But she had to.

The threshold to the living quarters was completely open. All she could see inside were stacks of crates and some rolled-up fabrics. Candles burned brightly from within. She could smell the faint scents of sweat and alcohol. As she approached the threshold, some primal instinct flared to life within her. Whatever was in this room, it was dangerous, and she shouldn't be there.

But Naro needs to know about it, whatever it *is.*

She mustered her courage and stepped into the backroom.

There was a clatter and *clang* and she jumped. Her dagger lay on the ground behind her, having fallen from her slack grip. There had to be ten or twelve corpses in this room spread all about as if they had died during their nightly routines. Three bodies were intertwined on a bed in various stages of undress. Two more were lounging across a couple of crates pushed together to serve as seating. Another had collapsed near some shelves that had plates and utensils on them, fresh fruit and smoked meat scattered across the floor.

She picked up her dagger and looked over the corpses, searching for some clues as to what happened and when they had died. She realized that they all had something in common—black veins across their faces and throats, black irises, and dried blood dribbling from their eyes and nose. These people had all overdosed on athra.

Her blood ran cold, and her eyes widened. She had seen one or two overdoses like this before, but never so many in one place.

Who are these people?

Ray looked around the room for some kind of identifiers when noticed the clothes they were wearing and the banners that were half-hung on the walls. Blue handprints were evident on their tunics. In the palm of each hand was a lidless eye, all staring at Ray. She crossed over to where a pile of fabrics lay and picked one up with trembling fingers. The fabrics were all shades of blue and she knew what would be on them when she unfurled it.

These were all sigils and markings of the Syrael Walkers.

But she recognized none of these people as her own.

Who were these people, and why were they dressed like the Walkers?

Off in the distance there was a loud *thud* as one of the doors was forced open. She heard voices from the storeroom along with the clatter of armor, weapons, and shields.

"Spread out! They're here somewhere," a thunderous voice boomed.

Panic threatened to overtake Ray's body, and she was overwhelmed with an immediate urge to flee. She nearly dropped the fabric and her dagger again but managed to secure her grip at the last moment.

What in the Protector's grace are the city guards doing here?

She stood in the middle of the room, easily seen from the opposite end of the storeroom. There were only two ways out of the storehouse—up the ladder or out the front door. She shuffled backward. If the guards were here, they would go to the ladder and search the tunnel. She would be caught almost immediately. The entrance to the tunnel was across the room from her to the left of the threshold behind a dark blue curtain. A curtain with the Walkers' sigil on it. Her stomach churned.

She was going to get caught.

Her back hit the wall and her heel bumped against an oddly protruding stone, shooting pain up her leg. She leaned against the wall and reached down to rub her heel when it suddenly gave way, and she fell backwards. All the air in her lungs was forced out as she hit the ground. She gritted her teeth and suppressed a scream of pain. Ray opened her mouth and took deep, quiet breaths, trying to regain her composure. The back of her head throbbed as she forced herself into a sitting position and gingerly reached around to feel for lumps or blood. Thankfully, she found nothing.

Ray didn't understand what she was looking at. She could see into the living quarters, but it was as if she wore a veil. Something was between her and the room. She blinked to try to clear her vision, but the distortion was still there. She could make out lines in the distortion, almost like blocks of stone... Her eyes widened. It was as if the wall were see-through. An illusion.

Guards wearing blue and green gambesons poured into the room and immediately began calling out to each other, pointing at the bodies.

"Sir, found them!"

"By the Protector, it's a massacre."

"Look for survivors."

They all spread out, inspecting the dead bodies and the room. Several grumbled and muttering under their breaths as they opened the crates.

"Damn Walkers. Killed themselves on their own haul."

"This has to be enough evidence for the king to smoke the rats out, innit sir?"

A couple of the guards approached Ray. She felt a couple of tears rolling down her cheeks. She didn't want to get captured like this. She didn't want to get captured *at all*. Naro would be so disappointed in her. She was only supposed to be a pair of eyes, not involved in this.

The two guards stopped near the wall and looked around. "Nothing over here, sir," one of them called out.

Ray didn't understand. *They can't see me?*

She pulled herself to her feet.

This is unreal.

Walls didn't just disappear when someone leaned against them, only to reappear seconds later. What was going on? This had to be some elaborate trap, but she didn't understand how it worked.

But she was safe.

She let out a slow, quiet exhale. She was safe.

The guards continued ransacking the room and talking to one another. One of the guards touched his fingertips to his lips, then his heart, then his forehead, a common sign of respecting the dead.

"Rats don't deserve it," another guard growled.

"That's for the Protector to decide," the first responded with an even tone.

Ray would have to wait until they left before she could attempt to leave, so she decided to take in her surroundings of the mysterious room she had fallen into. There were no candles, but the light from the living quarters was just bright enough for her to see. It wasn't a large room, more like a short hallway. On one end was the illusory wall and on the other was a ladder that went down.

Down?

She crossed over to the ladder and looked down the hole, but she could see nothing, it was pitch black. She looked back over her shoulder at the guards, wondering how long they would be in the storehouse. She considered climbing down the ladder. Perhaps it was a cellar of some kind... but that was impossible. Below the storehouse was the Docks District. Perhaps this ladder connected to another safehouse down there.

Then why haven't I heard of this before?

"Smoke out the tunnel," the captain of the guard told his men. "Bring the athra supply back to the barracks. We'll return tomorrow to clean this place out."

Ray's stomach dropped, and her blood ran cold. On occasion, the city guard would raid the storehouse and light fires in the tunnel to burn away the ladder and choke any poor soul who happened to be climbing up it. They were always careful to keep the fire contained to the tunnel, lest they destroy the rest of the building, but the smoke would still be a danger to her. Two of them were lifting a crate and hauling it out of the room—the athra supply. A few of the other guards disappeared into the tunnel with some crates. The smell of fire and smoke filled the area. As the guards left, one of them looked back at the corpses and spit on the ground. He mumbled something under his breath, but Ray couldn't hear him.

With the smoke spreading, she had little time to spare. Her eyes watered and breathing became difficult, but she had to wait until there was no more rustling or creaking of armor. The doors opened and closed several times. Soon voices could no longer be heard. She reached out to touch the illusionary wall and felt nothing as her fingers passed completely through. Ray stepped through the wall and into the living quarters. No guards remained, which she had been hoping for. They would be back by sunrise, though, to continue their investigation. She had to get to Naro and tell him what had happened in the warehouse. Without the tunnel, she'd have to go back into the streets and either find another route up in the Gutters or take her chances on the Golden Path.

But first she needed to get out of the storehouse without suffocating.

The rest of the way was clear, but she was wary of the front door. She didn't know if they had stationed guards outside of the storehouse until they could return, but she would have to take her chances.

She crouched down by the front door and slinked over to the window. The guards had left the candles burning inside, so she had to take great care with lifting the curtain to not draw attention to herself. Ray crammed herself into the corner to look at the front door as much of it as she possibly could. With dexterous fingers, she lifted the edge of the curtain to look out into the night. No one was standing outside of the door that she could see. Ray gently lowered the curtain. The view hadn't been the best, so she was still gambling her life by leaving the storehouse. She looked down at the dagger in her clenched fist. *I don't want to use this.*

She took hold of the door and pulled slowly, bracing herself for any shouts or attacks. But the coast was clear. With no one standing in her way, she bolted into the night, taking in deep gulps of fresh air.

The best way up is going to be on the Golden Path, she thought.

With the guards hitting the storehouse tonight, she wasn't sure if the other hidden paths up would be safe. Before she got to the road, though, she needed to lose her daggers. During the day she could have passed upward into the city with them, but the guards took no chances at night. If weapons were found, they would get confiscated, and the people who had them could get into trouble. Ray couldn't chance that. She had to appear as docile as possible. Leaving her three blades behind a couple of crates, she continued on her way.

It was easy enough to leave the daggers behind. They were just standard blades, no special make or markings. Other gangs like the Iron Hawks liked to dress up their weapons, so people knew who they belonged to. The Walkers didn't need to flaunt their weapons or their clothing. For all intents and purposes, anyone on the street could be a Walker. Tonight, however, Ray hoped that the guards wouldn't make such an assumption when she tried passing through to the Crafting District.

She backtracked down to the docks to access the Golden Path properly. It would do her no good to sneak onto the road halfway up, lest she risk getting caught by the guards. She took her cloak off and bundled it up under her arm. The rest of her clothes were unassuming enough. Boots, pants, shirt, vest, and a coat. All the things a normal citizen would wear during colder weather. She ran a hand through her hair and ruffled it up so it would appear windblown. She racked her brain for a quick and easy story to tell when she was inevitably stopped.

The road twisted through the lower tiers of Auora on an upward slope. It passed over the Gutters and the tier where the soldiers lived. Most folks referred to it as the Barrier since the city treated the Gutters as if it were plagued, and the soldiers were the only buffer between them and safety.

"Halt!" came the expected call as she neared a watch post on the road.

Ray slowed her pace and stopped as two guards approached her, torches burning brightly in their hands. The guard on the left raised his light to get a better look at her face.

"What are you doing out so late?" the guard asked, his free hand sliding to the hilt of his sword.

"And what's that in your hands?" the other inquired as he gestured toward her cloak.

"I's working on one of my pa's boats." Ray's voice came out barely louder than a mumble as she deepened her voice and tried her best to sound like a boy instead of a girl. Although she was a woman now, just barely, she had never really grown into her body. She was still lanky and skinny, and her chest rather flat. It was handy when she needed to fool the guards into thinking she was a boy. She unfurled the cloak and held it up for inspection. "It's jus' my cape. Didn't wanna leave it on the boat."

The guards looked at each other and stepped toward her. "Where does your pa live, and why's he sending you out so late?" the first one asked.

"Arms out for an inspection," the other grumbled, handing his torch off to his companion.

Ray spread her arms. "We have a house above the Crafting District. Pa's a woodworker, I'm learning from him. He carves pretty things on the boats sometimes if a customer asks. He gave me this one to work on."

The guard holding the torches scoffed. The other continued his pat down. Although Ray had been through this process many times over, she was still uncomfortable with the touch of the guards.

The guard sniffed and made an ugly expression. "How come you smell like smoke?"

"Kept my lantern too close while I's workin', I s'pose," Ray managed to respond.

The guard grunted then turned back to his companion. "Nothing."

The other guard scoffed again, handing the torch back over. "You're good to go. Don't stay out so late down there, though. Unsavory folk come out at night."

"Yessir." Ray bowed her head and continued up the Golden Path, never once looking back at the guards.

As the road curved and wrapped around the island, she slipped her cloak on and pulled the hood over her head. Streets protruded from the Golden Path. She was in the Crafting District now where many shops and workspaces lined the roads. All was quiet. No one was crafting that late at night. Naro's safehouse was nestled in the residential area of the Crafting District, so she turned off the Golden Path and made her way toward one of the ramps that led up to where the houses were. The Crafting District was similarly stacked with houses, made with stone walls and solid wood unlike the ratty boards far below in the Gutters.

There were many boarding houses here where crafters from faraway lands could rent living quarters while they were in town to make or sell their goods, several of which Ray was familiar with. The Walkers had contacts with many of the cities outside Auora, and would frequently meet up at the boarding houses or the taverns nearby to discuss trade agreements.

Other homes in the district were modest standalone homes where a crafter would live with his family. Almost all the crafters in Auora were some kind of smith, be it weaponry or woodworking. These men and women made good, honest money with their craft. Sometimes Ray wondered what it would be like to be a shop hand at one of their stores, but she knew it wasn't the right fit for her. She had been born in the Gutters where her parents and their parents before them had been born. Most folks born in the Gutters never made it any higher than that.

Naro's house was tucked away into the cliffside. It was two stories tall and rather plain, the bottom story made entirely of stone. The walls of the second story were made of timber from the Imalarii Woods. Fencing wrapped around a small side yard where a couple of crates were stacked. No crops grew because the yard never really saw the suns.

There was one lit candle upstairs in the far-left window above the yard. Ray knew that was where the lookout would have been stationed. She lowered her hood as she approached the gate. It creaked as she opened and closed it. Two dogs crossed from the back of the yard to her. They let out a couple of quiet barks, sounding more like deep snorts of air than true barking. She stretched her hands out to let them sniff her better. They immediately recognized her scent—she frequently visited this house—and circled around her as she made her way to the side door.

While the outside of the house was plain, the inside was anything but. Ray entered the kitchen, which was mostly counters, cupboards, a large stone oven, and a roasting pit. The smell of exotic spices filled the air, reawakening her hunger from earlier. Jars and sacks of goods from other cities and territories crowded the countertops. Inside the oven a small fire burned, and a couple of clay pots were on the rack. A woman chopped dried fruits nearby. As Ray came inside, she turned around.

"Not your night to be here," the cook grumbled, pointing the knife at Ray. It was Hilthe, one of the women Naro employed to tend his home and provide his meals.

Hilthe was an older woman with graying hair and wrinkles all over her face, but she had a sturdy frame and knew how to use a butcher's knife. She was like a grandmother to the younger Walkers like Ray. Although Hilthe had been warned not to get too attached to any of them, she still went out of her way to bake pastries if some of the young ones had watch duty at Naro's house.

"I got something for the boss. Is he here?" Ray responded, not minding the weapon. Hilthe was dangerous with a blade, but never toward the Walkers. Ray knew she was just grumpy that she had been interrupted during her morning work. *Is it dawn already?*

"Aye. And he's already up, I reckon," Hilthe responded, turning back to her cutting. "Before you go, grab another pot and put it up here for me."

Hilthe was going to make her food. Judging by the fruits and spices within Hilthe's reach, Ray assumed it was porridge. Her stomach growled at the thought of it. It had been several days since she'd last had Hilthe's porridge. She hoped that there were still some cadra berries from last time. Her gaze swept across the room, and she saw a stack of clay pots near the doorway leading to the dining hall. She grabbed one and set it down gently beside the cutting board.

"Thank you, Hilthe," Ray said sweetly, pressing a kiss to the woman's head. Hilthe grumbled wordlessly and continued with what she was doing. Ray left the kitchen and headed further into the house.

On the lower floor there were three rooms, four if she counted the entryway by the front door—the kitchen, the dining hall, and the lounge. The only way to get upstairs from the kitchen was through the dining hall. The dining hall was what Ray imagined the royal dining hall was like, with paintings hanging on every wall and beautiful benches and a table filling the floor. The table could easily seat ten or twelve people. Naro always sat at the head of the table in a chair with a tall back and plush blue cushions. She'd probably be eating in this room later once everyone had been called for breakfast.

From the dining hall there were two exits to the lounge and the front entryway. The lounge took up nearly half of the floor and was where Naro would sometimes receive visitors. It was a cozy room and it always made Ray feel warm and sleepy. During her shifts at the house, she spent her downtime in the lounge. Naro had commissioned a painting of the night sky on the ceiling, so she would lay down on the floor or one of the plush couches and stargaze. The windows were covered with heavy drapes from Lithalyon to block out light. Several lamps were scattered throughout the room, candles burning low.

In the entryway was a staircase leading up to the second floor. Ray quickly navigated through the bottom floor and up the stairs where there was a door on each of the three walls surrounding her. She knew the doors on the left and right were bedrooms for other Walkers to use and patrol from. The door straight ahead led to Naro's room.

As soon as she reached the top of the stairs, she crossed the landing and knocked on Naro's door. From the other side, she heard voices hush. She hadn't been concerned with waking him up, but who would have been in his room at this time of night?

"Enter," Naro commanded, his voice muffled.

Ray opened the door and immediately sunk into a bow, an apology on her lips. "Sir I'm sorry, I didn't think—"

"It's alright, Ray." Naro said with a voice thick like honey.

Ray looked up and in the dim candlelight saw that Sabyl, one of Naro's two lieutenants, was in the room with him. She had an ugly frown on her face, but she usually did, so Ray couldn't determine what they might have been talking about. Sabyl was a plain woman with black hair and brown eyes. She was in her early thirties and had been with the Walkers since childhood, much like Ray. She looked up to Sabyl sometimes when they were on amicable terms. That wasn't too often because Sabyl always acted like she had a stick for a spine.

"I thought you had the night off," Sabyl growled.

"Yeah, well, some news can't wait," Ray snapped back. She had learned long ago that if she was ever going to win Sabyl's respect that she needed to grow a backbone of her own.

Naro sighed, a sound Ray imagined a parent would make when their children were bickering, and they wanted nothing more than to disappear into the night. It was a sound that Ray tried to avoid at all costs. Her stomach knotted and she immediately backed down. Sabyl stood her ground, her eyes not leaving Ray.

Naro turned to look at Sabyl, waiting patiently until she looked back at him. He inclined his head toward the door which elicited a scowl from the woman, but she understood his order. She strode past Ray who had to turn to avoid bumping shoulders with the older woman.

"I'm sorry, Naro," Ray mumbled after Sabyl left.

"You'll command respect from her one day," Naro replied. "She knows this, even if she doesn't admit it."

She took in his words but didn't think much of the meaning behind them. Naro knew many things. Ray didn't quite understand how, but he would often make casual statements about someone's future that came true. The world had told her that magic was gone, but Naro was clearly magic-touched. He kept his talents to himself and a select few others, though. The world was not ready for him to reveal himself; that was what he often told Ray.

"Why did you come tonight, child?" Naro asked, looking at her. In the gloomy light his mismatching eyes looked the same dark colorless shade, his bronze skin closer to the color of night. He was almost like a shadow. It was a rather fitting look for the leader of the oldest gang in Auora.

"The storehouse in the Gutters was raided tonight," Ray said, drawing confidence from Naro's presence. "Someone framed it to look like it was ours."

Naro leaned back in his chair and was silent for a moment. "They found athra there."

Ray nodded.

"This game is getting dangerous," he murmured, more to himself than to her. "More dangerous than a pair of eyes need be in."

They locked eyes again.

"After you get some rest, tell Sabyl everything you've learned about the athra outbreak. I'm going to find you a different assignment. It's grown beyond your suit of talents." Naro's quiet voice was somehow both authoritative and soothing. It softened the blow of his decision.

Ray couldn't keep her face from twisting into a disappointing frown. "But Naro, I—"

"Trust in me, child," Naro said, and she stayed silent. "Is there anything else you need to tell me?"

He always knows when there's more.

"I found something at the storehouse, and I'm not sure who else knows about it," Ray began, uncertain of how to describe the illusory wall and the ladder leading downward. "When I was investigating the storehouse, the guards showed up. I thought I was going to get caught, so I panicked, and I... fell through a wall."

Naro didn't seem to mind. He waited patiently for her to continue and explain what she meant.

"I-It was like the wall wasn't really there. When I got up, I could see through the part I fell through, but the guards couldn't see me. I have no idea how it was even possible... And the place I fell into, it was a small corridor. One end was the fake wall, and on the other end there was a ladder that went down."

"Down?" Naro repeated.

"Yeah, but I didn't check it out... because of the guards..." Ray mumbled.

"Most intriguing."

"Should I tell Sabyl about this, too?"

Naro was silent for a few moments, which troubled Ray. *Doesn't he want his lieutenant to know about this?*

"For now, let this stay between you and I," Naro told her. "Get some rest, Ray. I will have your next assignment ready when you wake."

Ray bowed and left the room, closing the door behind her. Her mind raced. She was no longer supposed to investigate the deadly athra strain. She wasn't supposed to tell Sabyl about the fake wall.

What's he thinking?

It wasn't her place to question him. She quickly silenced her thoughts as she went into the bedroom to the left of Naro's room. No one was in there, which she was thankful for. The room had three beds in it and made it feel very cramped. There were a couple of smaller tables scattered around the room to place belongings on and a giant armoire containing clothing of all stations, but beyond that there wasn't room for much else. She tugged off her boots and threw herself down on the bed closest to the door, all the energy leaving her body. After an uncomfortable moment of laying still, she pulled off her belt and placed it on the table. No more dagger sheaths to poke her in the back. The suns would be rising now or very soon. She had been up all night without realizing it. She threw an arm over her eyes and quickly fell asleep.

CHAPTER 111: SETH

Seth winced as he looked down into the chambers below. It was rare for him to enjoy watching his father work anymore. More and more he watched with a hint of disbelief or disgust. *Surely there was another way for him to achieve what he wanted to do? Without needing to...*

One of the men below screamed, and Seth shivered. Below in the chamber, there were three raised platforms built out of wooden slabs. On each platform was a spellsinger flanked by two soldiers with towering shields. The shields were meant to keep any harm from coming to the spellsinger. Their numbers had been dwindling since Seth's father began experimenting more frequently, and the academies couldn't keep up with the demand for new spellsingers. The *Zsikui* assured him that he was getting close to finding the answers he sought.

Hopefully he finds it before anything else drastic happens, Seth thought bitterly.

His father stood in the middle of the platforms wearing dark green ceremonial robes, his brown hair covered by a matching dark green hood. He shouted wordlessly, moving between the three platforms with speed that Seth hadn't seen in a long time. Perhaps that meant it was working. A blue cloud formed in between the platforms as the spellsingers chanted louder and louder. One of the shield-bearers on the southern platform sank to his knees, the burden of the cloud becoming too much for him. Seth's father ran to his side and hoisted the shield up, using his own weight to help support the heavy burden. Although Seth couldn't hear the words, he knew his father was spilling a string of threats and curses at the soldier for even *thinking* about falling to his knees and potentially ruining all their work.

The cloud grew, and its center darkened. It looked like a hole opening in the air, but where it opened to, Seth had no idea. He wasn't sure he wanted to know.

Seth's father let out another victorious roar and abandoned the shield-bearer. He trudged his way toward the center of the chamber, his steps heavy as he tried to push back against the force the cloud was exuding.

"Yes, yes, a little more!" he shrieked, reaching a callused hand out to the black center of the cloud. The shadow of the cloud darkened his tan skin, giving it a dark umber color.

The spellsingers were wailing their chants with no more regard given to their volume or tone. Each of the three had their arms extended toward the ceiling, beckoning for something to come to them. Seth's eyes moved between each of the platforms, studying the spellsingers and their shield-bearers. As he looked at the southern platform, he noticed the kneeling shield-bearer had lost his grip on the towering shield above him. It swayed to the side and fell off the platform with a loud *clang*. The spellsinger was startled and broke off her chant to look at the shield-bearer.

Without her voice aiding her fellow spellsingers, the cloud wavered. A deep snarl echoed throughout the room, and Seth looked around in panic. The other shield-bearers and spellsingers looked afraid, but not Seth's father. He was almost touching the cloud—nothing else mattered to him.

Something bright jumped out of the cloud and landed on the silent spellsinger. She let out a panicked scream and fell backwards, scrambling to get off the platform. The standing shield-bearer turned to her, drawing his sword, but it was no use. The bright light consumed the spellsinger as she cried out in fear, and then it was gone. Her corpse was left behind, her skin blackened and burned. The shield-bearers looked upon her with horror in their eyes. Seth's bottom lip quivered, and he forgot to breathe. His eyes flicked to his father who was now reaching for an empty spot in the room. The cloud was gone.

Seth's father screamed again, but it was different. This was a guttural, deep, *enraged* scream that filled the room just as the otherworldly snarl had moments ago. He spun around to look at the southern platform, where one shield-bearer stood tall, his torso turned with sword in hand. The other kneeled on the ground, shield forgotten. Seth's father crossed the floor and climbed the platform, grabbing at the charred corpse of the spellsinger, and lifted it off the ground with alarming ease.

"You are *lucky* that the *Zsikui* aren't here to witness such *catastrophic failure!*" he screeched, chucking the corpse across the room toward the spot where the blue cloud had vanished. It wasn't often that he invoked the name of their hosts, the scaled serpentine people who made the pyramids their home. "We almost *had it*, I—"

His father stood rigid on the platform, his back straight and his head bowed. Seth wasn't sure what his father was focusing on, but he could tell he was avoiding looking at the other people in the room.

Is this another one of his lapses? Has he forgotten where he is?

Seth didn't dare call out to him. He had learned his lesson in bringing his father back to the mortal realm. He hoped that one day his father wouldn't return from wherever his mind wandered.

"Leave," came the simple, quiet command. Seth's father raised his head and looked around the room at each shield-bearer and spellsinger. "We will try again another night."

Seth exhaled slowly. The shield-bearers and spellsingers left as quickly and quietly as they could, not wanting to be in his father's presence for a moment more. The scent of burning flesh wafted up to the balcony and he winced. Seth wished he could retreat like they were doing, but he knew he had to stay. His father always knew when he left early, even if the experiment ended in failure.

"My son, did you see what just happened?" his father called out to him, looking up at the balcony.

Seth resisted the urge to flinch and look away. "Yes, Father."

"This was a failure." His father's voice was soft, but Seth knew not to be deceived by it. He straightened and leaned against the railing. His eyes met his father's, and he held his gaze steady. "Can you tell me *why* this was a failure?"

Seth pursed his lips. A stray strand of blond hair fell across his face, but he didn't sweep it back. His father wouldn't be pleased by the distraction, not during one of his 'lessons'.

Failure... Why had the experiment failed? "One of the spellsingers stopped chanting," Seth answered.

Although he wasn't close enough to hear it, Seth saw his father grinding his teeth. "And why did she stop?"

There was a moment of silence between them, which Seth hastily ended. "The shield-bearer dropped his shield." The words were pulled from his lips, and he knew he would regret saying them.

His father smiled. Perhaps "smile" wasn't correct... His lips were indeed curled upward, eyes crinkling at the edges, and his face full of joy, but it wasn't a bright joy. It was dark, cruel, and Seth knew exactly what fate the shield-bearer would face. He wanted to curl up into himself and hide away from that smile. He blinked.

"Yes, my son. And he will pay for his wrongdoings."

Seth tried to swallow but found the lump in his throat preventing him from doing so.

With a snap, his father turned and walked toward the door. "I will meet you and the rest of the family for dinner. You're dismissed."

Seth waited until his father had left the room before he moved his hands to the wheels on his chair, his grip tighter than normal. As the door closed, he let out a shaky breath. Dinner would be in a handful of hours. He would need to develop an appetite before then, so as not to disappoint his father at the table. Even at nineteen—a man full grown by all standards—Seth didn't want to risk his father's ire over something so simple as a meal. He tugged the wheels back and guided himself through the crumbling arch into the hallway. There were only so many places he could escape to before being summoned to the dining hall.

He opted to go to the colonnade and try to clear the smell of charred flesh from his nostrils. His home was no longer as hospitable to him as it was when he was a child.

Before Father's experiment.

He and his twin sister Octavia had spent most of their childhood climbing through the ruins and exploring the gifts that the *Zsikui* had given their people, the Provira. Now he was bound to the highest floor in the largest pyramid where his father and mother made their living quarters. A colonnade surrounded the outer edge of the living quarters and was mostly intact. There were a handful of spots where the walkway had crumbled, dropping down into the pyramid below. When he was younger, he had been able to climb over those holes with relative ease, but now he was forced to return indoors to make a complete lap around the colonnade.

As Seth left the observatory balcony, one of his family's stewards stepped in line behind him. The stewards were like shadows that trailed after him wherever he went. His father had organized the group during one of his moments of clarity, insisting that his son must be taken care of and protected at all costs. While some of the stewards had voluntarily signed up for the service, others were coerced into the role with threats of death. His father had made all of them swear a vow of silence as well, except for the *Zsikui* who had graciously donated their time and efforts into looking after Seth. They were the only ones permitted to speak to him, and they often regaled him with tales of when the Asaszi were powerful and feared, when their people could turn into great wyrms and breathe fire, and how they would help the Provira rise to the same greatness that the Asaszi once knew. Seth wondered if they realized that he didn't share his father's ambitions—not that he would ever dare voice those thoughts.

The air outside was heavy. As Seth worked the wheels on his chair, his palms grew damp. A thin line of sweat broke out against his hairline. The lands far below the ruined pyramid were the remnants of a decayed city overrun by the surrounding jungle. Gnarled trees sprouted from the small square huts, crumbled stone scattered all around like dust. The *Zsikui* had told his family about their history, how during the Eldest Days the pyramids had stood taller than any tree in the jungle. Since then, the pyramids had fallen, and the jungle had grown. Seth wondered what it had looked like before the jungle had reclaimed the land.

The jungle was lively today. Birds called out to each other from varying heights. Twigs snapped and branches shifted under the weight of the forest creatures. The wooden wheels of Seth's chair rattled against the uneven stone of the colonnade. Beneath the noise was a low hum. He had asked one of the *Zsikui* what the hum was, when he was a child. The *Zsikui* had let out an amused hiss and told him it was the sound of magic trying to free itself from the ground. He became enraptured with the idea of magic, but as he grew older and witnessed the experiments Amias conducted, that wonder turned to resentment. He hoped that magic would stay trapped underneath the earth forever more.

Loudest among the jungle noises was a single bird, cawing to the others. Seth angled the chair so he could look out into the forest and try to find it.

"That kytling is quite the *noisssemaker* today," the steward said quietly behind him.

Seth let out an agreeable huff, eyes narrowing as he scanned the treetops. The kytling usually stood on the higher branches with its chest puffed out as it sang its song. He couldn't find the familiar tuft of yellow feathers.

The steward came to stand by his side. "It mussst be farther back in the forest."

"I suppose," Seth replied, slumping back in his chair. Watching the kytling had become a hobby of his on the sunnier days. Living near the top of the pyramid meant Seth could see where the tree line broke and the suns shone down on the land. The kytling enjoyed the suns, as far as he could tell. He never heard its song on the darker, rainier days. He wondered where the kytling went on the days the suns stayed hidden behind the clouds.

Wish that I could disappear on those days, too, Seth thought bitterly. He looked down at his lap, his legs, and then shut his eyes tight. *Wish that I could fly away from all of this.*

He dragged his eyes open and grabbed onto his wheels, abruptly backing up from the ledge and continuing down the walkway. He heard the steward let out an annoyed hiss as they backed away quickly to avoid their feet getting run over. If Seth were in a better mood, he might have apologized, but he just wanted to get back inside and return to his chambers where he could be completely alone. While the stewards were ordered to follow him everywhere he went, none were permitted to go into his room—only if he summoned them.

"I would like to speak with Octavia before dinner. Please send her to my room," Seth said over his shoulder as they approached the door to his room.

"Yesss Lord Kharisss," the steward responded as they turned away from him and returned to the rest of the pyramid.

Seth lifted a hand and pushed the door open. He waited for it to swing all the way open before passing through the threshold. Once he was inside, he twisted his upper body so he could push it shut. He sighed and looked around his room.

Stone surrounded him. The walls, the floor, even the bed, were made from the same beige stone as the rest of the pyramid. He had one exterior wall in his room. It slanted inwards and had a square window carved out of it. Even in his chair, he could look out the window with relative ease. The faint sounds of the jungle carried into his room. The sky darkened as afternoon clouds drifted in. Rain would begin soon, and then Seth would only hear the patter of droplets hitting the pyramid and the trees swaying in the wind.

He wheeled himself toward the stone bed. Four pillars stood at each corner. In other rooms, like his twin sister's, the pillars were used to create canopies out of decorative silks and linens. In Seth's room he used them as grips to pull himself into and out of his bed. When he was younger there had been green and red silks wrapped around them, creating the illusion of a comfortable nest. One night shortly after the accident, Seth had tried pulling himself into bed using the silks. They slid off the stone pillars and he fell to the floor with a pained cry. The stewards standing outside had rushed in and carried him off to be tended to by one of the *tsurii*. When he was brought back to his room, the silks had been removed.

He hauled himself onto his bed, hitting the blankets with a grunt. He looked up at the green and red canopy overhead. His father insisted on leaving it hanging, saying the *Zsukui* would be offended if every piece of silk had been removed from the room.

Before Seth's mind had a chance to run away with that thought, his eyes settled on the only piece of furniture that wasn't made from stone—his bookshelf. When he was a child, his father had helped him build it so he would have a place to store his books in his new room. As he grew older, his mother gave him books from her own library, or those that she found in the market. The shelves were now overflowing with books from her.

He tried to lose himself in the feeling of warmth that washed over him, but something kept him from it—the sight of his lower body lying limply on the bed. Seth shut his eyes tightly, feeling the familiar prick of tears near the bridge of his nose.

It had been five years ago when it happened, shortly after his fourteenth birthday. He could recall everything from that day in vivid detail, often seeing it in his nightmares. Another experiment with spellsingers. In that same room. There had been a cloud there as well, although it had been bright red and almost transparent. He and his father stood on a platform above the cloud, looking down. Seth could almost see the floor through it, but not quite. It didn't look the same. The stones were brighter in color. He bitterly remembered feeling so excited to be standing next to his father, helping him with his latest experiment. He couldn't remember what it was for; he just remembered them standing, then sitting, legs hanging off the platform, his father speaking softly to him, a hand on his shoulder, warmth spreading from the tips of his ears down to his toes, his wiggling toes, and that warmth replaced by heat, hot, fire around him, his legs, he—

Seth opened his eyes with a sharp inhale, the skin around his eyes wet with tears. His door had opened.

"Brother, you—" His sister's voice came from around the door. Octavia stepped into the room and saw him on the bed, and she was by his side in an instant, worry in her voice. "Seth, what's wrong?"

He glanced at his sister kneeling by his bed. "Tav, I-I didn't realize—"

"Are you hurting, is it your legs...?" She reached for his hand, wrapping her fingers around his wrist. She looked him over with such concern that Seth immediately felt guilty for the tears on his cheeks. He took hold of her hand and gave a gentle squeeze, drawing her attention back to his face.

"No, my legs are fine. Nothing is hurting," he told her and sat up. "Today has just been... *taxing.*"

Octavia leaned back from the bed but her grip on his wrist didn't lighten up. "Was it the experiments?" she asked quietly.

Seth nodded, eyes lowering to their hands. He twisted his left hand in her grasp, so he was holding her hand between his. The two shared a silent moment. There were no words that Octavia could say that would ease Seth's mind and they both knew it. *Even though she knows these experiments are dangerous, she'll keep defending Father until her last breath.*

The twins were close, but there was a divide between them. Octavia was entirely devoted to their father and his cause. Seth couldn't fault her for it.

Before the accident, Seth had also gone down that path blindly. He thought his father a great man, smarter than any other and capable of doing anything he set his mind to. He had wanted nothing more than to please Amias and make him proud. After his legs were crippled, Octavia told Seth that their father would heal him, fix him, and he allowed himself to be deluded by her words. He didn't want to lose one of the only people he could trust, so he never challenged her devotion to Amias.

"How has your day been?" Seth asked and looked back up at his sister. It was like looking in a mirror. Blond hair falling past their ears, eyes pools reflecting muddy brown water, a splash of freckles across their noses.

Octavia tucked a strand of hair behind her ear with her free hand. "Training continues." She fidgeted with her earlobe. "I bested Arcyr'ys today in the sparring ring."

Seth gasped and squeezed her hand. "Arcyr'ys? The same *Pyredan* Wynn?"

Octavia grinned and nodded. "I'm sure I'll suffer from it tomorrow during chores."

He took in her appearance for the first time, realizing that she was still in her sparring clothes—tan cloth pants, cropped top, and wrappings around her hands and feet.

"I'm surprised he didn't send you off to the pits immediately after." Seth laughed as his sister relaxed.

"The thought definitely crossed his mind, but I was civil about it. Offered him my hand and bowed afterwards. Plus, Osza and Astohi were there."

The names of the Asaszi sent an odd shiver down Seth's spine. "Does Father know they were there?"

Octavia nodded and bit her lip, trying to fight back another smile.

Osza was queen of the Asaszi, and she was almost never seen outside of her private chambers. When she was, their father was always by her side. Astohi, her mate, made more frequent appearances in public, but only slightly, and again, always with their father.

"What were they doing there if Father wasn't with them?" Seth asked, his back stiffening.

A knock on the door interrupted their conversation, and they turned toward the sound. "Lord, Lady Kharisss, time for dinner," Seth's steward announced, his voice muffled behind the wood.

"Thank you. One moment!" Octavia responded before looking back at Seth. She rose to her feet, her hand still between his. "May I?"

Seth nodded, shuffling closer to the edge of the bed. She was the only person he allowed to touch him, especially for something he deemed so humiliating. He let go of her hand as she bent down in front of him and wrapped her arms around his waist. He in turn wrapped his arms around her neck, and she lifted him up and into his chair with grace.

She straightened up and tugged on the hem of her top. "Come along, brother," she said, opening the door for him. Seth tugged on the wheels of his chair and exited the room with his sister.

<hr />

The dining hall was decorated extravagantly because Osza and Astohi would be dining with them tonight. Green and gold silk banners had been woven around the giant candelabra, every candle lit and burning brightly. The stone table had vases of fresh flowers placed on top of it. Around the table were six chairs, one on each end, and the others filling the long sides. Ribbons had been threaded and tied onto the backs of each chair. Their father was already sitting at one end of the table, and their mother was seated to his left. Osza sat on the opposite end of the table with Astohi to her right. That left one empty side of the table for Octavia and Seth. Servants lined the outer edges of the room, each holding a different platter or bowl of food while others held jugs of wine and water. They waited for the twins to take their seats.

"Good evening, children," their father announced, beckoning for them to approach the table. He had changed out of his ceremonial robes and into a fancy black robe embroidered with gold lace and tiny gems. The past one hundred years had not been kind to Amias Kharis. Up close Seth could see the wrinkles, crow's feet, and scars on his father's face. At his temples his dark hair had turned gray, reflecting the stress of his experiments and his old age.

Beside him, their mother, Evelyn, was dressed in a matching black dress, her chestnut hair swept up in a tight bun revealing her pointed ears. Next to their father she looked young enough to be his daughter. The Elviri blood in her veins was strong, aging her gracefully. She smiled at her children, her gray eyes and pale skin glowing under the candlelight. She was like a beacon of light within the snakes' nest.

Seth rolled over to one of the stone chairs, fear briefly crossing his mind. *Surely Father doesn't expect me to move into one of these for the meal?*

"Good evening, Father," Octavia responded, nodding toward both their parents and their guests.

She swooped in front of Seth and grabbed the stone chair, lifting it off the ground and pulling it to the side so he had room to approach the table with his wheelchair. Although she did a wonderful job hiding her strain, Seth knew that she could only hold up the chair for so many seconds before she had to place it back down. Seth also knew that by doing this for him, she had indirectly issued a challenge to their father: Seth wouldn't be humiliated in front of the guests. Octavia would never dare do that in the presence of the Asaszi unless she was sure she wouldn't be punished for it. *Something happened in the sparring yard today for her to gain favor with Osza, Astohi, and Father.* The gears in Seth's head turned, but he had little time to process everything.

Octavia took her seat to the left of Seth in between him and their father who barely managed to hide his dissatisfaction. To Seth's right was the displaced stone chair and Osza. The Asaszi queen wore a simple gold circlet that held her black hair back and out of her face. A golden shawl hung across her shoulders. Her sharp, angled face was turned toward him and his sister. He met her golden gaze, and it was like facing a venomous snake. Her serpentine ancestry showed—thin lips that barely hid fangs underneath, two slits for a nose, and two small earholes along her hairline. Jade scales covered her body. She blinked slowly at him before looking back at their father. Her forked tongue slipped from her mouth, and she hissed quietly.

Their father clapped his hands once, and the servants busied themselves with serving the food and wine. Seth's plate was filled with various roast meats and stewed vegetables.

"Your presence is most appreciated this evening, Osza," their father said, his sour expression fading. "I understand that you and Astohi were present for my daughter's training this afternoon?"

Osza exchanged a glance with Astohi and then nodded. "Yesss, Amias. Your daughter shows promissse." Because of her lack of contact with anyone outside of the Asaszi, Osza took care to make sure her speech was more than just a pattern of hisses. "Assstohi and I think that it isss time ssshe devoted herssself to your causssse."

Seth was mid-drink when Osza finished. He held the cup to his face to mask his look of surprise. *So that's why they had been observing her today. It was her final test before her initiation. I should have put the pieces together sooner. If Osza and Astohi are pleased with her performance, that would mean—*

"Then we shall host the permutation ceremony tomorrow evening." Their father was practically beaming, and so was Octavia. Their mother was trying to look positive as well, but Seth knew she was just as uneasy as he was. "And we'll make my daughter the youngest *pyredan* since the Provira arrived in Moonyswyn!"

Seth's stomach churned. On the one hand, he feared for his sister. To announce her devotion to their father so publicly... But if her permutation ceremony would happen tomorrow, did that mean his father intended on pushing back his experiments? Would the shield-bearer from earlier be spared?

"Amiasss, what about your *experimentsss*?" Astohi asked, his golden eyes narrowing into even thinner slits. With his head turned toward the other end of the table, there was no mistaking the poise of his serpentine head. He was ready to strike if the wrong words were spoken.

Seth's father locked eyes with Astohi, unblinking. "The success of my daughter far outweighs the disappointment of the experiments."

Osza let out another hiss, one far more dire in meaning. "Failure?"

His father looked at her. "Efforts to create an opening in the tomb aren't going as planned. The Provira who make mockery of the title of shield-bearer cannot perform their duties during the rituals. It is... most disappointing."

Osza's golden slits were unblinking. Her face was neutral unlike that of her mate. Her tongue flitted out, tasting the air before she spoke. "Pity." She wrapped her taloned fingers around the cup before her and drank.

The room went silent save for the sounds of utensils on plates and the drinking of wine. Seth wondered how long he would need to stay at the table before he could excuse himself and return to his room. Being in the same room as his father and Osza made his stomach twist and turn uncomfortably, and he was having difficulty forcing down food. The news of his sister's permutation just made things worse. He wanted to escape as soon as he could.

"And what about your progresss on your son's legsss?" Astohi asked.

Seth froze as his fork pierced through a piece of meat. Another piece sat heavy on his tongue, and he forgot to chew. He felt Astohi's eyes boring into him, and he wanted nothing more than to shrink away into the darkness of the jungle.

Amias cleared his throat. "It is my understanding that High Priestess Szatisi has made progress with some of the spellsingers. I will meet with her before my travels to Iszairi to evaluate her work."

What?

Seth's heart thumped so loudly he nearly missed Osza's pleasant hiss. "Very good."

He carefully looked up from his plate and at his mother. *Did she know that Father was doing this? Surely not or else she would have told me.*

This had to be news to her as well. His mother, bless her, was perhaps the only person in the world that he could turn to at a moment like this, and he was furious that it had to be done in such a public setting. Evelyn's gray eyes were downcast at her plate. Now was not the time. Could he request that she come to his room after dinner? No, that would make him look like a child in need of his mother and Amias would ridicule him for it.

"There is also word from Tetherphin, one of the *envoys*," Amias went on with greater control and enthusiasm. Good news that he could deliver himself, eager to please the *Zsikui.*

Osza and Astohi's tongues flickered out in curiosity. Seth's mother and Octavia also looked up at the mention of the envoy.

The corner of Amias's lips curled upward in a smile. "He has arrived in Elimere, and the Elviri are none the wiser for it."

Seth's mother let out a quiet gasp. The Asaszi blinked slowly. Octavia hung onto their father's words, waiting for more.

"He has heard word that one of their highborn has been touched. He will hold his position until he finds them."

"How can we be sure?" Seth blurted out.

The attention of everyone in the room snapped to him, and Seth immediately lowered his gaze to his plate. He exhaled and looked back up at his father. Seth saw the faint outline of veins bulging from his neck. In that moment, Seth was thankful for their guests, their presence curbing their father's wrath.

Seth cleared his throat and clarified, "Father, how can we trust that what he's heard is true?"

"Tetherphin would never lie to his lord," Amias hissed through clenched teeth.

Seth didn't risk holding his father's gaze. Although his father hadn't really answered his question, he knew better than to risk challenging his response.

Did Osza or Astohi notice the lack of an answer?

They were, perhaps, the only people who could openly call out Amias. And yet they never did. Seth should have known better than to hope, even for a moment.

The room filled with tense silence again without the sound of utensils scraping and wine-drinking. After another moment, Seth decided he had had enough.

"Father, may I be excused?" he asked. When he didn't receive an immediate response, he knew that his father was waiting for him to look up. He decided he could afford one moment of bravery and deny his father the satisfaction of making eye contact. He placed his utensils down on the table and pushed his plate away to make his point.

After another moment of silence, his bravery paid off. "Yes. Go," came his father's curt response.

Seth gripped the wheels of his chair and pulled backwards, putting space between him and the table. As he swiveled toward the door, he spared one glance at his mother and sister. Octavia would be able to hold her own for the rest of the evening with Osza and Astohi in attendance. Seth wished he could speak to his mother. He rolled out of the dining hall before his cowardice resurfaced.

It wasn't any easier climbing into bed a second time, but he managed. That had been after he found a pair of silken sleep pants tucked into one of his drawers and pulled them on, casting aside his day clothes. Now laying back on the bed, he ran a hand through his blond hair and eased out any tangles that had formed during the day. He tugged on the blankets beneath him until he was underneath them. Seth sunk deeper into the bed, surrounded by silk and linens that buried the stone beneath. He pulled one of the several pillows to him, pressing it against his chest and face.

He let out a shaking sob that went down all the way to where he lost feeling at his knees. Sleep wouldn't come easy tonight. He tried to focus on breathing in and out, not letting the sobs wrack through his body. He listened to the sounds of the jungle outside, hopeful for rain, but instead was met with the buzzing and chirping of bugs that nearly drowned out the faint familiar hum underneath it all. The hum of magic. He scoffed, rubbing his eyes. Magic was gone, and he hoped that his father would never be able to find a way to bring it back.

Seth had witnessed the work of High Priestess Szatisi shortly after the accident when he was fourteen. His father had held him against his chest as he lay on a stone slab. Szatisi had poured something dark over his bare legs, adding a blue tinge to his skin. The three of them watched his legs, waiting for something to happen. At first it was faint, but then the feeling hit him full force. He had screamed and thrashed against his father's grip. Burning, burning, *burning*. His legs had felt like they were on fire. He had grabbed onto his father's arms, his wrists, anything he could reach as he pleaded to make it stop, to make it go away, get rid of them, get it off, *get it off*—

And then he had been submerged in water. The feeling faded. His legs no longer felt like they were on fire—they felt like nothing. They still felt like nothing. Seth wished his father had cut them off all those years ago. But he had insisted. He had said he would find a cure. Seth looked down at his legs, covered by linens, and cursed. There was nothing that could fix his legs. They were dead. The curse lingered on his lips as he faded into sleep.

CHAPTER IV: MUNNE

ELIMERE: DAY 14, MONTH 11, YEAR 13,239

Munne's eyes flew open, and she cried out. Her heart thumped wildly as she tried to regain her breath. Screams still echoed in her head as she fought to keep them out. She shut her eyes, inhaling slowly through her nose. As she exhaled, she sat up in her bed. Moonlight filled the room, its luminous tendrils crawling up the silken linens of the bed. Across the room her dirtied armor lay on a painted bench, waiting to be cleaned.

Munne shook her head. "I'm not in those caves," she whispered. "It's just a dream."

The words seemed true enough, but she could still hear the screams even if they were now no more than a whisper, feel the dank walls of the caverns closing in around her. She still saw the shadow of the enormous creature that chased after her. Her heartbeat remained erratic, and her eyes watered up, tears threatening to spill over.

She swept the blankets off and stood, no longer feeling at ease in her own room. She walked over to the balcony and threw the doors open, letting the moon's light wash over her. Her eyes raked over the city of Elimere, taking in the sight of all the pale wooden homes and shops below the manor. Traces of the earlier celebration lingered in the streets. The lanterns that the people had launched into the sky earlier that evening had returned to the ground and were scattered across the roads. To the southwest, the main plaza was still lit up with lanterns, and some members of the orchestra were still playing. She could hear the roaring of the waterfalls that flanked the manor.

Shortly after her troops arrived at the south border of Promthus, Munne started having nightmares nearly every night. Dreams of people crying and begging for help, for protection from the shadows. They were lost within a pitch-black cavern, and she would run through its twisting corridors trying to find them. She always tried to find them, but the dream ended the same way. She arrived too late, and the screaming began. The shrill cries and screeches of people being tortured echoed all throughout her head and all she could do was stand there and watch as those people flickered before her eyes. She saw one bloodied face after another, and soon enough it was more than she could handle, and she woke up in a cold sweat. She could still hear the screams as she stood on the balcony.

It wasn't like she hadn't heard the cries of the dying before, but these were different. Every time the screaming started, something inside of her lurched, and she felt the need to run and find the one screaming and protect them from harm. The desire transcended any sense of loyalty she felt to her court or to her soldiers. She needed to find this person and take care of them because her very existence demanded it. Tonight had been different, though, for a creature chased her as soon as she ran. A shadow of the creature loomed in front of her, and she dared not turn around to see what it truly looked like. An overwhelming sense of dread followed her into the waking realm.

Munne leaned against the railing and took another deep breath. She closed her eyes and shook her head, trying to get rid of the sounds. Leaves fell from the trees as winter neared the valley. The cold mountain breeze relaxed her mind but made her muscles tense, and her wounds from battle seemed to flare up all at once. The dangers of the half-breeds were very real. She had felt their anger and passion on the battlefield. She returned home with scars to prove how dangerous these monstrous anarchists really were.

She opened her eyes, suddenly feeling very exposed and cold, and returned to her room. She gathered up a blanket to wrap around herself. When she returned from her vigil earlier in the night, she had stripped herself of all her clothes and tossed them to the side, before crawling into her bed and falling asleep.

Munne looked back out onto the balcony to see where the moon lay in the sky. It was just beginning to fall from its peak, so sunrise was still a few hours away. She turned back to her room and decided to go for a walk to the archives. Being surrounded by books brought her great comfort, which she sorely needed right now. She grabbed a dark blue robe and a pair of slippers from her armoire before leaving.

Her feet padded softly across the floors as she departed from her suite to the nearest flight of stairs that descended to the lower levels of the manor. There were a few guards making their routes in and around the manor, but none asked any questions. This wasn't the first time she was up in the middle of the night walking the halls.

"It's good to see you again, Lady Vere'cha," one of the guards said quietly as she passed by him in the hall.

"It's good to be back." She nodded and gave him a polite half smile, pulling her robe tightly across her chest. Although many rooms in the manor had fireplaces for the colder months, the hallways rarely received any of that warmth.

It took her no time to get to the archives. The room smelled of old parchment and earth. It was a dark chamber, the only light sources coming from torches with smoldering flames. There were three floors in the archives that descended underground beneath the manor. The first floor had many tables and chairs and was meant to be where visitors would bring their books to study. Stained glass windows stretched from floor to ceiling, each depicting an aspect of the goddess of knowledge, Belleol.

As Munne came around a corner, she saw Elvarin sitting at a table with piles of books surrounding him. A dish holding a candle was next to his arm, the flame low. She made her way to his side, and glanced down at the book that was lying open in front of him—she could make out a passage about Lithalyon's development in the early years of the Second Sun.

"Sleep has eluded you once more, hasn't it, my lady?" Elvarin asked, not turning his head from the book.

"As it has with you," Munne replied as a smile tugged at her lips. She placed her hand on his shoulder and squeezed gently. "Why are you awake at this hour, Elvarin? I would have assumed you'd be resting after the celebration."

He turned to look at Munne, abandoning his focus on the book. His face was warm and friendly upon first glance, but as she studied him, she saw the dark circles around his eyes and wrinkles beginning to form across his face. "I was able to slip away shortly after the vigil began. Besides, there is always work to do." The corners of his eyes crinkled, his lips curving slightly. "What about you, friend?"

"These nightmares are going to be the end of me," Munne murmured, leaning against the table.

Elvarin twisted in his chair until he was facing Munne. She had written to him after the first week of having the same nightmare every night. There had to be a reason for it, so she asked him to investigate the archives when he had some time to spare. She trusted him with her affliction since they had developed such a close friendship in their early years as Warlord and Lorelord. The only other people who knew of it were Cesa and her triple.

She crossed her arms, a grimace spreading across her face. "I wish I knew what was causing this. I know you've been busy with your own studies of late, but..." She let out an exasperated sigh before looking at Elvarin. "Have you found anything?"

Elvarin frowned. "Aeglys has been keeping me busy with her own research, I'm afraid."

"A royal archivist would demand the service of the Lorelord?" Munne arched an eyebrow, amused.

Elvarin chuckled and shook his head. "I offered my assistance. She was close to Sariel, so I like to assist her when I can. I think for both of us, it feels like Sariel is still with us."

Munne nodded, her eyes darting around to the books Elvarin had sprawled out on the table before him.

"Have you tried communing with an mindwalker of Lithua? Perhaps they could find a way to ease your mind."

She turned to look at Elvarin. Lithuan mindwalkers often met with soldiers when they returned from battle to help ease their minds and cope with their trauma. "This isn't the same kind of affliction that my soldiers normally face. There must be something more to it."

"It was merely a suggestion. Don't sound so gruff about it." Elvarin glanced back to his books, beginning to flip through the pages again. "What about a pilgrimage? When was the last time you walked in the godswood?"

She leaned against the table, sighing. "Before I left the valley. I do need to make a pilgrimage."

Elvarin reached out and squeezed her hand, offering Munne a reassuring smile. "Remember to have faith in the gods, Munne. They hear our words and offer us guidance, even though they have left this mortal plane."

She squeezed his hand in return, the corners of her lips curling into a smile. "Thank you for your counsel, Elvarin. Hopefully, this will help me with curing my nightmares."

"Hopefully so. At least one of us needs to sleep." Elvarin winked before letting go of her hand. "Goodnight, Munne."

"Goodnight, friend," she called out quietly as she left the archives.

As Munne passed through the main foyer, she looked up. A portion of the ceiling had been carved out so the suns and stars could shine their light into the manor. She could only see the brightest of the stars tonight. Clouds hung low, hiding all the others. Perhaps there was a storm rolling in. She didn't mind if it rained tomorrow when she visited Ceyo's godsite, but her horse would fare better if it didn't.

She climbed the stairs to the third floor, and headed toward the southeast where her suite was located. The doors to her receiving chambers had a mural of the valley on it with the three towering mountain peaks surrounding it. Purple and red flowers were painted around the mountains, framing the valley in a lush spring setting. She pulled one of the doors open and hurried inside, suddenly eager to return to her bed. Exhaustion seeped through her limbs.

Munne shivered as she entered her bedchamber. The air in the room was cold. She pulled her robe tighter and walked toward the fireplace near her bed. She had forgotten to light it when she returned from the feasting earlier in the evening. Frowning, she walked to the other side of her bedchamber and pulled out a large, patterned quilt from one of the armoires. The quilt had been made by her father's mother as a gift for Munne's birth. It smelled of cedar, reminding her of her childhood and nights she would spend with her friends staying up late at night telling ghost stories.

She spread the quilt out on top of the other blankets on her bed. She kicked off her slippers and pulled her robe off before slipping under the blankets. Her bed had gone cold in the time she walked around the manor. She shivered and curled up into a ball, trying to retain as much warmth as she could. She prayed a wordless prayer to Nole for the ease of falling asleep again, and to Aeona for a comfortable slumber.

Soon after, she was fast asleep again.

◆

Birds perched on the balcony outside Munne's room, singing cheerfully to greet the day. Munne rolled over so her back faced the door to the balcony. Her eyes opened slowly, adjusting to the morning light spilling into her room. She had neglected to draw the curtains last night before returning to bed. Munne grumbled and rolled onto her back, throwing her arm over her face.

The smell of baked goods and cooked meats wafted into her room. Her maids must have brought food to her dining chamber. *A hot meal is a good reason as any to get up.* Munne climbed out of bed and stepped into her slippers again. She picked up the discarded robe off the ground and put it on, drawing it across her body. She looked around the room to see if the maids had entered while she slept. The hearth was still empty, and her dirtied armor still sat on the painted bench. They hadn't been in her bedchamber, and for that Munne was grateful. *I'll need to clean my armor before today's ceremony.*

Ever since the war began, Munne hadn't been sleeping well. The nightmares may have been a recent addition, but she was always a light sleeper, and tended to sleep past the suns rising out of the sky. There had been a few occasions where her maids had come into the bedchamber to start a new fire and pick up her discarded clothes, and Munne nearly leapt out of bed and onto the maid in a frenzy. The poor maid had been scared half to death. From then on, Munne made them promise not to enter her bedchamber while she was still sleeping. The maids were more than happy to agree with that decision.

Munne left her bedchamber and entered her dining hall. It was modest compared to other suites in the manor. Her table could seat six, and there was only one fireplace in the room. Behind a pair of doors a small balcony jutted out above the gardens. Her father had a table that sat twelve people comfortably and had a fireplace at either end of the room. Munne didn't know what she would do with that space if she took the Hunting Throne.

When I take the Hunting Throne, she reminded herself.

Two of her maids were finishing setting her table. A small bowl of sweet porridge was placed next to Munne's empty plate. There was a tray of fruits and cheeses nearby, as well as a plate of various cuts of roasted pork, and a plate of pastries. Munne smiled as she caught sight of spiced honey rolls. There was only one seat prepared to the right of the head seat. Munne never felt comfortable sitting at the head of her table when she was by herself.

"Good morning, Lady Vere'cha." One of the maids smiled and pulled the chair from the table. "And welcome home. Please, have a seat. Everything is freshly made."

Munne returned the smile and sat down, pulling the seat forward. The two maids stepped away from the table, moving to take care of other chores around the room. The dark-haired woman, Namyr, went to the hearth to start a fire while the fair-haired woman, Laenis, poured Munne a cup of water.

"How were things in the valley while I was gone?" Munne asked Laenis and put together her breakfast plate.

"The Harvestmath festival was truly wondrous. We had some visitors from Castle Auora during that time, and they brought some ales and wines from the city," Laenis said, and Munne could tell she was happy to be around her again. "Not enough visitors that we needed to use your guest chambers, though."

"Very good, very good." Munne ate a few spoonfuls of the porridge before setting it down and reaching for the fruit. "Was any of the royal family present?"

"No, m'lady, it was only advisors and emissaries," Laenis responded and bowed her head.

"Ah, well, I'm due for a visit to Castle Auora after the winter season has passed." Munne frowned a little, but it passed as she picked up and bit into one of the spiced honey rolls. She couldn't help but smile and close her eyes, savoring the flavor of the fluffy pastry. "Please tell the bakers that I'm eternally grateful for the honey rolls this morning."

"Of course, m'lady." Laenis grinned. "Oh, and then there was a strange group of foreigners who arrived two days ago. They don't look like any visitors we've received in Elimere before."

Munne raised an eyebrow. "Traders from the Black Lakes?" She took another bite from the honey roll. The Barauder of the Black Lakes very rarely made an appearance in Elimere. They preferred warmer climates, and often traveled to Elimaine instead.

"I don't believe so," Laenis turned her back to the table and leaned against it. "They are staying at The Moonlit Grove on the southern edge of the city. My brother is courting one of the barmaids there, and he saw them arrive when he visited her two nights ago. I'm not sure if he's met a Barauder before, but I think he would have mentioned their teeth or scales."

"Are they merchants? Did they bring any goods to trade?" Munne inquired, her interest piqued.

Laenis shook her head. "Oryn said that if they did, they had already brought it to the Eyreti Bazaar before arriving at the inn."

Munne frowned. *Visitors who aren't here for politics normally bring goods for trade. What brings these strangers to the valley?* "Please remind me of this when I return from the ceremony. I'll speak with some of the town guards and have them keep an eye on these visitors of ours."

Laenis curtseyed and took her leave, heading toward the receiving chamber.

"Oh, Lady Vere'cha," Namyr said and turned to face Munne, the fire having sufficiently started. "Before I forget, Lord Elvarin sent word that he would like to share your hearth this morning. I can prepare a second seat, if you wish."

Munne looked down at what remained of the spiced honey roll, then up at the table. There was certainly enough food for the two of them to eat together. Munne was surprised that he was awake so early, considering he was still awake last night when she took her walk around the manor.

"Very well. If Laenis hasn't left yet, have her relay the message. You can prepare his seat," Munne told her.

"Yes, m'lady." Namyr curtseyed and slipped into the receiving chamber.

Munne placed the remains of the roll on her plate and stood up. If Elvarin was coming, she could wait to eat the rest of her food with him. She paced around the dining room, clasping her hands behind her back. Her feet took her to the lone fireplace. She watched the flames dance and crackle within. In a few weeks, the *Ema'nala Ena'deth* would occur throughout the city. It was a time for remembrance of the past year and preparation for the year to come. In the main plaza, a mural of the two suns would be put on display for Elviri to come and meditate on their musings. *I hope to still be in the city for the celebration. I have so much to reflect on this year.*

After a few moments, Munne heard footsteps in the receiving chamber. She turned back to the dining room and saw Elvarin walking in behind Laenis, already dressed for the day. He was wearing a gray tunic and pants underneath a blue robe. Munne crossed to Elvarin, her arms spread for a hug. He smiled and wrapped his arms around her.

"Thank you for allowing me to share your hearth this morning," Elvarin said, sitting at the second prepared seat at the table.

Munne returned to her own seat, gesturing at all the food before them. "Please, eat as much as you'd like." She returned to nibbling on her honey roll and watched him pull pieces of pork onto his plate, as well as some chunks of cheese and fruit.

They ate in silence for a few moments before Elvarin looked up at Munne. "I, ah... had a reason I wanted to speak to you this morning," he said quietly, averting his gaze to Laenis and Namyr. They stood by the doors to the receiving chamber, their hands behind their backs. "Could we perhaps do so in private?"

"Oh, yes, of course," Munne mumbled. She hadn't expected this from Elvarin, but she turned to dismiss her maids all the same. "I should be leaving for the morning ceremony soon. You two are, of course, welcome to return and resume your duties then."

The two Elviri women nodded and left the suite.

Munne turned back to Elvarin. "Shall we get some fresh air?"

The two walked over to the doors that led to the balcony and stepped outside. The waterfalls echoed around them, the sounds bouncing off the manor. Munne breathed in deeply through her nose, enjoying the smell of the fresh autumn air. The view from this balcony faced south, so she could see everything in Elimere beyond the manor. The main plaza in Elimere blended in with the rest of the city. The decorations from the previous night had been taken down.

"What did you want to talk about?" she inquired.

Elvarin shifted his weight between his feet, and Munne saw uneasiness in his eyes. He was going to tell her something she didn't want to hear. *What has he learned?*

"I found something last night in the archives after you left," he said slowly, resting an elbow on the wooden railing.

"Is this about the dreams?" Munne crossed her arms. *Surely any new information is good, but why does he look so nervous?*

"Yes, ah... I found a journal that belonged to a soldier during the Elviri-Asaszi wars at the beginning of the Second Sun. He spoke about these peculiar fever dreams." Elvarin lowered his voice. "He wrote that he made camp with a group of refugees from a Proma village who were having fever dreams, very similar to the ones you described in your letter."

Munne frowned, her eyebrows knitting together. "Proma were having these dreams?"

"Yes, but that's not all..." Elvarin grimaced, pushing himself away from the railing. "The leader of the refugees, some kind of holy man, said that a black demon had caused these fever dreams. The refugees had never seen the creature in person, but the holy man swore by it. He described the demon in a way that the soldier wouldn't repeat in his journal, but that night the soldier had the same fever dream as the refugees."

"Black demon? That's a very vague description," Munne said.

"The soldier had these fever dreams every night. Days later, he began raving about the shadow of an evil creature, how it stalked him through his nightmares, how it had cursed him."

Munne's eyes widened, but she said nothing. *Could it be the same creature I saw last night?*

Elvarin continued, "It was terribly difficult to get through the rest of his journal. Toward the end, he was describing what that shadow looked like. The description matched the *Ardashi'ik*."

The *Ardashi'ik* was an evil creature of myth, one left behind in the Eldest Days. Few tales were passed through the years, but those Munne had heard told of a massive creature black as the darkest night with wings that could blot out the suns. Priests and other holy men occasionally spoke about the *Ardashi'ik* and how the gods triumphed over it in battle, a testament to their power. In recent years, some scribes had found traces of the myth in the archives alongside records of war and entries in diaries, leading to a gnawing fear that there was more to the myth than they thought. Fragments of her nightmare, of the shadowed beast, flashed across her eyes.

Was that the shadow I saw? She felt a wave of panic swell up inside of her, filling her with an overwhelming sense of dread. "The *Ardashi'ik* doesn't exist." Munne said, as if that would waive the problem away.

Elvarin opened his mouth as if to respond, but he thought otherwise. His silence did nothing to ease Munne's concern.

"Elvarin, it doesn't exist. Surely this was just the ravings of a madman?" She tried to rationalize what he had said, but she wasn't sure that she believed the words she was saying.

"I would like to believe it was just the diary of a madman, friend, but it concerns me that the descriptions between the two of you match so well, at least in the beginning of his journal."

Munne returned to her seat in the dining room. Elvarin was just on the edge of her line of sight, following her back inside. She sat in silence for a moment, staring down at her plate. *It's just a madman's book. It means nothing. The dreams are just my mind twisting the horrors of this damned war and mimicking it in the dream world. I'm just hearing the screams of the battlefield—what soldier hasn't? My urge to run is just my base instincts telling me to go. I share nothing in common with this soldier from many lifetimes ago.*

"How did it end?" Munne asked abruptly.

"It stopped very suddenly, I..." Elvarin shifted in his seat. "I'll need to compare with other sources from the time and see if I can find anything else out, or happened to him," he muttered, almost to himself. "But I told you I would let you know what I found." He looked back up at Munne, an apology written on his face.

She frowned, not sure what to make of this information. Her heart pounded in her chest. She needed to stand up and leave the room, but she didn't want to seem rude to her guest.

Elvarin reached out across the table, trying to take her hand in his. Munne caught just a glimpse of his movement and pushed away from it, panicked.

"I-I'm sorry, but I need to prepare for the morning ceremony," Munne said, a blank look on her face. She got to her feet. "Please, eat what you'd like."

"Munne..."

She turned to look at Elvarin, saying nothing. It took all her power to not run out of the room and back to her bedchamber.

"I will let you know what I find." With his response, Munne turned, forcing herself not to run.

Munne shut the door of the bedchamber behind her. She needed to distract herself from the new findings and get ready for today's ceremony. She couldn't wear her armor because it hadn't been cleaned yet—her own fault. She should've taken care of it last night before going to sleep, but she had been too consumed with her grief. She started digging through the various robes that were hanging in one of the armoires. *I'll have to wear one of my dress robes to the ceremony... but I'm visiting Ceyo's godsite in the mountains after, so I'll need something to ride in. Perhaps my riding gear...?* She began searching for it, becoming more frantic when she couldn't find it immediately.

Munne found her riding gear neatly tucked away in one of the chests. She sighed and tore off her robe to get dressed. Soon enough she was ready to depart. *I just needed to grab my gloves and necessities from the study.*

Her study was on the opposite side of the dining hall from her bedchamber. As she made her way through her suite, she saw that Elvarin had already gone. Inside the study was her desk along with multiple bookcases that held her own small library. The books were cherished volumes from her childhood, stories of Ceyo from the Eldest Days and fantastical tales of brave Elviri knights and maids. It was important to her to have a room where she could simply be Munne Vere'cha, lover of fine stories and pastries, and leave her duties as Warlord and heir to the Hunting Throne behind. It had been several months since she had last retreated into her study and shut the rest of the world out. *I need to make time to sit in here and unwind.*

On her desk was a pair of brown leather gloves next to her coin purse. She scooped both up and left the study. The spread of food was still on the table in the dining hall. She grabbed another spiced honey roll and left her suite.

The suns were warm as she left the manor. A slight breeze drifted from the waterfalls, turning the comfortable day into a chilly, brisk one. Munne didn't mind—her coat kept her warm. She ran her hand through her hair out of habit and realized she hadn't done anything with her hair amidst her frenzy. It fell to her shoulders without any decoration, unbefitting of her station. Silently she chided herself.

Munne's path took her to the Hall of the Dead for today's ceremony to oversee the departure of the dead, along with the high priest, her father, and some of the other higher-ranking officers. As she passed by one of the bakeries on her path, the scent of sweet and savory pastries wafted through the air. If Munne hadn't eaten earlier, she may have stopped to purchase something. This bakery, as well as many others close to the hall, prepared food earlier than usual to accommodate the influx of people in the area.

As she neared the hall, the streets became more crowded. People chatted about the festivities the evening prior, and about travel plans for the last stretch of autumn. Visitors usually didn't stay in the valley during the winter months. Those who traveled from Elimaine and Elifyn to observe the ceremony of the dead usually returned home over the next couple of days before the weather drastically changed. Others discussed plans for the day, if they had chores that needed attending to or shopping that needed to be done. As Munne passed them, several clusters of townsfolk lowered their voices. It was unusual for the Warlord to not be dressed in some kind of dress robe or armor, and to arrive only moments before the ceremony began. Munne could tell as they laid eyes on her that she would be the subject of their next conversation.

Near the steps of the hall were two lines of six carriages, each carrying three caskets. A priest from the hall sat at the front of each carriage, dressed in familiar dark robes. The sight chilled her blood and calmed her nerves. *Soon they join Azrael in eternal peace.*

Kieron stood on the steps of the hall along with Huntaran and the three lieutenants of the army. Kieron and her father were wearing dress robes, the lieutenants in polished armor. Munne immediately felt a twinge of guilt for not wearing her dress robes, but she quickly pushed that feeling away. She climbed the steps and took her place next to her father close to the doors. They all glanced over her before returning their gaze to the doors. Each one of them had a stoic expression. Still, she could tell that they were thinking about her choice in attire. No one would dare make a scene during the ceremony, but Munne knew either Kieron or Huntaran would pull her aside later and chastise her for not dressing the part. She quickly glanced at the gathering crowds to see if Cesa was there bearing witness to her poor attire choices but didn't catch sight of him.

The doors to the hall opened, and she shifted her gaze back. The high priest emerged from the hall riding on a black stallion. He brought the horse to a stop at the top of the stairs, looking out at the gathered crowds. "Welcome all. Today your soldiers march one last time, to their resting place. As they pass through these streets, may they feel comfort, knowing we support them from beyond the veil."

He urged his horse forward at a steady pace. Out of the hall came several more priests atop horses. They stopped at the top of the stairs, waiting. From either side at the bottom of the stairs, the twelve carriages moved forward. There was no noise aside from the creaking of the carriages, the horse hooves hitting the ground, and the waterfall tumbling down at the edge of the valley. Munne's eyes never left the carriages, not until they disappeared around a curve in the street.

The townsfolk broke up and filled the streets after seeing the carriages off. Many glanced up in Munne's direction, expecting her to descend the stairs and speak with them about their deceased loved ones. When Cesa had been Warlord, he'd always tell stories about the soldiers to bring comfort to their families. Her mouth dried out, and suddenly her tongue felt heavy in her mouth. She wouldn't be able to speak to these people today. Something inside of her was telling her to run, run away from the valley. The townsfolk were looking up at her expectantly. She needed to breathe.

"Elviri of all provinces, thank you for being here this morning," Munne called out. The lieutenants all turned to look at her, their stoic expressions cracking. This was abnormal, not part of the routine. "Your loved ones fought bravely and didn't deserve this fate. But I assure you..." A knot formed in her throat, and she forcibly swallowed. "I assure you that we will have our vengeance."

Huntaran's eyes widened, and he reached out to grab his daughter's arm, but Munne moved quickly. She descended the stairs and walked as fast as she could toward the stables. *Duties be damned. I need to leave the valley and calm my mind.*

No one dared try to stop Munne as she made her way to the stables. The stable hands were in the middle of feeding the horses when she barged in. She went straight for Alathyl, her gray mare and began saddling her up.

The stable hands were startled by her sudden appearance. One of them approached her. "Lady Vere'cha, we weren't expecting you—"

Munne turned to the stable hand. "No need to panic. I'm just taking Alathyl for a morning ride."

The stable hand seemed to relax, but Munne could tell he was still on edge. After all, why would the Warlord be barging into the stable to retrieve her horse when she should be attending a sacred ceremony?

Munne finished preparing Alathyl and then climbed onto her back. She charged out of the barn and up the winding path that led out of the valley. The leaves were beginning to fall. They had turned color two months ago before Munne had left for Promthus on her latest campaign. After spending time at the godsite, she would need to find a spot in the woods to lay down and enjoy solitude in nature.

Munne was going to visit the first godsite of Ceyo a short distance to the south from Elimere. That was where Ceyo was born in her mortal life. All the gods had been born mortal and journeyed to the north to ascend to godhood. The places they were born were marked as sacred, and the Paladins of the Gods were responsible for preserving the sites.

As Munne approached the grove where Ceyo's cabin stood, a gust of wind blew through the woods. She stopped her horse, straightened her back and closed her eyes. She inhaled deeply, the scent of earth and pine mingling in the air. Nearby, several birds sang their autumnal songs. It was a welcome change from the valley.

Munne opened her eyes. She slipped off her horse, reins in hand. She led Alathyl toward the modest cabin. Sunlight poured into the forest grove, basking the cabin in warm light. Red and yellow leaves littered the ground. There were no paladins near the cabin, which she found a bit odd but was thankful for the solitude. She would have time in peace with Ceyo. There was a hitching post close to the cabin where Munne secured Alathyl's reins.

It wasn't until Munne turned to face the godsite that she felt the cold of the mountains. Her riding coat wasn't enough to protect her from the gusts of wind blowing through the trees. She quickly crossed over to the cabin and pushed the door open. The inside was cold as well, but at least the wind couldn't chill her here.

The inside of the cabin was sparse. There was a wooden frame of a bed on the opposite side from her with animal hides tied to each post to create a place to lie down. More fur pelts lay on top of the bed, as well as two straw pillows. The bed was for pilgrims and paladins who chose to stay the night at the hallowed ground with the intention of humbling them before the presence of the gods. Munne was no stranger to the discomfort of the bed. She had stayed the night in Ceyo's cabin many times before.

To the left of the bed was a small stone fireplace with a simple wooden bench in front of it. Firewood had been stacked next to the fireplace in the corner of the cabin. A wooden altar with elaborate runes carved into the stand was erected on the other side of the fireplace. On top of the altar was a bust of Ceyo carved out of white marble. The bust was of her upper body, cutting off right under her chest. Her hands were raised in front of her, palms open. The goddess's eyes were closed, her lips parted slightly.

Munne approached the altar, a shiver running through her. The altar was built so that the worshippers would kneel in front of the bust and place their hands against the goddess's. Munne knelt in front of the altar and removed her gloves. She placed them on the ground next to her and raised her hands to meet Ceyo's. She closed her eyes.

The first thing she noticed was the silence. The wind wasn't blowing against the windows, nor were the birds singing in the trees. Even the cold had vanished around her. Was she now warm? She hadn't lit a fire before kneeling before the altar. Munne opened her eyes and met the gaze of Ceyo. Rather, she met the gaze of the marble bust of Ceyo, whose pupilless eyes were now open. Munne blinked. *Shouldn't the statue's eyes be closed?*

"*Be at peace, Munne.*"

A wave of comfort and ease washed over her. She blinked again, focusing on the bust before her. She projected a thought, "*Thank you for communing with me.*"

"You came here with a purpose."

Munne thought she was nodding her head, though she couldn't feel the movement. *"I seek guidance. I have been having nightmares as of late, and I don't know where they are coming from."*

There was no response. Munne changed her focus and looked beyond the bust of Ceyo. Her eyes widened. Beyond the bust, there was nothing. The cabin had slipped away.

"You ask for something that I have not seen since before the Passing."

Something faintly warm stirred against Munne's hands. She looked down but saw nothing out of the ordinary about the marble hands pressed against hers. When she shifted focus back to Ceyo's face, the goddess's eyes were closed again.

"There is a danger in this request, and yet it must be fulfilled. You do not walk alone, Munne. You will meet your guide to this dark place."

A twinge of panic struck Munne, and her breathing became labored. *What dark place? Could this be related to the one Elviri's journal, and the mention of the Ardashi'ik?*

"Munne!"

Munne blinked, and she was back in Ceyo's cabin. The goddess's eyes remained shut, and the marble was cold to the touch. Munne fell backwards on the cabin floor. To her left were two panicked Elviri women. One kneeled beside her while the other paced the length of the cabin.

"Munne, what in the creator's name are you doing?" the kneeling Elviri demanded, placing her hand on Munne's shoulder.

Warmth emanated from the woman's touch, and Munne fully returned to consciousness. The hand belonged to Mayrien, an Elviri close to her age and a member of her triple. Her brown hair was braided and hung over her right shoulder, her hazel eyes bright with fury. She was wearing a regal set of riding gear with the Elviri army emblem emblazoned on the chest and back of the outer jacket.

"Mayrien, I—"

"You nearly gave your father a panic attack, damnit, and on such a solemn day," Mayrien sighed angrily, letting go of Munne's shoulder.

"You are also late to the war council," the other Elviri murmured, not looking at Munne. The Elviri had short blonde hair that just barely reached past her ears. She was dressed in her own regal set of military riding gear—Araloth, the third member of her triple.

"Araloth..." Munne closed her eyes and pinched the bridge of her nose. "What time is it?"

"Close to midday," Mayrien responded, standing up. "We would have been here sooner, but your father decided we needed to bear witness to his anger in your stead."

Munne looked at Mayrien, then at the bust of Ceyo. She opened her mouth to speak but the words never left her lips. *It was already midday? I left the valley in the early morning, and the ride to the cabin was no more than fifteen minutes. Where had the time gone?*

Araloth and Mayrien were Munne's two most trustworthy allies, and two of her closest friends. The three of them formed a triple in the armed forces shortly after Mayrien and Munne elected to join the army after their lifepath rotations. Araloth had been a sect officer under the infantry and cavalry division and was looking to advance to the rank of lieutenant over her division. Mayrien came from one of the royal families in Elimaine whose history was closely tied to the Elviri Army. She naturally took to archery, seeing that her elders and ancestors were commonly found in high-ranking positions in the archery division.

When Munne met Mayrien in their lifepath rotations, the two began a healthy competition to see who was better at the given lifepath and became close friends thereafter. The two originally were in a marksman triple with a third Elviri, Yaris, but he chose to join the siege weaponry division and the women were without a third member. Araloth took notice of their sparring sessions and decided to add front-line experience to their training, and they became a triple with Araloth as their leader.

"It was the nightmares." Munne managed to get the words out. The fiery rage in Mayrien's expression died down immediately. Araloth stopped pacing and turned to look at Munne with sympathy.

"I'm sorry, friend. We didn't realize it had gotten so bad," Araloth murmured, kneeling next to Munne. Araloth offered her hand, and Munne took it. The two stood up together, Mayrien rising next to them.

Munne chuckled. "I learned something new this morning, and I was hoping Our Lady would be able to give me guidance." She looked at Ceyo again, her smile fading.

"Did she speak to you?" Mayrien asked quietly.

Munne nodded, averting her gaze to the ground. Ceyo had spoken to her in the past, as had some of the other gods. Usually, they spoke in riddles and showed puzzling images, which made communion difficult. Priests and acolytes of the gods spent their years trying to decipher these riddles and provide insight. This message from Ceyo was the clearest one Munne had ever received, but it unnerved her that it was still so vague. It unnerved her more that so much time had passed. She had only placed her hands against Ceyo's moments before Mayrien and Araloth showed up. A shiver ran through her body. She pulled her gloves on. The day hadn't gotten any warmer.

"I didn't realize so much time had passed. We should be on our way."

"We should, but—" Araloth's voice was firm yet understanding. She was still the leader, despite the shift in power when Munne was chosen as Warlord and replaced Araloth as official leader of the triple. "Munne, we should discuss this further after the council."

Munne looked up at her elder and nodded. "I agree. Perhaps over dinner... and drinks." A grin flashed across her face. Araloth's expression softened, throwing her arm around Munne's shoulders. The three exited from the cabin and mounted their horses. Munne looked at the sky through the leaves. It was indeed midday. Munne had somehow lost two to three hours at Ceyo's godsite. The goddess had never pulled her away for that long before. Something was amiss.

You will meet your guide to this dark place.

Munne closed her eyes and shook her head. She would think about this later in the company of good friends. For now, she needed to clear her mind and prepare for the war council with her father and other advisors. *Ceyo, please aid me with this tribulation.*

CHAPTER V: SETH

Seth awoke to the patter of rain hitting the side of the pyramid. He rolled onto his back, rubbing his eyes. The skin felt puffy beneath his fingers, and he grumbled. *Did I really cry myself to sleep? What am I, a child?*

He pushed himself up into a sitting position and looked around the dark room. Only a few dim rays of light entered the window. Closing his eyes, he took a deep breath and listened to the rainfall. Seth needed to speak to his mother today about what transpired at dinner. Maybe she had asked his father about his work with the high priestess after they returned to their chambers. Although his mother didn't hold the same sway over Amias that Osza and Astohi did, she still knew how to coax information from him when needed. And Seth desperately needed information. He needed to be calm when he met with his mother. It would be no use fighting with her.

He opened his eyes again. Rain fell. Tree branches rustled. Underneath it all came the quiet hum. *Mother will be in her library today.*

Seth shimmied to the edge of the bed, pulling his wheelchair over. With delicate movements, he grabbed onto one of the stone pillars and thrust his body forward, twisting his torso so that he sat facing forward in the chair. He let out a strained huff and rolled the chair around the room, searching for something to wear. He had one set of stone drawers nestled in one of the corners, and a towering armoire that stood watch over his bed. The bottom row of drawers was only touched when the stewards came into his room, since he couldn't easily reach them. Similarly, the doors to the armoire were always left open so he could access the clothes within.

Seth found a gray tunic folded inside one of the drawers. He tugged it on over his head and opted for a pair of black linen pants that had also been tucked away in the drawers. Shoes hadn't been an issue for him since he was fourteen. Even when he was younger, it was a struggle to keep shoes on his feet. He loved to run around and feel the cold stone, wet grass, and wooden mats under his heels. He missed those sensations.

Seth opened his door, disrupting the train of thought his mind had started to go down. Now wasn't the time for reminiscing. Two stewards waited outside his room garbed in robes that covered their bodies head to toe. None of the Asaszi were assigned to him today. That was good. It was less likely that word of his conversation with his mother would get back to his father. Or at least, it would take longer for the message to be delivered.

Holding his chin high, Seth rolled past the two stewards. He heard one of them pull his door shut, and they fell in line behind him as he made his way to his mother's library.

The library was one of the few gifts that Amias had given his wife. It was a retreat where Evelyn could hide away from the world and its cruelties. She had, in turn, given this gift to her children when they were old enough to sit on her lap and listen to her read them stories of faraway lands. Seth had many fond memories of sneaking into the library late at night when he couldn't sleep, and his mother finding him in the morning, sleeping in one of the chairs, curled around a book.

Thankfully, the library was on the same floor as the living quarters, so Seth was still able to visit it after the accident. His taste in books had changed as he had gotten older, gravitating away from the myths and stories of heroes from the Eldest Days in favor of educational texts teaching him about the world. Still, he enjoyed visiting the library and finding something to read. He passed through the threshold, two stewards trailing behind him, and saw his mother sitting in one of the chairs. Her legs were pulled up underneath her, tucked underneath the skirts of her dress, and she cradled a book in her hands. Her long black hair was pulled back into a knot, a few strands falling across her face.

"Good morning, Mother," Seth said, a smile passing over his face.

She looked up from her book and smiled. "Seth, what a pleasant surprise. How did you sleep?" She repositioned herself and leaned forward in her chair, placing the book on the small table next to her.

Seth averted his eyes and let out a shaky laugh. "It wasn't the best... I was hoping I could talk to you? About last night?"

Her smile wavered. Confusion and panic crossed her eyes before she blinked and nodded. "Absolutely, dearest. Let's sit by the window?"

Seth pursed his lips and wheeled himself to the other side of the room. The stewards waited by the entrance. There was only one window in the library, but it took up nearly the whole wall. One could see the entire slope of the pyramid, down to its roots where small stone huts and crumbled ruins stood. There was little distance between the huts and the edge of the jungle where vines and branches had twisted through the buildings.

Seth's mother took a seat in one of the chairs by the window, smoothing out the skirts of her dress. She offered him another smile. "Last night?" she asked.

Seth nodded, positioning his wheelchair across from her. She took his hand and squeezed gently. "How long has he been working on it?" His voice was quiet.

His mother held onto his hand tightly. "I don't know... That was the first I have heard of it as well," she murmured, stroking the top of his hand with her thumb. "I've had my suspicions, with all of his visits to Iszairi, but every time he returns, he's always in such a foul mood that I..." Her voice trailed off.

Seth sighed, letting his head fall against the back of his wheelchair. "I wonder if he even planned on telling me about it, or if it would be a surprise, like—" He forced his throat to close around the word. He wouldn't go down that path, not with his mother. Not now.

"Oh, Seth..." His mother sighed, squeezing his hand again before letting go. "I wish I had answers for you. I don't want a repeat of that, either. I couldn't stand to see you hurt again."

Seth looked back at his mother. She was looking out the window, her lip quivering. He and Octavia were the first children of Amias and Evelyn to live past their tenth birthday—Szatisi had told them as much on their eleventh birthday. Their parents never discussed the other siblings. Their mother refused to talk about it. Based on how protective she was over them, especially after Seth lost his legs, he could infer what happened to the others.

"What about... Octavia?" Seth introduced the question carefully, watching his mother for her reaction. Thoughts of his sister's ceremony mingled with Amias's promise of a cure, leaving him with an aching heart. *He's giving us both what we desire, and the cost will be great.*

She turned her head to meet his eyes. "I tried to convince him to delay the ceremony until he returned from Iszairi. It... didn't work."

Seth pursed his lips. He wished his mother had succeeded. *Maybe there's still time to convince Octavia how stupid and insane the ceremony would be. Mother can help convince her. No... neither of us will be able to convince her. Octavia is loyal to Father, loyal to the point that she'll willingly offer her body, her entire self to this pointless cause of his—*

Seth tightened his hands into fists and slammed them against the armrest of his chair.

"Seth?" Evelyn asked, panic in her voice.

"S-sorry, I..." He shook his head and forced his hands to relax. After a moment he spoke again. "Why do they do it?" Her brows knitted together in confusion. "The"—he gestured toward his ears—"*ceremony.*"

She frowned and spoke slowly, choosing her words carefully. "The Asaszi say it's a sign of devotion to your father's work. To mold themselves into your father's perfect image."

"But then they don't look like Father. They look like Elviri. And I thought we hated the Elviri." His face felt hot as he continued to dwell on it, thinking about the fanatic hate his people felt toward their ancestors. He and his mother had pointed ears due to Evelyn's strong Elviri heritage. Amias and Octavia, along with the majority of the Provira, hadn't. "Wouldn't any kind of resemblance to the Elviri be a bad thing?"

"Your father believes that our people are meant to become 'what should have been'. The Asaszi tell him so."

He continued to linger on the hatred instead, missing what Evelyn said. "Why do we hate the Elviri, anyway? Just because they wouldn't let us stay in their lands?"

She reached for his hand again. "The Asaszi say they have committed other atrocities, and there were so many wars fought in the Eldest Days," she said.

Seth pulled away from her grasp. "How do we know what they say is true?" he asked.

That elicited a loud *sssshhh* from his mother before she grabbed his hand and pulled him close to her. "Don't even *think* about voicing those kinds of thoughts, Seth. The Asaszi have been gracious hosts, allowing us to stay here with no expectation of repayment," she whispered sternly.

He held her stare, partly out of fear. He had never seen his mother react in such a negative manner before.

After another moment, her voice grew quieter. "But I understand your frustration. I've tried studying the Elviri-Asaszi Wars, but... they have no books, nothing written about them. Only their spoken word. If only I could go to the libraries in Elifyn..."

His eyes widened. "Mother, you can't be serious," he whispered.

"Your father talked about them often when building this library." There was a fondness in her voice as she looked around the room. "He said if it weren't for the Asaszi and their lack of written records, he would have built me a library to rival even the Great Library in Lithalyon."

Seth couldn't help but look around the room as well. He tried to imagine a library larger and grander than this one, but his imagination failed him. "What else did he say about the libraries?"

A smile crossed her lips. "That there are rows upon rows of books, covering thousands of years of history, culture, and art. There are scribes who put in a lifetime of work in those libraries, yet still there is more to learn." She sighed wistfully. "He also spoke of books bound in beautiful colored leathers with intricate lettering etched onto the covers." She picked up the book she had been reading—a collection of pages roughly bound together between plain brown leather. There were no markings on the cover to indicate its contents.

Seth frowned, seeing the disappointment cross over his mother's face. He looked around the room again. For a moment he could feel his wonder and excitement for his mother's library losing its strength. In its stead rose a new desire, an urge to go beyond the pyramid and seek out something more extraordinary.

There was rustling near the door. Seth and his mother snapped their heads toward the noise. One of the stewards had been adjusting their skirts. Seth looked out the window at the sky. Dark clouds filled the horizon. It would be a day of rain. As quickly as it came, his newfound desires slipped away like a leaf in the wind. His mother's library would have to do.

"I wish things were different for Octavia," his mother said, "but this is the path she's chosen, and we need to support her. Through everything."

He didn't have a response to that. Instead, he watched the clouds outside.

———◆———

In the hours leading up to the ceremony, Seth spent most of it in his room brooding about his sister. The rain had continued from the morning into the afternoon, so he wasn't able to stroll on the colonnade. His mother's words echoed in his head.

"We need to support her. Through everything."

He scowled and angrily fidgeted with his silk blankets. *I can't support her decision to side with Amias. He's jeopardizing the safety of so many Provira. How can she stomach the idle destruction of our people? We've been at war with the Elviri and Proma for over a hundred years, and it's only by sheer luck that we haven't all been killed. How can she support that war?*

His thoughts shifted to the other discussion he and his mother had. It was like a breath of fresh air to hear something other than his father's narrative about how glorious the Asaszi were. Seth had never heard someone openly question the Asaszi before, and he was glad to know he wasn't the only one who hesitated to accept what they said. He was concerned, though.

How long has Mother questioned the Asaszi? How has she kept silent for so long? Has she tried voicing her concerns to Father? No, she couldn't have, Seth knew. Amias would have punished her for it.

His thoughts wandered to the libraries she talked about. He wished he could see them with his own eyes, trace his fingers along the spines of all the books. He wanted to look up and see nothing but rows and rows of books, containing more knowledge of this world than he ever thought possible.

Not that I would ever be allowed to leave the pyramid, he thought bitterly. Amias would keep him trapped forever under the excuse that the Elviri would kill him if he ever left. Maybe they would. Arcyr'ys had mentioned to his father that fighting was getting worse on the border. Maybe one day the Elviri would send an army and storm the jungles to find them and kill them all.

Or maybe that's just what Father and the Asaszi want us to think.

When the stewards knocked on his door, he shooed the thoughts from his head and climbed into his chair. When he returned from his mother's library, he went ahead and changed into clothes for the ceremony—a green silken robe that had been given to him by the *Zsikui* last year on his eighteenth birthday. Curling patterns were woven into the arms and back of the fabric with golden threads. He rubbed at the fringes as he squirmed in his chair. After his time in bed, the robe was now wrinkled, which was something his father would normally get angry over. With the ceremony, though, Seth was confident that his father would be too preoccupied with Octavia to worry about his son's appearance. He hoped for that, anyway.

He opened the door and rolled forward.

The ceremony took place in the same room as Amias's experiments. There weren't any spaces large enough to accommodate the number of people who would be attending the ceremony. Although the room had been cleaned thoroughly in preparation for this event, Seth could still smell the charred corpse from yesterday's experiment. He felt ill at the thought of it.

Seth took his place on the balcony as he always did for his father's experiments. He wasn't alone this time. His mother and his stewards were there as well. Down below in the chamber, members of the army and the *Zsikui* had gathered. One of the platforms had been dragged into the middle of the chamber where Amias and Arcyr'ys stood. They whispered to each other. Behind them was a brazier with a bright flame burning within it. On one of the other platforms, Osza and Astohi sat on two elegant chairs that had been brought to the chamber specifically for them. They were dressed in luxurious silks and gaudy jewelry. Four of their personal guards flanked them.

Surrounding the platforms were soldiers and serpents alike, all murmuring and hissing in anticipation of Octavia's arrival. Her popularity amongst the troops was unsurprising. She was pretty and charismatic, even Seth knew this. What *was* surprising was how much the *Zsikui* adored her. Seth had heard whispers of their approval over the past few weeks, how they expected her to succeed their father as leader of the Provira forces.

How many of the Zsikui *have dared to say that around Father? He certainly won't be relinquishing his hold over the Provira any time soon, no matter how much he claims to love Octavia.*

Octavia appeared in the threshold of the room, a smile glowing on her face. She wore a white silk gown that clung to her shoulders with sleeves draping down past her fingertips. She wore a crown of blue and green flowers, her blonde hair tucked behind her ears. Beside her was High Priestess Szatisi dressed in ceremonial robes. The murmuring and hissing of the crowd turned its attention to the two women, and cheers erupted throughout the room. Seth heard his mother gasp quietly at the sight of her daughter.

"She's so beautiful," Evelyn whispered. Seth couldn't take his eyes off his sister. Indeed, she was beautiful, but the gnawing fear in his stomach knew better than to be fooled by the cheers of the crowd and the smile on his sister's face.

Szatisi held up her hands to the chamber in a greeting. The crowd cheered louder in return. She lowered her arms and turned to Octavia, gesturing for her to enter the chamber. As she took her first step forward, the soldiers' cheering became deafening. They continued as she made her way to the platform in the center of the room where Amias and Arcyr'ys were waiting. Szatisi followed behind her at a distance, ensuring all the attention was on Octavia. Seth's stomach tightened as his sister got closer and closer to their father.

"We must be happy for her," Seth heard his mother say, but the words didn't register in his head. How could he be happy for Octavia, knowing what was about to happen? He felt his mother's hand wrap around his, and she squeezed tightly. A lump rose in his throat, but he forced it back down.

Seth forced himself to look around the chamber. His eyes first flickered to Osza and Astohi. The two Asaszi were sitting in their chairs, no emotion crossing their faces. They were focused on Octavia as she approached the middle platform. Seth followed their gaze, taking in the sight of General Arcyr'ys Wynn. Arcyr'ys wore his tarnished and dented armor. A cord held back his brown hair. His facial features were soft, and Seth saw something resembling pride in his eyes. Surely Octavia could see it as she drew nearer still. That would only add to her happiness.

And finally, Seth's gaze turned to his father. Amias stood perfectly still, his hands behind his back. His black silk robe covered everything below his neck. His hair was tied back as well, the fading blond a stark contrast against the robe. Normally, for a ceremony like this, he or the other officiating general would wear a plain cotton robe—something easily disposed of. Not for Octavia's ceremony, though. This would be a moment to cherish by all... except Seth and his mother.

Octavia climbed the steps, taking care to lift her skirts so she didn't step on them. Her eyes never left their father. Szatisi allowed her to climb the steps first before following suit. While Octavia stopped in front of Amias, Szatisi crossed over and stood beside him, opposite of Arcyr'ys. Amias turned to face the priestess and bowed. They exchanged words that Seth couldn't hear over the crowd below. Or perhaps he had tuned it out. He didn't need to hear the words he'd heard several times before, especially not when they now were about his sister.

Szatisi reached into her robes and removed a curved dagger. Seth's stomach twisted again. The blade itself was made from the sharpest steel, better than any of the army's weapons. The handle was made from malachite and onyx, shaped to look like a serpent bearing its fangs. Szatisi offered the dagger to Amias, the hilt facing him. He removed one hand from behind his back to accept the dagger. Amias wore dark gloves underneath his robes, perhaps so he would not get blood on his hands.

Too late for that.

Amias turned to Octavia. His mouth moved, reciting words of the ceremony, and Seth could only assume his sister was responding in turn.

"*Pyredan! Pyredan!*" the crowd chanted.

Szatisi and Arcyr'ys stepped forward, moving from Amias's side to Octavia's. His sister sank to her knees, raising her hands up in front of her as if in offering. The skirts of her gown pillowed around her. Szatisi and Arcyr'ys took hold of her wrists and pulled her arms out so that she was offering her whole self to Amias. Seth could no longer see her face, but he knew she was still smiling. He tried to swallow but found himself unable to. He felt his mother's hand trembling in his own—or was that him?

Amias held up the dagger and the crowd went berserk. He turned and held it over the flame in the brazier. Some continued cheering *pyredan* while others began chanting Octavia's name. Seth wanted to close his eyes, but his father would know if he did.

He always knows.

Amias reached out and gripped the tip of Octavia's left ear with his free hand. After another moment, he lowered the dagger and carved away the upper curve of her ear, the top of her ear now forming a point. Even this far away, Seth could see the bright red swell of blood spilling from the wound onto Octavia's white dress. If she screamed, Seth couldn't hear her.

She's strong, though, and stubborn. She wouldn't scream at the pain. She'd revel in it. He was horrified at the truth of his own thoughts.

Amias raised the scrap of flesh into the air as if it were a trophy. He then threw it onto the ground in front of Octavia, and then proceeded to cut off the upper curve of her right ear. If Seth had eaten at all earlier in the day, he would have thrown it up.

After Amias tossed the other scrap onto the ground, Szatisi and Arcyr'ys released Octavia. She slumped forward, barely catching herself with her arms. A hush fell over the crowd as they waited for her next actions. Seth caught himself holding his breath as well. *Please let her be okay.*

Octavia rose to her feet, collecting the remains of her ears from the ground. She hobbled forward a few steps and threw them into the brazier. The crowd erupted into wails and cheers. She turned to the room, a smile plastered across her face as droplets of blood fell onto her dress, staining the white silk.

Seeing her smile like that was the final straw for Seth. He ripped his hand away from his mother's, grabbed onto the wheels of his chair, and left as quickly as he could.

The colonnade was empty underneath the moonlit sky. Insects sang their nightly songs in the distance. The forest never truly slept. Seth continued rolling his chair forward. He could not tell if there were stewards following him or not. He did not care.

As he completed a lap around the colonnade, he saw someone leaning against the balcony, looking out at the forest. Seth slowed the roll of his chair, warily approaching them.

"Hello, my son."

Seth wanted to scream and throw himself from the balcony, but he was stuck in his wheelchair. Hands shaking with rage, he forced himself forward toward his father.

"Your sister made me quite proud tonight," Amias said with a smile on his lips. He was still wearing the black robes and gloves from the ceremony. Seth made sure to keep his distance. He didn't want his father reaching for him. "I'm hoping you will make me proud as well, once your legs have been restored. You're long overdue for a coming-of-age ceremony of your own."

Seth's blood ran cold, and he couldn't control himself. "*What?*"

"Szatisi and I spoke before the ceremony. She draws nearer to a perfected draught that will restore your legs to their former glory. And once that has been done, my son, we'll begin preparations for you and your sister to claim your places by my side—her at the head of our army, and you carrying on my legacy with the spellsingers." Amias inhaled deeply, tilting his head back. *He's basking in his own glory.*

Seth couldn't find the words to respond with. He looked out to the forest, racking his brain desperately for a response. *What kind of ceremony is he talking about, though? My ears are already pointed. Surely Father won't cut up my body if it already resembles his "perfect vision"?* The thought made his skin crawl.

"Our family will be the start of a new dynasty, one that will last thousands of years," Amias continued, still not looking at Seth. "Neither the Elviri nor the Proma can stop us. They will finally pay for their betrayal, and we will take our rightful places beside the Asaszi as rulers of Daaria."

Seth's eyes widened, fear keeping his mouth shut. *He's a monster.*

Amias stretched out his hands and then gripped the balcony again. "I depart for Iszairi the day after next. It's almost time for our experiments to be tested at the Tomb of the Prince. Szatisi and I will meet tomorrow to prepare for the journey, and to further discuss the healing draught for you." Amias finally turned to look at Seth, a smile stretching across his thin lips. "After all these years and to be so close to victory... It will be good to have my children at my side when we finally cast down those who have wronged us."

Seth gave his father the nod he was waiting for, averting his eyes away from Amias's face. He wasn't sure if he would ever be able to rid his mind of the sight of that smile. He tried to focus on something else, the dark forest, the singing insects, the crumbling walls, but that smile kept pushing its way to the front of his mind.

"Get some rest, my son. You will need to gather your strength for when I return from Iszairi." Amias approached Seth, reaching out to place his hand on his shoulder. "It will be good to see you as a full-grown man."

Seth closed his eyes, bracing for the feel of the heavy gloved hand against the silk covering his skin. *He mocks me.* Warmth seeped through the material, and he wanted nothing more than to burn the robe. His father had tainted it with Octavia's mutilation.

After a moment that seemed to stretch for hours, Amias removed his hand from Seth's shoulder. "Stewards, escort my son back to his room." He spoke to the space behind him, his voice strong.

At his command, two stewards appeared beside Seth. One took the handles on the back of his chair and pulled him inside, away from his father. Seth couldn't find the strength to take control of his wheels, nor could he look away from his father out on the balcony. Seth's last glimpse of his father was him standing there, gazing off into the forest.

———————◆○◆———————

The hallways were empty but sounds of celebration and festivity echoed from the experiment chamber. The sounds followed Seth all the way back to his room, where he could just barely hear them. He wondered if his mother had retreated to her own room, or if she stayed behind to smile and watch Octavia celebrate her ceremony with the other soldiers in solidarity. She was stronger than him, so he expected she remained behind. Seth loved Octavia, but he wasn't strong enough to support her through this. Perhaps tomorrow, after her wounds had been cleaned, and she was no longer in that tainted dress... Just the thought of the white silk made him heave.

As he lay in his bed, his robes tossed and discarded in a corner of his room, Seth tried to force his mind onto a different topic. He didn't want to have nightmares about his sister tonight. He thought back on his day, trying to pull at least one good memory from it.

His mother's library, and the libraries in Lithalyon.

He closed his eyes, trying to imagine a library larger than his mother's. He pictured rows upon rows that stretched up to the sky. Books of all topics filled the shelves. He ran and weaved through the bookcases, marveling at their pristine condition and the smell of dried ink. The childish thoughts brought him some level of comfort. *Mother spoke about wanting to learn the history of the wars. The Elviri must have their own records of what happened. Can we trust what they've written? Surely, we can trust them more than the people who demand mutilation in exchange for loyalty. What do I have to lose, just to read those books?*

The library was just a fantasy, though. He would never travel to Lithalyon. His face pinched into a tight frown, and he pressed the palms of his hands against his eyes. His damned legs would never carry him away from here.

Before he could lose himself in his misery, Seth had a thought. *Szatisi will be in Yiradia for another day or so until Amias leaves for Iszairi. She'll go with him then and aid him with his work at the Tomb of the Prince. Has she brought the draught with her to Yiradia? Is it possible that I could get my hands on it...?*

His mind raced with cautious excitement as several possibilities for the next two days formed inside his head. He didn't let himself hope, but he did let himself wonder about a great many things—the soaring heights of Lithalyon's library, the twisting paths within the forest, and most wonderful of all, his feet beneath him as he walked. For the first time in a while, he was able to fall asleep soundly with no nightmares to disturb him.

CHAPTER VI: RAY

When Ray awoke, it was just past midday. Someone else had entered the room and claimed a bed while she was asleep. She couldn't tell who the sleeping person was as she gathered her gear and boots, quietly pulling everything on.

The house was livelier now that it was midday. Laughter and chatter drifted from downstairs. Minnie, another of Naro's housekeepers, shuffled out of the room opposite Ray, her arms full of linens and clothes.

"Can I help you, Minnie?" Ray asked as she pulled the door shut behind her.

"No don't trouble yourself sweetie. This is a normal load for me, it is. I'll be fine," Minnie crooned, turning so she could see Ray.

Although her body was young, Minnie's spirit was as old as Hilthe's. Minnie came from the Gutters and had lost all three of her children and nearly herself to sickness last winter. Naro happened across her in the market not too long after her oldest had succumbed to the illness where she had been begging for enough money to pay for a ship to take her onto the Hourglass Lakes so she could spread her children's ashes on the water. Where others had shunned Minnie because of the potential for disease, Naro offered her his arm, took her aboard his ship, and gave the grieving mother a chance to honor her dead children. Soon after that, she was working for him as a housekeeper.

"Alright then. Have a good day!" Ray called out as she descended the stairs. Ray liked Minnie, although she always got sad being around her.

Four or five people lounged downstairs, all Walkers, sitting and chatting. From what Ray could hear, they were discussing boat shipments, which was one of the legitimate methods Naro used to make money. He ran a modest shipping company that carried goods to and from all corners of Daaria. He had a separate identity for that line of business, and nearly all his employees were honest men and women. Some were Walkers, though, to ensure certain shipments would or would not arrive in certain locations.

Ray cut into the dining hall where Sabyl and a hooded Walker were huddled together on one side of the table. She couldn't make out what they were discussing, but she raised a hand in greeting to them both.

Sabyl looked up and made eye contact with her. "Fetch your food and come join us. Naro said you have information for me," she said, all traces of aggression gone from earlier in the morning.

Ray nodded and continued into the kitchen. She knew better than to assume Sabyl was friendly toward her at this point. She was acting on orders from Naro, so both of them were obligated to play nice and work together.

Better give her my best, Ray thought. *It'd be nice if I could befriend Sabyl and earn her trust.*

Inside the kitchen, Hilthe was working alongside another woman, Rhia, to prepare the meals for the rest of the day.

"Good morning!" Ray spoke in a sing-song voice.

Both women looked at Ray and grumbled about how it was clearly afternoon now, do young ones not know how to tell time anymore?

"Your porridge is over there," Hilthe said, pointing at a pot with her stirring spoon. She worked diligently over a large cauldron of stew while Rhia chopped and prepared vegetables to toss in.

"Thank you, ladies," Ray told them.

She crossed the room and grabbed her pot and a spoon, ensuring not to get in Rhia or Hilthe's way. She planted another kiss on Hilthe's head and made her escape to the dining hall before she got swatted with a spoon. She took a seat across from Sabyl and the hooded person she recognized as Yari, Sabyl's second in command. The two were close, having grown up together on the streets. Both had a penchant for petty theft, and one time the law caught up to Yari after he nabbed something from a fancy pottery artist. No one knew exactly how it happened, but Yari lost his voice after a particularly long stay with the city guard. After he was released, the two found their home within the Walkers.

Both turned to look at her, but it was Sabyl who spoke. "That athra investigation must be getting hot." Sabyl knew that Ray's main job within the gang was to observe and report. Ray was never involved in anything else apart from listening, watching, and some sleight of hand. Sabyl and Yari, on the other hand, were expert thieves and they knew how to use the swords that hung from their belts.

Ray squirmed in her chair a little bit and shoveled a spoonful of porridge into her mouth to buy her a moment to respond. She cracked a smile when she tasted the cadra berries in the porridge, but quickly dropped the expression and spoke with a serious tone, "We're being framed for the athra but not sure by who."

She went over the previous night's expedition in great detail, except for the part where she found the hidden wall. She obeyed Naro's request to omit that detail. Sabyl and Yari listened intently, nodding at certain moments. When she finished, they turned to each other, and Yari whispered something about the Red Court that Ray could barely make out.

The Red Court's usually pretty underhanded with their tactics, but they haven't ever been a threat to us. At least not since I've been around.

Sabyl looked back at Ray. "Thank you for the report. It sounds like someone is trying to force the guard to act. We'll poke around today and try to find something. Where were you getting your information on the street?"

"Primarily from Laurel, but I've watched some dealings and overheard a lot of things in the market," Ray replied. Being one of Naro's lieutenants, Sabyl knew about Laurel's identity and relation to Naro. Yari probably knew by extension, and even if he didn't, there weren't many people he would tell.

Sabyl nodded and rose to her feet. "Got it. Thanks, Ray."

She's just doing her job. We both are, Ray reminded herself. That didn't stop her lips from curling into a small smile at the older woman's words of appreciation. *But I guess I will take whatever victory I can.*

With that, Sabyl and her partner were gone. Ray took her time finishing her porridge. She would need to check in with Naro before she left, to see if he had come up with her next assignment. She shifted around uneasily in her seat. Her thoughts would continue to linger on the athra strain, especially now that Sabyl and Yari were involved. *I doubt there's anything Naro'll give me that will grab my full attention. I hope Sabyl and Yari can find a quick resolution to this problem.*

She returned her pot to the kitchen, opting not to bother Hilthe and Rhia as they shuffled around the warm room. As she headed back toward the stairs, she noticed the boaters had left. The house was considerably quieter now. She climbed the stairs and knocked on Naro's door.

"Come in," came his honeyed voice from the other side.

Several candles burned, and dim light filled the whole room. In the back corner of the room was Naro's exceptionally large and luxurious bed. Silks, furs, and other sorts of comfortable blankets covered the mattress. A massive armoire stood in the opposite corner, intricately carved from Imalarii wood. On the doors was a mural depicting an Elviri goddess—Ray didn't know which one—standing among her devotees. Several rugs covered the floor, all with different colors and patterns from various cultures across Daaria. To her left was his desk covered in documents and trinkets. Naro sat behind his desk, a quill in hand. His dark hair was pulled back into a bun, a few loose strands hanging down the side of his face. In the light, Ray saw the blue hues in his hair and could easily make out his colorful blue and green eyes. He wore a loose white shirt, the sleeves pushed up to his elbows. His bronze skin practically glowed in the candlelight.

Ray closed the door behind her and waited for Naro to finish what he was doing. She had long ago gotten over her guilt of entering his room while he was at his desk. He was very forgiving and never made his guests wait too long.

After a few moments he set his quill down and looked up at Ray, leaning back in his chair. "I trust you found Sabyl?" The hint of a small smile rested on his face.

"Yeah, I told Sabyl about the warehouse and everything I knew, and she left with Yari not too long ago." She inhaled sharply but paused before continuing. *Surely it would be okay to discuss what I heard from Yari?* "Could the Red Court be behind this?"

Naro steepled his hands and touched his fingertips to his chin. "The thought has crossed my mind. They could have brought the athra into the city, but I don't think the Lords and Ladies Crimson were responsible for last night's scene. They understand the value of keeping the Walkers around."

Ray crossed her arms, her brow furrowing. "Well, what if one of the other two got their hands on some of this athra and wanted to take us down a peg?" she asked.

Naro arched an eyebrow. "You think the Hawks or Disciples would do this to us?"

Her nose wrinkled, and she shifted her weight between her feet. "Well, maybe not. Not right now anyway since they had their spat a few weeks back. But who else?"

Naro grinned in response and leaned forward in his chair. "Who indeed?"

They played this game often. He was testing her, allowing her the chance to learn what it was like to think as a gang leader or a lieutenant. Normally, she enjoyed this game, but usually the game wasn't centered around a drug trafficking problem that could destroy the gang.

He swept an arm across his chest, ending their game and dismissing the topic. "But that's not a question we can answer right now. It's time for your next assignment. I have a project that's already underway that could use your help. A bit of a research project, but they're almost ready to take action. I think this could better your skills and learn something new."

Her curiosity was piqued. She knew better than to take his word at face value, though, so she asked the question, "What exactly is this research project on?"

The faint smile turned into a mischievous grin, his eyes lighting up with delight. "We are going to kidnap Princess Niamnh."

Ray's eyes widened and she made a conscious effort not to let her jaw drop. "The princess, sir...?"

"Right before her eighteenth name day."

Several thoughts raced through her head, most of them questions of why Naro would put this plan together. *What good can come of this? Won't this provoke the guards into an all-out war against the gangs, the Walkers in particular? We'd be putting the regular townsfolk at risk. The city won't be safe.* For the first time she wondered if her leader wasn't all right in the head. *The Naro I know wouldn't put the Walkers in peril like this. But surely he's got his reasons?*

Very briefly her thoughts dwelled on Princess Niamnh. King Nelle had kept his eldest daughter hidden away from the world since the passing of

Queen Annalah five years ago. Rumor was that the princess was feral, or had some kind of disease, so the king kept her locked away to spare himself the embarrassment. She hadn't made a public appearance since the queen died. She had two older brothers, but one had perished in the fighting to the south against the Provira two years ago, and the other had disappeared beyond the Wall to the north last year. Princess Niamnh and her younger sister Celia were the only ones of the royal line who remained.

And Naro wants to kidnap *her?*

It took her a few moments to pull the words together to ask him a question. "What... benefit would that bring to the Walkers?" She spoke delicately, treating it like another one of their games. She tried not to vocally challenge his decision but rather understand it. Naro could be reasoned with and talked into or out of anything in a discussion, but he didn't take outright defiance.

Naro stood and walked around the side of his desk. "Child, do you remember the night we met?" he asked.

Ray wrapped her arms around herself, suddenly feeling very vulnerable. Although Naro was an important part of her life—her lifeline, her *everything*, really—the day they met was like a dark stain on a pretty tablecloth. She could recall the memory with just the slightest nudge, and suddenly she was thirteen again, pilfering through the rubbish outside this very house. She thought she had been careful, but suddenly out he came, rambling on about some ray of sunshine appearing before him. He was mostly naked, covered only by a pair of dark trousers. Smeared across his face and chest were remnants of baybalm powder. His dark hair hung wildly around his face. His pupils were dilated, and he grabbed her shoulders, looking wildly into her eyes. One blue, one green.

What a ray of sunshine, he had cooed to her, tightly grabbing her shoulder with one hand, the other hand gently caressing her hair.

Sabyl came out of the house, panic written across her face. *Get back inside, boss!* she had snapped at him, grabbing him, and trying to pry him off the scrawny youth digging through his trash.

Ray had been so frightened she hadn't even pushed back against Naro. Some of the baybalm got onto her face. It had a faint sickly-sweet smell to it, and it made her stomach churn.

Bring the sunshine in, won't you, darling? We need some sunshine, Naro had asked his lieutenant while his head lolled back to meet Sabyl's gaze.

Free from Naro's grasp, Ray made a move to run. Sabyl scowled and moved with lightning-fast reflexes. She spun and shoved Naro toward the house, then turned back to chase after Ray, snatching her wrist. *Let me explain.*

I don't wanna go nowhere near him! Ray snarled, thrashing against Sabyl's grip.

Sabyl turned Ray around and took hold of her shoulder. *Let him clean himself up and explain. We can offer you a home.*

Ray's mother had been gone almost a year at that point. She knew the struggles of living on the streets without any kind of support. She knew the gangs existed, but always told herself she was too good to work with them.

At least come inside and eat some porridge. Hilthe can make you a bowl. Sabyl's voice had been quiet and nurturing. A side of her that not many got to know. It got Ray inside the door, and she found herself eating porridge and talking about where she came from.

Sabyl kept her company, even after the conversation ended, and about an hour later Naro came into the dining hall all cleaned up, as if nothing had ever happened. He wore a gray silken shirt with a dark vest over it, looking very much the master of the house. His dark hair had been brushed and pulled neatly back into a ponytail, a few loose strands hanging over his ears. He was practically a different person, but Ray recognized him from his eyes. One blue, one green.

He had taken a seat across from her at the table. Not at the head of the table, but in one of the common folk seats. Ray was immediately on edge, but he placed his elbows on the table and folded his hands together.

We got off on the wrong foot. Allow me to make amends and introduce myself anew. My name is Naro, and I would like to offer you a place within the Syrael Walkers.

"I'm not fond of the memory either," Naro murmured, pulling her attention back to his face in the present. "But that day, I was searching for something. And while I didn't find what I was seeking, I did recruit an exceptionally talented scout." He grinned, and she couldn't help but do the same.

But what had he been searching for? It's no secret that Naro indulges in baybalm on occasion, but how could that hallucinogenic help him search for anything? Her confusion must have been evident on her face because he continued speaking before she could ask a question.

"Visions are such precarious things." He chuckled. "That information has only been divulged to my lieutenants, so I would appreciate your discretion on the topic. Although I'm sure you have an inkling as to what I'm referring to."

"You have visions about people," Ray said, the words feeling strange on her tongue. Although it was practically common knowledge among the Walkers that Naro could see things, no one ever talked about it. Any time he made mention of someone's future, everyone just kind of assumed it was normal and went about with their day. Ray in particular shrugged this knowledge off because it reminded her too much of their ugly introduction.

Naro nodded and continued. "Oh, it goes beyond just *people*. I've had visions of the future of Promthus, of Daaria itself. The gift of foresight is a very dangerous thing." He spoke so lightly of something so heavy. So *impossible*.

"But how? Isn't magic gone?" she blurted out. She felt stupid for even asking such a thing, but... *It's true, isn't it? Aren't visions some kind of magic?*

Rather than give her a concrete response, Naro simply winked at her. A feeling of dread washed over her. In that moment, the world grew larger and darker. She felt small and vulnerable.

Naro returned to his seat, searching through his papers. "Ajak has been assisting me with the preparations for this plot. Most of the work has already been done, but there is one thing I would ask of you."

If anyone would be working with Naro on this mission, it would have been Ajak. It was no secret that Naro had been grooming him to become a lieutenant one day. Perhaps this mission was his final test. Ray liked Ajak more than she liked the other lieutenants, Sabyl and Aldrin, and she wanted him to succeed, but she still felt uneasy about the whole situation.

"What do you need me to do?" Ray asked.

"It's a simple task, really." He held up a piece of paper and offered it to her. "Take this letter to the herbalist's shop near the Honeyed Bee, up in the Market District." Naro opened a drawer in his desk and withdrew a nondescript leather coin pouch. He tossed it to her with a wink. "Part of a *'healing remedy for our sister'*."

Ray understood. She would need to put on other clothes, something be-fitting a normal citizen. Not a dock worker or Gutters rat. She glanced down at the letter and made out a few of the words, something about sending a daughter to pick up blueleaf. She wondered if she was legitimately acquiring blueleaf, or if this was a front for something else Naro had ordered. She would find out soon enough.

She pocketed the coin pouch. "I'll be back."

Naro returned to his paperwork. She had been dismissed.

Ray left his room and returned to the bedroom on the left. She opened the giant armoire and began digging around for an appropriate disguise. She needed a dress befitting a young lady of the elite citizen class. Or at least a wealthier crafter's daughter. She picked out a soft gray dress, matching slippers, and a green shawl to wrap around herself. Her hair was a mess and the safehouse didn't have a washbasin or supplies to fix herself up. She would have to settle for a nice hat or bonnet. She found a bonnet made of emerald green lace and cloth that almost matched the shawl. It would have to do.

She made quick work of changing into her new clothes, tying the bonnet strings loosely under her chin and smoothing down her skirt. She pulled the coin purse and letter out of her street clothes, then tucked the clothes into the armoire for her return. To finish the ensemble, Ray picked up a beautifully embroidered bag and shoved the items inside. Better to go ahead and take care of Naro's errand now rather than make him wait.

Leaving the house was easy, but she had to carefully plot a route to get from the safehouse to the Golden Path in the least conspicuous manner possible. She was dressed as a wealthy young woman, and those types were not often found beyond the main roads in the Crafting District. Naro's safehouse was tucked far away into the district, farther than a wealthy young woman would be seen. The afternoon suns lazed about through the sky. She had plenty of time to get to the herbalist's shop.

Her first stop was a storefront for a nearby woodworker. She couldn't re-member his name. She slipped into his shop from the back and then exited onto the street. The other patrons paid her no mind, and no one called after her when she left. Ray held her chin high, a small sway in her step. She certainly didn't feel like a lady, but she supposed it was working because no one gave her odd looks. The Golden Path was easy to get to from here, and then it was a straight shot up to the Market District. The guards didn't stop her, or many others, as they traversed between districts.

The Path curled around the Crafting District and climbed upward over another tier of housing mainly for traders and crafters. Supports for the Golden Path were stacked on top of buildings and into the rock of the island. It leveled out upon reaching the Market District. Here the Path turned into a main highway of activity, cutting through several marketplaces before climbing higher still into the Sky District. The Honeyed Bee was toward the ascent into the Sky District, so she had further to go.

As Ray crossed through the marketplaces, she let her gaze wander at the various stalls and storefronts. Today was just as noisy as the day before with crafters and traders peddling their wares. Several children were screaming and shouting into the crowds, trying to sell their parents' goods. Ray humored some of them, gawking at their stalls before moving on. She passed by several indoor marketplaces as well, the scents of grilled meats and perfumes wafting out. She made a mental note to count exactly how much coin Naro had given her and see if there was any left for snacks on the way back.

The Honeyed Bee was, like most other establishments in Auora, very tall and not very wide. There were perhaps six floors total. The bottom two were dedicated to food and drink with the top four floors reserved for private rooms and halls. Ray was very familiar with the establishment. The Walkers had their fair share of business pass through its doors. Naro either owned the tavern or was very close to the owners.

Next door was a building that housed the herbalist's shop, appropriately named the Green Emporium. It was located on the third floor of the building. The remaining floors were occupied by other stores. Circular stairs were situated right inside the front door of the bottom floor, which belonged to a pottery shop. There was an eclectic blend of everyday pots and dishes, and fancier pieces meant for noble households. The thought of having a dedicated porridge bowl crossed her mind, and she had to suppress a giggle. Such luxury! The second floor belonged to a famous local candlemaker. Her nose was assaulted by no less than ten different scents from several burning candles. She never understood the obsession with scented candles. Naro would occasionally light some, but more often than not, he would just use regular unscented candles.

The third floor was her destination. Stone planters crowded the windows. The display tables were filled with dried plants, small planters, and various tools used to take care of the plants. The shopkeeper stood idly in the back of the room. As Ray got off the stairs and entered the store proper, his face lit up.

"Good afternoon, ma'am. Welcome to The Green Emporium. Is there something in particular that you're looking for today?"

Ray nodded and withdrew the letter from her bag. "Hello, yes, my family sent me for this." She handed it over to the shopkeeper and crossed her arms. As the scents of the candle shop below faded, she could smell the new scents of the herbalist's shop—dirt, mint, sage, and other plants.

The shopkeeper unfolded the letter and read it over, nodding a couple of times. "Ah, one moment. One of my blueleaf plants blossomed just this morning." He went behind a countertop to pick up a small wicker basket and a pair of shears, then moved over to one of the planters. He cut off a couple of sprigs of a beautiful bush with small blue leaves. He tucked the sprigs into the basket and then turned back to Ray. "It will be ten for three sprigs."

Ray withdrew the coin purse from her bag and pulled out the appropriate number of coins, which was... exactly what was in the bag. Naro didn't intend for her to stop on the way back, then. Her mood dropped, but she took care to maintain appearances for the shopkeeper. She pretended the bag was heftier than it was and made a small show of handing him the ten coins. They exchanged polite smiles and goods, and then she left with haste.

On the way back to the safehouse, she sighed wistfully as she passed several street food vendors that she ordinarily would have stopped for. *Oh well, another time, another place.*

She used the same woodworker's shop to slip back into the backroads of the district. A waft of smoke streamed lazily into the air from the kitchen. It would soon be time for supper. Ray wondered what Hilthe and the others would be cooking today.

She entered through the front door. The house was quieter today. No one sat in the lounge discussing trades or rumors. She couldn't see anyone in the dining hall either. With a shrug she climbed the stairs. Naro's door was closed, as usual. She raised a hand to knock, but it swung open before her knuckles touched the wood. On the other side of the door was Naro, a cheeky grin on his face, and Ajak standing further into the room. She couldn't prevent the look of surprise from blooming across her face. She quickly composed herself and put on a neutral expression.

"Right on time, as predicted." Naro chuckled with a knowing look, stepping to the side to let Ray in. She silently cursed herself as she crossed inside.

A small square table had been pulled into the center of the room. On top of it was a petite black cauldron, a few phials of liquid, and a large wooden spoon. Ajak was standing close to the table, his hands tucked into his pockets. He had a mop of shaggy brown hair atop his head in a loose bun. His skin was dark but not as dark as Naro's. She caught a glimpse of amusement in his warm brown eyes.

"Thanks for retrieving that for me, my dear." Naro plucked the basket from her arm and set it down on his desk. "It'll come in handy later."

Ray crossed her arms and looked curiously between Naro, Ajak, and the cauldron.

Naro saw this. He saw everything. "Ajak and I were preparing for the job you've just been assigned to. Ajak, care to get our Ray caught up on the inner workings of our plan?"

"Of course, boss." Ajak smiled and pulled his hands out of his pockets.

He crossed the room and placed a hand on Ray's shoulder, leading her out of Naro's room and into the bedroom next door. He let go of her and took a seat on one of the beds, his legs sprawling apart.

"Boss tells me you were assigned to this job just this morning," he said.

Ray crossed over to an armoire, feeling herself slip back into a normal routine. The thought of Ajak left her in pieces but being around him felt natural. Being physically near him made her feel safe, even though the thought of being *with* him made her want to run and hide. All her conflicting thoughts vanished as she opened the armoire and dug out her street clothes. *Focus on the work.* She stepped out of the slippers and pulled on her leggings under her skirts. "Yeah, but I don't know much beyond, well, *kidnapping*," Ray replied.

Ajak crossed his arms behind his head and leaned back on the bed, so he was looking at the ceiling. "Alright then. Well, welcome. Looking forward to working with you. It's been a while since we worked together."

Ray turned away from him, growling playfully. "Not all of us are busy climbing the ranks." She started to pull the dress over her head, careful not to tug too hard on the fabric.

"Yeah, well, now we can do that together." She heard the smile in his voice.

She was thankful she was facing away from him because a blush spread across her cheeks. She finished removing the dress and put her linen shirt on, not caring so much about the rest of her clothes. Dinner was still at least thirty minutes away, and there wasn't much else to do in the house besides talk. She would put her shoes and vest on when it was time to go downstairs.

Ray crossed over to the bed and sat down on the opposite end from Ajak, her legs on top of his. He shifted around on the bed, getting into a more comfortable position to accommodate them both. He placed his hands on her shins, patting them lightly.

"Forgot how scrawny you are," Ajak teased.

"Funny, I was gonna ask when you got so pudgy." She retorted with a giggle.

He glared at her and lunged forward to grab and tickle her sides. She brought her knees up in defense, swatting one hand away and grabbing the other.

"Joking, joking!" she cried. They exchanged smiles, and he leaned back slowly. She held her defensive position for a moment before relaxing as well. "Mostly joking, anyway. You been spending a lot of time up top?"

"Yeah, it's been nice. Been making friends in high places," he responded, a mischievous glint in his eyes.

"Sure, *friends*," she threw back at him. *Well, that was rather quick. Normally it took longer for Ajak to bring up his* friends *in our conversations.*

"Not all of them are like that," he murmured, shifting around so his back was against the wall, her legs across his lap. "And you know they don't hold my attention like—"

"But they hold it all the same."

Uncomfortable silence blossomed between them. Neither of them moved. Ray looked away from him to the armoire.

"Ray—"

"Don't."

"Give me the chance to apologize," Ajak insisted. He moved into her periphery and placed a hand on her knee. "I don't like hurting you. I want us to be—"

"Partners. I know." She looked down at her lap and folded her hands. Ajak had been pursuing her for a couple of years now. *He's not a bad guy, I just...* "I don't want to be one among many."

He flexed his hand, his grip on her knee tightening for one moment before he relaxed. Silence again.

"Tell me about the job," Ray murmured, turning to look at Ajak as their eyes met.

"Boss really outdid himself on this one," Ajak said, his tone veering into business territory. "We have an inside man, a way in, and an ironclad escape route."

She cracked a small smile. "Good to hear."

"It's been brewing for almost two years now. Started out with just the boss. He brought me in at the beginning of the year, mainly to scout things out and point him to places we should keep an eye on. I found us a boatman. Boss found the inside man. Err, I think it's a man. Knowing the boss, it could be anyone."

They both chuckled, their bodies relaxing again. Ray found Ajak comforting. She liked sitting with him like this, feeling his hands on her. She wasn't stupid enough to deny that she liked Ajak. She just wished he would find another girl so she could firmly and definitively shut those feelings out.

"Everything's starting to come together, though. That brew he and I were making earlier? That's the brew we'll knock the princess out with."

Ray raised an eyebrow. Brews like that didn't last longer than a month or so, depending on how it was kept. Naro would no doubt ensure its freshness, but even he wouldn't be able to stop it from losing its strength eventually.

"So how do we get in?" she asked.

Ajak smirked. "Remember that one poor bloke we brought in last summer? Mainly keeps to the docks? He's got a twin working in the castle kitchens."

"A willing twin?"

He shrugged. "Willing enough."

"And that'll have to do." She smiled grimly.

"Yeah. So, we'll go in through the kitchens, then get an escort up to the princess's room to deliver an evening meal. The final route out of the castle isn't set in stone yet, but we'll know a few days prior. Boss is getting that information for us. Once we're out, though, we're crossing the lake."

Ray was impressed by his casual tone. Ajak really had embraced Naro's teachings. He would make a fine lieutenant. She listened attentively as he went on about the plan and all the work he and Naro had done on it. She was left with a nagging feeling in her gut, though. *Why is Naro bringing me in so late in the game? What role am I actually serving?*

After Ajak stopped talking about the job, they just sat together in silence for several minutes. Ray fixated on the armoire and the costumes hidden within. Rhia called them down for dinner. He helped her up and they went downstairs together. The table was quite full tonight. Several Walkers hovered around, and a couple helped Rhia bring the food from the kitchen into the dining hall.

Naro was already sitting at the head of the table, dressed in finery. He wore a royal blue jacket with tiny beads and jewels sewn into the lapels, shoulders, and cuffs. A beautiful cravat was fastened around his neck with swirls of purples, blues, and greens all over. Ray had caught glimpses of this cravat before and knew it had a dragon on it somewhere, but with the way he was wearing it tonight she couldn't see it. Underneath was an unassuming black silk shirt, but Ray was sure it cost more than any amount of gold she had ever held in her hands. Perched behind him on his chair was a wide-brimmed hat with a billowing feather fastened to it. The hat itself was made from dark blue velvet, and the feather belonged to a bird that Ray had only heard stories of. It was kind of an olive color with blue swirls and circles that resembled an eye.

A peacock feather, she recalled. Naro had told her about it a long time ago. It came from Lithalyon if her memory served her correctly.

He was dressed like a king, and from his seat at the head of the table, he was quietly surveying his kingdom as it bustled all around him.

Ray and Ajak claimed a pair of seats on Naro's left in the middle of the table. The other Walkers had claimed their seats as the food was passed around. Rhia sat opposite Naro at the other end of the table, something he had insisted upon for every seated meal. Whoever worked in the kitchen would be his equal at the table. Ray doubted that King Nelle ever let his servants join him at the table.

"Been a while since he dressed like that, huh?" Ajak whispered in her ear.

She had been staring at Naro, and she felt her cheeks flush. Naro wasn't looking at her, but she was sure he knew. She busied herself with filling her plate from the dishes being passed around.

Everyone else was chatting about the day, and about whatever activities would fill their evenings. Ajak cracked jokes with some of the other men at the table. Ray overheard some of the girls gossiping about some nobles. A couple of other Walkers spoke in low voices about the Iron Hawks. Through it all, Naro was silent. His elbows were propped up on the table, his hands folded into a bridge his chin rested on.

It was a rather simple dinner tonight. Some roast pork, potatoes, and greens. Must have been because there was a crowd. It all tasted delicious.

"Come join me in my room after Ajak leaves." Naro's voice was so soft that she must have been the only one to hear it. "There's something I want to show you before I depart for the evening."

Rather than look over to him and draw attention to herself, Ray simply nodded and kept eating her dinner. As the Walkers finished their dinner, Rhia got up and brought a pot of honey pudding in from the kitchen. As the pot was passed around, most took a serving—or two—while others abstained, Ajak among them. He stood from his seat and made an elaborate bow.

"Goodnight, friends! May your evening be nearly as exciting as mine own," he said with a flourish of his hand.

Laughs and jeers spread around the table as Ajak dramatically exited the room. A couple of other Walkers followed him. Ray stayed behind, partly to enjoy a scoop of the sweet pudding, partly to drown her sorrows in it. Ajak's words from earlier rang hollow as he departed. *So much for not hurting me,* she through bitterly.

Tonight, the pudding was more like custard, but delicious, nonetheless. Ray loved Rhia's sweets and wondered if there would be enough for another bowl in the morning for breakfast. As she ate, she leaned back in her chair and enjoyed listening to the others—her family—talk about the events of the day, the sweetness of the pudding, and where they'd be off to after dessert. She didn't pay attention to any one conversation, instead content to simply be a part of the familial scene.

The chatter died down as the meal concluded. Naro stood up and nodded his head to Rhia. "Thank you as always, Rhia."

Others echoed the statement, Ray included. Naro grabbed his hat and left the room, strutting like a noble.

When she finished eating, Ray took her dishes into the kitchen and added them to the pile of dirty dishes. A couple of the younger Walkers—boys no older than twelve—were helping Rhia wash the dishes.

Ray smiled at Rhia. "The pudding was great tonight."

"Custard, dear," Rhia corrected.

"It was great!" Ray reaffirmed as she left the room. The two boys giggled behind her, and she heard Rhia scold them and direct them on how to properly clean the knives.

Ray crossed through the house and headed upstairs. Naro's door was closed, but she wasted no time in opening it and entering. He stood over the cauldron on the table alone, holding the basket of blueleaf. Another phial was on the table, small and orb-like. The contents were a murky brown color. Naro tore up some of the leaves and tossed them into the cauldron.

"Stir, please," Naro politely commanded.

Ray nodded and did as she was told.

Naro placed the basket on his desk and then picked up the mysterious phial. "I trust Ajak told you about this?"

Her brow furrowed. "Mostly. He said it's a sleeper, but I don't understand why you'd add the blueleaf to it," Ray said.

The corner of his mouth curled upward. He held the phial in front of his face, swirling the glass gently. "The sleeper is the base of the potion, yes. We want to incapacitate the princess. But there's a second component to it as well, something much more important. What's blueleaf used for?"

"Headaches." Her response came without a thought.

"Yes. What else?" He lowered the glass and looked her in the eye.

She was silent as she racked her brain for the answer. She didn't often deal with blueleaf or other herbs, but she had a little bit of knowledge. Sometimes Naro had her pick things up from herbalists' shops or stalls. It was a common task that many Walkers performed. That way it was harder to trace the purchases back to him.

Oh. "You take it sometimes after you've seen things."

A thoughtful look passed over his face. "Yes, after the visions. I chew on it to neutralize the effects of the visions."

Ray nodded and continued to stir. The liquid inside the cauldron smelled like dirt and not much else. Blueleaf lacked any kind of odor, and often neutralized the smell of anything else it was combined with.

"You know the rumors about our princess?" Naro asked, taking the stopper off the phial. He poured the contents into the cauldron. It turned the liquid from a watery blue into a sickly green but just as quickly it faded back to the blue. A sweet aroma wafted up from the cauldron but quickly faded as the liquids combined. She continued to stir.

"She's got something inside her head," Ray said. Her thoughts turned dark. It was perhaps one of the biggest secrets of the crown. Everyone knew something was wrong with Princess Niamnh, but no one knew the exact truth. Everyone had their own theories as to what was wrong with her.

"That she does. A Doshara," Naro confirmed, his voice solemn. "Tell me what you know of them."

Ray's face twisted into a disgusted sneer before she forced herself back to a neutral expression. "Doshara. Vengeful soul-takers. They turn people into monsters who must be put down like rabid dogs, then jump into another person to start the cycle over." She paused and then her jaw dropped, overcome with shock. She nearly let go of the spoon. "Wait, the princess has a Doshara *inside* her?" Naro nodded. "Then... Why are we kidnapping her? Aren't we putting ourselves at risk of getting infected?"

"No, he's not interested in us."

He?

Naro waved a dismissive hand in the air as if he had heard her thoughts. "No, it goes beyond that. We're doing this to save the city."

"Save... the city?" she repeated slowly.

Naro reached out and gently placed his hands on hers. "I'll explain it in further detail later. But for now, that's all *you* need to know."

Does Ajak know this? She had a sinking feeling that he did not. *What have I gotten into?*

"Go out and enjoy tonight. Starting tomorrow, we're on lockdown until after the kidnapping is complete." Naro's voice was soothing, but she heard the command underneath. "Report back here at first light. I'll have your next set of instructions then."

She didn't think she could enjoy herself, but she had no other choice. Naro held her hands for another moment before taking the spoon from her and tapping it against the edge of the cauldron, knocking off all loose droplets of the potion. She took that as her cue to leave.

CHAPTER VII: MUNNE

The ride back to the valley was silent, but Munne found great comfort in being with Mayrien and Araloth, especially when it was just the three of them. The triple had been through several journeys and battles together, and there was no other pair that Munne trusted more with her life. They traveled much faster going back than when she departed the valley that morning. This war council was very important. It would have representatives from the other races present to discuss their next plan of action against the Provira. Munne hoped the foreign dignitaries wouldn't feel slighted at her delayed arrival and start to the meeting.

A vain hope. They'll be judging me harshly while they wait for me.

When they reached the main path coming out from the valley, they encountered several riders and carriages heading south. Visitors were returning home following the march of the dead. Munne felt the need to draw her hood up and obscure her face, but she knew there was no point. Just the sight of Mayrien and Araloth would confirm who their third rider was. Munne thought it would be a greater slight to try to hide her actions now instead of owning them. She remained hoodless as she entered the valley.

The streets were crowded, as was normal for the early afternoon. Townsfolk shopped, and visitors gathered last-minute items for the journey home. It was also time for the midday meal, so the bakeries and dining halls were filled with guests. The midday meal would be served at the war council. Munne wasn't sure if she would have the stomach to eat anything just yet.

The war council was held in the Meeting Spire, which towered over most of the buildings in the valley. It was almost as tall as the Hall of the Dead and made of the same dark stone. The spire stood halfway between her father's manor and the road leading south out of Elimere. Nearby were the guest houses, reserved for foreign diplomats. Representatives from Promthus, the Black Lakes, and possibly other cultures would be present at the council, as well as leaders from the Elviri provinces.

The three Elviri dismounted from their horses at the stables near the spire. Araloth held back for a moment to speak to the stable hands while Mayrien and Munne proceeded inside.

"I'll catch up in a moment," Araloth called to her companions. She turned to the stable hand and said, "Please make sure these horses are returned to..."

Munne only caught the first part of Araloth's sentence before the doors to the spire closed behind her. Under normal circumstances when she wasn't running late, she would have taken Alathyl to the main stables near the southern exit from the valley and enjoyed the walk to the spire, taking in the sights of so many people carrying on their normal lives.

Their simple routines and lack of diplomatic council meetings is enviable. Would that I could do away with the meetings altogether.

The inside of the spire was made up of many staircases and rooms. There were seven total floors in the building, each with varying sizes of meeting halls. The first floor of the spire was a reception area where representatives gathered before their meetings, and they could enjoy artwork by local Elviri artists. On certain days, if the meeting was important enough, members of the orchestra would come and play music while the representatives waited. There was also a kitchen on the first floor where meals would be made if a meeting ran for a long time. The war council was both important enough and would run for a long time.

Mayrien and Munne reached the second floor, where the three lords met regularly with their patrons. Normally Munne held war councils on this floor when it was just between her and the other Elviri, but today's council would be on the third floor, which housed the largest meeting hall in the Spire. The doors were closed, which meant the meeting was already underway.

They began without us? Munne exchanged a curious glance with Mayrien.

Inside the room on each of the walls were lit fireplaces. A large wooden table stood in the center, taking up a majority of the floor. A map of Daaria was carved into the table with small figurines representing various militaries on top of it. All the attendants were sitting around the table, except for one

Proma man who stood at the end closest to them. Munne recognized him as Rhorek Gondamire, the knight-general of the Proma army. He was a tall man with broad shoulders, wrinkles on his face, and golden blond hair. The sigil of the Proma royal family was embroidered into the chest of his dress robes—a golden crown atop a blue hourglass-shaped lake. He had been in the middle of speaking when she entered the hall and had spun to see who came through the doors. He bowed his head in her direction, acknowledging her presence. The other attendants turned their attention to Munne and Mayrien as well, though none spoke any greeting.

On the left side of the room were all the Elviri—Kieron and his triple, Caedwyn, Faelwyn, and Lindenwen, leader of the Paladins of the Gods. Three empty chairs remained where Munne and her triple were supposed to sit. On the right side were their guests, emissaries from Promthus, the Black Lakes, and the Imalar Woods. Rhorek was joined by three of his men, though Munne couldn't recall their names and ranks. Beside them sat one Imalarii who she recognized as Eldo Talltree, one of the guild masters from the Imalar Woods. On his right were three Barauder from the Black Lakes. Their dark blue and green skin was more accustomed to the swamp-like environs of their home. Underneath the candlelight of the hall, their faces and hands looked dry. The Barauder weren't yet involved in the war with the Provira, although two of their leaders, S'raak and Lagazi, advocated for their people to join the fray. The third leader, Druuk, had been more conservative, and challenged the opinions of the older women. The Barauder had traveled to Promthus and the Elviri provinces to discuss their involvement in the war, at the behest of S'raak and Lagazi.

Huntaran sat at the far end of the table. If she hadn't been looking in his direction, she would have missed the last guest in the room. Away from the table near the fireplace was another Elviri man. He wore pale yellow and red robes with three swirls embroidered onto the chest with red thread. He was a mindwalker of Lithua. Guilt and anger flared up within her as she and Mayrien went to their seats.

What's a mindwalker doing here? He should be at the healing houses, not here attending a war council.

"Thank you for joining us, Vere'cha," Huntaran said coolly from his seat at the head of the table, closest to the entrance. He wore a stoic expression, but she saw traces of anger and frustration in his eyes.

She bowed to him, and then to the rest of the room. "I apologize for the delay," she replied, and then took her seat at her father's right side. She felt the gaze of the Lithuan mindwalker on her, but she ignored him.

Mayrien followed as did Araloth, having slipped into the room while everyone's attention was focused on Munne.

"Apologies for the delay, my friends." Huntaran echoed Munne's apology to the rest of the room. "Let us continue our discussion. Rhorek, I believe you were giving us an update on the southern border of Promthus and Moonyswyn."

The Proma knight-general regained his focus and cleared his throat. "Yes, the border skirmishes have been rapidly escalating. Outposts near Merrioff have been overrun in the past two weeks." A grimace crossed Rhorek's face.

Munne knew exactly which outposts Rhorek referred to. She had been there when the first was lost. The others must have been taken after the Elviri retreated to Elimere.

"We've begun evacuations of the rest of the farmlands surrounding the city. The walls of Merrioff are strong." Rhorek held his head high, but the fear was in his eyes.

To Munne's knowledge, the walls of Merrioff hadn't been tested before. Not against the Provira, anyway. Merrioff was a modest town nowhere near the size of Elimere or Auora. Munne had passed through it several times during the war. She knew farmers from the south had already begun evacuating before Rhorek gave the command. They had filled the homes and inns in the town when she and her army passed through. If there were more to come, she wasn't sure if the town would be able to house everyone for long.

"Guild Master Eldo, I summoned you to this council so that we may discuss the possibility of increasing the number of woodcrafts sent to Promthus, particularly to the town of Merrioff."

Huntaran turned his attention to the single Imalarii man in the room, who sat between the Proma and the Barauder. If they had been standing, Eldo would have come up to Huntaran's waist. The Imalarii had curly brown hair and warm brown eyes. He was dressed in a green tunic and pants and had a small pudge to his stomach. Although he appeared very meek and vulnerable, Munne could see the outline of muscles on his arms underneath his sleeves. She was certain she was looking at a master archer. The Imalarii had never been involved in any wars or conflicts with the other races of Daaria. They preferred to trade goods and crafts. However, a renowned bowyer wouldn't just craft weapons—he knew how to use them.

Father must have sent for Eldo while I was away, Munne thought, *but why wouldn't he have waited for my return? That should have been a decision for me to make.*

"Aye, that is something I've discussed with my guildmates," Eldo replied, tapping his fingers on the table.

Huntaran bowed his head and met Eldo's gaze. "And what would the Imalarii ask for in return?"

Eldo held his gaze for several moments before responding. "We don't wish to draw attention to ourselves. We have done nothing to provoke the ire of the Provira. However, Imalarii craft is very distinguishable. If the Provira notice that we have provided Merrioff with weapons, they'll get angry." Eldo paused, his gaze shifting between Huntaran, Kieron, and Munne. "The Imalarii have asked me to petition for protection along the border, as long as the Provira are a threat to us, in addition to compensation for the timely crafting of these new weapons."

Huntaran glanced between Kieron, Caedwyn, and Faelwyn, awaiting the chieftains' responses.

Kieron nodded his agreement almost immediately. *It makes sense—he won't turn down newer weapons for the soldiers stationed in Promthus, especially with the war escalating.*

Caedwyn and Faelwyn leaned in close and exchanged whispers before turning back to Huntaran and giving their approval as well. Their agreement was not a surprise, but the speed in which they delivered their answer was. Most of the compensation the Imalarii asked for would be coming from Elifyn up front with Elimere and Elimaine assisting with repayment thereafter. It wasn't necessarily a risky move for Caedwyn and Faelwyn to make, but the luxurious lifestyle of their people may take a hit for a few weeks.

This isn't something they would just agree to without discussing with the other noble families in Lithalyon. How long has this trade agreement been in development? Why is this the first I'm hearing of it? Anger continued to bubble and churn within her stomach.

"The Elviri are in agreement. What say you, Knight-General Gondamire?" Huntaran called out.

Munne and the others turned their attention to Rhorek. He was already bobbing his head enthusiastically. *Does he have the men to spare for this? The Proma have faced the brunt of the Provira forces so far. They've lost many more lives than we have.*

"It seems we are in agreement, then," Huntaran said to Eldo, the corners of his lips curling into a polite smile. "We will prepare a small force of troops in the coming days and send them to the Imalar Wood before the first snowfall."

"And I will send word to my men in Trent to increase their southern patrols," Rhorek chimed in.

The agreement was made almost too easily. Munne shifted around uncomfortably in her seat. Her father had no doubt gone around her to introduce these discussions while she had been away and was making decisions that *she* should have been making. *What else did he do while I was gone?*

Huntaran turned his attention to the rest of the table. "Friends, I have also gathered you here to discuss the different paths we may take in the coming months with the Provira." He looked at each member of the council before settling his gaze on Rhorek. "The conflict must be brought to an end, preferably with minimal bloodshed."

He paused to allow the council to murmur words of agreement. Munne contemplated raising her voice to discuss the idea of sending a larger force to southern Promthus to drive the Provira out once and for all. She could tell by the way Huntaran watched the table that he wasn't through with speaking, though, so she would have to wait.

"I fear too much blood has been spilled already. As *Se'vi*, my first priority is the safety of the Elviri, and my second priority is maintaining the peace in Daaria. Rhorek, you wrote to me that the Provira delivered a message to Castle Auora shortly after the attacks south of Merrioff. Would you please read this letter to the council?"

Munne's blood ran cold, and she felt a distinct shift in focus in the room. *What kind of a letter could the half-breeds possibly write that would elicit such a reaction from this council?*

All eyes were now on Rhorek. He stood, a frown plastered on his face about delivering the message to the council. He pulled a fine scroll from his coat. Munne couldn't recognize the broken seal from where she sat.

He unraveled the scroll and cleared his throat. "'People of the Proma, we write to you as a gesture of goodwill from our lands and our Lord Isyth.'"

Munne's eyes widened. Mayrien physically recoiled at the name. Faelwyn and Caedwyn exchanged worried glances while Kieron and his triple shifted uncomfortably in their seats. *Our ancestors had erased that name from the annals of history, along with the rest of the damnable Asaszi. Where did the Provira learn of that name?* She immediately turned to her father whose expression was blank.

Rhorek looked over the Elviri with an uneasy stare. He seemed reluctant to continue, but he managed. "'We thank you for the provisions you have sent to the outposts we recently acquired at the northern border of Moonyswyn. We will accept these as tokens of goodwill for our proposed ceasefire. We write to you to invite members of your court to our western border to discuss the terms of this ceasefire, and to ask that you deliver this message to your allies so that they may receive the same invitation. We will look for you on the last day of Our Lord's Year, at the shores of the River Ys. If we don't meet under a peaceful banner, the new year will begin with blood. Praise... praise to Our Lord Isyth.'"

The words were foul in the air. All the Elviri had looks of disbelief and rage on their faces, except Huntaran and the Lithuan mindwalker. Munne's eyes never left her father's face. *He read the letter before the council, that much is obvious. What scheme has he plotted for this gathering?*

"Thank you, Rhorek. You may leave the scroll on the table," Huntaran said. Rhorek grimaced and tossed the scroll onto the table far away from him. It hit the wood and slid further away from the Proma. "Friends, this news is indeed dire. The Provira have discovered something which we sought to hide from this world, and we don't know how they found it. We believed all traces of the Asaszi had been destroyed thousands of years ago. I understand that your initial desires will be to take up arms, march into Moonyswyn, and eradicate the entire rainforest. My years as a student of history would caution against such action. We must learn what knowledge the Provira have obtained, and why they would speak such a cursed name."

"We are already engaged in combat with them. This isn't the time to retreat and think about what they've done!" Munne exclaimed, leaning over the table. The council was taken aback by her sudden outburst. Some gazes darted to her, while others were on her father as they waited for his reaction.

"Now is the proper time to evaluate what our foes are doing and make a decision on how to handle them before they bring the war to us in the new year," Huntaran responded.

"You want to tuck our forces away in libraries and read about men of the past? You want to let the Provira and Asaszi come to us?" Her voice rose with each sentence.

"I won't spill any more blood needlessly." Huntaran raised his voice to match Munne's, his stoic expression crumbling underneath his frustration.

"Blood has already been spilled, and blood will continue to spill if these half-breeds are left unchecked!" Munne scowled. She stood up and pointed her finger accusingly at the unraveled scroll. "That message is a threat, and it must be dealt with."

Huntaran slammed his fist on the table. "As *Se'vi* I am ordering you to stand down, Vere'cha!"

Munne's jaw went slack, and she was brought out of her anger for a moment. Her father had never used his rank to silence her, not since she accepted the title of Warlord. They had their disagreements, but her father always respected her position of authority, especially when it came to military matters.

Huntaran opened his hand and placed it on the table. He spoke with a calmer voice now. "We won't raise arms against the Provira, not until we know what we are facing. Aeglys, one of our royal archivists, has been charged with researching past wars between the Elviri and Asaszi. I plan on sending an envoy to treat with the Provira, in an attempt to gain information we otherwise won't find in our studies."

Elvarin had mentioned assisting Aeglys in her studies. Was this what he had been researching last night?

Voices cut through Huntaran's words before he finished speaking. Mayrien and Kieron's triple were in an uproar. The three Elviri were on their feet, as were Rhorek's men. Kieron twisted between trying to calm his triple and glaring at Huntaran. Lindenwen simply had a look of shock on her face. Rhorek was silent. Faelwyn and Caedwyn spoke to Araloth, but Munne couldn't distinguish their words. She couldn't find words to express her anger at her father. Some of the Elviri and the Proma shouted angrily at Huntaran.

"You cannot think we'll just lay down our weapons to these monsters!" one of Rhorek's men shouted.

"*Se'vi*, the Provira cannot be trusted!" Faerendyl hissed.

"We spent thousands of years trying to banish traces of the Asaszi. We must do so again!" Telimar, one of Kieron's triple, shouted.

The three Barauder in the room were notably silent, but Munne saw the fear and concern in their eyes as they looked at one another.

Enough! Munne pushed herself away from the table. She placed her hand on the wall and leaned against it, running her other hand through her hair.

The Lithuan mindwalker rose during the outburst. Munne twisted her head to look at the man, prepared to yell at him to sit back down, that none of this concerned him. He placed a hand on her shoulder and met her eyes. The gentle touch and concern in his gaze compelled her to hold her tongue. This mindwalker was well trained in his studies, which frustrated her. She wanted to yell, but under his gaze she knew that it would achieve nothing. She frowned, placing her free hand on her waist. The mindwalker removed his hand and gestured toward the table before walking forward.

Huntaran glanced at the mindwalker before turning his attention back at the gathered council and slammed his fist on the table again, trying to quiet the crowd. Everyone's voices tapered off, tentatively willing to listen to what he had to say.

"I intend to send Anumil, a Lithuan mindwalker, to meet with the Provira. He has been trained in the language of the body and has spent many years learning about the Eldest Days. He is capable of learning what the Provira have discovered. I hope to placate the Provira by sending a spiritual envoy, rather than an armed envoy," Huntaran said and stood beside Anumil.

"Who will go with him, Father?" Munne asked quietly.

Her father met her eyes. "I'm placing Lindenwen and her paladins in charge of Anumil's journey. They will keep him safe and protect him from any harm."

Munne wanted to lash out and scream, but she kept her face void of any emotion. Her father was overriding her authority as Warlord by sending the paladins as an escort instead of soldiers from the army. Even if his intention was to keep the peace, Anumil wouldn't be safe with the paladins. The Paladins of the Gods were never supposed to be true soldiers.

"And where will your soldiers be while Anumil is treating with the Provira?" Munne's voice betrayed her, and she uttered the words with contempt.

Huntaran was silent, contemplating his daughter. "There is work to be done at the Imalarii border, and I think it would be appropriate for the Warlord to ensure our allies are protected."

A knife twisted in her stomach. Although he hadn't posed it as an order, Munne knew that was what her father meant. She simply bowed her head, knowing her words would betray her again if she opened her mouth.

Huntaran turned his attention to the Imalarii man sitting at the table. "Guild Master Eldo, our Warlord will gather a number of her troops and depart for the Imalar Woods as soon as possible. Would you like for her to act as an escort, or travel separately?"

Most eyes focused on Eldo. "While I appreciate the Elviri honoring their end of the deal," Eldo said and straightened. "I think it would be wiser to travel separately, so that any potential Provira spies don't see us together. I would like to avoid confrontation with the Provira for as long as possible." He paused and looked between Munne and Huntaran. "I will leave in the morning."

"Very well. She will depart in two days' time, and her triple will follow in a few days' time with a small division of troops." Huntaran said. "Friends, let us adjourn for now and share the midday meal together. I have arranged for a venison roast to be served in the dining hall of the main guest house. We may resume discussion of our trade agreements after the meal."

The other council members rose to their feet and shuffled out of the room with Huntaran leading the way. There would be no further discussion between Munne and her father. Munne wanted to escape this room as quickly as possible, but she waited until all the guests left. It was just her and her triple left in the room.

Araloth broke the silence first. "Munne, I think we should—"

"I need to go to the archives," Munne interrupted. She turned to Araloth, reaching out for her hand. "There's something I need to find."

"But what about the midday meal?" Mayrien asked, leaning forward so she could speak directly to Munne and Araloth.

Munne turned to look at Mayrien, letting go of Araloth's hand. "What about it?"

"You'll be expected to attend. You know this." Mayrien frowned.

Munne shook her head and stood up, pushing her chair back. "I'm not going."

Mayrien scoffed and tossed her head back, rolling her eyes. Araloth stood as well, grabbing Munne's hand again. She spoke quietly, but there was a sense of urgency in her words. "Munne, you can't walk away from your duties as Warlord."

"My father has made it clear that he is taking over my duties as Warlord," Munne muttered, walking away from the table toward the doors. Araloth followed. "He has already decided my punishment by sending me away to the Imalar Woods. What worse thing could he do if I don't attend this meal?" She knew as soon as she said the words that her father could do much worse. It wasn't unheard of for a *Se'vi* to strip one of the three lords of their title. Would her father do that, though? Munne decided not to dwell on it and chose to strengthen her resolve to go to the archives. "You should go to the meal. Don't get punished for my choices."

"What do you hope to find in the archives?" Mayrien asked as Munne's hand touched the door handle.

Munne tightened her grip on the door handle but stopped. "Answers to my nightmares. I'll tell you about it over dinner at the Moonlit Grove. Dress as civilians. I don't want to draw any attention to our conversation." With those words, Munne left her friends in the Meeting Spire and rushed to her father's manor.

CHAPTER VIII: RAY

The first rays of light poked at the city around Ray as she rubbed the sleep from her eyes and entered the safehouse. She had walked around the city for most of the night. Thoughts of her mission raced around in her head, which had kept her feet moving. It wasn't until she had started falling asleep during her walk that she decided to rest at one of the other safehouses in the Gutters.

I hope there's porridge again this morning. I'm getting hungry.

Ajak was already sitting at the dining table with a steaming mug of tea in front of him. His hands were in his lap and his eyes were half-closed, his clothes all tussled up. She thought she could smell some kind of perfume on him—someone else's. He looked like death. Where had he been last night? No, it didn't matter to her. She snipped the budding jealousy at the root. Better not to dwell on what Ajak did at night.

She sat down across from him, propping her elbows on the table and resting her chin on the palms of her hands.

"Minnie's in the kitchen," Ajak mumbled, not looking up from the table.

Ray let out an affirmative grunt and headed into the kitchen. Minnie moved between countertops and the oven, muttering to herself. Every time she crossed the room, she brought some kind of utensil or container with her.

"Good morning, Minnie," Ray said loud enough to catch the woman's attention. She sounded like she was still half-asleep, and she might as well have been. She didn't normally wake up this early.

"Hello, dearie. Would you like a cup of tea?" the woman asked.

Ray nodded, propping herself against one of the countertops. Minnie put down the pan she was carrying—probably for cooking bacon—and moved over to the pantry shelves. She grabbed a large tin and a spoon, then came back over toward Ray.

126

"Pass me a mug, dearie."

Ray pulled a mug out from the cabinet next to her and passed it over to Minnie, who took it over to the oven and ladled boiling water into it. She returned and opened the large tin, taking a heaping spoonful of dried leaves and dumping it into the mug.

"Give it a stir and add whatever you'd like." Minnie nodded over to a couple of other containers of dried fruits and herbs.

"Thank you, Minnie." Ray decided to add a mix of dried apples and mint to her tea, something to wake her up and give her some needed energy.

After she was done, she exited back into the dining hall. Ajak was hovering over his own mug, staring into its contents. Ray thought about asking him how his night was or making an off-handed comment about how terrible he looked, but she didn't want to hear his response. Instead, she mimicked his pose and leaned over her own mug of tea, breathing in deeply to savor the mingled scent of mint and apple.

There was a comfortable silence hanging over the room. Minnie shuffled about in the kitchen, but beyond that the house was empty. Ray listened to herself breath in and out through her nose. She could hear Ajak's breathing too if she focused on it.

When Naro entered the house, she knew right away. Ray heard the front door opening and closing, his boots on the floor as he approached the dining hall. When he crossed the threshold, Ray had to catch herself from making a face. He looked even worse than Ajak, and he was *smiling*. His jacket was thrown across one of his shoulders. His cravat hung loosely around his neck and his shirt was unbuttoned far enough to reveal the top of his chest. His hat was missing. He swayed with every step and had to lean heavily against his chair when he got to the table.

"Good morning," Naro said louder than normal, his voice hoarse. His hands groped at the top of the chair, and his jacket fell to the floor beside him. He threw a casual glance at it and then returned his gaze to Ray and Ajak.

"Good morning, Naro," Ray responded, trying to muster up more energy than she had to spare. She wished the tea was cool enough to drink, but she would have to wait.

"Morning," Ajak mumbled. He picked up his mug and drank deeply.

"We have a very exciting day ahead of us today." Naro pulled the chair out from the table and took a seat.

Minnie came bustling out of the kitchen with another mug in her hands. She too must have heard Naro's entrance. She placed it down in front of him and hurried back to her duties.

"I want you two changed and ready to go to the Sky District within the hour," Naro told them, his words slurring together ever so slightly.

Ray looked between Ajak and Naro. *Can these two clean up fast enough to blend in up there? How did Naro even make it back here in one piece?* "What are we doing in the Sky District?" she asked.

A sloppy grin spread across Naro's face. "We're going to meet the princess."

"Are you sure that's a wise idea?" Even Ajak seemed taken aback by the idea. He had physically recoiled in his chair, holding his tea close to his chest.

"It's perfect. And we're only going to be watching. No interfering." Naro picked up his mug and downed it in seconds. He leaned back to gaze thoughtfully into the mug, speaking to himself. "The Imalarii know how to make a strong morning tonic."

Ray chose not to dwell on his personal musings. They had their plan for the day. In fact, it was work that she was very familiar with—tailing people, observing them, and making note of their behavior and actions during the day. *But why are we doing this now? Wouldn't Naro have done this a long time ago, during the earlier stages of his planning? If we already have the herbs to brew the sleeper potion, then surely that means we're kidnapping her soon.*

"So, we're just gonna get a look at her?" Ajak asked, sounding a little more awake than before.

"Well, you want to make sure you get the right girl, don't you?" Naro countered, and his gaze shifted from the mug to Ajak.

Ajak held his stare for a few moments and then nodded. "Makes sense," he mumbled.

Her thoughts finally caught up to what Naro was asking of them. They were going to *see* the princess today, in the Sky District? It had been several years since the princess was last seen by the public. *Has the Doshara altered the way the princess looked?*

"The king's letting her leave the castle?" Ray asked, not realizing she spoke aloud. Ajak gave her a confused look.

Naro merely smiled as he stood up, his chair scraping the ground as it slid back. All traces of his stupor had vanished. He was the imposing gang lord once more. "We'll leave within the hour. Make sure you're dressed."

He plucked his jacket off from the floor and slipped into the kitchen. He came back out a few moments later and headed upstairs. Ray and Ajak exchanged glances and then got up. She needed to dig through the armoire again and find a new outfit to wear today. The gray dress was too drab for the Sky District. She would need something with more embroidery, more jewels.

She and Ajak climbed the stairs after Naro and then split off into separate bedrooms. Inside the room Ray picked two Walkers talked quietly to each other. They paused to wave at her, then continued their conversation. She vaguely remembered their names, Wyatt and Dol. They were both teenagers close to Ray's age, but they primarily worked for Aldrin, the other lieutenant of the Walkers. Wyatt was sprawled across one of the beds with an arm slung over his face. Dol sat on the ground next to the bed, her head resting against the frame. Ray couldn't remember if they were a couple or not.

"Aldrin's got me in the Pike and Pint almost every night looking out for those bastards," Wyatt groaned. "We had good intel that they'd be there. But people are still disappearing."

Dol shook her head and murmured back, "That ain't right."

Ray crossed to the armoire and dug through the contents. There were a handful of dresses hanging on one side. Most of them weren't fancy enough to wear into the Sky District, so her choices were limited to a cream-colored gown with frills or a green gown with ample amounts of embroidery and lace.

"Normally, Aldrin's intel is better than this." Wyatt's complaining continued.

Dol's voice dropped to a whisper. "Maybe he's being double-crossed?"

There was silence between the two of them.

"If he is, his *friends* are playing a dangerous game," Wyatt muttered. "No one crosses the Walkers like that."

Ray frowned. She wasn't as familiar with the work that Aldrin was doing, but if there was some kind of double-crossing going on, was it possible it was connected to the athra? That thought didn't sit well in her head. All she knew about Aldrin was that he was a Provira, perhaps the only one remaining in Promthus. He was just a child when the Provira were exiled from the city over a hundred years ago and had joined the Walkers when his family left. Naro had been the one to raise Aldrin to lieutenantship, so Aldrin has obviously proven himself trustworthy. Why else would Naro have kept him so close?

She continued shuffling around clothes. She really didn't want to wear either of the gowns because they were too cumbersome. Perhaps she could wear a fancy tunic and tuck her hair underneath a hat to look like a page or a lord's son. That would be a true disguise. With the new idea in mind, she dug through the clothes once more and found a dark purple tunic along with a matching foppish hat. She also needed to find a shirt, leggings, and a pair of boots, but those were in greater abundance. She began to change.

"Hey, Ray, what've you been on lately?" Dol called from behind Ray as she finished lacing up a pair of boots.

"Been doing the usual, just watching places. People," Ray responded.

"You gonna go watch the rich today?" Dol had a hint of excitement in her voice, seeing the tunic in Ray's hands. She was a year or two younger than Ray and was fascinated by the Sky District.

"Yeah, boss has me tailing a couple of different people today." The lie came easy enough. Typically, she would have been tailing people, gathering information. She was sort of doing that today, she supposed.

Dol took in Ray's outfit and wrinkled her nose. "You look lordly enough."

"Easier to move around if you're a little lordling," Ray retorted.

Dol shrugged and leaned back against the bed, reaching up to rub Wyatt's shoulder.

Ray left the two of them alone and crossed the hall into the other bedroom where Ajak was laying down on one of the beds. He had already changed and wore something similar to Ray—a dark crimson tunic. He wasn't wearing a silly hat, though. In fact, it didn't look like he had done anything with his hair yet.

"What's the deal with Aldrin's crew?" she asked, sitting down on the bed across from him.

He rolled onto his side to look at her. "I don't know all the details, but people've been disappearing from taverns."

"What kind of people?"

"People from smaller gangs, and others who fancy themselves the adventuring type. The city guard is looking into it too from what I remember."

She had heard of that before. There was some group running a con offering people the chance at riches if they traveled to the land of Kherizhan, far to the south of Promthus. Ordinarily this wouldn't be a problem, but none of the people who took this group's offer returned to Auora. It had been going on for two or three years. She wasn't sure how closely the guard was investigating, considering it had gone on for so long. What was curious was why Naro had one of his lieutenants looking into it.

"Have any of ours gone missing?" she asked, her brow furrowing.

"Maybe one or two kids, but I don't think anyone else has." Ajak pulled himself up into a sitting position. "Hey, give me a hand with my hair."

Ray moved to the other bed and the two prepared his hair in silence. She brushed it for him while he made two braids to frame his face. He finished the look with two bronze beads at the end of each braid.

He threw a glance over his shoulder and asked, "Lordly enough?"

She stifled a laugh and nodded, trying not to pay too much attention to how attractive he looked.

They spent the rest of their time sitting together in silence, wanting nothing more than to go back to sleep. About thirty minutes later, they heard Naro's door open and took that as their cue to get up and meet him outside on the landing.

Naro was in a completely different outfit from the night before. It was more reserved and becoming of a rich merchant or nobleman. There were multiple layers to his outfit, all the colors muted and unassuming. He wore a gray shirt underneath a dark blue tunic. On top of it all was a dark green cape with slits for his arms. Gold buttons lined one edge of the cape. He wore a pair of plain leather gloves that reached up to his elbows, and a pair of knee-length boots to match.

"Come, we'll take the stairs," he told them, beckoning for them to follow him into his room.

Ray looked at Ajak quizzically, but he was already walking after Naro. She frowned and adjusted her hat.

Once they were all inside the room, Naro shut the door and crossed over to the massive painted armoire and opened one of its doors, digging around for something. She heard a very faint *click* and then he took a step back.

"Come," Naro commanded softly.

Ajak entered the wardrobe without question, disappearing into the wardrobe between a gaudy green overcoat and a black cape. Naro waited patiently for her, although she couldn't read the expression on his face.

"Stairs?" she questioned, eyeing the wardrobe warily. "Is there some kind of secret passage behind there?" She was no stranger to hidden passageways, but as far as she knew there were none in this safehouse. *What secrets is Naro keeping in his wardrobe?*

He only responded with a wink, so she gathered her wits and stepped into the wardrobe, pushing her way between the same overcoat and cape. Ray kept one hand in front of her, feeling for the back panel. Rather than collide with a solid wall of wood, a hand took hold of hers and gently pulled her through. She had to stifle a scream, reminding herself that Ajak had just entered ahead of her, so it must be his hand. On the other side of the clothing was Ajak, a mischievous glimmer in his eyes.

She had stepped through a doorway in the wall onto the landing of a massive spiral stone staircase. The stairs twisted and stretched up as far as Ray could see, which chilled her to the bone. Lit torches on the walls illuminated Ajak and herself in a strange blue light. *I've never seen blue flames before. What is this place?* The doorway leading back to Naro's room was like a large hole that had been expertly carved out of the stone. Next to the hole was a door, which she assumed covered it when the way through was closed.

"Did you know about this?" she asked, her voice barely a whisper. She knew better than to call out in a corridor like this. Her voice would bounce and echo off the stones.

"Only since last week," Ajak replied, leading her toward the stairs.

Naro exited the armoire and stretched his arms upward before gesturing to the stairs leading up. "Shall we?"

He took the lead, the other two falling in line behind him. The door behind them slid shut, separating the cozy bedroom from the corridor.

"Where does this go?" Ray whispered.

"As far up and as far down as I would like," Naro replied without so much as a glance over his shoulder.

She frowned. *What does that mean? Is there some kind of magic at play here? But that would be impossible.*

Well, now she wasn't quite sure what was and wasn't possible. The thought made her skin crawl.

"I'm a merchant. You two are brothers. I'm visiting your family from my time in Hyndur and Lithalyon. You're showing me around the city." Naro rattled the fake backstory off with ease.

Ajak jumped in without hesitation. "You're a distant relation that we're trying to sweeten up because we want access to your worldly connections and money."

"Despite having money of your own?"

Ajak flashed Ray a wolfish grin. "More could never hurt."

"Yes, then you shall spend the day *impressing me*." Ray heard the challenge in Naro's words. He wasn't referring to their characters, although that certainly would help them out. He wanted to see what Ajak and Ray were capable of today. She tried to focus on that challenge rather than the dark gaping maw beside her. *How far* down *does this staircase go?*

Her legs began to tire as they continued to climb. There were several landings that led to other doors and holes in the wall, although she couldn't tell where they led to. There were no distinct markings or signs. *Of course there won't be markings. This place shouldn't even exist. Should it?*

Finally, Naro came to a stop in front of a wooden door with a flower carved into it. He reached into his cape and withdrew a small golden key. On the other side of the door were tools and baskets. They were in a storage room of some kind. Naro gestured for them to enter, so they did. He closed the door to the stone corridor and locked it, returning the key to his person.

"Go on. It's a private garden," Naro said.

Ajak shrugged and crossed over to the other door, opening it and letting sunlight stream into the room. Sure enough, they were looking at a beautiful courtyard. The three of them exited what Ray now identified as a tool shed. The scent of flowers and fresh air brought a smile to her face, and she realized that the mysterious staircase hadn't smelled like anything, not even burning wicks or stale air.

She knew better than to ask more questions, but Protector above, she was curious. *Whose garden is this? Are we in the Sky District now? Who else knows about that staircase?*

"—didn't go this far up last time." She heard Ajak mutter under his breath. He looked around in shock, his cool facade gone.

Naro walked past them to a garden gate that was angled in such a way that the tool shed couldn't be seen until someone was already in the garden proper. Ajak and Ray picked up the pace. Perhaps he would humor them later and let them ask questions about the mysterious stone staircase and the beautiful garden. For now, though, she had to focus on the task at hand and impress Naro with her skills.

<hr/>

The suns shone brightly by the time they got to the streets of the Sky District. It was fairly busy being so early in the morning. Clusters of noblewomen took a stroll around the neighborhood, their arms linked and their voices floating around them as they spoke of intrigue and scandal among the upper crust of society. Groups of men strutted about, visiting relations and acquaintances to discuss business.

ay, Ajak, and Naro had no trouble blending in. They stood on either side of Naro, leaning in every so often to point at some building or person and murmur a quip about it. The Sky District itself was rather small, being at the top of a man-made mountain on an island, but the architecture was rather impressive. Miniature mansions were stacked high toward the sky. Typically, the bottom couple of floors were dedicated to indoor gardens and parlors where guests could take in the sights of the family's wealth. Some of the mansions were wrapped around beautiful courtyards, like the one they had emerged from. There were other non-residential places in the Sky District, like the music hall and art museum. The rich people of Auora appreciated the finer things in life.

Ray had been to the Sky District before but only ever in disguise. Being in a place of such beauty and riches left her with confusing thoughts. On the one hand, she could simply stop and stare at everything and take it all in and never be satisfied. That way of life was a mystery to her, one that she definitely wouldn't mind experiencing. On the other, these were the people who scoffed at the wellbeing of the Gutters. They didn't share their wealth and raise up their fellow man; they kept it all for themselves, locked away in their little haven at the top of the island.

They meandered around the Sky District for close to an hour before Naro exclaimed, "Come, I mean to rest my feet and enjoy something to eat. I believe you mentioned a café nearby?"

Ray hadn't, in fact, mentioned a café, but she recognized the cue. They were going to sit down and watch the surroundings of a café that Naro had already picked. She and Ajak agreed boisterously and acted as if they were leading Naro off in a direction when it was in fact him leading the way from behind.

The café wasn't too far away. It was nestled in a small square of shops, some of the rare few in the Sky District. On either side of the café were art studios that housed a rotation of artists from Auora and beyond. Painters came to the studios to perform their work with an audience behind them ready to throw coin purses at their feet. Across the square from the café was a seamstress's shop. A couple of city guards were outside the shop, speaking quietly to one another.

Once Ray spotted the pair of city guards, she became aware of just how many other guards were nearby. Most were from the city itself, but there were two men from the castle, easily identified with their shining plate armor. This must be where they would see the princess today.

Ajak and Naro talked idly in the background while Ray took in her surroundings, trying to get familiar with the layout of the square, the different entrances, where the guards would be posted. The royal family hadn't left Castle Auora for over five years. There was no telling how strong a force would be accompanying the princess and whoever else had left the castle. Ray was a child the last time any royal family members left the castle. She couldn't recall much beyond her mother trying to get them a spot to view the royal carriage and catch a glimpse of the king and queen. She couldn't ask Naro questions now since they were already on the field.

The destination was a seamstress's shop. Her mind began processing the sights and sounds around her, posing questions that she would need to find answers to. *How many guards from the castle would be here today? How many of the princess's Sworn Swords will be with her? Will other noble ladies be with the princess? Will other gangs be sending people to watch the princess, or potentially try to harm her?*

Ray looked around to try to find other people in disguise. Naro had gotten his information from somewhere, and she had a strong suspicion that it wasn't from a vision. Wherever he had gone the night before, that was where he learned of the princess's trip.

"*Brother*, your food is going cold." Ajak's voice pulled her back to reality. She glanced over with a stupefied look on her face, then remembered. Disguises. They were to be brothers, and Naro a merchant they were trying to impress. Naro sat opposite them, sipping on a cup of steaming tea.

"My apologies." Ray tried to make her voice sound deeper. "I was lost in thought."

"Thinking of girls, no doubt." Ajak smirked. "But that's not an appropriate topic of discussion. *My* apologies." He turned his attention back to Naro, and they continued talking about the southern roads and towns.

In front of Ray was a plate of smoked fish, candied bacon, and a few jam tarts. She had her own cup of tea, the faint scent of lavender wafting over. She picked up a jam tart and took a bite, nearly moaning in delight. Ajak gave her a sharp nudge in the side, and she shot him an apologetic glance. *That wasn't a very manly sound.* Her cheeks flushed with embarrassment, and she busied herself with her food, remembering to hold her fork and knife a certain way and dab the napkin on her mouth in between bites.

They didn't have to wait long for the main event to begin. More city guards entered the square, lining every exit. A few ladies were escorted out of the seamstress's shop by a pair of guards, no doubt to empty the building before the princess arrived. Passersby exchanged annoyed glances as they navigated around the guards, but others shared exciting discussion about the princess's outing. No one would be able to come or go without the guards' notice, which was why Naro ordered another round of delicacies from the café and got comfortable in his chair. It was a rather nice day outside despite being on the chilly side. Every so often a cold breeze blew across the square and sent small shivers up Ray's spine. Winter would soon be upon them.

Other patrons of the café started to talk about the event as well. Ray tuned out Ajak and Naro's banter about Merrioff and listened.

"Madame Gweneth must be making the dresses for her eighteenth birthday."

"Has the king announced a tourney yet?"

"I've heard she looks like her mother young again."

One of the serving girls, a mousy brunette, brought a large tray of warm meat pies and pastries to their table. She curtsied then raised the skirt of her red dress and left. "Now then, tell me more about your father's proposal," Naro said before taking a bite of a meat pie.

Ajak responded but Ray wasn't paying close enough attention to make out the words. The longer she sat in that chair, the more she felt like an outsider.

Of course I'm an outsider, I'm a rat in fancy clothing.

But the feeling of not belonging went beyond that. She wasn't sure why she was sitting at this table with Naro and Ajak who knew how to blend into higher society without notice. She knew how to slip around unobserved, but this mission felt vastly beyond her skills. Her stomach twisted uncomfortably. She tried sipping her tea to untangle that knot, but the lavender liquid had gone lukewarm and didn't taste very good anymore.

She looked around for one of the serving girls dressed in red, trying to meet their eyes and get their attention.

"What is it, brother?" Ajak whispered to her.

Her eyes snapped to his face. She could see a glint of annoyance in his brown eyes. She wasn't acting out the disguise well enough. The knot in her stomach tightened even more.

"I'd like more tea," she managed to mumble.

Ajak let out a small *hmph* and raised his hand in the air, snapping his fingers a couple of times. A serving girl came over almost immediately. Without taking his eyes off Ray, he told the girl to bring them a pot of lavender tea and fresh cream.

The girl nodded and left with a quiet "yes, sir."

"My apologies, I..." Ajak trailed off as a commotion stirred in the square beyond their table.

Noble lords and ladies stood on the edges of the square, gawking and talking loudly as a host of knights wearing plate armor with crowns emblazoned on their chests came parading in from the south road. Ray recognized four of the knights among them as Sworn Swords—knights who were sworn to one specific member of the royal family—based on the royal blue cloaks that billowed behind them. In the center of the retinue of Sworn Swords and knights were two girls that Ray could only catch brief glimpses of. One girl was tall with white hair and bronze skin dressed in heavy blue petticoats. The other girl was much shorter, no older than ten, with blonde hair and paler skin. They must be the princesses.

"What a lovely appearance," Naro murmured from across the table.

Both Naro and Ajak watched the escort closely, no doubt counting every knight, watching to see who was assigned which post. There was a hungry look in Naro's eyes that sent a chill down Ray's spine.

She looked back at the princesses and their knights. Most of the knights took positions around the seamstress's shop while the four Sworn Swords went into the building with the girls. Tension decreased outside after that, but only slightly. People were allowed to continue about their day, but no one was allowed inside the seamstress's shop. Most who had gathered around the square stayed put, eager to catch another glimpse of the princesses after they'd been sequestered away within the castle for several years. *I wouldn't mind another glance either, so I have something firm to commit to memory.*

"Quite an exciting day," Ajak commented nonchalantly.

Ray murmured something in agreement. "It's not every day that you see royalty on our streets."

"Then this visit has been most fortuitous indeed. Let us drink to our good fortune!" Naro exclaimed, allowing his voice to carry through the café. One of the serving girls perked up and approached the table once more, the same brunette from before.

"Yes, my lord?"

"Can you provide us with a list of the wines in your cellar?" Naro asked, turning his attention to her. His voice was calm and soft. For a moment it was as if they were back in the safehouse, and he was asking a casual question to one of their own.

The serving girl smiled and nodded. "Of course, my lord. We have vintages from Trent and Lithalyon today. If you are looking to celebrate a special occasion, I would recommend one of the red wines from the Elviri city. We have but a few left."

"An excellent recommendation. The Lithalyon vineyards hold a special place in my heart. We'll take a bottle." Naro flashed her a charming smile before turning his attention back to Ray and Ajak.

The bottle arrived at the table, along with three goblets. The trio continued to eat, drink, and casually discuss the ins and outs of the city while the princesses dallied inside the seamstress's shop.

It had been no more than twenty or thirty minutes before Naro frowned and gently placed his goblet on the table. He tilted his head to the side and cast a sideways glance toward the opposite end of the square.

"Sir?" Ray spoke softly, as much in-character as out.

"Trouble," Naro whispered.

Ray and Ajak exchanged a worried look and glanced in the direction Naro had been looking at. Sure enough, there was shouting and a commotion, and it was coming closer. Several guards chased a pair of hooded figures down the street, swords drawn.

"Thieves! Stop!"

"Get them!"

Behind the chase came a woman and two men dressed in robes and finery. Members of the church. The woman shrieked, "The idols! They stole the idols!"

The two thieves burst into the square, each carrying a gold miniature statue. One quick look around and they realized how much trouble they were in. Both had hoods and masks on, so she couldn't get a good look at either of their faces. *Do they belong to one of the gangs? Or are they just a couple of stupid unlucky souls?* One of them pulled something from their sleeve and held it up to their face. A shrill whistle pierced the air and then they were back to running. They were headed in the direction of the ramp down to the Market District, but the way was blocked by at least four city guards with more closing in around them. The pair didn't slow their pace.

Three of the guards suddenly collapsed, arrows sticking out of their chests.

"Above!" another guard screamed.

Ray nearly jumped out of her chair as she spun to look to the rooftops. She caught a brief glimpse of an archer ducking out of view. *Had they been up there this whole time? Did I miss them earlier when I was looking around?*

Chaos broke out in the square.

The thieving pair must have been able to get past the line of guards, but now the city guards split off into two groups: one to pursue the thieves and the other to get to the rooftops. The guards outside the seamstress's shop raised their shields, taking a defensive position to protect the princesses inside.

Naro and Ajak got out of their chairs and crouched on the floor, trying to get out of sight from the archers. Ray ducked down and crawled over to them. The rest of the café was in a panic. People screamed and fell to the floor while others ran out into the streets.

"Whose were they?" Ajak hissed at Naro.

Ray looked to her leader for guidance but only saw rage in his eyes, his lips curled into a menacing frown. Her blood ran cold. She was still reeling from the scene, but it was abundantly clear that Naro had not expected this turn of events.

"Death's," Naro muttered darkly. He inhaled and changed his expression back to neutrality. "We need to get out of here. I have work to do now."

What about our plan? What about *the plan? We saw the princess, yes, but what next? What was supposed to happen, before those thieves showed up? Damn them, now it's going to be difficult getting out of here.*

Ajak and Ray glanced around. There were a few guards in the café, directing people away from the patio and archways and further into the building. Men and women pushed each other around, trying to get as far away from the streets as possible. Screams and accusations filled the air.

"Don't touch me!"

"Get inside!"

"Ana, where are you?"

Across the square, knights and guards surrounded the entrance to the shop. "Shields!"

The guards formed a defensive barrier around the princesses with their shields surrounding them and above them.

"Go. Now," Naro ordered.

Ajak and Ray stood up with Naro behind them. Ajak took the lead and made for the exit, navigating his way through the sea of bodies. Many people were bumping against them, trying to carry them further inside. Ray used her smaller stature to her benefit, twisting and turning against the other patrons and newcomers from the streets to follow Ajak.

"Move!"

The mass of knights marched away as the trio broke free from the café's chaos. Ray couldn't help but glance over at the knight as they made their exit. For one brief moment, she caught sight of Princess Niamnh's ghostly gray eyes. She looked terrified, her eyes darting all around. The princess saw something, and she became fixated. A look of recognition and awe crossed her face before she was pushed along with her Sworn Swords. Ray frowned and turned to look at what the princess had seen—

Naro?

A hand pressed against Ray's back, and she picked up the pace, hustling after Ajak. They were running down the street in a matter of moments. Ajak made for the garden shed and stopped to tug on the gate, but Naro grabbed him by the shoulder and pulled him away.

"Not back to the safehouse?" Ajak asked, voicing the same question that was on her mind.

"No. Follow me."

Naro led them past the garden and away from most of the manors. They slipped into an alley—albeit a much cleaner alley than she was used to—and Naro stopped in front of one of the doors. He pulled a key from his cape, twisted open the lock, and gestured for them to get inside. Ray thought they were in the back of a shop, but what kind she wasn't certain. It was a small room no larger than the shed in the garden, but it was empty. No distinct smells or sounds. Just stone walls surrounding them, and the wooden door that let out into the alley.

Naro closed the door and locked it, all light vanishing from the room. Ray heard him move toward one of the walls, tapping against various stones. There was a low grinding noise as stone slid against stone. Blue light filled the room from a single torch, just like the ones in the stone corridor from earlier. *More blue flames?* Her head spun from all the confusion, but she pushed it all away. Part of the wall had slid open, revealing a ladder that went down beneath the building.

"Go," Naro commanded.

Ajak quickly crossed over and descended the ladder, Ray following at his heels. They descended into another stone room dimly illuminated by the blue flame. Ray could make out the shapes of a bed, several cabinets and wardrobes, and a table with chairs. As soon as Naro's feet touched the floor, he began moving around the room, lighting lanterns. Neither Ray nor Ajak spoke. She had no idea what was going through Naro's head, but she was scared. She had never seen Naro like this before.

Once he was done illuminating the room and checking for various belongings, he approached the two of them.

"Sir, may I ask what's going on?" Hesitation laced Ajak's voice. He didn't want to ask the question, but she could tell he felt compelled to.

"You may not," Naro responded firmly. "All will be revealed later tonight. You two are to stay here and wait for my return. Do you understand?"

Ray nodded alongside Ajak, but she did *not* understand. *Who were those thieves? Why is Naro leaving us here? Why can't we go back to the safehouse?* She looked at the ground, unsure if she wanted to meet Naro's gaze at that moment. *Just trust him.* Without another word, Naro left, and the two of them were alone in the mysterious stone room.

CHAPTER IX: SETH

Despite being unable to avoid his father the previous night, Seth didn't see him the next day. He received no summons, no letters, and no news on Szatisi's healing draught. He was relieved.

Seth spent most of the day with his mother in her library. After settling down with their books, silence filled the room. Seth had picked up a tome written by one of the Asaszi nearly two hundred years ago. They wrote about the decay of Yiradia, and how the forest was working to reclaim it. Though his eyes followed the words on the page, they departed his mind as soon as he went past them. He continued to think about his plan from the night before, if it was possible to steal the draught Szatisi was working on.

How long will Father be gone from Yiradia? Previous trips of his ranged anywhere from five to ten days, depending on the success of his work. He seems confident with this upcoming journey, so perhaps this one will last longer than most. Seth allowed himself to cautiously hope for it.

He was still unsure about how he would pull his plan off, or if he was just reminiscent of his childhood. He couldn't tell his mother about his idea of stealing the draught, let alone ask her for advice, even if he thought she would be sympathetic to his cause. He couldn't put her at risk. He frowned, his grip tightening on the Asaszi tome.

His mind wandered to his sister. His beautiful sister who just went through a horrible mutilation at the hands of their father. Octavia willingly chose to go through with it. Surely that meant she wouldn't be sympathetic to him if he were to approach her with his plan. She may even turn him in to Amias. Besides, they hadn't spoken since her ceremony.

She's probably too taken with her soldiers to care about me anymore. His stomach twisted, and he forced in a sharp breath. *But Tav wouldn't just discard me like that, would she?*

The light in the library dimmed as storm clouds rolled across the sky outside. The stewards ignited some of the candles, restoring the light. He closed his eyes as they moved around. *If only they'd hurry up and leave.*

The sound of raindrops hitting the side of the pyramid came from the window. When Seth opened his eyes again, the stewards had returned to their post. He looked back down at the pages before him. The firelight flickered across the parchment, dancing in the faint breeze that blew through the room. He let himself get lost in its dance.

Though most of the Asaszi make their nests underneath the pyramid, Szatisi does have a room on this floor because of her position as high priestess. I wonder if I could get into her room somehow and look for any notes about the healing draught. How could I get away from the stewards? I might be able to bribe a few of the Provira stewards, but the Asaszi won't let me out of their sight. The plan proved difficult to formulate, but he persisted, nonetheless.

⸻⸱◦⸱⸻

The next morning, Seth received an invitation from his mother to join her and Octavia for breakfast. The steward delivering the invitation didn't mention if Amias would be joining them or not, which gave him pause. He ultimately decided to go, though, and made his way to his mother's chambers. When he entered the small dining room, he was relieved. His father wasn't there. And although the memories of two nights ago were still fresh, he could face Octavia now that she had been cleaned up and her hair covered her ears. What was left of them.

Seth felt his own ears heat up—*anger? fear?*—and he averted his eyes from the table. Neither his mother nor his sister noticed. The three of them chatted idly about how one another slept, the weather outside the pyramid, and which creatures they heard this morning when they awoke. Soon they finished their plates of meats and greens, and their conversation lulled into silence.

"Tav, would you take a walk with me?" Seth asked the question before he even had a chance to process the words.

Octavia looked up at him, and he saw a flash of fear cross her eyes before she smiled at him. "Of course. To the colonnade?"

He nodded, pushing himself back from the table. "Thank you, Mother."

Evelyn remained seated, but she gave Seth a warm smile. "Enjoy your stroll."

As he pushed himself forward to leave the room, Octavia followed closely by his side. The two walked together to the colonnade in silence, the stewards trailing further behind than usual. It was some small comfort that Octavia had joined him, but he struggled with what to do next. Looking at his sister, even with her fresh wounds, he was overwhelmed with his desire to talk to her and rekindle their friendship. *I need to tell her about my plan.*

Outside, the forest was loud and awake with birds and insects. Seth saw a handful of colorful feathers through the leaves. A family of spotted monkeys was climbing through the branches. There wasn't a cloud overhead, although that would surely change as the suns passed further across the sky. He instructed the stewards to stay at the entrance back inside so he and Octavia would walk alone. And so, they obeyed.

Seth was the first to break the silence. "How are you feeling?" he asked, ignoring the pain in his chest.

Octavia let out a sigh, looking down at her feet as they walked. "Happy, but also worried that you wouldn't speak to me," she replied.

He tilted his head and frowned. She's *worried about* me? "Tav, you know I—"

"I know, and we've always been through everything together, but... the other night was different." She spoke with haste.

He closed his mouth, his silence an agreement with her statement. That night was different, and it marked where their paths truly diverged. She was now on their father's side. But Seth aimed to test that, even after her ceremony of devotion. After all, Amias had never explicitly stated that his son couldn't leave the pyramid... The words came to him. *Perhaps I can convince her.*

"Father says Szatisi will have a healing draught ready for me to take soon," he began, picking his words with care. "He leaves for Iszairi tonight, but when he returns, he expects me to drink the draught and then have my own ceremony." The word felt wrong in his mouth, but he pressed through it.

Octavia stopped and turned to face him. "Oh, brother, that's…" Her voice was filled with excitement, but also doubt.

Seth smiled at her. "It's good news, yes. But I… I need to ask something from you."

"What is it?" she asked, more doubt seeping into her words.

"There's somewhere I want to go, and I need your help getting there."

Her brow furrowed and she waited for him to elaborate.

"I want to go to Lithalyon."

Octavia stopped in her tracks, which forced Seth to grab his wheels. "Seth, you can't be serious."

He pivoted to face her, mindful of the edge of the walkway. "Why not? I've been trapped up here in this pyramid for years. I want to get out, Tav. I want to see more of the world."

She threw her arms out, scowling. "Because it goes against Father's orders, and you know that. No one's allowed outside of Moonyswyn—"

"Except for spies and warriors," he interrupted, prodding a finger against her stomach. "People like *you.*"

Octavia swatted away his finger and stepped out of his reach. "People who know how to protect themselves. Something that *you* don't know how to do."

Her words stung him, and he physically recoiled. *It's not my fault that I never learned how to fight. If Father hadn't—no, I can't go there.* "But if I *did* know how, it could work."

"No, it's too dangerous." She was walking back toward the stewards.

"What if I had help?" he blurted out.

That stopped her again. He rolled toward her and grabbed her hand.

"I wouldn't be leaving the pyramid like this." The words spilled from his lips rapidly. "Remember what Father said at dinner the other night, about Szatisi? Well, after your ceremony he told me she's almost finished crafting a healing draught that will fix my legs."

Octavia's eyes were fixed on their joined hands. "Why not wait for her to deliver the draught to Father?"

Her words hit him hard. He hadn't considered what his life would become if Amias was the one to give him the draught. *He'd expect me to train with Octavia, no doubt. But what else would he expect, no, demand of me?* "Do you think Father would give me any degree of freedom once my legs are restored?"

The twins stood silently on the colonnade for several moments. Seth's heart raced. With everything out in the open, all he could do was wait for his sister's response. *Please don't tell Father. Please help me, Tav.*

Octavia knelt beside his chair. "Why do you want to go to Lithalyon so badly? If the Elviri found out who you are, they'd kill you without question. What could be worth that risk?"

Getting away from Father is worth that risk. "I want to see the library."

She laughed, squeezing his hand tightly. "Of course, the brains to my brawn. It makes sense that you'd risk your life for some books."

She was joking, he was sure of it. He pressed on anyway. "Please, Tav. It's been miserable being confined to this floor of the pyramid since I was a kid. I'm a man grown, or as much of one as I can be."

Her laughter died in her throat. "Seth, even if you get that draught, what makes you think you'd be able to get out of the pyramid?" she murmured, casting a few glances over her shoulder. Her voice grew quieter. "That... that the draught would even work?"

Seth leaned back in his chair, deciding to use her trust of their father as leverage. "Father insisted that it would. He's so confident in whatever it is Szatisi has done."

"If he thinks so..."

He opted not to respond to that. Instead, he softened his voice. "I need your help if I'm to get out of here. You know this place better than me, and you know who will be on patrol."

Her hand was limp in his. He looked up and saw that she was looking past him out toward the forest. There was something painful and sad in her eyes.

"Tav, please," he repeated.

Octavia squeezed his hand once more before pulling hers away. "I'll think about it, brother. I can't commit to this, not now."

Seth went to protest, but she spoke over him.

"I won't tell Father about your desire to leave. Just... let me think. Please." Without another word, she turned and walked back toward the entrance, back inside, where the two stewards were standing.

Seth watched her go, his stomach twisting. He could trust that she wouldn't tell Amias about this conversation, but he wondered if he had pushed her too far or spoken too soon. He supposed he would know soon enough, with Szatisi and his father leaving that evening. There wasn't much more he could do. He stayed on the colonnade for a while longer, but soon became tired of the sounds of the forest and returned inside.

<hr/>

Rather than returning to his room, Seth took his time wandering the halls of the pyramid. The ones he could reach, anyway. Although he knew the layout of the upper floor well enough, he had never looked around with the intention of sneaking out. It delighted him to see his home in a new light. Each corner and alcove suddenly became a new spot for him to hide in during his escape.

What kind of disguise should I use? Should I pretend to be a guard on patrol, or maybe one of Father's spies departing for an important mission? He was both thrilled and terrified of these new questions he found himself needing to answer. He could just go ask Octavia and—

His hands hesitated on his wheels, and his roll slowed. The stewards adjusted their pace behind him. He wouldn't be able to ask Octavia. At least, not yet, *if ever?* Seth picked up his pace again. He would need to come up with answers on his own, and if he was lucky, he would have a chance to discuss them with his sister.

First thing's first: a disguise. Start with getting out of the pyramid, I'll figure out the rest later.

The stewards took up their post outside his door as he entered. The first thing he searched for was a pair of shoes. In his current condition he almost never wore shoes, but if this healing draught worked, he would need a pair. Tucked away in one of the drawers he rarely used was a pair of leather boots, given to him earlier that year by his father.

Father did that on purpose, I'll bet. Seth ran his hands all over the boots to see how they held up, and then slipped the left one on. He struggled to get his foot in and adjusted properly, but after a moment the boot was snug. *These will make do, I suppose.*

He continued to drudge through drawers and pull piles of clothes onto his floor. Soon he had a small collection of pants, shirts, and robes that he could take his pick from. As he sifted through those, his stomach churned.

Will any of these suffice? Will people recognize me in these clothes? He tried to pick clothing that wasn't obviously owned by royalty. *Or whatever they call us. How many of the guards would recognize me from sight alone? I'll be standing, though... who could possibly recognize me like that?* A different thought dawned on him. *Would they think that I'm Octavia?*

A shiver coursed through his body. Disguising himself as his sister could get him to the bottom of the pyramid without issue, but what would happen if the guards saw him escape into the forest?

Word would no doubt spread about it, but what would they say? Would I be putting Octavia in danger? Aren't I already putting her in danger just by asking for her help?

He pushed himself away from the dressers, the small pile of clothing slipping from his lap. His hands trembled as he moved toward the window, looking out into the forest. Dark clouds loomed on the horizon. The forest was quieter than usual, save for a lone kytling that called out louder than all the other birds. Seth could see the kytling on the edge of the forest, perched on a low branch, fluttering his yellow feathers. Seth wished he could stretch out his own wings and take off, never to return. He allowed his mind to venture past the pyramid and think about the city of Lithalyon, separated from him by miles of rainforest and river.

Maybe instead of just visiting the library and returning, I could leave for good. If this draught works and my legs are restored, I could find work in Lithalyon. My ears are pointed enough that I could pass for an Elviri. And surely the Elviri aren't as cruel towards their own as Father is toward our own kind. But what about Mother and Octavia?

The smile faded from his lips, and his thoughts turned dour. Although there was a small chance that he could convince his mother to leave with him, he knew he wouldn't be able to convince his sister. A wave of sadness passed through him, and his body grew heavy. He loved Octavia. He wished that things could have been different for them, and they could have had a life separate from their father. It didn't matter at this point. Their choices had been made, and Octavia had sided with their father.

But Seth dared to hope that Octavia would help him with his request. Perhaps if he could find something in the library in Lithalyon, something to convince her that their father was journeying down the wrong path, she would listen. Seth allowed himself to have hope in this.

I'll sneak away for a few days to learn as much as I can about the Elviri and who they truly are. There must be something in their library that proves that Father is on the wrong side of this war, or that the Asaszi are truly horrible beasts. If I can find that and bring it back to Tav, then perhaps we can find a way to truly escape, for good, with Mother and—

There was a knock on his door.

Seth quickly pulled himself into a seated position as the door opened, revealing Octavia.

Octavia? Has she changed her mind so quickly? We just spoke earlier this afternoon.

"Hey, Tav," Seth said, his voice wavering.

Octavia closed the door, blocking out the light from the hallway. The room was plunged into darkness. She took a few steps forward, her boots clicking on the stone floor. She wore the jade and gold armor of the Provira army, but her helmet was gone. She held something in her hands, but he couldn't make it out.

"Hello, Seth." Her own voice was quiet but firm. "I've decided to help you, but you must do everything I say without question."

He felt his heart soar up through his chest and into his throat. *She can get me out of the pyramid and on my way to Lithalyon.* "O-of course, thank you, I—"

Octavia's voice rose in volume. "I can't stay for long. Father is about to depart with Szatisi, and I must see him off. I'll return to say goodnight to you afterward."

"What are you holding?" he asked.

"I'm sorry you're not feeling well," she said, completely disregarding his question. "I'm sorry it took so long, but I had the kitchens brew this tonic for you. I'll bring you your dinner later."

She turned back toward the door and stopped as she reached for the handle with one hand. With the other, she placed the item on the table next to the door. Seth couldn't make out what it was in the dark. The door opened and light poured through. It was a glass bottle of some kind. But then Octavia was gone, and the room was dark once more.

Seth frowned, very put off by his sister's comments. *I'm not sick. What's she playing at? And what's in that bottle?*

He pulled himself into his chair, gripping the wooden wheels and moving himself toward the table. Now that his eyes had a chance to adjust to the darkness in his chamber, he could make out the features of the bottle more clearly. It was a crystal jade decanter with a decorative serpent stopper standing proudly on display. The liquid inside was dark and nondescript, filling no more than a quarter of the decanter. Pulling the stopper out of the decanter, he braced himself for the pungent smell of a healing tonic, yet no smell assaulted his senses.

What is this, then, if not a healing tonic? It's too dark to be water. Unless she... is this Szatisi's draught? Seth sat frozen in his chair. He dared not move for fear of the moment shattering and him waking up in a cold sweat. *Is this a dream?*

His eyes darted to his window, where the moon was hidden behind more storm clouds. A quiet rumble filled the air. He felt a trembling run from his shoulder, past his elbow and into his fingertips. All he needed to do was raise the decanter to his lips and drink.

Seth hadn't moved from his place by the table when Octavia returned nearly an hour later carrying a tray of soup and water. He was fixated on the decanter while rain fell, and thunder grew louder.

"Oh, you poor thing, let me help you," Octavia crooned as she shut the door behind her. She hurried to his side, setting the tray on the table.

"How did you get this?" Seth asked quietly, his eyes never leaving the decanter.

"After she left her room to meet up with Father, I was able to slip in and grab it," Octavia responded with a whisper.

Could that be true? Had it been so easy to steal this priceless potion from the priestess, just like that? "The stewards think I'm sick, is that part of the plan?" Seth turned his attention back to his sister.

Octavia nodded. "They won't come into your room until you're feeling better. Only I will."

"What about Mother?"

His sister frowned. "I'll figure out something to say to her. That you're contagious, or you asked her not to come in." Seth opened his mouth to protest, but Octavia held up her hand and shook her head. "It'll take about six hours to get to Lithalyon, and you have an entire library to dig through, so we need to move quickly. You need to drink."

"You're not coming with me?" The question fell from his lips before he could stop himself.

Fear and worry crossed Octavia's face. "I can't. I have to stay here and make sure no one finds out you've gone. But I did secure your passage to the city. Anrak, one of Father's spies, is going to help. So please, Seth, *drink the damn potion.*"

Seth looked again at the decanter. The cure. His hand trembled as he lifted it toward his face. The liquid sloshed against the crystal as he tightened his grip around it. He inhaled deeply to calm his nerves. *Will this taste like anything, or will it be flavorless as well as odorless?*

He raised it to his lips, hand shaking, and drank a few droplets of the liquid. A bitter tang filled his mouth, and he nearly spit it out. Instead, he forced himself to swallow, and he felt his throat begin to heat up. As the liquid coursed through his body, he felt the heat travel from his throat, down his spine, and into his thighs. The heat pooled in his knees for a moment, and he nearly cursed.

Of course it wouldn't work! I let myself get caught up in a childish fantasy, I put Octavia at risk, and now we'll have to face the wrath of Father and Szatisi when they return. How could I have been so stupid?

He closed his eyes, stinging with the all-too-familiar sensation of tears, but then the heat pushed past his knees. Eyes now open, he watched muscle magically form over his atrophied legs. The heat traveled farther down his legs, until he could feel everything from his kneecaps to his toes. He could *feel* again.

My legs...

The heavy thudding of his racing heart was all Seth could hear. He wanted to shout out in excitement, to call his sister to his side, but he refrained at the last moment. It wasn't time for celebration—it was time for escape.

Seth turned and looked for his sister, who stood at the foot of his bed, jaw agape.

"Your legs just... *changed.*" Her voice was barely above a whisper.

Can I stand? Will I... will that work, after all these years? Even with bearing witness to the magical miracle, Seth still found himself harboring doubts of the effects of the healing draught. With trembling hands, he pushed himself out of his wheelchair and onto his feet. The stone floor was cold beneath his skin. He wiggled and stretched out his toes, amazed by the sight. *I never thought the cold would feel so* good *against my skin.*

His legs wobbled beneath his weight, and he took a few unsteady steps forward. He reached out and grabbed the window ledge to stabilize himself. He snapped his head back to look at his sister, his face frozen in shock.

He saw the same expression mirrored on his sister's face. Tears formed in the corners of his eyes and for the first time he didn't try to hold them back. *Finally, after so many years... I can walk. I can* live.

"Oh, Seth..." she murmured, voice cracking.

He let out a breath, and then laughed. "Tav... I can't believe this..."

Octavia rushed over to him and embraced him in a tight hug. Tears seeped into the fabric of his robe. The rush of excitement overwhelmed him, and he started bouncing on his toes, enjoying the feeling of his heels touching and lifting off the floor.

Octavia rubbed at one of her eyes before regaining her composure. "I know. I know. We need to hurry, though... Do you have something to change into?"

Seth nodded, looking over at the small pile of clothes he had gathered on his bed. Octavia turned her back to him and he quickly disrobed, pulling on a pair of leather leggings, a dark green sleeveless tunic, a hooded cloak, and a leather belt. The last thing he put on were socks and shoes—the same leather boots he had pulled out earlier. Slowly, he took a seat on the edge of the bed and pulled them over his feet. It was much easier this time, being able to control his legs, feet, and toes. The boots hugged his feet and calves, pressing the cloth socks snugly against his skin.

Never thought I'd miss the feeling of shoes, considering how often I went without them as a child. When he finished, he stood up again and walked over to Octavia. "I'm ready."

As she turned, she pulled him into another embrace. They leaned into one another, resting their heads on the other's shoulder. Seth heard Octavia inhaling sharply, shuddering under his touch. She was crying. He held her close, his own tears falling. He shut his eyes and let himself savor this moment with his sister, fearing its soon-coming end.

"Listen very carefully to me," He felt her breath on his neck and hair as she spoke, and he couldn't stop the shiver running down his spine. "Anrak is waiting for us at the stables. He's leaving for Auora, but he'll be passing through Lithalyon. I asked him to escort you, a promising recruit named Calydrian, to the Elviri city and ensure you make it inside the walls without issue."

"Calydrian," Seth echoed, committing the name to memory.

"I told Anrak that Calydrian is going to Lithalyon to get information on the Elviri city and see if a raid is possible. That he will only be gone for two or three days. And that he'll be bringing a report back for my father." Octavia's words were pointed, and Seth understood the meaning.

Seth pulled away from his sister's embrace with great reluctance. As he unwrapped his arms from around her, she caught his hands and held onto them tightly.

"You have to bring something back for us, Seth."

The implication of her words sent chills through his body, and his stomach tightened. *She's not talking about her and me; she's talking about her and Father.*

She continued, averting her gaze. "It's the only way I can protect you if Father finds out you've gone. If you help his cause, he can't be mad at you for defying his orders. You have to trust me."

He looked down at the floor, stretching his toes. Conflict raged inside of him. On the one hand, Octavia had brought him the draught. Surely this meant she was supportive of what he was doing. But what she was asking from him, the way she looked away from him when she spoke...

"I'll try my best," Seth mumbled, unsure of what his "best" would entail.

Octavia squeezed his hands and let out a sigh of relief. "It's time to get out of here."

He watched her eyes glance between him and the window. When her gaze returned to him, he gave her a confused look.

"There's really only one way down from here besides the door," she said, letting go of his hands. "And I didn't have time to grab a rope, so we're going to have to make do." She moved to the bed and started to gather up the silk blankets.

"Wait, what?"

Octavia crossed over to the window and peered out, over, down the side of the pyramid. She grumbled something to herself and began twisting the blankets into a rope.

Rope? "I'm going down the side...?"

"Yes." Octavia said sternly, tugging tightly on the knot she had just formed. "So, gather your things and help me tie these sheets into knots."

I've only had my legs restored for a few minutes and my sister is tasking me with scaling down the side of the pyramid. He had to stop himself from laughing at the absurdity of the situation. *Better to risk life and limb than stay here. At least if I fall, it'll all be over.*

He picked up one of the satchels near his drawers and stuffed some other clothing into the bag. Looking around the room, he thought about what else to bring. His eyes settled on the decanter. There was still a lot of liquid left in it.

What if the effects wear off? And I'm left crippled once more? His heart seized painfully in his chest for a moment, and he had to remember to breathe.

I must bring the decanter with me.

He walked over to it, picking up the serpentine stopper from the table. He gently returned it to the decanter, and then placed it in his satchel. He glanced over his other belongings, and settled two notebooks, a quill, and an inkpot.

Clothes to wear, draught to drink, and notebooks to write down my findings. That should be enough for the few days that I'm gone. "I think I'm ready."

"Then come help me with this rope."

Seth returned to Octavia's side, and after being handed a fistful of blankets, twisted and tied them. While very much occupied with the thought of climbing down the pyramid, he managed to ask his sister, "Am I going all the way to the bottom? With these?" He lifted the blankets up as if to make a point.

"No, just to the ledge below this one. That will put you in an alcove that's not usually patrolled at this time of night. Come on." When she finished the next knot, she got up and tied one blanket around the stone pillar closest to the window. She gave it a firm tug to test the fabric and the pillar, satisfied when neither the fabric tore nor the pillar shifted. After securing the makeshift rope, she led Seth to the window and handed him the end. "I'll meet you down there, I promise."

Seth took the silken rope in hand and gazed out the window. Rain fell steadily from the sky, and a low rumble of thunder echoed in the distance. *What a night for climbing.*

He swallowed, forcing down the lump that had formed in his throat, and hoisted himself onto the window ledge. Droplets hit his shoulder and leg as he twisted around to crouch on the balls of his feet, facing his room. With a grimace he yanked his hood over his head to shield himself from the rain. He threw his satchel over his shoulder and squeezed it lightly between his arm and his side.

"Try not to let go, okay?" Octavia murmured.

Seth let out a nervous laugh but didn't respond.

With great care he shuffled backward until he felt the edge of the ledge underneath his right foot. He inhaled sharply and shifted his weight to his left leg, his grip on the rope immediately tightening. Octavia nearly jumped out of her skin trying to get to him fast enough, grabbing the rope as well.

"Sorry, j-just hit the edge, is all," he mumbled, looking down at his hands. His knuckles had gone white. Octavia exhaled through her nose. He strengthened his resolve and looked back up at his sister. "I-I'll meet you down below. Promise."

Octavia's lips were firmly pressed together. She nodded once before turning to go to the door. After she departed, Seth closed his eyes and took a deep breath. The hood and back of his cloak grew damp from the rain. A rumble of thunder came and went. He slid his right foot backward until it went over the edge and was firmly against the slope of the pyramid. He released his breath and moved his left foot.

The climb down wasn't easy, especially with the storm growing nearer. Seth nearly lost his grip when a bolt of lightning flashed through the sky, followed by a loud crack and boom. The rain seeped through his clothing and chilled him to the bone. Thankfully his boots were able to grip onto the pyramid, and slowly, inch by inch, he made it to the window below his. The silks held firm, and he trusted that they wouldn't fray or untangle with his weight.

His left foot found the opening. He went to take another step down the wall and instead found a gap. His leg went slack, and he scrambled to pull it back onto solid stone. He let out another shaky breath. Once more he started to descend, now anticipating the opening. He instead searched for the side of the window, so he could lower himself down onto its ledge. With his right foot, he found the ledge. Confidence resurged in him as he stood upon a flat surface. He lowered his left foot to meet his right, and he sank down into a squat so he could slide through the window into the pyramid.

He nearly collided with a large vase as he climbed inside. It stood tall and proud in front of the window, blocking the view of the forest outside. *Did Octavia move it here for me to use as cover?* He sank to his knees and peeked around the vase into the corridor, clutching onto his satchel.

Very little torchlight spilled into the alcove from the corridor beyond. He watched the corridor for any passing guards but saw none. He stayed where he was, though, and waited until Octavia rounded the corner and stood across the alcove from the vase.

"Calydrian, are you there?" Octavia called out softly.

Seth nodded his head, remembering the alibi she had provided. "Y-yeah, just... getting some air." He fumbled through the words, rising to his feet.

"You'll be getting plenty of it soon. Oh, first... Here." She pulled out a small bag from her jacket and tossed it to him. He caught it, noticing the jingle and clinking from within.

He gave Octavia a quizzical look. "Coins?"

"For the city. Come on, Anrak is waiting for us." She beckoned for him to follow.

It had been many years since Seth explored the lower levels of the pyramid. Not much had changed, but it was still a surreal experience to be walking through the halls again. Memories filled his head of going down to the base of the pyramid with his mother and sister to greet their father after his trips to Iszairi, Kherizhan, or one of the border outposts. He and Octavia would race down to the entrance hall where they would jump on their father and tell him about their adventures while he was away, their mother laughing behind them. Seth felt a bitter twist in his stomach as those memories dissolved from his thoughts. Those days were behind him, locked away with his youth. There would be no more good memories of his family. Not with his father, anyway.

The torches burned brightly at the pyramid's entrance. Octavia pulled her hood over her head, and he took her cue to ensure his own hood was tightly drawn against his face. They passed two door wardens dressed in scale mail and black robes. He couldn't see any inch of their skin, despite the torchlight. He couldn't tell if they were Provira or Asaszi. He wasn't sure which would be worse.

Octavia glanced at one of the wardens and nodded, and the warden returned the nod. They didn't even spare a glance at Seth. His sister kept a fast pace as they left the pyramid and headed north toward the stables. Seth considered looking back at the pyramid, but the darkness and rainfall kept him from seeing it in all its splendor. Despite the rainforest taking back its land, the pyramid of Yiradia was beautiful. Perhaps on the return journey he would be able to fully take in the sight of it.

They didn't see another person until they reached the stables. Most of the citizens of Yiradia lived inside the pyramid, or in the portion of the village to the east, where the rainforest hadn't yet overtaken the huts and other structures. The stables were kept on the northern side of the pyramid where there was easier access to the ancient roads that led toward Promthus and Elifyn. Much of those roads had been retaken by the forest or were destroyed by the Asaszi years ago. Only the hardiest of scouts were able to pass through them. Tonight, Seth would become one of those scouts.

It's been several years since I last rode a horse, but if walking and climbing came to me easily, then surely, I'll be able to ride out of here without any problem.

The stables loomed ahead, lights glowing from within. The stablemaster's hut stood nearby, similarly illuminated. Octavia stopped outside the stables and gestured for Seth to come close.

"Remember, Calydrian, you only have two or three days to bring something useful back to us," Octavia murmured.

All Seth could do was nod. A lump had formed in his throat. *Two days. This library better be easy to find inside the city.* Panic started to bubble within him, but he forced himself to take deep, steady breaths. *There will be time to worry about that later. Focus on getting out of the rainforest first.*

Octavia opened the door to the stable and led him in. Inside the structure was well-lit, and Seth saw several varieties of horses in stalls. They shifted about restlessly and quietly snorted, no doubt bothered by the storm outside. There were two other people in the stables beside the siblings, presently engaged in a conversation of their own. Marus the stablemaster, who Seth remembered from his childhood, spoke with a shorter man who was hooded and facing away from Seth. Marus was a hale and hearty man, standing taller than most men Seth had seen. He was unsure of his age, but he could see gray streaks running through his brown hair.

The other must be Anrak, the man Octavia had spoken of, Seth thought.

"Good evening, Marus, Anrak," Octavia said to the room, raising her hand in greeting. Seth stayed behind her, keeping his eyes on the floor.

The two men turned to her and returned the gesture. Marus left Anrak and disappeared into another part of the stables. Anrak crossed the room to Octavia, extending his hand out to her. Octavia reached out and grabbed hold of his forearm, and he did the same.

"*Pyredan* Octavia," Marus said gruffly, looking her over. Seth stood behind Octavia, and quickly became the target of Anrak's focus. "Is this the one?"

They released each other's arms and Octavia took a step back, standing beside Seth. "Yes, this is Calydrian."

Anrak stood a little shorter than Seth and Octavia, but he was more muscular. Black stubble covered his tan cheeks and chin, his brown eyes flickering in the torchlight. Seth parted his lips to offer Anrak a greeting, but the other man spoke first. "You said he's got promise?"

"From what I've seen, yes. I'm sending him on this mission to see what he's worth." Octavia's voice was calm and steady. She patted Seth on the back. He let out a small chuckle and swayed forward a bit.

Anrak looked him over with a careful eye, and in turn Seth did the same. The spy wore plain leather armor underneath his dark cloak. At his waist was a sheathed sword. There was a gleam of hardness in his eyes, and for a moment Seth feared that he would be found out after only minutes of being in his company.

Instead Anrak let out a grunt. "Infiltration is a tough first mission, but if he can't make it back, then that's one less mouth to feed."

And at least I'll finally be free of Father, Seth thought darkly.

Octavia grinned and nodded. "That's the intent."

Anrak returned the grin and stepped forward. "Well, Calydrian, there are many miles to cover between here and the border, and we want to get there before the suns come up."

Seth nodded, unsure of how to respond. Anrak wrapped an arm around his shoulders and led him off into the stables.

"Not much of a talker, eh? Just fine for me. Never liked talking during my travels." Anrak grumbled. "Marus! We're ready."

The stablemaster was standing in front of a stall where a stocky gray horse pranced around and stomped the ground. "This beast of yours is more stubborn than you are, Anrak."

Anrak guffawed. "Not wrong, Marus, not wrong. I'll take care of the saddle."

Marus grunted in response, then turned to Seth. "You ridden before?"

"It's been a few years, but I remember how," Seth answered. He could remember riding around Yiradia with Octavia and receiving basic training from one of the *pyredans* when they were children. He couldn't remember his first horse's name, or what happened to it after he lost his legs five years ago. Frowning, he shook the thoughts from his head.

"Hm. Alright, come here, kid," Marus said, walking off toward another stall. Seth hurried after him. In the stall was another gray horse, but this one was much shorter in stature than Anrak's horse. He stood near the back of the stall, already saddled, watching Marus and Seth intently. "He's called Nar. Good fella, he'll take care of you."

Marus opened the stall and gestured for Seth to enter. His mouth ran dry. It had been so long since he had ridden a horse. He swallowed nervously and approached Nar, his hand outreached toward the horse. He huffed and then bucked his nose into Seth's hand. His hesitation melted away, and he found the confidence to climb up into the saddle. It took him two tries, and he could have sworn he heard Marus chuckling from outside the stall, but he managed. His actions were a bit clumsy, but more for a recent practice. The muscles in his legs still seemed to be working fine, miraculously so.

I can't believe this is going so well.

Seth led Nar out of the stall, swaying from side to side as the horse walked. Childhood memories of old stirred in his mind, and he took comfort in holding the reins. He leaned forward and stroked Nar's mane, murmuring quietly to the horse. "We'll make some new memories, right, Nar?"

Nar snorted in response.

In front of him, Anrak was perched on his own horse. "Come on, kid. We ride."

Marus pulled open the large door at the end of the stable. Rain still fell steadily outside. "Careful of the thunder."

"Thank you, Marus," Anrak said over his shoulder as he urged his horse out of the stable. He whistled out two notes, and Nar took off after him with Seth holding tightly onto the reins.

If there was thunder, Seth couldn't hear it over the hoofbeats of the horses. As soon as they cleared the stable, Anrak took off at full speed and Nar followed. There was little Seth could do to control the horse, so instead he let Nar lead, and he made sure he didn't fall off. He kept his head low toward Nar's, wary of low-hanging branches in the forest. They weaved in and out of the trees, often deviating from the path where vines and foliage had created an impassable web. Though it was dark, Anrak led them true, avoiding treacherous portions of the road where roots pierced through the ground or branches hung too low.

Rain continued throughout the night as they made their way through the rainforest. Seth strained his ears listening for any signs of wildlife, but between the noise of the storm and Nar's hoofbeats, he could hear nothing else. He also tried keeping track of the passage of time, but the constant bobbing and swaying on the back of Nar distracted him. He let himself get swept up in the sound of hoofbeats, the feel of his legs pressed against Nar's sides, and the wind on his face. During his five years of being bound to the wheeled chair, Seth never thought about riding another horse. Touching the ground with his feet seemed impossible enough, let alone doing anything else with his legs. But now that he was atop Nar, flying through the rainforest, he realized just how much he missed riding as a child.

This is exhilarating.

CHAPTER X: MUNNE

The wars between the Elviri and Asaszi had bled into the Second Sun, even after the last of the Elviri gods had vanished from the mortal plane. Elvarin said that was when the journal was written, so Munne knew that the journal would be kept in the same place as the other scrolls and books from those warring times. With any luck, Elvarin would either have returned the journal, or he would be here in the archives, continuing his research.

Sunlight filled the archives. There were a handful of Elviri present in the archives today, Elvarin being one of them. He sat at the same table as the previous night, the same stack of books dumped on the table's surface. Munne went straight up to him. She placed a hand on his shoulder, and he jumped.

"Sorry, friend," Munne murmured, sitting in the chair next to him.

Elvarin took a deep breath and smiled. "It's alright. I may have been a little too enchanted with this book."

Munne arched an eyebrow and lifted the left half of the book so she could see the cover—*Cultures of the Rainforest*. She gently placed the book back down. "Assisting Aeglys with my father's tasks?" Her father's words from the earlier meeting echoed in her head. Aeglys has asked for Elvarin's help with her research. *Does Elvarin know why Aeglys is researching the Asaszi?* Munne would need to discuss this with him, but her focus was elsewhere.

Elvarin's smile faded, and he leaned back in his chair. "Yes, she came to me a few days before your return to ask a favor from me."

"It's my turn to tell you that it's alright," Munne sighed and removed her hand from his shoulder. "In fact, if you hadn't agreed to assist her, you wouldn't have found that journal." Elvarin practically squirmed in his seat. Munne's brow furrowed, and she crossed her arms. "What is it?"

"I should have recognized the journal sooner," Elvarin grumbled, looking away from Munne. "It belonged to one of your ancestors. A third son of the Hunting Throne."

Munne tilted her head in confusion.

Before she could speak, Elvarin continued, "I haven't had time to research him yet, but there should be a record of him in one of the volumes on the Hunting Throne. His name was Malion."

Munne's lips pressed together in a tight line. Elvarin turned toward her and waited for her to speak. *More reading. Should I start with the journal or the ancestry tome? Dinner will be in about six hours. If Elvarin was able to get through the journal last night, then I should have time to read both books before meeting Araloth and Mayrien. That is, if this entry in the ancestry tome is easy to find.*

"Are the ancestry tomes still kept on the bottom floor?" Munne finally asked.

Elvarin nodded. "There should be four or five tomes dedicated to the Hunting Throne during the first two thousand years of the Second Sun."

Munne rose from her seat. "Do you still have the journal?"

Elvarin lifted two books from the top of his pile and removed a small leatherbound journal. He placed it on the table close to Munne and then gently placed the two books back on top of the pile.

"Let me know if I can help you with anything else, friend."

"Thank you." Munne picked up the journal and departed for the lower floors.

The second floor of the archives held books that covered most of the Second Sun. Chandeliers hung throughout the floor. Sunlight poured down the stairs and illuminated the area surrounding the staircase. There were hardly any tables on the floor but still an ample number of chairs tucked between the rows of bookcases. Across the top of the bookcases were grooves where grips from ladders could be placed to reach the highest shelves.

Munne continued down to the lowest level, one hand gently sliding along the banister. The smell of musty scrolls hit her first, and then the scent of earth. The air was stagnant, but it provided some degree of comfort to her. The lowest level was only lit by the candelabras and chandeliers placed throughout the floor. It was where the ancient histories of the Elviri were kept. There were no tables and hardly any chairs on the lowest level.

She had spent many hours in the archives with the scribes during her lifepath rotations. Her favorite subject to study had been the creation stories and everything leading up to the first Elviri-Asaszi war. She was fascinated with how the Elviri developed, unhindered by war and strife, with the assistance of the gods. Though there were many impressive feats during the era of the Second Sun—with more to come, surely—it lacked the same grandiosity of the Eldest Days.

The ancestry tomes were proudly displayed in one of the corners of the third floor. There were books that traced all the powerful lineages back to the Eldest Days. The books detailing the history of the Hunting Throne were placed on their own bookcase, which had been glamorously carved with intricate runes. There were fewer tomes, about twelve in total, detailing the Eldest Days, despite the era lasting hundreds of thousands of years. The older tomes weren't bound like the modern books had been. Instead, they were piles of parchment with holes pierced through the top left corners and were held together by strands of silken rope and a piece of tanned leather serving as a cover. The sigil of the Eldest Days had been carved into the covers of the older tomes—a shining sun rising above the horizon with flames lashing out below. There was also lettering carved into the leather cover detailing the contents of the tome.

The books of the new era were bound completely in leather and had spines to secure the binding. The sigil of the Second Sun—one sun in front of a second, smaller sun—was carved into the spines of the books. There were twenty-six books in total that covered the Second Sun. Munne pulled the first five off their shelf, one at a time. The leather felt warped and worn from centuries of sitting on display beneath the earth. She carried her small pile of books to one of the only chairs on the floor and set the pile down beside it. Munne sat in the chair, and it creaked. She pulled the journal from the top of the stack and opened it to the first page.

Twenty-sixth day of the eleventh month: I purchased this journal from the valley yesterday before I left. I intend to write in this journal as I travel across the Telatorr Mountains and into the plains of Promthus, to aid our

brothers-in-arms in retaking their villages from the Asaszi beasts. I write in this journal at the behest of my beloved, so that she may know I am always thinking of her when we are apart. This journal will be my wedding gift to her, so that she may know that our love can overcome all obstacles...

Munne's ancestor, Malion, went on at length about his relationship with "his beloved", who he never referred to by any other name. He finally ended the entry, and then began a new one on the next date. He wrote each day during the journey from Elimere to Promthus, describing the marching and the relaxing. The way of the army was much the same then as it was in the present. Munne smiled as she read about how Malion would scout ahead of the troops and help clear the pathways of snow and fallen tree branches.

Third day of the twelfth month: We arrived on the western shores in excellent time, all thanks and praise to Aeona for keeping the winter frost at bay long enough for us to descend to the plains of Promthus. Tonight, we will stay in Ferilin, the largest town on the western shore. Tomorrow we will ride south and make our way around the lake, taking back every village and farmstead from the devilish fiends. I hope to be done with our quest in time for the bitter cold to come and go, and for the frost to melt away from the flowers of the valley so that our wedding may be celebrated by all life...

There were no years recorded for each entry, which she found a little odd. Malion's travels went on for a little over a week before he reported any kind of attack or incident.

Twelfth day of the twelfth month: We have come across the first settlement that has not shown signs of bustling activity. It seems as though some kind of trouble passed through here, although we have not gotten close enough to tell. If the Asaszi had started on the eastern shore, which seems likely, they must have been working their way toward the west with their conquest. They must be near here, if this is the first place we have come across that appears suspicious. Maybe this will be an easier journey than anticipated, and I can return home for an early spring wedding. Oh, what joy if it were true!

The settlement seems to be little more than a group of farmsteads in a cluster. We only saw five structures on the horizon as we approached. After the midday meal, I will be exploring the structures with my triple, along with four other scouting triples. The rest of the troops will stay back and await our return. It's strange, although we have not stepped foot inside those buildings, there is something dark about this place. The other farmsteads and villages had shown signs of life—cattle and sheep roaming the lands surrounding the buildings, smoke rising from roofs, and sounds of tools working the land. This place has none of that. As we approached, there was nary a trace of cattle along the road, nor was there smoke on the horizon. The horses have been difficult to handle since we drew closer to this place. The men are starting to worry, but we the scouts would venture into the village soon enough to discover its secrets.

His handwriting changed with the next paragraph, continuing about the twelfth day of the twelfth month. His handwriting was messy, as if trying to record as much as possible before he was interrupted. Ink was smudged across the page, making the handwriting difficult to read.

There's evil here. The farmers were in one of the houses. They kept talking about a demon. It was keeping them awake at night. They hadn't slept in days. The Asaszi had been there, but they bartered for their safety. The Asaszi took their livestock in exchange for their lives. They were crazed, dried blood on their hands. The walls had been scratched repeatedly. How could they do this to themselves? We leave at dawn, although I don't know if I can sleep tonight. The farmers are going to be taken back to Ferilin tomorrow, but tonight they sleep in our camp. One of them is watching me, though I dare not look at him. I am writing with haste so that I may tuck this journal away soon and try to sleep.

The next entry was written with neat penmanship.

Thirteenth day of the twelfth month: I don't think there's a man or woman in this camp who was able to sleep properly last night. The horses certainly didn't. They paced and whinnied all night, making it almost impossible to sleep for longer than a handful of minutes at a time. The one farmer is still staring at me, but I have put significant distance between us. I break my fast with my triple while he sits with the departing healer on the other side of camp. Still, it unnerves me to feel his gaze upon me. Why does he continue to stare?

There was another change in handwriting—he was writing again in haste.

I return to my journal sooner than I anticipated. The farmer approached me as we finished our meal and began readying the horses. He said something about "it" chasing them every night. I asked him to speak clearly so that we could understand him. When he looked at us, there was something dark in his eyes. I wasn't looking at a mortal man. He pointed at me and said it would chase me too. I fear learning what he meant by that.

The farmers and scouting triple left the main forces later on the thirteenth day. Malion didn't report any other strange occurrences for the day, but the troops fanned out and searched for the Asaszi nonetheless. It was the decision of the general to split the troops into two smaller groups and send one back toward Ferilin to stop the Asaszi before they attacked their next target. That group departed shortly after the scouting triple. Malion was placed in the group that continued onward toward Trent and the eastern shore, continuing his journal entries into the next day.

…It kept me from sleeping through the night. Every time I would drift off, the screaming would start again. All sorts of terrible screaming. Who was I hearing? What was happening to these poor souls, and why is this misery targeting me? Was I hearing the screams of those poor farmers? I wonder if they had lied, and the Asaszi were coming to them in the night and subjecting them to all variants of torture. It would explain the horrible state they were in when we arrived. Why, then, would they lie when we came to their farmstead? Would they not want to reveal what these monsters were doing to them, and see justice be served?

I am sorry, my beloved, for allowing this unsettling dream to take up so much of this entry. I pray to the gods that this dream doesn't return, and that my mind is simply creating illusions and thoughts based on the horrid sights I witnessed at the farmstead.

Munne's thoughts jumped to her own nightmares and the screaming she had heard night after night. Her vision clouded and her heartbeat accelerated. For a moment she couldn't see the words on the page in front of her. *Surely this is just a coincidence.* Both her and her ancestor served in the armed forces, they had both seen horrors that most would go their whole lives without. Surely it was just a coincidence.

She blinked and she began reading again. On the fifteenth day, he wrote that he had the unsettling dream again.

The screaming returned last night. I tried to block it out, but those screams pierced through my defenses and filled me with such dread. I thought I could let out my own scream just to make it stop, but then I saw movement in front of me. I tried to blink and raised a hand in front of my face. I could see the movement, although very faint. I could make out the faintest flicker and blur of my skin moving. It was as if I were in a cave, or somewhere else, swallowed by darkness. I could feel beads of sweat running down the sides of my face. Had I been running? Was I running away from the screaming? The dream was over before I had the chance to gather my bearings and make any sense of it.

As the days progressed, Malion wrote less and less about his travels and his beloved, and more about the unsettling dream. It had quickly turned into a nightmare as his eyes adjusted to the darkness and he realized this dream was taking place underground in a vast tunnel system. Every night he was running, sweat dripping off him, while he was forced to listen to the sounds of people screaming and crying for help. Munne's heart pounded as she read more of his journal. The dreams were almost identical to her own, like Elvarin said. She glanced at her hands and noticed her knuckles had turned white from her grip on the journal. She parted her lips to take in a deep breath, trying to calm herself.

Nineteenth day of the twelfth month: It's cold here, despite the warmer climate. I can feel the cold sapping my energy when we stop for meals. Would that I could return to the valley and be reunited with my beloved. Alas, I am cursed to search for an enemy that eludes our every step while the suns are in the sky, and I am cursed to run from an enemy that hides his face from me while the moon is in the sky. Sleep doesn't come easy. I have this nightmare every night, sometimes multiple times before dawn breaks. Perhaps a night in a civilized place will put my mind at ease. At least there will be beer...

I was glad to see the walls of Trent. Our search, no matter how fruitless, was finally over. Now we would begin the journey home, which would take us across the lake rather than around it. We would go to Castle Auora and pay our respects to the Proma king before returning home.

The next line had been scratched through repeatedly, but Munne was able to decipher most of the words.

*It was my duty as son of the **Se'vi** to do this.*

Munne parted her lips and let out a small sigh. She sympathized with her ancestor, knowing all too well the heavy burden it is to be a child of the Se'vi. *But why cross that line out? Was he trying to hide his identity?* The journal continued.

Trent was a fairly large city—nothing like the valley, though. It was supported by the farmsteads surrounding the lake and acted as the middle leg in the trading network between the farmers and Auora. Some of the men chose to sleep in tents outside of town, while others purchased beds for the night. I made sure I had brought enough coins with me to pay for a bed. I plan on having plenty of food and beer before going to bed, so that hopefully this dreadful curse will leave me alone tonight.

Twentieth day of the twelfth month: I saw it. I saw what the farmer was talking about. The demon. He chased me through the tunnels last night. His black shadow loomed in front of me. If I had been terrified of this nightmare before, then there are no words to describe this new rank of fear. I will talk to the healers today about this and see if there are any herbs I can take to soothe my mind. How long will this go on?

Malion didn't write for the rest of the twentieth day, nor the twenty-first. The next entry in his journal was on the twenty-second day. He wrote about the barracks in Castle Auora and how uncomfortable they were compared to the barracks in Elyr Tym, Elimaine's main city. He spoke about how Elviri soldiers were cared for much better than the Proma, if the Proma indeed slept and broke bread within the castle. He made no mention of visiting the healers, or of the demon.

The next four or five entries were alarmingly normal. Malion hadn't spoken of the nightmare for several days. *Was the demon no longer chasing him at night in his sleep? Had he found something to rid him of this terrible blight?* Munne flipped through the pages with a sense of urgency, skimming through the entries where Malion discussed returning to Ferilin. There was one sentence that struck her as odd compared to the rest of his normal behaviors.

He is still watching me.

Munne wasn't sure if Malion was referring to the demon or the farmer who had been brought to the city of Ferilin. Malion never again mentioned Ferilin, or any part of Promthus once he crossed west into the Telatorr Mountains. He mentioned that snow covered the roads leading to Elimere, the occasional reindeer spotted in the woods, the ropes that cut into his skin during the night, and that the flowers would indeed be blooming for his wedding to his beloved.

Munne paused and reread the entry. His handwriting was jagged and sharp, as if he had struggled to maintain a grip on his pen.

Fourth day of the first month of the new year: One of the soldiers was kind enough to wrap two blankets around me last night, after I had complained of the cold that morning. The general told me there was nothing they could do about loosening the rope wrapped around my wrists. He was straightforward with me. They were doing it to protect the other soldiers. I could not blame them, even as I sat awake in the cold all night with snow falling on my face. I could not sleep. Would not sleep. I asked them to let me have my journal tonight so that I could write to pass the time. Writing in the cold is very difficult, and very time-consuming. This is good. It will keep my hands busy and keep them from stiffening. This was for the best. I cannot wait to return home to my beloved, whom I am so—

Munne flipped the page and jumped, almost dropping the journal when she saw a crude drawing of a pair of large eyes on the page. The eyes were wide open and had been traced over several times. The lines were sloppy and hastily drawn. Even though it was only a drawing, she felt an overwhelming sense of dread looking at the eyes. She bit her lip and lifted her hand to flip the page, wanting the eyes to go away—to make the eyes go away. It needed to *leave*. In her haste, she flipped through multiple pages, the eyes gone from her sight.

Day eleven: He keeps watching my beloved. He's staring at her. Does he not know it's rude to stare? He needs to stop. I need to make him stop. He must leave this house. I escort him through the front door and yet he returns.

He must stop. He needs to leave. My beloved doesn't want to look at him. She won't say it aloud, but I can feel it. I can feel her willing him to leave. He needs to leave this house. He needs to leave leave leave leave leave leave leave leave leave leave leave leave leave leave leaveleaveleave-leaveleaveLEAVELEAVELEAVELEAVE

The rest of the two pages were covered in the same word—*leave*. Munne felt the same sense of dread with the pages as she did with the drawing of the eyes. She needed to put the book down and get rid of it, but she needed to know how it ended. She went to flip the page again, but her wrist was heavy with the weight of it. Munne couldn't bring herself to do it, but she needed to.

I need to turn the page and get rid of this, get it to leave, get away from me, get out and—

The clattering of the leather hitting the stone floor scared Munne out of her trance. She was standing, and the journal lay on the ground a few feet away from the chair. *When did I stand up?*

Hands shaking, she picked up the journal and tucked it under her arm. She wanted nothing more than to leave the archives. For a moment she considered picking up the stack of ancestry tomes and bringing all the books back to her study, but quickly banished that thought.

I'm not bringing this evil into my sanctuary. I'll come back here to research what happened to Malion later, and then talk to Elvarin about all of this. She hurried to the stairs and climbed them two steps at a time, eager to be gone.

As she reached the top floor of the archives, she noticed that there was less sunlight in the room than before. She glanced over at the stained-glass windows to see the suns were going down. Several hours had passed while she was down below on the third floor, which wasn't surprising considering how engrossed she had gotten with Malion's journal. *Araloth and Mayrien will be at the Moonlit Grove soon, though, and at this rate I may be late if I don't walk faster.*

Munne climbed the stairs to the upper levels of the manor and flung the doors open as she headed for her bedroom. Laenis entered the dining hall from the study and Munne raised her free hand in a greeting to her maid.

"Will you be taking dinner in your suite tonight?" Laenis asked after Munne.

"Not tonight, I have other arrangements," Munne responded, disappearing into the hallway to her bedroom.

Munne tore off her riding coat and changed into a simple brown tunic and cloak to blend in with the townsfolk.

She pulled the cloak around her shoulders and tied it off. Munne turned to a jewelry box and pulled out a leather cord to tie her black hair back with. A plain leather satchel hung from one corner of the taller armoire. She grabbed it and tucked Malion's journal into it before departing. As she left the manor, she pulled the hood of the cloak over her head.

The streets weren't nearly as crowded as they had been the night before. People walked around the different plazas, enjoying the company of friends and family. Smells of roasted meats and hops filled the air. Munne wound her way through the streets of Elimere, heading toward the southern edge of town.

The Moonlit Grove was one of the larger inns and taverns in Elimere, purely because of its location. The inn was located across the street from the main stable house. It stood four stories tall, with the main level reserved for the tavern and kitchens. Smoke rose steadily from around the side of the building, and Munne heard cheer and merriment coming from inside. She pushed open the door and quickly scanned the inside for her companions, hoping she wasn't late.

Mayrien and Araloth were nowhere to be seen. Munne let out a quick sigh of relief and then hailed one of the serving maids, requesting a table for three on the outer wall. The maid escorted Munne to an empty table with four chairs. Munne took in the maid's appearance—tan cap with long blonde hair underneath, brown eyes, rosy cheeks, tan dress with white apron—and made sure to memorize every detail about her.

Munne sat down and looked around the tavern again, ensuring no one was paying her any mind. When she was certain she wasn't being observed, she pulled her hood off and moved her hair across her left shoulder. Her triple had visited the tavern a handful of times previously, but not in disguise. *Better to talk to my friends here without anyone recognizing or bothering us, than meet in the manor. There are too many ears listening there, ears that don't need to hear about my* affliction.

The maid returned to the table with a stone mug and a pitcher of ale. She placed the mug in front of Munne and then filled it with ale. "Anything to eat, ma'am?" the maid asked.

"Bread and meat for now," Munne replied, her voice more gruff than usual. "I have two others coming. They'll want food, too." The maid nodded and left.

Munne picked up the mug and took a swig of ale. The tavern was mostly full tonight. Many of the patrons weren't natives of Elimere. Some tables were friends reuniting over drinks, while others were merchants discussing their sales at the Eyreti Bazaar. There was a trio of musicians on the small stage. One sat in front of a drum, another strummed a lute, and the third sang a song about the oncoming winter. It was pleasant enough, but her attention was on the other patrons.

As her gaze swept across the room, she noticed a group of four travelers in the far corner with their hoods drawn and cloaks covering their bodies. Munne caught glimpses of their faces and hair. One of them seemed to have streaks of red in their hair. Another looked gaunt and frail with silver locks framing their face. Two of them weren't facing Munne's direction, so she wasn't able to get a good look at them.

As if they felt her gaze, the person on the left turned to face the tavern floor and made eye contact with Munne. She was startled to see olive skin, a curved nose, and two mismatching eyes—one green, one white. There was a jagged scar across the white eye, the skin pale and pink in comparison to the rest of his face. He blinked slowly and then nodded to Munne.

"Hail friend, how was your pilgrimage through Elimaine?" Mayrien's voice cut through Munne's thoughts.

She forced herself to turn and look at her two friends approaching her table. Mayrien wore a pretty, nondescript blue dress with a gray cloak wrapped around her shoulders. Her hair was tied into a simple knot, a few strands falling across her face.

"It, um, went well," Munne told her, nearly forgetting to use the same gruff voice she used earlier with the maid.

Mayrien sat down across from Munne, blocking her view of the strange man and his strange group of companions. Araloth took a seat on Mayrien's left side in between her and Munne. A brown cap concealed Araloth's hair, a green coat and brown pants her chosen attire for the night.

"Have you already ordered something to eat for us?" Araloth asked quietly, pulling her chair closer to the table.

Munne nodded absentmindedly and tried to catch one more glimpse of the strange man with the scar. Mayrien gave her a weird look before the maid came back around to their table with two stone mugs in one hand and a pitcher of ale in the other. She placed the mugs down in front of Mayrien and Araloth and poured ale into them.

Mayrien turned to look at the maid, a smile on her face. "May I also get a glass of local red wine?" she asked, folding her hands together. "I love getting a glass when I visit the valley."

The maid straightened her back and nodded before leaving the table again.

Mayrien looked back at Munne, a puzzled expression on her face. "What were you looking at?"

Munne shook her head and drank. The ale was cool but lacking flavor.

Araloth pulled her mug close to her chest. "Do you want to discuss the meeting from earlier?" she asked.

"Definitely not," Munne grumbled. "Although we probably should."

"Will we be traveling with you?" Mayrien asked.

"That will probably be the only respite from this, this…" Munne failed to find the right word to describe her feelings. *Betrayal? Torture? Mockery?*

"Were you able to find what you were looking for?" Araloth went on, trying a different topic. She took a drink from her own mug.

"Yes, I did… And I'm not sure that was such a good idea." Munne grimaced. Her companions waited patiently for her to continue. She looked around the room, once again ensuring no one was looking at their table. "These nightmares… I'm not the first person to have them. One of my ancestors had the same dreams."

"Which side of your family?" Mayrien whispered.

"My father's." Munne frowned. "And I don't know much about him. His name was Malion. He was a third son to the throne, and he lived during the Elviri-Asaszi Wars at the beginning of the Second Sun."

Mayrien wrapped her hands around her ale and tilted her head to the side. "I don't think I've heard of that one."

Munne glanced at Araloth, shifting in her seat. "He was part of the troops that marched into Promthus."

"Which time?" Araloth arched an eyebrow.

"It would have had to have been after the massive plague that swept through the lands, when the Elviri were reclaiming villages for the Proma. It was odd, though, because he never mentioned the plague." *Maybe the farmers had caught the plague and that's why they had acted so strangely toward Malion?*

"I think that was the only time we reclaimed any villages, right?" Mayrien asked, staring at Araloth.

"The only time I recall, yes," Araloth muttered, taking another sip of her drink.

Had there been a different war, with a different purpose? Why would that have been omitted from the history books? Munne's stomach clenched, and she was overwhelmed with the desire to leave. Her fingers fiddled with the front of her satchel, reaching in to stroke the leather journal inside. She pulled her hand away. She shouldn't touch that right now. She should have left it in the archives. Why did she bring it with her? Now it would be watching her, staring at her. It was always watching.

Munne squeezed her eyes shut and forced herself to speak. "His nightmares turned into something worse." She opened her eyes, her heartbeat accelerating. "He started seeing a demon in his sleep. The *Ardashi'ik.*"

Mayrien and Araloth exchanged a worried glance. "Friend, have you seen it, too?" Araloth whispered.

As Munne opened her mouth to respond, the maid returned with a large plate of meat and a basket filled with breads and rolls that she placed on the table in front of them.

"Let me get you something to eat with," the maid said and scurried off. She returned just as quickly, placing three forks and three knives on the table. "Will you be needing anything else?"

"Not right now but thank you," Araloth said with a deeper voice.

The maid nodded and left them to their food. The meat smelled delicious, but Munne wasn't sure she would be able to eat. She forced down another gulp of ale, watching Mayrien and Araloth tuck into the bread and meat. Both still looked at her with sympathy but waited for her to continue. They had always been patient companions, even when they were younger.

"For the first time last night, yes," Munne finally said. She wrapped her arms around her stomach and held onto herself tightly. "I'm not sure what this means."

"Elvarin will figure it out, I'm sure of it," Mayrien murmured, offering Munne a smile.

Munne managed a very quick flash of curled lips. Her eyes darted to the tavern floor. *It was always watching. Is someone watching me?*

"Friend, you need to eat something," Araloth said a little louder this time, pushing the basket of bread closer to Munne.

Munne reached out and grabbed one of the loaves from the basket—rosemary and olive. She tore off a chunk and chewed on it, her eyes glazed over in thought. There wasn't much more to their dinner conversation. They were drowning in the background noise of the tavern goers and musicians. The musicians now played a song about an Elviri squire falling in love with one of the royal maidens. Some of the patrons sang along, raising their mugs in the air. Others cheered and clapped, encouraging the music.

Araloth and Mayrien finished the meat, coaxing Munne to take a few bites. She was able to stomach them as well as another rosemary and olive roll.

"I should head back to my suite," Munne mumbled. "If the nightmares come tonight, I'll need plenty of time to fall back asleep."

Mayrien cast her a sympathetic look. "Do you want us to walk you home?"

Munne shook her head. "Quite alright... I'll be okay."

She pulled her hood up and stood. She pulled out some coins from her satchel, and her hand brushed against the leather journal. It felt like an icy shock, and she jerked her hand away. She forced herself to reach back into the satchel and grab a couple of gold coins from it. She placed the coins on the table and hastily left the tavern, eager to get some fresh air.

Outside the suns had set. Lanterns were lit across the town. People were still in the streets, heading home from their evening meal. It was significantly colder outside without the suns. Munne pulled her cloak closer to her body and picked up her pace. A gust of air blew through the streets, and she shivered. She would need to light a fire in her hearth tonight.

As Munne approached the manor, she decided to first walk through the gardens to kneel before Belleol and Ceyo's altars and ask for guidance before she laid down for the evening. Perhaps the gods would take pity on her and spare her from the nightmares, so that she may get some rest and collect her thoughts in the morning. She also considered stopping at Lithua's altar to pray for patience for her journey to the Imalar Woods.

The gardens were dark with a few lamps scattered throughout. The hedge walls stood about six feet tall, creating a beautiful maze of flowers and plants. The gardeners of Elimere took pride in the gardens. They scoured the mountains for cold-hardy flowers that would bloom even in the harshest of winters. Along the bottom of the hedges were stone planters containing those flowers, along with various herbs and shrubbery. Vines with tiny white flowers wrapped around the lampposts and iron-wrought benches along the paths. Statues of the gods filled the gardens, each with a small altar placed on top of the base of the statue.

Belleol's statue stood at the end of one path carved out of a silver-gray marble, the god sitting on a bench with an open book in her hands and vines with white flowers were wrapped around her wrists. She looked down at the book and had a wreath of blue flowers on top of her head. The base nearly came to Munne's waist and an ornate stone tray resting between Belleol's feet. Munne approached the statue and kneeled in front of it, placing her hands on the base. The stone was frigid cold and drained the heat from her skin.

"I pray to the Wise Sage and Seer, please guide my thoughts tonight," Munne whispered. "Let my mind be at peace, and not wander."

She bowed her head and closed her eyes, hearing the waterfalls roaring in the distance, and the bugs chattering in the gardens. A gentle breeze blew, and she heard the rustling of leaves and petals. She repeated her prayer silently to herself a few more times before climbing to her feet and opening her eyes.

178

She looked up at Belleol, her blue eyes meeting the smooth silver marble of the statue's. She stood there for a moment, allowing herself to relax. The gods would guide her path. She took comfort in that.

Munne turned back down the path, heading for Ceyo's statue. Her statue stood in a large open space and was easily twice as tall as Belleol's, if not larger. She held her sword triumphantly in one hand and her scepter in the other. Her hair had been carved to fan out behind her as if the wind were blowing through it. She wore gauntlets and her famed breastplate. The actual piece of armor was kept preserved in one of the museums in Elimere. From the waist down, she wore a billowing skirt. The contrast in armor and dress displayed Ceyo's dual roles as both diplomat and warrior of the Elviri people. Around the edges against the hedge walls were stone benches. Behind the statue was a small waterfall that trickled into a pond. Ceyo had a wreath of white flowers placed atop her head. Vases filled with assortments of blue, white, and purple flowers were placed on the base. At Ceyo's feet was an altar made of a small pile of stones, each painted and carved with runes.

Munne couldn't reach the altar when kneeling, so she stood in front of the statue and placed her hands on either side of the pile of stones. She bowed her head, closed her eyes. "I pray to the Guardian, Ruler of All, please guide my thoughts tonight."

A spark of warmth flowed through her fingertips, creeping up her arms. Munne opened her eyes and looked up at the towering goddess with wonder. Her marble eyes were smooth and steady, looking ahead at the valley.

"Thank you, blessed ruler," Munne murmured, a smile spreading across her face.

The goddess was silent.

Munne slowly pulled her hands away, savoring the warmth from the statue's cold stone. The gods would be with her tonight while she slept. She decided she would pray before Lithua's altar the morning she departed from the valley once again. That would give her another day to prepare what she would ask the goddess for.

CHAPTER XI: RAY

It had been hours since Naro left Ajak and Ray to hide in the underground room. What they were hiding from, Ray wasn't certain, but she had a feeling that they were lying low for a reason.

"How long until he gets back, d'you think?" Ray asked Ajak.

"No telling," Ajak grumbled in response.

True enough, she knew. "Mission successful, at least? We saw the princess."

"Yeah, but who knows if boss'll feel the same?"

Ray conceded and looked around the room. There wasn't much to do besides rummage through the cabinets and boxes, and even then, they didn't find much. She had long since abandoned the foppish hat she was wearing, along with the purple tunic. Ajak had ruffled up his own clothing, no doubt to get more comfortable. After a while he gave up on looking around and slumped into one of the chairs by the table. She had continued to look around, but the place was practically empty. Inside one of the boxes were some hard tack rations and a jug of water, but no fresh food. She wondered if the place belonged to the Walkers or someone else, or if it was abandoned entirely.

Above them came the grinding of stone, and Naro climbed down the ladder carrying two large knapsacks on his back. He wore different clothes, his gaudy merchant disguise abandoned for a plain black silk shirt and dark leather pants. He tossed the knapsacks on the ground in between Ajak and Ray.

"Ray, there are clothes for a barmaid in one of those sacks. Change, go to the Honeyed Bee, and tell Marcos that you are on shift tonight in the Lavender Room," Naro ordered, his voice soft yet firm. "The rest will be for Ajak and myself. We'll follow to the tavern shortly."

"Yes, sir," Ajak murmured. He leaned forward and grabbed the other knapsack and began sifting through it.

Ray nodded and crouched down, beginning her hunt for yet another disguise. She gathered up all the components of her outfit—a long-sleeved brown dress, soft leather boots, and a dark blue bonnet—and changed in the back of the room. Ajak and Naro turned their backs and murmured quietly to one another. She overheard the names of some of the other big gangs but couldn't make much else out.

When she finished changing, she crossed back over to them. "Any other orders, sir?" she asked.

Naro turned to her, uncrossing his arms, and placed a hand gently on her shoulder. "For now, just keep your eyes open and ears listening. Remember everything you hear and see in the Lavender Room. There will be time for questions and discussion soon enough."

Eyes and ears. Her shoulders sagged with relief. After all the strange events over the past two days, she was happy to return to her roots. She nodded and then took to the ladder. If nothing else, she could handle being a pair of eyes and ears.

Up above, the suns had begun to sink low in the sky. There was a slight chill in the air that grew stronger. She would need to hustle to the Honeyed Bee to get out of the cold. It took her a moment to find her way back to the main streets, but once she did, she kept her head low and hurried toward the ramp down into the Market District. It wasn't odd for a barmaid to be in the Sky District, but she wanted to minimize her time there. She needed to blend in.

After the earlier events with the princess' outing and the thieves' escape, there were several people out on the streets chatting excitedly. As she moved through the streets, she listened for gossip and news.

Two men were walking beside her, absorbed in their own discussion of the event. "They chased them all the way to the Crafting District!" one man spoke with a boisterous laugh.

"Did they catch them, though?" the other responded warily.

"The treasures they stole from the church were returned a couple of hours ago."

"Praise the Protector!"

That didn't answer the question, though. I wonder who those thieves were, and if their heist had been planned or a horrible accident at the wrong time. Ray shrugged off the questions and quickened her pace. *I'll get more information on that later.*

The Honeyed Bee was already full of warm, lively bodies. Ray had spent several evenings in the tavern blending into the background, taking note of the various merchants, lords, and craftsmen who struck deals in the lower levels. The top four floors were more of a mystery to her. Those rooms were invite-only, and she had never been fortunate enough to receive one.

Until tonight. Who else will be upstairs tonight?

She slipped into the lowest floor and made her way to the bar where Marcos, a round red-cheeked man, was serving drinks to various patrons. She caught his eye and leaned over the counter so he could hear her.

"I've been told I'm on duty in the Lavender Room tonight," Ray said.

Marcos nodded and tossed a dishcloth over his shoulder. "Aye, you are, and the guests'll be arriving soon so get to settin' the table!" His response came easy enough, even though she had never directly spoken to this man before.

"Yes, sir." Ray nodded and hurried off toward the stairs. She wondered if there would be others working with her tonight. Although not entirely accustomed to working in a tavern, she hoped to have someone to lean on in case she got overwhelmed. She wouldn't be on the main floor, which meant less patrons overall, but there was no telling what kind of people would be in the Lavender Room tonight.

Most of the people who worked at the Honeyed Bee were genuinely employed and earning coin. Every so often, though, there would be a Walker or two working under cover. It appeared that the normal staff knew this and accounted for it in their work. Ray had even worked in the common rooms below a handful of times. The staff at the Honeyed Bee never asked questions, and never asked for names. They simply relayed instructions and patiently guided the rogues through the evening.

Near the stairs was a painted sign detailing which rooms were on which floor. The Lavender Room was on the fourth floor, along with two other private rooms. She hitched up her skirt and climbed up the stairs, wasting no time getting to work. The fourth floor was decorated lavishly with beautiful paintings hanging on the walls and plush patterned rugs stretching across the floors. She poked her head inside the Lavender Room to get a lay of the land. A square banquet table filled most of the room with enough seats for twelve. A dark maroon tablecloth covered the surface. The walls were painted a pale lavender color, the namesake of the room.

Twelve, then. She made the mental note and hurried back toward the hutches to gather the appropriate dishes. *Naro and Ajak will be among them, but who else would be present?*

Another girl slid next to Ray and started pulling down goblets. She wore a black dress and matching bonnet. A few strands of blonde hair fell close to her ears. She looked no older than Ray, but she carried herself with an air of authority. She must be one of the head servers.

Without looking away from her work the girl asked, "Which room?"

"Lavender."

The other girl nodded and rattled off their tasks. "Right. We're partners tonight. The room'll have twelve guests in it. The kitchens are already working on the meal. We're to put out cups for both water and wine, but do not serve either until all the guests have arrived. There's a small tray of pasties and greens that'll come up after all the guests have arrived, so put out small plates. The kitchens already have the big plates."

Ray nodded and filled her hands with six glass goblets for water. Her partner for the evening grabbed the other six. With deft hands and a quick pace, they had both sets of cups and the small plates set up in little time.

"What wines are we serving?" Ray asked once they finished.

"Honey and red. I'll grab them from the cellar, you get the water pitchers." With that the girl left, heading for the stairs. Ray followed although her path diverted on the second floor where she stopped to grab two pitchers full of water.

When the other girl returned to the Lavender Room, she handed Ray a bottle of red wine and said, "Tonight, you're Red, and I'm Honey. Understand?"

An easy enough way to avoid names and avoid having to create a persona. Ray nodded. "Yes, Honey."

"Good. There are two bottles of each, which we'll probably go through as soon as the guests arrive. I'll get more if it's needed. Same with water." Honey placed her bottle of honeyed wine on a small table near the door along with the spare bottles. "You focus on clearing plates and cleaning up. The food'll come up the shaft down the hall when it's ready. We'll serve it together."

Honey covered a few more instructions for Ray which were rather simple: don't speak unless spoken to, no outright laughing, and everything she heard was to stay in this room and never be spoken of again. Simple rules for private meetings such as this. Ray wondered how many meetings like this Honey had been privy to, but she knew she would never get an answer if she asked.

I must pay careful attention to what's going on, she reminded herself. *There's no telling who'll be sitting at this table or what they'll be talking about. I just need to look for clues. Remember who looks away or coughs politely when asked a question. Watch for any underhand trades. Listen for any names of interest, real or fake.*

They didn't have to wait long for the guests to arrive. The first was a pair of two very tall, muscular men wearing plain, nondescript clothes befitting of craftsmen going out to dinner after a day at the forge. Although there had been effort to clean themselves up, there were soot stains so deep on their faces, their skin looked a little gray. Ray never would have cast a second glance at these men if she were down in the common rooms. For them to be up here in one of the private rooms meant there was something noteworthy about them. Ray noted their faces, their frowns as they saw an empty table, their quiet muttering as they sat down on the same side of the table. She overheard one asking what alcohol they'd have tonight, and the other simply shrugged. Honey neither spoke nor moved from her spot, so neither did Ray.

The next group to enter the room was a trio of nobles, clearly plucked from the top of the Sky District. There were two women and one man, and they sat on the side opposite the craftsmen. All three were wearing crimson red capes with elegant clothing and jewelry underneath. The woman in the middle snapped her fingers at Honey and Ray as she unclasped her cloak and held it out behind her. Honey hurried over to the woman's side and collected her cloak, along with the cloaks of the other two as well. She took them out of the room to hang on hooks in the hallway.

The woman in the middle was clearly the one in charge. She was the most beautiful, had the most jewels draping her body, and looked down her nose at everyone else. Her skin was pale, her hair black as night, and she had the most piercing green eyes with an emerald gown to match. Around her neck was a gold pendant with a ruby set in the middle. Ray's stomach twisted anxiously as the woman looked around the room, traces of a sneer forming on her face. But Ray had to maintain her calm.

I'll do what I must to ensure this woman is pleased. I need to see what part she plays in this dinner.

The other two nobles weren't as impressive. The second woman had a widow's peak, and her nose was too large for her face. She had plain brown hair and brown eyes and wore a lot of gaudy baubles and gems. Her gown was the source of her beauty and prestige—a beautiful golden gown with ample amounts of embroidery, lace, and gems encrusted on it. The man was short and round, with dark eyes and receding hair. Again, it was his clothing that solidified his status. He wore a deep purple tunic with gold leaves on his chest. Two heavy chains of gold and silver hung from around his neck. Rings with large gems adorned his fingers.

The guests looked between one another, not saying a word. Honey returned to Ray's side, and the two stood with their hands folded behind their backs and waited.

Ray immediately recognized the next group of guests and had to actively force herself to maintain a neutral expression. Naro, Sabyl, Aldrin, and Ajak entered the room, all wearing elegant clothing in the dark blue and white colors of the Walkers. It was strange seeing Sabyl wearing clothes befitting a noble, but she held her chin high. She hadn't seen Aldrin in several weeks, so Ray was surprised to see him. His black and gray hair fell to his shoulders, covering his ears.

To hide his mixed-blood status, Ray thought.

Aldrin's green eyes shone against the dark colors of his robe and vest. Beside him, Ajak looked handsome in his dark blue doublet. The sight of him dressed in such regalia stirred something carnal within Ray. She tore her eyes off him to prevent the blush from spreading too far across her face.

Leading the three Walkers was Naro, who stood out from the others in a high-collared shirt of black silk underneath a sleeveless royal blue robe. Swirling patterns of eyes covered the robe in silver thread. A wide leather belt cinched his waist, the buckle molded into the shape of a lidless eye. His dark hair sat atop his head in a knot. He held his chin high, looking like a king before his court. The only thing missing was a crown.

This is a meeting of the gang lords, Ray realized.

Her eyes darted to the craftsmen and nobles—the Iron Hawks and Red Court. A chill ran down her spine. She had seen other gang members on the streets, but she never imagined she would be in the same room as their leaders. Would this be a diplomatic meeting? It had to be, why else would Naro bring Ajak and his lieutenants?

Was this Ajak's final test, or did Naro give him the position once I left the basement?

Naro sat in the middle seat on the side closest to Ray and Honey, his back facing them. Sabyl and Aldrin were on either side of him, leaving Ajak with the empty seat next to the Iron Hawks. Ajak inclined his head toward the Iron Hawks before pulling the chair out and taking a seat. One of the Iron Hawks grumbled and threw a look at Naro who didn't even acknowledge them.

The last of the guests arrived moments later—three men wearing dark gray robes and cloaks. These had to be members of the Disciples, religious fanatics who enjoyed bullying others on the streets for money and goods. All kinds of nasty rumors—and truths—had spread about this group. It was something of a miracle that they had lasted as long as they did, let alone become one of the major players in the city. The three men removed their cloaks, handing them off to Honey, and took their seats at the table. They were rather plain men with blond and brown hair. Ray realized she would have missed these three if she had been working downstairs. She wondered how many other gang members she had failed to recognize in the past.

"Many thanks for the short notice gathering," Naro said as soon as they sat. He steepled his fingers, placing his elbows on the table. "I know you all have other important matters to attend to, so I will make this brief."

No one else spoke. Ray watched their eyes as the gang lords looked around the room. The Disciples exchanged glances. One of the Iron Hawks crossed his arms and leaned back in his chair. The leader of the Red Court had her eyes locked on Naro, her expression unreadable.

Naro clapped his hands once. "Water and wine for the guests. And a tray of small bites."

Honey pushed herself away from the wall and Ray followed suit. They both took a pitcher of water and filled glasses before returning for the bottles of wine. Ray and Honey filled the guests' goblets, Naro's filled last. Honey placed her bottle back on the small serving table and then slipped into the hallway to summon forth the plate of pasties and greens. Ray took up her spot against the wall, her hands behind her back and head bent down.

Naro took a sip of his wine, an unspoken signal for the guests to drink as well. There was no toasting, no raising goblets to each other. It all felt very cold and distant. He placed the goblet back on the table and then looked at each guest at the table. The silence continued as Honey brought a large tray into the room and set it down in the middle of the table. Naro turned his head, his eyes following her. Once she was back at her spot against the wall, he reached out to grab a small pastry with cheese and jam smeared on top. Another unspoken signal. The rest of the table each grabbed one thing, and everyone took a bite before setting their food on their plates.

Ray found it odd that these other gang lords were so easily falling into step behind Naro. Was this just the etiquette of gang lords when they met? If another one had called this meeting, would Naro be following their signals to drink and eat? She didn't quite believe that to be the case.

Watch for any signs of discontent among them. Are they following along willingly? It was a tough room to read, however. None of the gang lords expressed any outward displeasure at being in the meeting—they all collectively maintained neutral expressions as they went through their rituals of first sips and bites.

"I thought I had made it abundantly clear that these ten days were to be free of events," Naro said softly, his voice sweet like honey. The pastry was still pinched between his finger and his thumb. His gaze bore into the small treat as he tilted it around the plate. "And yet this afternoon there was quite the stir in the Sky District, in the same square as Madame Gweneth's shop."

He set the pastry down, raising his head to look around the table. He raised his voice but only slightly, still maintaining his calm demeanor. "I don't care what business you get into. I don't care what scuffles you may have on the streets, how many guards you kill, or how many people get caught in your traps. But you *will* listen to me when I give an order."

Ray's blood ran cold. This wasn't the voice of one gang lord among his peers—it was the voice of a king over his subjects. *And since when does he not care about people getting hurt or killed? He must be bluffing, just trying to reason with these people.* With his back to her, though, she couldn't read his face to tell.

"There is to be peace for the next five days. No schemes, no heists, no work. The streets are to be *silent*. After the fifth day, the city is yours. Do you all understand?"

Ray's eyes widened ever so slightly. *"Theirs"? To what end?*

She adjusted herself and then dared raise her eyes to look over the gang lords again. The two Iron Hawks shared a look, one Ray knew well—hope and caution. On the Red Court's side of the table, the plump man leaned in and whispered something to his leader. She arched an eyebrow but otherwise said nothing.

One of the Disciples tilted his head back and dared speak. "We are only four. There are others out there—"

"And they will listen to their betters!" Naro snapped. "The streets *will* be silent. There will be no more engagements with the city guard, not one toe out of line." He looked around the table as if daring one of the others to speak up against him. The Disciple who had spoken had a sneer on his face. As he locked eyes with the woman from the Red Court, Ray saw her give the smallest nod.

A faint *ding* came from the hallway. Honey reached over and tugged on Ray's sleeve. Dinner was ready. They first circled the table, picking up the small plates. Some hadn't touched their food beyond the initial bite. A brief thought of sneaking one of the pasties crossed Ray's mind, but she shooed it away. *Not now.*

The two girls left the room and walked down the hall to the small box in the wall—the lift to and from the kitchens. Inside the box were four plates filled with roast chicken, vegetables, and a garlicky bread knot. Beside the wall was another small table, where Honey set her small plates down. Ray did the same.

"Chiefs first," Honey murmured, grabbing two of the plates.

Ray grabbed the others and followed the girl back into the Lavender Room. Honey went to the left to set her plates down in front of the leaders of the Iron Hawks and Disciples. *How does she know who the leaders are from these two groups? None of the men have any distinctive marks or sigils on their clothing.*

She blinked the question away and instead committed the faces of the two leaders to memory—the Hawk on the left, and the Disciple in the middle. She was thankful that Honey let her serve Naro and the woman from the Red Court, the more obvious leaders in the room. She set down the plate for the woman first, daring to cast a glance at the ruby pendant. It was a beautiful stone that had been smoothed and cut into the shape of a teardrop.

Ray didn't linger. She didn't want to draw attention to herself. She quickly moved to Naro's side and served him his plate. His eyes flicked up to meet hers, and for a moment, her breath was gone. She could only see a sliver of green from his left eye, and his blue eye was dark and cold like the Hourglass Lakes. Gone was the warmth she was so accustomed to seeing in his mismatching eyes. He looked ruthless and annoyed.

Is he annoyed at my presence? Am I overstepping my place as a serving girl? She looked away from his gaze and followed Honey back out of the room to get the rest of the plates.

As with the wine and pasties, the guests waited until Naro picked up his fork and knife to begin eating. Dinner was a silent affair, with only the noises of cutlery as company. No guest had to ask for more water or wine. Honey and Ray ensured cups were full, having memorized who drank which and being ever vigilant for signs of a drained goblet.

Once again Ray watched for any abnormalities, listening for any hushed whispers between the lords. On occasion, when they thought he wasn't looking, the Disciples would glance at Naro with a slight sneer on their faces. *But I'm his eyes tonight,* Ray thought. *I don't like the way they keep looking at him. Why did the other gangs allow the Disciples to acquire so much power? They obviously can't be trusted.*

There was no dessert after the meal. As soon as he finished his plate, Naro gently set his knife and fork down, and then dabbed at his cheek with a handkerchief. He looked around the table once more. His lieutenants had finished their meals, as well as the Iron Hawks. The other two gangs still had food left on their plates. Without a word, Naro stood. Aldrin, Sabyl, and Ajak followed suit, leaving their utensils on the table. Naro exited first with his lieutenants behind him.

The others gradually finished their meals and took their leave. The Iron Hawks drained their wine goblets before lumbering off toward the staircase. The woman of the Red Court cleared her throat, and Honey slipped from the room to retrieve their cloaks. Ray helped hand the cloaks to the nobles and pull back their chairs. They strutted from the room with their chins held high. Honey and Ray resumed their spots against the wall.

The Disciples were the last to leave. They whispered among themselves for a few moments, which Ray struggled to hear. There was no way for her to get closer to them, though, so she had to take whatever crumb of information she could get. She thought she heard one of them mention the Pike and Pint, but she wouldn't bet anything substantial on it.

Eventually one looked up at Honey and Ray. "Our cloaks," he called out.

Honey retrieved the cloaks, and Ray assisted with handing them to the Disciples and pulling back chairs. The three men left the room, and it was just Honey and Ray left.

"Stack the plates. I'll grab the cups," Honey ordered, and they fell into silent work cleaning up the Lavender Room.

Soon the table was cleared, the tablecloth swept, and the dishes sent down the lift. It felt good to do something with her hands as she played back the events of the evening. *Something's amiss with those Disciples. And could it be true that the thieves from earlier didn't belong to any of the main four? What if the Disciples had been lying about that?*

"Remember the rules," Honey said softly as they departed the Lavender Room, the commanding tone gone.

"I heard nothing," Ray responded, the corners of her mouth curling into a faint smile. *An easy enough lie. How many others have said it before?*

Honey gave her a curt nod. "Right. Check with Marcos before you go. I think he had something to tell you."

Ray returned the gesture and descended the stairs into the common room. Marcos was still serving at the bar, which was now considerably more populated than earlier. She navigated her way through a maze of drunks, talkers, and gropers to get to the counter.

"Marcos!" she called out, squeezing into a space between two heavy men to prop her elbows on the counter.

The barkeep spotted her, and his eyes lit up. He crossed over to her, acknowledging orders from other patrons along the way. "All finished?" he asked once he reached her.

The man on her left leaned back in his seat with a hearty guffaw, his back pressing against her side. She frowned but made no move to push back. "Yeah. You have something else for me?"

Marcos nodded. "Need you to make a delivery. Two blocks east, red door in the alley." He turned away for a moment and then returned with two bottles of wine.

Is this my exit strategy? She took the bottles and played along. "Thanks, Marcos!"

Ray slipped out of the Honeyed Bee and turned east toward the alley Marcos had described. *This must be a continuation of my disguise. Some extra step in the job? What else am I supposed to be observing tonight? I don't recognize this part of the Market District. Shouldn't I be getting back to the Walkers to check in with Naro?*

The alley around her was silent. She was in between a shop and an inn. The red door was attached to the back of the inn. The owner's quarters, or perhaps a not-so-secret room for people wanting to remain hidden. She knew inns across Auora had rooms like that—she had even stayed in a few when she was younger. She didn't recognize this particular inn or door, however. She stopped in front of it and knocked twice.

The door slowly creaked open, revealing a small room with a table and a couple of chairs. A single candle was lit on the table. She saw no other doors or ways out of the room.

"Hello?" she said into the empty room. "I have a delivery, for, um..." Her voice trailed off as she watched a single brick in the wall push out from its resting place. She tilted her head to the side, curious. *What was—?*

Part of the wall swung open, revealing a hidden door. Ajak was on the other side. He beckoned her inside, his voice low. "Hurry up. Close the door behind you."

She gathered her wits and stepped into the small room, shutting the red door behind her. She followed Ajak into another room, one even smaller than the first. The only thing inside was a descending ladder. She was becoming all too familiar with mysterious ladders.

She turned to Ajak, holding up the two bottles of wine. "What should I do with—?"

"I'll take them down." Ajak cut her off by taking them from her hands then nodded toward the ladder. "Down you go. Boss is waiting."

She swallowed nervously and began her descent, careful not to step on the hem of her dress. Down below was the main room of a small flat. She saw three doors leading to other rooms. Naro, Aldrin, and Sabyl weren't in the main room, but she heard their voices coming from the door on the far wall. Ajak came down the ladder behind her, bumping his elbow against her back.

"Go on. I'll get you something to eat."

Ray quickly crossed over to the room and entered. Inside was a simple bed with furs and blankets piled on top. There was a small desk against the opposite wall where Naro sat in the only chair in the room. Aldrin leaned against a wall while Sabyl paced around. Behind her, Ajak entered with the wine bottles and a cloth bundle. He handed one bottle to Naro, and the other to Aldrin. Ajak pressed the cloth bundle into Ray's hands. Naro wasted no time opening his bottle of wine and drinking deeply from it. Aldrin waited.

Inside the cloth bundle were a couple of buns, still warm to the touch. At the sight of food—fresh food, at that—her stomach awoke and began growling. She tore into the first bun and was delightfully surprised to taste a meat filling.

"You think they'll listen?" Sabyl asked in a pointed tone.

"The Ricard brothers and Lady Janna are smart enough to listen. It's those bastards in the gray robes that I don't trust," Naro muttered. He took another drink from the bottle of wine.

So, he's already wary of the Disciples.

Aldrin took his time uncorking his bottle. "You think the incident in the Sky District was one of them?" he asked.

Naro sighed. "I don't think it was any of the other three."

"Then why gather them and threaten them the way you did?"

"Careful, boy." Naro's tone sharpened, and he set his wine bottle down.

Ray's brow furrowed. *Why would he call him "boy"? Aldrin's the oldest person in this room, easily at least fifty years older than Naro or Sabyl.*

Aldrin tossed the cork aside, but still hadn't taken a drink. "Just seems like we should be out there punishing the ones who did it, not having fancy dinners with the people who didn't do it."

Sabyl crossed over to Aldrin and yanked the bottle of wine from his hand before moving to slap him across the face.

"Stay your hand, Sabyl," Naro told her. Ray heard the tiredness in his voice. Sabyl didn't strike Aldrin, but neither did she lower her hand. She glared daggers at the Provira.

Naro always praised Aldrin's frank attitude and courage to speak his mind—he had told her it was one of the reasons he made Aldrin a lieutenant. However, it seemed that Naro didn't want to hear Aldrin's thoughts at that moment. But Ray was inclined to agree with Aldrin.

What was *the point of meeting with the other gang lords tonight?*

"It's a lesson I find myself teaching time and time again," Naro murmured. He looked between Aldrin and Sabyl. "The Syrael Walkers are strong. Powerful. But we cannot control this city alone. Nor should we. And that is why we meet with the other three."

Aldrin scoffed. Sabyl's eyes darted to Naro, who gave her the slightest of nods. Without looking back at Aldrin, Sabyl struck a blow across his cheek. He recoiled and raised his hand to cradle his face. She stalked away to the opposite side of the room, taking a long swig from the wine bottle.

Ray and Ajak stared uncomfortably at their leaders. She had never seen anyone in the Walkers hit another so maliciously.

"You're strong, Aldrin. Powerful. You think you could control it all on your own?" Naro asked, his voice barely above a whisper.

Aldrin met Naro's gaze and didn't look away.

"Ray, Ajak, you're dismissed," Naro said curtly without casting a glance toward them. "You all are to stay here for the night. New orders will be given in the morning."

"Yes, sir," Ajak mumbled, grabbing Ray's wrist and leading her out of the room.

They moved to the door on their left, which led to a room with three beds all made up. There was little else in the room. Ajak and Ray sat down together on the same bed and leaned back against the wall.

"Aldrin had a point thought, didn't he...?" Ray murmured after a few moments of silence. Ajak grunted in response. She couldn't tell if it was to agree or disagree. "What are we doing here?"

His hair, which had been tied back into a ponytail, had begun to fray and fell loose around his face. He had taken off the silver neckerchief and unbuttoned the top two buttons of his dark blue shirt, his coat tossed to the ground. He looked exhausted. She was sure she looked very similar to him. "In this flat?"

"In this whole dinner scheme," she clarified, fidgeting with the sleeve on her dress.

Ajak tilted his chin to the side and met her gaze. "We're next in line for lieutenantship."

She shook her head. "Maybe you are, but not me."

Ajak took hold of her fidgeting hand and squeezed it. "Yes you. On the way over here, Naro told me that this flat is only known to him and his lieutenants. No one else in the Walkers knows about it. And now here you are."

"I'm sure he just wants me here to make sure I'm safe," she replied, looking away from him. "Not because he wants me to be a lieutenant."

"Ray, think about it. He told me that my mission—*our* mission—to kidnap the princess was the final step to me becoming a lieutenant. What do you think *you're* going to get out of it?"

Ray wanted to tell him she didn't know. That he was wrong. That there was another reason for her getting involved in all of this. She was only eighteen and had only ever been a pair of eyes on the street. She would make for a terrible lieutenant, having only ever listened and watched other people. She wasn't even that great of a thief. There were several other Walkers who were much better at thieving and sneaking and fighting. Ray had no idea how to deal with the rival gangs.

"I-I can't," she stammered. She didn't know what else to say. She tugged off her shoes and then held her knees to her chest, laying her head down against them while staring at the darkness.

Ajak didn't respond. Maybe he didn't want to waste his breath. Or maybe he was realizing that she wasn't cut out for it. She felt him shift and move beside her. He stood and she heard the rustle of clothes.

"Come on, let's get settled," Ajak said, nudging her leg with his hand. "I doubt Aldrin and Sabyl want to share a bunk tonight. Scoot over."

Ray sighed and crawled to one side of the bed, giving Ajak the space to get in beside her. The bed wasn't too terribly large. They would be sleeping shoulder to shoulder with just enough space on the edge to keep them from rolling off in the middle of the night. He slid under the blankets and lay on his side facing away from her. She stayed above the blankets on her back, staring up at the ceiling.

"Try to get some rest," Ajak murmured. "No telling what the boss'll have us do tomorrow."

Ray managed a small smile at that. It had barely been two days, but to her it felt like a lifetime had passed since Naro had taken her off the athra assignment and told her she would be joining the crew to kidnap the princess. She wondered how soon he would make the call to move forward with the plan if he decided to at all. The incident at the square had shaken him up, or at least made things complicated. She didn't know the extent of the damage, and she wasn't sure if she would ever know. She doubted even Ajak understood it.

He's right, though. Neither of us can hope to know what Naro's next set of orders will be.

She let out a quiet exhale and closed her eyes, wondering how quickly sleep would find her.

CHAPTER XII:
MUNNE

When Munne opened her eyes, she wasn't in her room, or in the nightmarish caverns that had become so familiar to her. She was in the woods, standing in a clearing. On the ground was a thin layer of crisp leaves, freshly fallen. She recognized the place, but it was missing the structure that gave it its identity—Ceyo's godsite. Her cabin was missing, and yet Munne swore she was at the same clearing where it should be standing. Fog spilled from the trees. The clearing felt different in this world, wherever that was. It felt foreign and unfamiliar. She looked up and the sky had a deep purple tinge to it. There was no moon in sight, and yet the clearing was fully visible.

"Goddess, where have you brought me?" Munne whispered as she walked around the clearing.

"You're somewhere safe," an ethereal male voice came from across the clearing, deep within the trees. Munne tried to find the source of the voice, but her eyes failed her. The forest was too dark.

"Safe from what?" she called out to the woods.

A gentle breeze came through the clearing, but she didn't shiver. She looked down and was surprised to see herself wearing nothing more than a sleeveless vest and pants. Her feet were bare, and yet she had not felt the leaves crunch underfoot. She didn't feel the cool air on her skin.

What is this place?

"Safe from the *Ardashi'ik*," the voice came from behind her.

She let out a startled cry and spun around, raising her arms defensively in front of her face. She shut her eyes out of instinct from hearing that name.

"I didn't mean to startle you," the voice said quietly, sounding much more solid. Munne lowered her arms and opened her eyes.

Before her stood an Elviri man wearing a black tunic and pants. His dark brown hair fell to his shoulders, thin braids framing his face. He had a very plain face, with brown eyes, a straight nose, and thin lips. His left arm was extended toward her, as if reaching to grasp her elbow. A sympathetic look rested on his face.

She instinctively took a step back, shifting her weight and pivoting with her upper body so she was in a defensive position. Her right hand curled into a fist, ready to strike if he came any closer. "Who are you?" she asked.

"Who I am is of no importance," he said, lowering his hand. "I'm here to guide you on the path set before you."

Munne's gaze swept over his body, assessing his stance and posture. He appeared docile enough, but she had never seen him before in her life. "Are you an agent of the gods?"

The man looked past Munne to the middle of the clearing. He walked past her, his hands behind his back. "Curious, how so much can stay the same." There was melancholy in his voice. "Even after so much time has passed."

She turned with him, keeping her distance. "Why won't you tell me who you are, or answer my questions?" Munne asked.

He turned, his eyes meeting Munne's. "Your journey to Kherizhan doesn't require it." His tone matched the firmness of her voice. "All that matters is that you heed my warnings and follow my instructions."

"What journey to Kherizhan? I'm doing no such thing," she said, holding her chin high. *Who is this man, to assume such authority over me? If he was sent by the gods, why doesn't he say so? Why else would we be here, at Ceyo's godsite?*

"You seek answers to your ancestor's plight, which you also happen to share. You aim to cast out the darkness, where he could not, and save yourself. The answers you seek lie in Kherizhan."

Munne's fist loosened, and she physically recoiled at his words, taking a couple of steps back. Ceyo's words echoed in her ears: *You will meet your guide to this dark place. Is Kherizhan the "dark place" the goddess was referring to? And is this man my guide?*

The man held her gaze for a few moments before walking away from her toward the center of the clearing. Munne watched him go, the frown slipping from her face. *He hasn't shown any signs of aggression or hostility, so perhaps I can trust him? We're meeting at Ceyo's godsite, so surely the goddess planned for this. Or perhaps this is a different kind of nightmare?*

Her muscles tensed, and she was suddenly on edge. She glanced around the clearing, trying to see what was hidden beyond in the woods. She could have sworn she saw a pair of eyes watching her from across the clearing—one green, one white.

She had seen those eyes before, very recently. Events from the previous day replayed in her head—the visit to Ceyo's godsite, the war council, the archives, the tavern—

The foreigner from the Moonlit Grove? Why would he be here?

Another breeze blew through the clearing, and with it came the faint sound of screaming. Munne twisted her head around, trying to find where it was coming from. She recognized the screams from her nightmares. *Perhaps this is just another nightmare, and the* Ardashi'ik *is waiting for me just beyond the tree line, watching me stand with this stranger, plotting to run in and attack me and—*

"Ah, *k'khryth n'rykiir ykanyryth*." The man spoke in a language unfamiliar to Munne—something she had never heard before.

Munne no longer heard the screaming. She snapped her attention to the man, but he was gone. In his stead was another Elviri man dressed in a hunter's garb with braided light brown hair and dark green eyes. She recognized him from the paintings and statues in Elimere. He was Huntlé, the man who became a god.

Munne took to one knee, bowing her head in reverence. "Great Hunter, I-I'm sorry, I didn't realize—"

Huntlé looked down at himself and let out a *tsk* before his body was engulfed in an odd shimmering light. He stood completely still, and yet his body vibrated and changed. Munne was both blinded by this light and completely able to see through it as if it weren't there. She raised a hand in front of her face. Perhaps it was her eyes playing a trick on her. She narrowed her eyes, trying to focus on his figure. Munne blinked, and suddenly Huntlé was no longer Huntlé. He was tall, brown robes covering his entire body. A matching wrap covered his head, hiding all his facial features except his eyes. She focused on his eyes, trying to see what shape and color they were. For a moment, she could have sworn his eyes were completely white.

"I cannot keep it at bay any longer. I have nearly drained myself. I can wake you, or let the darkness in," he said and crossed the empty space between them.

The closer he got, the more desperately she felt she needed to flee from him, panic swelling up inside of her. All her years of training and discipline were gone in the blink of an eye. She opened her mouth to speak, to tell him to back away from her or else she would attack, but no words came. He stopped mere inches from her, and it was like her entire body was on fire, screaming to run, but she couldn't force herself to move. He had to bend down to meet her gaze. She had never seen eyes like his before, devoid of color and pupils. Her chest tightened. He filled the entire space around her, and she thought she was going to suffocate. Out of the corners of her eyes she saw him reaching out to touch her.

The moment his hands touched her skin, Munne awakened. She jolted upright, throwing an arm out to catch herself. Her chest heaved, her breathing erratic. Munne covered her face with her other hand, closing her eyes. She needed to breathe. Breathe. Calm down.

Who was that man? He took the form of Huntlé, but also changed into two other men. Do the gods have that kind of power? Surely, they do. Then why have I never seen something like this before?

As her breathing evened out, she felt an overwhelming urge to leave her suite for the second night in a row. The floor was considerably warmer beneath her feet than the night before. She saw the fire still smoldering in the hearth. Grabbing one of the blankets from her bed, Munne wrapped it around her body. She stood and headed to the balcony door. She didn't step out tonight, but she did look up to the sky to see how late in the night it was. The moon was at its highest point in the sky. Midnight.

Munne sat on the edge of her bed. The shapeshifting stranger mentioned a journey to Kherizhan. *Her* journey to Kherizhan, whatever that meant. Why would she travel to the inhospitable mountains in the southeast? There was no purpose in going there. All routes into Kherizhan passed through Moonyswyn, so that would be a suicidal journey traveling through the lands the Provira inhabited. Lands that had once belonged to the Asaszi. The shifter also said that the clearing was safe, that she had been somewhere safe away from the *Ardashi'ik*. But she still heard the screams in that place. The shifter had reached for her, as if he wanted to touch her. Had he touched her? She looked over herself and saw faint red imprints of hands on her upper arms. Touching the imprint felt warm, and a calm washed over her.

She hastily removed her hands from her arms, and the calm feeling was gone. Panic and dread filled her once again. *How did these imprints get there? Is this the work of the gods, or something more sinister? If it's something sinister, why do I feel so at ease when I touch them?*

The image of the face looking at her from across the clearing appeared in her mind, the mismatching eyes sending a shiver down her spine. One green eye and one white eye.

At least this mystery can be more easily solved. I'm due for a visit with this foreigner at the Moonlit Grove.

———◈———

The walk to the Moonlit Grove was much faster now that the streets were sufficiently empty. It also helped that the cold made her walk faster. Only a handful of people were still out and about, indulging in drinking and other forms of merriment. The main door to the tavern was locked, but Munne knew she could access it from inside the foyer of the inn. She walked around to the main doors of the inn and entered.

The lights in the foyer were dim and dying. No one sat behind the front table since none of their guests were arriving or departing from the inn at that time of night. The tavern door on her right glowed with light. Munne walked over and gently opened it.

All the tables in the tavern were empty, save for one. It was the same table in the corner where Munne saw the strange group of travelers earlier in the evening. Only one of them sat at the table, and their hood was drawn. The hooded man was hunched, nursing a mug of ale. Munne had a feeling she knew which of the group it was.

She hurried over and sat on the opposite side of the table from him. He had clearly been drinking for several hours, so he was no serious threat to her. Even if he tried to attack, she could easily incapacitate him, or at least hold

200

him off until the guards came. She folded her hands together and placed them on the table, leaning forward.

"What business do you have in Elimere?" she asked.

The man lifted his head, revealing his mismatching eyes and jagged scar. The sight both disturbed and strengthened her. There could be no mistaking him for anyone else—his was the face she saw in her dream.

The man rubbed his chin with the back of his hand, taking in her appearance. He mumbled, "Trading, fair Elviri." He nodded politely in her direction.

Munne blinked as she looked him over. "What goods have you brought to trade?"

He met her gaze for a moment, and then looked back down at his drink. "Already answered those questions at the gates," he responded, his voice muffled by the mug as he drank.

"Where do you hail from?"

The man set the mug down on the table and leaned back in his chair. Munne saw the clothes under his cloak—a shirt that may have been white at one point and a tattered leather vest. "You look familiar."

His words gave her a brief pause. *Could he know about my dream? Otherwise, I can't recall seeing this man before. I would have remembered his eyes.*

"Yes, I could say the same for you as well. Perhaps from a dark clearing in the woods?"

She saw a spark of something in his green eye. *Realization? Pride?*

"Or perhaps somewhere darker, more sinister than an empty godsite," he said quietly.

Munne's hands squeezed together, her knuckles turning white. *He can't possibly be referring to the nightmares. Could this man be the shapeshifter? How else could he know what he knows?* Munne shifted uncomfortably in her seat, her hands loosening their grip.

"Who are you, really?"

The man crossed his arms over his chest. "I'm a simple caravan guide. And you're about to embark on your own journey, yes?"

Thoughts of Auora and the Imalar Woods swam through her head. That was Huntaran's intended journey for her, one that she was begrudgingly accepting of. But the shapeshifter—*this man?*—suggested another path lay before her.

Kherizhan.

Munne leaned further across the table so they could continue to talk quietly. "Tell me about Kherizhan."

He leaned forward as well. "It's quite a dangerous place to get to, unless you're traveling with someone who knows the secret ways. My caravan is heading there, in fact. We depart the day after next and will be making haste to arrive before the end of spring."

Her nose wrinkled, smelling the alcohol on his breath. "Why? There's nothing in those mountains." *Nothing except perhaps the cure to these nightmares.*

He grinned, revealing a golden tooth at the back of his mouth. "There's treasure."

Munne sat back in her chair. She crossed her arms and frowned. *He must be joking.* "No one has lived in those mountains for thousands of years."

"Ah, ah, that's where you're wrong, fair Elviri." He shook a finger at her and pulled something from within his vest. He tossed it onto the table, and Munne saw it was a small black disk, slightly larger than the gold and silver coins of the Elviri. A blue jewel sat in the middle of the disk, worn and faded with time. She looked up at the man, a questioning look on her face. "Go on, take a look at it."

She picked up the disk, turning it over in her hands. It was a heavy little thing, and the jewel could be seen from both sides. Sharp lines had been carved into one side of the disk. Perhaps it was some form of marking or writing? As her thumb brushed against the jewel, she felt a spark of warmth from within it. She held the disk up closer to her face so she could look at the jewel more carefully. Something rippled underneath the surface of the jewel. She flipped the disk over to see if it was just a trick of the light, but she saw the same ripple there as well. She stared at the man again, the puzzled look still on her face.

"The long lost Olaava left behind all sorts of magic little trinkets like that when they crawled under the earth all those years ago," he said, as if it were an explanation.

The Olaava were creatures of myth, disappearing before the end of the Eldest Days. Very little was known about them, even among the Elviri scribes.

Even if the Olaava had existed, surely their trinkets and treasures would have crumbled to dust in the thirteen thousand years since the dawn of the Second Sun. "How could this be considered magic, much less belonging to mythical creatures? Never mind that magic has been gone from Daaria for thousands of years. This is simply a blue gem set into black stone."

His grin returned as he snatched the disk from Munne's hands. He placed it on the table and rubbed the jewel with his forefinger with furious speed. As he pulled his finger back, blue light sparked from the jewel, growing larger. Munne realized it was *fire*. She stared at it in awe, baffled by what she was seeing. The man was smiling like a child with a toy as he danced his finger around in the air, and the flame danced with him. After a moment, he grabbed at the air with his fist, closing it shut. The flame disappeared. He looked back at Munne.

There was silence between them for quite some time. The man patiently waited for Munne to speak, but she had trouble finding the right words. *Magic is real, even if only in such a small trinket. Magic is returning to Daaria. How is this possible? Are the gods returning to us? Could some kind of treasure from Kherizhan help end the war with the Provira once and for all?*

Finally, she spoke, ensuring she had returned to a neutral expression. "And what if treasure isn't what I seek?" She knew that the man would easily be able to call her bluff, but there was more than just the promise of magical artifacts that kept her engaged with him. Her original purpose for entering the tavern was to seek out answers, not raise more questions.

The man laughed, tucking the small disk back into his vest. "Y'know, there are other people who would pack up their entire lives and run to the southeast at the hint of magic."

She doubled down on her bluff. "I have no purpose for it." The Elviri had maintained their power without magic for thirteen thousand years, so she didn't necessarily *need* any magical trinkets. It was a worrying thought, though. He spoke the truth. There were indeed others less fortunate than her who would scramble to take something that promised them wealth and power.

What if the Provira are searching for these trinkets?

His laughter subsided, and his expression became serious. "He said you'd find answers in Kherizhan, about the dreams you and I have been having."

Munne's blood ran cold. *He's not the shapeshifter.* "You were in the clearing with us."

"On the edge, yes. Truth be told, I wasn't sure you could see me," he murmured.

"How were you there?" Munne asked, her eyes still wide with trepidation.

He looked around the tavern, avoiding Munne's gaze. "I'm not sure, but when I laid down this evening, I felt something. *Someone.* I could tell someone else in the valley had these same nightmares—"

"So, you've heard the screaming." Her eyes became unfocused as she realized she was no longer alone in her suffering.

"Every night."

There was more silence between them. *Is he also going to Kherizhan to get rid of these nightmares? Does he know there's a cure there, or is he only going at the behest of the shapeshifter? Has he seen the* Ardashi'ik? Finally, she spoke, regaining focus. "If, perhaps, someone wanted to join you and your companions on your journey?"

He turned his head to Munne and leaned in close, his foul breath filling the air between them once more. "Two days' time. We leave at first light."

She sniffed and shook her head. "No, that won't do. I'll be leaving the same morning for Auora. I cannot be seen leaving the valley with you."

The man tilted his head, puzzled.

Munne held a hand up to him, as if to stop his thoughts from flowing. She wouldn't discuss her business with him, although she was almost certain he knew who she was. "I'll meet you in Auora within two weeks if the mountains are kind in passage. Where will you be staying?"

He looked her over one more time before responding. "The Pike and Pint. But if that's too seedy for a highbo—"

"That will do," she cut him off, glancing at the rest of the tavern. It was still completely empty. "I'll meet you at the Pike and Pint in two weeks. I'll come and ask after my cousin Dalys. Don't leave me waiting."

He chewed on the inside of his cheek and then slowly nodded.

Munne rose from the table, pulling her cloak tightly around her body. "Good evening, then, sir." Without looking back, she left the tavern and returned to her father's manor under the cover of darkness.

CHAPTER XIII: SETH

Anrak continued their fast pace for what felt like hours. Seth's entire body was sore, but he had little choice but to keep up with the spy. When the rain stopped, the sounds of the forest returned. Seth had never journeyed into the woods after the suns went down, and there were noises he had never heard before from creatures he couldn't even imagine what they looked like. His eyes strained to stay open, and exhaustion began to overtake him, dulling the aches in his body. The darkness crept into his peripheral vision, his sight becoming fuzzy. He was unsure if he could fall asleep on the back of a horse, but it seemed like he would find out very soon.

With the rain gone, Anrak slowed his pace to a steady trot, and Nar followed suit. The shift in movement jolted Seth awake. As he bounced in his saddle, he tried to reorient himself with his surroundings. The forest pressed in around them, and there was little room to leave the path. He hoped that either the forest would thin out soon, or the path would become less hazardous. It was a slim hope, though, and he prepared himself for the worst.

There was a distinct shift in the sounds of the forest. The familiar song of the forest birds overtook the strange chittering and buzzing of the nighttime insects and other mysterious creatures. As soon as he heard the birds, Seth looked up to see if he could catch a sign of either of the rising suns. There were no singular rays of light coming through the canopy, but the darkness seemed to let up. It looked like it was going to be another dark and rainy day today.

Anrak slowed his pace, so he matched Nar's speed. "We're almost to Lithalyon. Had to take a detour so we're approaching from the other side—their friendly side," he told Seth. Seth nodded and made a sound of acknowledgement. "Shoulda asked back at the stables, but are you pointed or rounded?"

Exhaustion prevented Seth from controlling his face as he gave Anrak a look of total confusion. Anrak returned the look, apparently confused by Seth's confusion.

"You daft? Your ears, kid. What shape?"

The look slipped from Seth's face. He shook his head and responded, "Sorry, pointed."

Anrak grunted in response. "Very good. You'll fit in just fine. There's a road up ahead that'll take you directly to the city. When they ask what you're doing, tell them you're on leave from your rotation, and you want to visit the museums..."

Seth absorbed the information Anrak passed along. The spy gave Seth a very basic lesson on Lithalyon, as well as the Elviri language, particularly with how to say, "*I'm more comfortable speaking in the common tongue.*" Seth repeated the words to himself over and over, hoping that he would get the pronunciation correct. He knew how to read Elviri writing from the very few books Amias had permitted Evelyn to keep in her library. He had forbidden Evelyn to teach their children how to speak the language, so this was Seth's first real lesson with the language. Anrak also stressed the importance of having his hood down when he approached the city, so that the guards would see that he had naturally pointed ears. They would be much more friendly to an Elviri-appearing individual approaching them from the west.

Seth's hands trembled as he digested all the new information being thrown at him. *I've come this far. The city is close, and with any luck I'll be able to get inside without issue. How fortunate that my ears are long and pointed!*

"*Mal'nyth en elda h'Daarivi.*" He repeated the Elviri phrases several times to himself to calm his nerves, to prove he had everything under control.

Soon enough a break in the tree line revealed a weathered stone road. Anrak paused at the edge, and Seth knew it was their moment of parting. After stepping on the road, he turned to thank the spy, but he was already gone. Seth was now all alone.

He took a deep breath and urged Nar on. The small horse snorted and trotted off in the direction Anrak instructed them to go.

As Seth approached the Elviri city, the forest opened to reveal towering circular walls, a portcullis, and a gatehouse. The walls were made from smooth brown stone and stood several stories tall. The gatehouse was a small but stately building next to the portcullis. Two guards stood outside of the gatehouse, each bearing a lit torch. The forest stopped several paces away from the walls, so Seth's approach to the gate could be seen from many angles. Torches lined the way, leading him directly to the portcullis and the guards. The hairs on his neck prickled and stood on end, and he promptly remembered to toss his hood off, the cloth brushing against the tips of his ears. He felt very exposed but was unsure of what else to do but follow the road. He fought to control the tremble in his hands.

One of the guards noticed him and raised their torch in a gesture to their partner. Seth nodded at them, unsure of what the proper greeting would be. The first guard approached Seth and asked a question in—what he assumed to be—the Elviri tongue. The all-too-familiar swell of panic rose inside of Seth, and he parted his lips to breathe in deeply. The second guard followed, glancing over Seth and Nar. A cold bead of sweat rolled down the back of Seth's neck, his cheeks flushing and his body temperature becoming irregular.

Seth tugged on the reins and stopped Nar. He opened his mouth and managed to stammer out the words Anrak taught him. *"Mal'nyth en elda h'Daarivi."* Even after repeating it to himself for several minutes, the language felt strange on his tongue.

The guards exchanged a look before they returned their gaze to Seth.

"Too much time around the Proma?" the first guard asked in the common tongue, his voice dripping with suspicion.

"A-After spending so much time with them, yes," Seth said, trying hard to control the waver in his voice.

"Where were you stationed at?" the second guard inquired, approaching Nar from the right and continuing their visual inspection.

They're checking for weapons. Seth racked his brain for the names of the cities in Promthus for the reports from the envoys and generals, for *anything*. He blinked. "South of Merrioff, near the border."

"Heard there was bad fighting there," commented the second guard. "But you must have been in good hands with the Warlord."

Seth had heard that title before. Amias had talked about the Warlord in several of his meetings with the *pyredans*. "She was. Truly an inspiration watching her on the field."

The first guard grunted. "I thought that station was mostly composed of soldiers from Elimere and Elimaine. If you don't mind me asking, why have you come all this way south?"

"I need some time away from the war... I wanted to spend my leave in the museums and libraries, t-to reconnect with the gods." The last few words were tricky. Seth only knew a little of the Elviri pantheon but not what they really meant to their people.

The guards seemed pleased enough with the response. The second guard headed back to the gatehouse. The first stepped out of Nar's path and spoke. "The suns will be rising soon. You best get inside and find somewhere to sleep."

The corners of Seth's mouth curled upward into a smile, and he was able to breathe easier. "Thank you." *I can't believe that worked. I must make a convincing Elviri.* He was surprised at how accepting he was of that idea. *Octavia would probably want to tear her ears off—*

With a loud groan, the portcullis opened, jarring Seth from that dark thought. He led Nar inside the walls of Lithalyon. As he passed through, his breath was taken away again. He had never seen a city of this size before, nor one so heavily populated. Houses and shops lined the pristine streets. There was no overgrowth of shrubbery or weeds, and there were streetlamps lining the roads. Trees and buildings coexisted without one dominating and overtaking the other. The level of care and work amazed him, but deep within he felt a twinge of sadness and guilt that Yiradia looked nothing like this. He wondered how beautiful the pyramid and village would have looked if the Provira and Asaszi had worked to restore it, rather than wage their war against the Elviri. Outside the city, the forest stood tall over the walls. Lithalyon seemed like an oasis amidst the trees.

As his eyes lifted to take in the rooftops and treetops, his attention was immediately drawn to the center of the city. A massive tree, taller than the pyramid in Yiradia, towered over Lithalyon. Its overgrown arms reached over the center of town, covering several of the beautiful buildings with shade and protecting them from the suns and moon. Lamps and windows glowed underneath the tree, and Seth could just barely make out the red hues of the leaves above. He had never seen red leaves on a tree before, nor one so massive. The sight of the tree filled him with awe.

He returned his focus to the city streets before him. The street was made from smooth stones and lined with stacked rocks in some places and large roots in others. Shops lined the road he was on. Some shops were made from the same smooth brown stone as the walls, but others were made from wood. It was all so diverse compared to Yiradia, where all the structures were made from the same stone. Nearly all of them were closed at this time of night—*morning*, he corrected himself—but upstairs some buildings had lamps and candles glowing within.

What goods do these people sell? How many live here in the city, and how many more were abroad fighting in Father's war?

As Seth exhaled, exhaustion washed over him. His arms suddenly became heavier to lift, and his eyes strained in the lamplight. Cramps formed in his thighs, pain spreading throughout his legs. Although it hurt, he was happy he could feel something past his knees. A cool breeze blew across the street, and he became very keenly aware just how dirty and drenched in sweat he was. The air was drier here, much less humid than in the rainforest.

I need to find somewhere to bathe and rest. Nar snorted, perhaps in agreement.

Seth looked around as the horse continued down the street, searching for signs or lettering that he could read. The books back in Yiradia didn't often talk about inns or stables, so he struggled to understand certain words and signs. He let out a frustrated sigh and looked for buildings with stables attached to them instead. Perhaps if he found one large enough, chances were it would be attached to an inn.

In between nearly all pairs of buildings stood neatly trimmed trees and shrubbery. Flowers grew in the space between the road and the shop doors. The intermingling of nature and living beings ceased to amaze Seth. He wondered if he brought knowledge about the city back to his mother and father if they would work with the Asaszi to restore Yiradia.

I'm not here for them, he reminded himself. Despite what Octavia asked of him, he was not here to gather *any* knowledge for Amias. He was here because he wanted answers for himself.

Before he could bog himself down with more morbid thoughts of his family, he noticed a building on his right that had a rather large stable attached to it, as well as a welcoming front porch. It stood three stories tall, and many of the windows had lights coming from within. Seth led Nar toward the building, desperately hoping that it was indeed an inn.

As he approached, a young woman exited the stables and walked to the front porch with a basket in her arms. Seth raised a hand in greeting, calling out to her in the common tongue. "Hello! Is this an inn, by chance?"

The woman looked at him with curious eyes, stopping in her tracks. Her lips parted, but she didn't speak for several moments. Once she did, she spoke slowly. "Hello... Yes, this is an inn."

She's not very familiar with the language, Seth thought. He cursed internally, but he had no other choice. He spoke to her again. "Do you have any rooms available?"

She nodded, taking in him and his horse. "Some rooms and some stalls. Come." She gestured for him to follow, and she turned back toward the stables.

He followed her eagerly, and Nar even picked up his pace. Seth stroked the horse's mane, murmuring reassurances that they would rest soon. As she walked, the woman scooped the basket underneath one arm. She stopped in front of an empty stall and extended her free hand toward it—an offering.

He slowed Nar and dismounted, landing clumsily on his feet. He had been riding for far too long, and he needed to reorient himself to using his legs. He quickly massaged both of his thighs, trying to abate the cramps, as well as his lower back. Almost as a reflex, he curled his toes just to make sure he could still feel them, as if landing on his feet moments earlier hadn't happened.

I can do more of this later, preferably in a hot bath.

Seth took hold of Nar's reins and led the horse into the stall, smiling at the woman. She offered a smile in return, but it was clearly strained and seemed like she was very confused by the action. He slung his satchel over his shoulder and began to remove Nar's saddle.

"Someone will take care of your horse. I will take you to a room," the woman said.

Seth looked up at her. "Yes please, thank you. One with a bath?"

Without a response, she left the stables, and he followed her once again. They climbed the stairs onto the front porch, and the woman led Seth inside. The main hall took up most of the first floor. Several wooden tables and chairs filled the room, and against the far wall opposite the stables was a large hearth. A fire burned low in its pit. On the other walls were several trophies of fish and creatures from the forest. Seth couldn't recognize what any of the creatures were. No one else was in the room aside from him and the woman.

They continued over to the staircase, up to the second floor. A long hallway with several doors stretched before them, and on the opposite end was another staircase leading up to the floor above them. The woman moved quickly down the hallway, stopping in front of one of the doors on the far end. She reached her free hand under her skirts and produced a ring of keys. She unlocked the door and pushed it open, taking a step back. She extended her free hand toward it.

Seth leaned into the room and peeked around. The furnishings were simple but intriguing to him. To his immediate left was a wooden tub, half-filled with water, along soap and a cloth robe. On the wall opposite the door was a window covered by worn drapes. A wooden bed with a large blanket was tucked in the far corner next to the window. Seth wondered what sort of material he would be lying on. He was only accustomed to lumpy blankets and furs. At the foot of the one bed was a wooden chest with two clasps, presumably for him to place his belongings in. On the wall opposite the bed was a table with a large unlit candle placed in the middle and two chairs.

He turned back to the woman and nodded. She inclined her head, lowering her hand. Seth moved into the room, but then stopped. He reached into his satchel and withdrew the sack of money Octavia had given him.

"How much—?"

"Five for one night. Two for one dinner."

"And for a bath?"

The woman's brow furrowed. "No extra. I'll send up hot water."

Seth reached into the sack and withdrew five coins, handing them over to the woman. She took them and tucked them away into one of her skirts. She worked the one key off her keyring, handing it over to Seth. He took it and thanked her. Without another word, she left for the stairs.

He returned to the room and closed the door behind him. Seth tucked the sack of coins back into his satchel, and after a moment he slipped the key in as well. He removed his satchel and placed it on the table next to the candle before moving over to the bed. Glancing it over, he pulled back the blankets to reveal a cloth mattress. Curious he pressed his hand into the material, gauging how comfortable it felt against his skin. It seemed much more comfortable than the stone bed he slept on in the pyramid. He might not even need to create a nest of blankets to raise himself off the bed.

While waiting for the woman to return, Seth sat at the table and continued massaging his thighs and knees. After several minutes, the woman returned, along with two men, each carrying large pails of steaming water. They poured the water into the tub, bowed, then made their exit, pulling the door shut behind them.

With great effort, Seth rose to his feet and hobbled over to the tub, dipping his fingers in to gauge the temperature—warm enough to soothe his aching body, but not as hot as the baths back in Yiradia. It would do for today, and more importantly, it would get him clean.

The bath felt good on his sore muscles, and he stayed in the tub until the water was cool. With great reluctance, he stood up and covered himself with the robe. He fished the room key out of his bag and locked the door, then turned to the room. A small rush of excitement passed through him. There were so many new experiences he was about to face in this city. His hands trembled with anticipation as he crossed to the bed and pulled the blanket further back, creating space to crawl under. As soon as his head touched the pillow, he lost consciousness, exhaustion finally overtaking him.

Rays of sunlight slipped past the drapes and danced across Seth's face. He wrinkled his nose and squeezed his eyes shut, wanting nothing more than to roll over and ignore the suns. As he moved, the mattress underneath crinkled and rustled, and his eyes flew open.

I'm not in the pyramid anymore.

He was in Lithalyon, in disguise, in the bed of an inn. He was going to find its libraries today. A smile spread across his lips as he reached for the blankets to toss them back, turning his torso to slide his feet across—

His lower body wasn't moving.

Seth pushed himself up onto his elbows, tearing the blankets back away from his legs. They were still there. He could still see his shins and feet sticking out from beneath the bath robe. But he couldn't *feel* them. Panic overtook him as his eyes darted around the room. *Why can't I feel my legs anymore? Did someone do something to me while I was sleeping? But I locked the door. Was it the bathwater? The soap?*

He parted his lips, breathing quickening to the point where he needed to suck air in through his mouth. From the back of his throat, Seth felt a scream clawing its way into his mouth. As he inhaled, preparing to unleash whatever noise forced its way out of him, his eyes locked onto his satchel.

The decanter.

Has Szatisi's cure failed?

Seth's mind raced. His father had been so sure that Szatisi's cure would work. Amias told him that it would work. He *needed* it to work.

Without his legs to assist him, Seth shifted his weight to his elbows and crawled out of bed. Fortunately, it didn't stand very high off the ground, so he could reach the floor without straining his muscles. He placed his elbows on the floorboards and pulled the rest of his body out, his limp legs making a loud *thump* as they hit the floor.

I can't get stuck here. In this inn, in this city. I have no means of escape. My wheelchair is back at the pyramid. I'll be discovered. Will the Elviri find me first, or Father? The thought of either group finding him filled him with immense dread. Surety of death either way.

What about Octavia? Or Mother?

The table also stood fairly low to the ground. He pushed himself up so he could reach the tabletop and pulled the satchel off. With fumbling fingers, he undid the clasp on the front and shoved his hand inside, searching desperately for the crystal decanter.

Where is it?

One of his knuckles brushed against the decanter. He grabbed it as if his life depended on it and yanked it out of the satchel. He removed the stopper, and then raised the decanter to his lips. He drank a little more than before but left most of the liquid within. His hands trembled as he replaced the stopper and closed his eyes.

Within moments he felt the same heat from the night prior, and he was able to flex his left foot. Soreness seeped back into his legs, but it wasn't nearly as painful as yesterday. Seth let out a sigh and leaned back against the bed. His heart thumped loudly in his chest as the adrenaline subsided. *So, it isn't a cure, not completely. It's still in progress...* He was thankful to find that out on his own, rather than in the presence of his father. Amias would have made him drink the whole decanter...

His face twisted into a grimace as he tasted the bitter, vile taste of the liquid. It was truly horrible, but he would have to drink it again, possibly many times, before he returned home and had to feign innocence. Like he hadn't tasted freedom just days prior.

I need to be careful of how much I drink and when. Best keep track of what time I drink it, and what time I lose the feeling in my legs. This decanter has to last until I get back to Yiradia.

Seth pulled himself to his feet and changed into a new set of clothes, preparing to descend to the lower level of the inn. He hadn't brought a journal or anything to write with, so that would be one of the first things he'd do. Food and drink were also needed. Before he left the room, he pulled back the drapes to see bright sunlight and busy streets in the city below. The massive tree dominated the skyline, standing taller than any other building in Lithalyon. Red and gold leaves cast a warm glow on the buildings underneath its boughs. He made a note to visit the tree before he left, for nothing else than to gaze upon it from a closer distance.

Seth gathered up the satchel and stepped out into the hallway. He locked the door behind him, slipping the key back into the bag and descending the stairs. He kept an eye out for any other guests or workers.

There were a handful more people in the main room than there were that morning. One person, a woman, stood behind the bar while a man swept the floor nearby. Two guests sat at a table close to the hearth, talking in low voices. Seth noticed that they had no plates or mugs in front of them. He would probably need to find food somewhere else. He nodded and crossed over to the front door, pulling it open and breathing in the city air. The first thing he noticed about Lithalyon was how sweet the air was. Despite the crowds of houses and shops, the lingering smell of flowers was in the air. The corners of his lips curled up into a smile, and he followed the road further into the city.

Seth caught himself looking around to take in all the different kinds of shops and people. There were mostly Elviri on the streets and in the shops, although there were a few Proma as well. Without looking closely at anyone's ears, it was like being back in Yiradia surrounded by Provira.

The races look so similar, no wonder it was easy for me to get into the city. But the Elviri appear to be so much more peaceful and happier than the Provira.

Guards patrolled the streets, but they would stop to idly chat with a store owner or browse their selection of goods. Children played outside their homes, their laughter floating through the air. Although he couldn't understand what most of the people were saying, it was pleasant to hear the chatter of people going about their everyday lives. Seth was overcome with awe and envy.

They all just mingle together, blissfully ignorant of what goes on beyond their walls.

He noticed a metalsmith's shop on the right side of the road that shared a forge with a glassblowing shop next door. The metalsmith paced around the forge, shuffling between several tools and tables. Seth veered off the road and climbed the steps outside the shop, passing through the open door. The inside was warm and crammed with several wooden tables stacked high with various goods for sale—cutlery, cooking pans, tools, and even some luxurious items like candle stands. As he inspected a display of horseshoes, he thought of the metalsmiths back in Yiradia. The only goods they produced were arms and armor.

The Elviri don't seem affected by this war. Are the Provira nothing but a nuisance to them? Is Father fighting a losing battle?

Seth left the shop, pushing such thoughts out of his mind. One metal-smith's shop wasn't an indicator of the entire Elviri army. Perhaps this one smith had not been paid to craft goods for the soldiers in need.

Continuing on, the road opened up into a large open plaza. Surrounding it were several bars and taverns with spacious gardens facing the plaza. The sound of laughter and boisterous conversation came from several of the establishments. Seth's stomach grumbled. With no particular place chosen, he set forth to get some food and drink.

He heard the common tongue being spoken by some of the patrons in a garden on the opposite side of the plaza. Two signs hung over the archway leading into the garden, one in the Elviri tongue, the other one in the common tongue with Rindel's Canopy painted on it with elegant penmanship. Stone tables and chairs lined the outer hedges of the garden. The center was clear and empty, perhaps for musicians to set up, or for revelers to dance. He requested his meal—a cup of tea and some dish called Rindel's Bounty—and handed over a couple of coins inside. He returned to the garden to sit. It didn't take long for someone to bring him his meal—a cup of steaming tea and a plate of meat-filled pastries and sliced fruits. Most of the food was unfamiliar to him, but it was delicious.

After savoring his meal, he returned to the plaza and gathered his bearings. It was past midday. To his right was the rest of the plaza, and the road he came from. To his left were three roads, two veering off toward the massive tree, and the third going back to the outer wall. He opted to follow the first of the two roads to the tree. From what he could see on the horizon, several large buildings stood underneath the tree. Perhaps one of them was the library he sought.

The buildings on that side of the city were older, and there were signs of the passage of time and reparations made. Where stones had come loose or chipped away, stoneworkers had replaced them with sturdier, more beautiful material. The colors of the old and new contrasted and painted a picture of its history. There was something prideful and elegant in how the Elviri cared for their lands, choosing instead to heal it rather than tear it all down. The tree standing before him was a living testament to that.

As Seth got closer to the tree, he realized that it stood on top of a small hill, most likely made up of its own roots. There were a handful of buildings on the hill with the tree while most were below. It seemed that most homes had gardens with several trees of their own, as well as a plethora of flowers. The road curved around the side of the hill, approaching the northern wall. There were more roots lining the pathways than stones as he got closer to the majestic tree. The air was even sweeter in this portion of the city. Red and gold leaves floated down from the sky, decorating rooftops and walkways with their colors. Seth couldn't stop marveling at the beauty of the city.

Although there were several large, attractive buildings in the part of town he had entered, he found himself drawn to one that stood several stories tall with many stained-glass windows and carvings. The surrounding grounds were filled with trees and flowers with several paths winding through them. The main entrance was a solid wood door with intricate symbols carved into it, and its handles were made from a gold precious metal, shining as if never touched. Drawn to the door, Seth pulled it open, taking in the sight before him.

The main hall was a large chamber open all the way to the roof. Sunlight poured in from all the windows, creating several colorful murals on the floor. Most were sigils of the different Elviri provinces—three mountain peaks, a pine tree paired with a crescent moon, and a curved tree paired with a sun. He recognized them from the descriptions in several of the *pyredans'* reports to his father. Above the entrance was the largest stained-glass window depicting two gold spheres—a larger one placed in front of one much smaller—on a blue background. Seth had heard his mother and father mention this one—the sigil of the Second Sun.

Further into the main hall was a large oaken desk in the middle of the room, and beyond that were rows upon rows of bookcases. His mother's description didn't do it justice. The library was gorgeous and filled with more books than Seth had ever seen in his life.

Where to even begin? I wish Mother was here to see this.

Two Elviri, an older woman sitting behind the desk and a young man close to Seth's age standing in front, were at the front desk having a conversation. They wore matching gold and green robes made from a very fancy material.

Seth approached them slowly, noticing they were speaking in the Elviri language. "Excuse me," he said in the common tongue, raising his hand to greet the two. "I'm looking for some books on a certain topic?"

The two Elviri turned to look at him. The woman had difficulty hiding her annoyance, while the young man had a slight smile on his face. "Which?" the woman asked abruptly.

Seth was taken aback, although he wasn't sure why. He had, after all, interrupted their conversation. "I-I'm looking for books on the Elviri-Asaszi Wars, as well as some writing material."

The woman looked up at the man, an eyebrow arched. "Lisanthir can assist you with that." She spoke as if that was the only answer Seth needed to hear. She looked back down at the desk and sorted through some papers.

Is he knowledgeable on that particular subject? How fortunate for me if so.

The young man, Lisanthir, picked up a pen and loose pieces of paper and turned toward Seth, allowing him to focus on his face. Black hair fell to his shoulders, curling slightly at the ends. Two strands of hair framed his angular face, a gold bead hanging from the end of each. Looking into his eyes was like looking upon the rainforest with many swirling shades of green. The way his lips twisted up into a smile made Seth's cheeks flush. He was immediately drawn to how attractive the Elviri was, something he had never noticed about any of the Provira in Yiradia.

"Here. I can show you to that part of our history section. I recently completed my lifepaths and began working in the library. The wars are some of my favorite years to study." Lisanthir's voice was quiet and warm. More welcoming than the other Elviri Seth had spoken to thus far. Seth took the paper and pen from him with an appreciative nod of the head. "Don't mind Scribe Haedras, she treats everyone with the same level of contempt," Lisanthir said with a wink and smile.

The woman glared daggers at Lisanthir. "*Esci enthi'ris dyrk.*"

Seth glanced between the two, knowing from her tone that she was insulting the other Elviri.

Lisanthir merely laughed it off and beckoned for Seth to follow him, walking further into the library. Seth followed quickly, avoiding looking in the direction of the angry woman, hearing her move around papers and books rather forcefully.

"What did she say? I-I didn't quite catch it…" Seth inquired.

"Something about the arrogance of youth—don't worry about her. She hates being placed at the front desk and answering questions, but Scribe Tollanor is on leave visiting the returning soldiers in Elimere…" Lisanthir glanced back at Seth and trailed off. "Pardon me, I can get carried away sometimes… Oh, and you'll have to forgive me. I don't frequently use the common tongue."

"You speak it well enough," Seth commented, looking around the main hall. The height of the bookcases distracted him. They stood several feet above his own head, and they were filled with bound books waiting to be opened. Stools and ladders were nearby to access the higher shelves. Gatherings of chairs were placed throughout the library for visitors to bring their newfound hordes of books to and curl up to read them.

Lisanthir chuckled. "Well, thank you, I suppose. Although it is strange that another Elviri would prefer speaking in the common tongue, rather than our own."

"Yes, I've… heard that a lot since I arrived," Seth mumbled. They reached the end of the main hall where two staircases framed the massive stained-glass window of the sigil of the Elviri lands.

"When was that?" Lisanthir asked, leading Seth up the staircase on the left side of the window.

"Just before dawn," Seth responded and placed his hand on the railing to guide, still looking out at the library.

Two wings branched off from the main hall, and Seth saw more stained-glass windows shaped like people in them although he couldn't tell who specifically. After a certain point, all he could see was the floor above them, so he shifted focus to the stairs and the young man in front of him.

And that young man was continuously throwing looks over his shoulder at Seth. He felt his cheeks flush again, and he immediately looked away, looking at something—*anything*—and settled on the stairs underneath his feet.

"I-I just got used to being around the Proma, is all," Seth said, almost defensively.

"Do you live in Auora? Or were you stationed in Promthus? I don't recall seeing you in any of the lifepaths, and we seem close in age."

They turned and climbed up another set of stairs to the third floor.

Seth began to get overwhelmed with the number of questions Lisanthir had for him. "No. Yes. I-I was given leave not too long ago, and decided I wanted to come to the libraries for a few days."

At the top of the landing, Lisanthir led Seth toward the left wing down a row of bookshelves. The ceiling above them was pitched, and several chandeliers hung from beams crossing the open space. Most of the candles were lit, but some had blown out and made it cozy and dim. There were hardly any other people in that section of the library.

Seth felt that he could curl up with a stack of books and not emerge from the library for several days. *If only.*

Lisanthir stopped and gestured to one of the middle shelves on a towering bookcase. "Starting on this shelf, you'll find several general history books on the Elviri-Asaszi Wars, mostly written by various Elviri scribes during the Second Sun. We should also have some journals from soldiers who were alive toward the end of the Eldest Days." He turned toward Seth, dropping his voice to a soft murmur. "If you're looking for any specific information, please let me know, and I'd be happy to assist."

Seth parted his lips to respond, but Lisanthir walked away before he could. He was left in between the rows of bookcases, his cheeks a deep scarlet. An electrifying chill raced down his spine. His gaze flicked between the spines of the books, the wooden floors, and the direction of the stairs where Lisanthir was currently walking.

What was that all about?

He shut his eyes and took a deep breath before turning back toward the books. He willed himself to focus on locating the first book he would read.

Seth ended up grabbing three books to start with and found himself a chair nearby to sit and read. The first book was rather small and provided more of a timeline of events rather than any detailed analysis of what happened. Seth already knew most of it from the books back in Yiradia. He didn't spend much time flipping through its pages.

The second book focused more on the development of Elviri culture at the end of the Eldest Days, particularly the development of Lithalyon as a beacon of art and music. The library's history was detailed in the book, as well as the development of the wall surrounding the city. Although he took great personal interest in this book, he ultimately put it to the side in favor of the third book, *The Downfall of the Asaszi.*

The prose was intriguing, and heavily biased against the Asaszi. There was a plethora of details about the tactics the Elviri used to invade the rainforests of Moonyswyn and eradicate the Asaszi at the end of the Eldest Days. There were mentions of the Asaszi leader, but he was given no name; he was simply referred to as a living demon. With his death, the Asaszi all but dissolved with their forces killed or scattered to the wind. The author also included mention of a "cursed she-beast" whose "plans" were rendered useless, and how fortunate that was.

Who are the demon and the she-beast? The books back in Mother's library never mentioned them. Perhaps I could inquire...?

"I thought you might still be here." A warm voice called out to him from the end of the bookcases.

Looking up, he saw Lisanthir holding a lantern. Seth tried to swallow but found that his throat had run dry. His tongue felt heavy in his mouth. "Oh, ah, yes, I've just been reading..."

Lisanthir chuckled softly, walking closer to where he was sitting. Something inside of him twisted and pinched. "The suns will be setting soon. Not that the library actually closes, but most people depart at sunset," he said.

"O-Oh. I suppose I should gather my things." Seth stood, acutely aware that he didn't, in fact, have things to gather. Hunger gnawed at his stomach.

"You're welcome to stay if you'd like. I just wanted to check in and see if you needed anything before I left." Lisanthir looked over the books that Seth had picked out, arching an eyebrow at the book Seth held in his hands. "Ah, one of the praised volumes by Beywyn. Is this your first time reading his work?"

Seth glanced down at the book in his hands and then back up at Lisanthir. "Ahh, yes, it is. The title caught my attention."

"It's quite a sweeping statement, isn't it? *Downfall of the Asaszi*. It sounds so final. But that's where Beywyn was wrong."

It was Seth's turn to raise an eyebrow. "What do you mean he was wrong?" he asked.

"Well, it was certainly a downturn for the Asaszi. But it wasn't the end. That came over a thousand years later in the third, truly final war between the Elviri and Asaszi."

That wasn't covered in any of the books he pulled from the shelves. He opened his mouth, shut it almost immediately, but then decided to go ahead and ask. "Do you... Could you elaborate? I mean, it wasn't covered in any of these books. I don't know much about it, to be honest."

A spark appeared in Lisanthir's eyes. "Well, I was leaving here to get dinner somewhere. You could join me, if you'd like, and we could talk about it?"

Before he could second-guess his actions, Seth nodded. "That would be lovely. My name's Calydrian, by the way. Pardon for not introducing myself sooner," he said and walked up to Lisanthir.

"Calydrian," He was rewarded with a smile that brought about the now-familiar spark of heat inside of him. "I know where we can go for dinner." For the second time that day, he followed the handsome Elviri through the library.

CHAPTER XIV: SETH

Lisanthir took Seth to a tavern near the library. It was built from old stones and was surrounded by four older trees. The tavern, the Four Adavas, was aptly named after its surroundings. It was a rather cozy establishment with a small indoor dining area. The outdoor dining area was much larger and where most of the patrons were seated. Lisanthir had asked which area Seth would prefer, and he opted for the outdoor patio. They crossed through the interior, and Seth noticed the paintings hanging on the walls. Some were of beautiful landscapes while others were of smaller subjects like flowers or people. The smell of roasting meats and baked goods wafted through the air, and Seth's stomach grumbled loudly.

I haven't eaten since I left yesterday, he realized.

They passed through the doors to the outdoor patio, and Seth once again marveled at the way the Elviri melded nature with their surroundings. Above their heads was a lattice canopy laced with blooming white and yellow flowers. Luscious green ivy wrapped around the wooden posts. The tables and chairs were made from metal with intricate floral patterns. Candles were lit on every table. In one corner of the patio, a couple of musicians were playing an upbeat tune. Several patrons cheered and tossed them coins. Servers wove between tables, delivering mugs of drink and plates of food. Lisanthir waved to one of them, and they gave him a smile and gestured toward one of the tables farther away from the musicians. Lisanthir turned to Seth, a look of inquiry on his face. Seth nodded in return, and they sat at the table.

"I dine here fairly often." Lisanthir had to raise his voice to be heard over the music. "I have friends who work here, both in the kitchens and on the stage."

"Oh! You could recommend dishes for me, then," Seth responded, smiling to hide his panic. *I don't recognize half of these foods. What will taste good?*

"Certainly. What kind of food do you like?" Lisanthir asked.

"Well, I always enjoy warm baked bread, and I'm partial to citrus."

"Good taste! What about meats?"

Seth contemplated his answer before speaking. "I prefer pork to chicken or beef. Fish is nice, too."

"I think I know what to order, then." Lisanthir waved down a server and conveyed his request in the Elviri language.

A few moments later they had two mugs of local red wine in front of them, along with a large, decorative wooden board loaded up with fresh fruit, various sliced cheeses, chunks of warm baked bread, and an assortment of fresh cured meats.

Lisanthir thanked the server as Seth began plucking fruits and bread off the board. As he chewed on a slice of bread, he saw Lisanthir watching him, a corner of his mouth curled up into a slight smile.

"Sorry," Seth mumbled around the bread. He paused and swallowed, finding it suddenly difficult to do so. "Didn't eat enough at midday, I suppose."

Lisanthir chuckled. "No, please, be my guest. I was just going to ask if you needed help identifying what was what," he said.

Seth looked over the board, realizing he didn't recognize everything that was on there. He had known what the orange slices were before he began eating one and recognized a couple of the berries as well. Bread was bread, so that didn't matter as much, although the chunk he took a bite out of had a citrus-like flavor that was very pleasant. He didn't recognize the cheeses or meats, nor any of the other fruits.

He pointed to the cured meats. "What about these?"

Lisanthir explained what everything was, and where it grew within the city. Blue grapes, blackberries, orange-honey bread, olive bread, two different cuts of cured pork, and a cut of cured fish.

"It's a shame that we can't trade our fruits with many other places," Lisanthir said with a frown. "I suppose there's always the Proma border towns. And the Icarites will sometimes pass through and trade our fruits for various crafts and goods." He sighed.

Seth watched him pick up a slice of the meat and one of the cheeses, stacked them on one of the chunks of bread, and took a bite from it. It looked rather delicious, so he started picking up the components to assemble one himself. The musicians ended their current song, and the other patrons clapped and cheered. After a moment they quieted down and returned to their own meals and conversations.

"Ah, but we were going to discuss some bits of history," Lisanthir said during the lull. He looked up at Seth. "I suppose during Beywyn's time, it did seem like the end. He saw the second sun climb into the sky. Surely a sign from the gods that it was all over."

Seth had discussed that before with his parents, although it was a long time ago. Before the accident. He was reading one of the books in his mother's library, an epic tale of Ysillis the Gladiator. It had only mentioned one sun in the sky, not two like he was used to. After approaching his parents about it, they explained that at the end of the Eldest Days, a second sun rose into the sky and ushered in a new age meant for mortals—the end of the gods' time on Daaria.

Lisanthir continued, "There was a third uprising from the Asaszi about one thousand years into the Second Sun. It was primarily directed at the Proma. The Elviri weren't really involved until the Asaszi began spreading a plague across Promthus. That forced their hand during the time of a *Se'vi* who wasn't... in the best place to lead a war."

A plague? Seth recognized that. His face lit up with pride—one of his father's lessons was finally paying off. But surely that wasn't what Lisanthir had meant by the final downfall of the Asaszi, not after so many of their sweeping victories. "Oh, when the Asaszi almost destroyed Auora? After slaying the current king? I think they also nearly killed one of the Elviri heirs."

Lisanthir's eyes widened, and he seemed to see Seth in a different light. "Yes, it was. I thought you were unfamiliar with it?"

Seth's confidence wavered. "Oh, um, I read about it while I was abroad. A long time ago," he replied.

"I didn't think the Proma kept records from that time in history." Lisanthir settled back in his chair, leaning back from the table.

"Um, I don't recall if it was a book written by one of the Proma or not."

"Well, I suppose there are things we can learn from each other." Lisanthir flashed him a grin before popping a berry into his mouth.

That smile both calmed and excited Seth. He brought his mug of wine to his lips, taking his time with his drink.

"So, what else do you study in your spare time?"

Seth lowered his mug. "I know a lot about Moonyswyn," he said without thinking. He saw Lisanthir raise an eyebrow. *Wait, no, bad.* "W-well, as much as someone can on the frontline. I'm also interested in the mythology and ancient characters of the Eldest Days."

"Myths and legends are some of my favorite stories to read. When I'm not busy with other work, that is."

Much to Seth's relief, they stuck with the topic of mythology and other more mild interests during the dinner. Their server brought out their main plates not too long after the charcuterie board. Seth only knew what was on his plate because he and Lisanthir discussed it prior to ordering—a roasted cut of fish with vegetables from the local gardens. The name of the fish had sounded familiar to him. Maybe the Asaszi cooked it back in Yiradia? It tasted very good, regardless. Their mugs of wine were refilled once or twice, and Seth couldn't recall another dinner where he felt this relaxed and warm. He was rather starting to like Lithalyon.

"Come, let me walk you back to where you're staying, Calydrian," Lisanthir said with a slight slur as they left the tavern.

Seth blushed but took no action to hide it. "Oh, you don't have to. It's somewhere near the front of town, I think... I'll manage, don't worry."

Lisanthir let out a *pah* and started walking in the direction of the town center. "I've decided that you're my guest in this town, so I want to ensure you are taken care of. Go on, lead the way."

Seth's stomach twisted in a most pleasant manner. "Alright then, follow me."

They walked through the streets of Lithalyon together while Lisanthir told Seth all about the various shops and prominent members of society. The Hill District, as the area around the massive tree was called, was home to the affluent citizens of Lithalyon, as well as the art galleries, museums, and places of study. The Chieftains, Caedwyn and Faelwyn, lived in a manor directly underneath the tree.

As they passed through the plaza in the center of the city, Lisanthir explained that many events were hosted there for various festivals and gatherings.

"In fact, our celebration of *Henayth'mar* starts tomorrow. The chill of winter doesn't quite reach us here, but our farmers still put on a grange display of local produce. There'll be much eating and dancing, and if you're so inclined, I would be honored to take you to the celebration." Lisanthir stopped and brushed a strand of hair behind his ear.

A harvest festival sounds lovely. If the Asaszi hosted one, there'd be nothing but roots and leaves. Nothing pretty to look at. Wait, Lisanthir wants to take me *to the festival?* Seth blinked and realized they were standing outside of the inn he was staying at. "This is where I'm staying," he blurted, a bit more abrupt and awkward than he anticipated.

If he upset Lisanthir, he couldn't tell from his facial expression. Instead, the man looked over the inn before *tsking*. "Not a terrible place to stay... Are the beds comfortable?"

"Enough, yeah," Seth responded, looking at the ground. He really hoped he hadn't upset him.

"Well... This is where I make my leave." Lisanthir took a step back and bowed before Seth. "Thank you, Calydrian, for joining me for dinner, and allowing me to walk you home."

"Thank you for the company," Seth murmured, a smile on his face.

Their eyes met for a moment before Lisanthir turned and departed.

Seth turned toward the inn and entered, feeling as if he were walking on clouds. The smile remained plastered on his face as he climbed the stairs to the second floor. At the landing, he lost his footing and stumbled a bit, catching himself from falling at the last moment. He sighed and pushed himself up. As his weight shifted to his feet, he stumbled again. The smile faded from his face and his eyes narrowed.

Surely, I didn't have that *much to drink. What's happening?*

He cautiously took a step forward and realized that he could barely feel his foot or his toes. The feeling crept further up his legs. Panic overtook him as he realized Szatisi's cure was wearing off again. He gritted his teeth and moved as quickly as he could into his room, placing a hand on the wall to support himself.

Seth closed the door behind him, removed the decanter from his satchel, and placed it on the table before he collapsed on the bed. All feeling in his feet had disappeared. He scowled, panic subsiding and replaced with frustration. At least he had gotten through the day before it wore off. Hopefully, he would have enough to get through the next day. He opted to not drink any tonight because what would the use of his legs be while he was sleeping? He had to save every last drop of the liquid for when he was awake.

He worked his shoes off, and then his shirt, and then dragged himself under the blankets. He laid his head back onto the pillow, closing his eyes. Sleep eluded him for several minutes, which gave him time to listen to the inn and his surroundings. Though his window was closed, he heard faint murmurs of people walking through the streets. He heard the muffled sound of music coming from the common room below. Footsteps of varying speeds and weights moved up and down the hallway outside. It reminded him of the pyramid and how he could hear the sounds of the rainforest outside. Similar but different. It lulled him into a comfortable rest, and shortly thereafter he fell asleep.

<hr />

When Seth awoke, he wasn't surprised at his inability to move his legs. He just reached for the decanter and drank a few precious drops. Soon he was wiggling his toes and pulling his boots on. After another night of rest, he felt that he was ready to focus on the library and uncover some kind of useful information. *But what would be useful?* The history of the Elviri-Asaszi wars was certainly intriguing, but he wasn't sure if it held the answers he sought. Or what his sister sought. Not that he wanted to help her or their father.

Will Lisanthir be at the library today? The young Elviri's laughter filled his head, and he wanted nothing more than to hear it again. *It was so nice to spend an evening with someone and just enjoy conversation and food. I could never do that back home.*

Seth passed through the main room of the inn quickly and quietly, placing a few coins on the counter for the man behind the counter. Today he brought his satchel with him, including the decanter, so that he wouldn't run the risk of losing feeling in his legs before he made it back to the inn. Outside the birds sang, and Seth nearly stopped in his tracks. He had heard birds singing before, but these birds were different from the ones in the jungle. Unlike the kytling and his companions, these birdsongs were melodic and sweet. Very pleasant. He wondered how his kytling was doing back at Yiradia.

Decorations were being hung in the central plaza—garland, silks, and banners displaying winter finery. Farmers and crafters put together different displays. Wagons filled the streets as the city prepared for the festival. Seth tried his best to stay out of anyone's way, but he caught himself staring after various carts and groups of people. One couple was riding in on a large wagon, the back filled with many orange, green, and yellow gourds. Several other Elviri helped unload the gourds, talking and laughing while comparing sizes. A herd of children were helping decorate various stalls. It was incredible how the Elviri all came together to prepare.

And they did this often? Impressive. We've never done anything like this back in Yiradia. A pang of sadness hit, and he resumed his walk with haste.

The celebration wasn't limited to just the town square; the rest of the city joined in as well. As Seth crossed into the Hill District, he noticed more decorations strewn about on the lampposts and garden walls. Red leaves floated down from the towering tree, littering rooftops and walkways. Blue and gold banners hung from several balconies and windows. He knew he would never see anything as colorful and pleasant back home.

Even the library underwent a transformation for the festival. Some of the scribes were outside hanging garlands and glass ornaments in the trees. Another pair stood by the main door, each holding a different banner to display. He passed by them quickly, not wanting to interfere with their work.

As he entered the library, his eyes immediately darted to the front desk, searching for Lisanthir. The Elviri stood the desk, looking up to see who was entering the library. When their eyes met, Seth inhaled sharply. His stomach tightened just as painfully as it had yesterday. *What kind of magical grip does this town have over me, that an Elviri has stirred these kinds of feelings in me? I didn't think I was capable of feeling this kind of affection for anyone, let alone one of the "enemy". Not that I really consider the Elviri my enemy anymore. But would Lisanthir think if he knew where I'm really from?*

Lisanthir smiled at him, and all his doubts washed away. "Calydrian! Good morning," he called as he approached Seth.

"Good morning, Lisanthir," Seth responded, keenly aware of how his name rolled off his tongue. He felt good saying the Elviri's name, it gave him comfort. He wished he could hear how his real name sounded coming from Lisanthir's lips.

"Continuing your reading from yesterday?" Lisanthir asked.

"Actually, I want to look at some of the other historic books, not just about the wars." Seth caught himself talking very quickly, more so than usual. "W-would you be able to show me where those are?"

Lisanthir smiled again. If he had any comment about Seth's speech or request, he kept it to himself. He led the way back into the library without another word. They stayed on the lowest level and turned toward the left wing past a couple of rows.

"The histories are typically near Aeona," Lisanthir said as they came to a stop, mindful of the other patrons.

Seth looked at the back wall and realized who the people in the stained-glass windows were—the Elviri gods. He stared at a blonde woman surrounded by bright blue and yellow shapes. Her eyes were closed, and in her hands, she held a star. That must be Aeona. Seth couldn't remember what her domain was, and the window did nothing to help with that.

Seth felt a squeeze on his upper arm. He looked down to see Lisanthir's hand grasping his arm gently. "Let me know if there's anything I can help with, okay?"

He looked up into the Elviri's eyes and found himself unable to respond. He managed to nod, which elicited another smile from Lisanthir. He couldn't help himself but grin in return.

After what felt like a lifetime, Lisanthir pulled his hand away from Seth's arm, almost as if he forgot it had been there. The Elviri cleared his throat. "I was wondering... You never gave me a response last night about the festival." Panic must have flashed across Seth's eyes because Lisanthir chuckled. "The festival begins tonight. I'd like to take you if you'll be around. I know you were only staying here for a few days for your studies, but—"

"Yes, I'd really like to. Yes," Seth interrupted before he could stop himself or think about his response.

Lisanthir beamed at him. "Great! I'll come back shortly after sundown to walk you to the plaza." Without giving Seth a chance to think about the exchange, he left him in the middle of the histories.

Seth opened and closed his mouth several times, trying to fully process what had just happened. Even his thoughts were incoherent. All he knew was that his skin felt like it was on fire, and he hoped the flame never went out.

Seth eventually regained enough sense to acquire a small stack of books and find a quiet alcove with a table and candle stand. As Seth opened the cover of an ancient tome, a small slip of parchment fell out. He watched it float to the floor before bending over to pick it up. The parchment felt old and brittle, and he feared it would crumble beneath his fingers. He held it up so the nearby candlelight fell across it. As he flipped the parchment over, he saw the faintest outline of jagged lines and dots. *Asaszi writing.* Seth narrowed his eyes and tried to translate.

Underneath the Syk'thas. Volume six. page thirty.

Seth rose, glancing around with sudden anxiety. *Where did this parchment come from? Who wrote this? What is the note referring to?*

He found himself moving without thinking. Rushing down the aisle, he looked up at the stained-glass windows. *Syk'thas.* The word translated loosely to "usurper". Although the word "usurper" was common enough in Asaszi history, only one had been given a special title—Ceyo, goddess of the Elviri. It wasn't difficult to find the window in her likeness. It was in the middle of the wall of windows, her red hair glowing softly in the mid-morning light. Seth passed by several rows of bookshelves and tables as he walked to the back wall.

As he approached the last row of books, he turned and looked for "volume six", whatever that was. Although it was only glass behind him, he felt the intent gaze of Ceyo as he browsed the books. The section seemed to mostly be reference materials, ranging from atlases of the Elviri lands to dictionaries for children learning their writing. The titles seemed to blur together as his fingers trailed along the leather spines of each book—*Rivers of Elifyn, Writing Elviri Script, Elimaine Wildlife Volume VI, A Traveler's Guide to the Elimere Mountains, An Atlas of Elviri Lands*—

Seth stopped. He took a step back and then turned on his heels, his hand hovering over a rather large tan book. He pulled it from the shelf and let his gaze linger on the cover. *Elimaine Wildlife Volume VI: Godsites.* There wasn't an author's name, nor any other kind of marking. The other books in the series were missing as well. He opened the front cover and thumbed through the pages. Elegant Elviri script filled the pages, detailing the different birds seen flying overhead near the godsites, the types of deer in between the trees, and the insects crawling over the stones. He marveled at the dedication the author—whoever they were—had when writing everything down. He admired a rather beautiful drawing of a bird with its wings spread before turning to the next page, which happened to be the thirtieth page of the book. In the margins was another scribbling in Asaszi script. Whoever had written it—certainly not the author of the book—had gone through the difficulty of making the jagged language look similar to the Elviri script, more elegant and curved. If he weren't familiar with the language, he might have thought a child was scribbling down a few words from the page, perhaps to mimic the author's handwriting.

Fool. He destroys us. Rhono gone. I'll be next. Must store notes somewhere.

Underneath it in much smaller writing were a few more words.

Two-hundredth page - read.

Seth's brow furrowed as he flipped ahead in the book to the two-hundredth page. There was a small illustration of a bird perched on a branch. Its beak was long and curved, nearly as long as its neck. He hadn't seen a bird so scrawny and long before. Next to the illustration was an entry titled, "The Resting Places of Ophala and Langlir". He read through the section, looking out for any other Asaszi script left behind. The section described a small clearing in the northwestern section of the Elimaine Forest where the Elviri had built a godsite for the two demigods. Seth was unfamiliar with the Elviri mythology, but the name Langlir stirred up some long-forgotten memories within him.

Where have I seen that name before?

The section went on to describe the bird in the illustration, the aphet, and how it would frequently be found in the clearing. A separate paragraph described the bird's behaviors, which included singing late in the afternoon, and protecting snakes that happened to slither through the clearing. The author recalled a time when they observed a snake bathing in the sunlight, and a hawk was circling overhead. The aphet the author had been studying suddenly took to the sky and screeched at the hawk, who was easily twice the size of the scrawny bird, but the aphet managed to scare it off. The author hadn't known it at the time, but the snake was pregnant, and gave birth a few days later. They always saw the aphet hovering nearby, looking over the mother and her children.

Written in the margins was more Asaszi handwriting, mimicking the Elviri script.

See? Now check his book. Page fifty-four.

What does that mean, "his book"? The aphet? But I'm holding the book that's dedicated to the bird, along with the other creatures in the Elimaine Forest. Seth looked back over the passage in the book, searching for any additional clues or mention of other individuals—

Oh, of course. Langlir.

He closed the book and tucked it under his arm, moving quickly toward the stairs. He had passed the section on the Elviri deities on his way to the historical section earlier. Adrenaline pumped through his veins, and he couldn't help but let his lips curl into a small smile. He had always been fond of riddles and puzzles, and it felt *good* to be chasing after one right now. In the back of his mind, though, he couldn't help but worry about the author of these notes, and what their intentions were. Who was meant to find these? What would he find at the end of the trail? His pace quickened as he contemplated the potential answers.

The section on the Elviri deities was much larger than Seth realized. The smile slipped from his face as he paced up and down the rows of books. *Is Langlir even considered a deity if he was just a demigod? Had he done anything of note that would prompt the Elviri to write books about him? Surely, he did, if he had a godsite. They wouldn't build one for someone unnoteworthy, would they? Father would say yes.*

Something bubbled up within Seth at the thought of his father. He reached out to the nearest shelf to steady himself and take a deep breath. As he stood back up, he happened to glance at the books closest to his fingertips. One was dedicated to the songs written by the goddess Lithua. The other was simply titled *Langlir*. His heartbeat quickened, and he scrambled to grab the book from the shelf. The cover was very plain, similar to the other books he had acquired so far—another tan, authorless book. He opened it and flipped through the pages, looking carefully for another Asaszi note.

What page did the previous note say to go to? Ah, yes, page fifty-four.

The page of interest was the last page of a chapter with only a few sentences covering the top portion of the page. Below was a wall of text written in the Asaszi script. The harsh, jagged lines were a stark contrast to the beautiful, curved script above it.

Rhono fiercely believed the key to the Tserys was through his mother. That's why Amias was so quick to support him and join the Zsikui. Fools.

Seth's eyes widened, and his hands began to tremble. *Amias? My father? And could this "Rhono" be the same one that mentored my father when the Provira left Promthus over a hundred years ago?* So many thoughts raced through his mind, but he forced himself to focus on the written words.

The Zsikui know nothing about the Tserys, despite what they say. Rhono and I know what's hiding in that mountain, yet he convinced himself he could create something to control it. That's why Amias clung to his every word. And turned on him when Rhono began to descend. Although I wonder how much of that was Amias's doing and how much was Osza's. Nevertheless, Rhono is dead, and Amias thinks he holds the key to freeing the Tserys. But I know he's wrong. And I refuse to guide him to the correct answers. Amias will make a terrible leader for our liberated peoples, I realize that now. It's too late for me to make a difference. I know he knows of my growing disdain for him. I'm certain that an accident will occur soon, either truly or crafted. I must leave my research to be discovered by one more capable than I.

And that's where it ended. Seth frowned, and then started back at the beginning of the added section, searching for any kind of clues for what came next.

I must leave my research to be discovered by one more capable than I.

He sighed and closed his eyes. *Whose words am I chasing after? They clearly were writing about Father, with the mention of the* Zsikui *and* Osza. A small part of him felt vindicated knowing that someone else believed his father to be dangerous, but *who? And when was the last time I heard anything about Rhono? I think Mother talked about him a few times when I was younger, but I don't remember the context.*

He groaned and opened his eyes, looking back down at the book in his hands. The library would be no help in trying to search for Rhono. It had been sheer luck that he found these notes written by a mysterious author. He had to focus on the puzzle before him. Someone who knew his father, who had disagreed with him, had left a series of notes scattered across several books in an Elviri library, along with their research... Research about what? The *Tserys?*

Amias thinks he holds the key to freeing the Tserys.

What did Seth know about the *Tserys?* He was born near the end of the Eldest Days, and the Asaszi prospered under his leadership, although it was very brief. He was more powerful than even the Golden Emperor Tser, which was why they gave him the title of *Tserys.* The Elviri deities went into hiding upon learning of the *Tserys's* power. An emissary of the deities, a former slave of the Asaszi, journeyed to Moonyswyn and challenged him to personal combat. The two slew each other, and shortly after the second sun rose into the sky and ushered in a new era for Daaria.

But if the Tserys *is dead, then what's Father trying to "free"? Whatever it is, that must be what's at the Tomb of the Prince in Iszairi. Why else would he be traveling there so frequently?* A shiver ran down Seth's spine as he pictured the sinister cloud from several nights ago, and the otherworldly noises that came from within it.

And what does any of this have to do with Langlir?

Sighing, he searched for somewhere to sit. He supposed he would have to read the book to find out since his mysterious scribe had left nothing for him to go off.

CHAPTER XV: MUNNE

Munne slept through the rest of the night without any further incident. When she woke the next morning, she struggled to piece together the events of that evening. *The shapeshifter and the caravan guide are not the same person, and yet both are telling me to go to Kherizhan. What do they know? What awaits me in that desolate place? If I decide to go,* she quickly reminded herself. To go there would mean going against her father's orders, something she hadn't done before.

As Munne pulled herself out of her thoughts, she found her hands resting on her arms, right over the imprint the shapeshifter left on her. Her skin was still pink, as if the handprints were burned into her flesh. With great reluctance, she removed her hands from her arms and got out of bed.

She was supposed to leave for the Imalar Woods tomorrow, at the behest of her father. It wasn't the first time she left the valley within days of arriving, but this time certainly left a bitter taste in her mouth. Her triple would be joining her, which alleviated some of the frustration. However, if she were to abandon her assignment to the Imalar Woods and instead travel to Kherizhan, she needed to set a plan in motion that would keep her under the guise of following her father's orders until it was too late for the Elviri to dispatch someone to stop her. She needed to meet with Araloth and Mayrien before the traveling party left the valley and figure something out. She sent Namyr to their quarters to deliver a message, asking them to join her for breakfast tomorrow morning.

Today Munne needed to finish her ancestor's journal and look him up in the ancestry tomes, no matter how uncomfortable it made her. She needed to know what happened to him.

After finishing her morning meal and getting dressed for the day, she made her way down to the archives, preferring to read the journal there than in her own chambers. She brought her satchel, which had Malion's journal tucked away inside. Several groups of other noble Elviri passed by her during her walk. She offered each of them a smile and a greeting. As soon as they met her gaze, they looked away, whispering amongst themselves. The smile fell from Munne's face. Although she wasn't necessarily comfortable around the other highborn Elviri, they usually returned her greeting.

Has something happened? Did word get out that I abandoned the war council yesterday? While not totally unheard of, it certainly was a controversial action for her to have taken.

"...don't know if she could handle the stress," came a whisper nearby.

Munne turned and saw a small group of Elviri noblewomen hustling away from her. *Are they referring to me?* Her stomach tightened. She turned back to the hallway and made her way to the archives as quickly as she could.

The archives didn't provide the same sense of comfort as it had previously. A shiver ran down her spine as she entered the great hall. Munne grabbed hold of her satchel and quickly made her way down to the third floor. The smell of earth and scrolls filled her head, and for the first time those smells made her a little nauseous.

Munne closed her eyes and shook her head, willing her ill feelings away. *I need to be strong.*

She made her way to the chair she had been sitting in yesterday. The five ancestry tomes she removed from the shelves were still stacked neatly nearby. She removed the satchel from her shoulder and reached inside to pull Malion's journal out. She took a seat and began flipping through the pages, returning to where she left off.

leave leave leave leaveleaveleaveleaveleave LEAVELEAVELEAVELEAVE

Munne found the strength to turn the page. The next one was dated as the second day of the fourth month of the new year. After reading the date, she quickly checked the spine of the journal to see if any pages had been ripped out to account for the sudden jump in time. From what she could tell, it was fact the very next page.

Why hadn't he written anything for two and a half months?

Second day of the fourth month: Lithwyn and I were wed yesterday as the flowers of the valley bloomed. She was radiant in her golden gown with

lilies in her hair. We moved to our new chambers in the Se'vi's *manor last night—a lavish improvement from my previous chambers. There are several rooms here, in addition to our bedroom and living areas. Father and Mother will expect us to fill those rooms with children of our own. Oh, how I can't wait to be a father. Lithwyn will make such a wonderful mother, and our children will help rule the Elviri. I won't achieve it in my lifetime, but maybe one of our children will become Warlord. With my eldest brother ascending the throne, my second brother's wife serving as Writlord, and Lithwyn's uncle serving as Lorelord, the line of the Hunting Throne would be as strong as ever! Oh, what a lovely and wonderful thought.*

Malion made no mention of the beast, or of his nightmares. Munne reread the entry to make sure she didn't miss any sign of things being off or wrong with him. *Had he found some kind of relief from the nightmares? If he did, why hadn't he mentioned it? Damnit, Malion. What chance do I have without your answers?* She had difficulty swallowing. The next several entries were very similar, where he went on at length about his wife and their future together. It was quite sweet, but Munne couldn't help but feel a growing sense of dread as she continued to read.

With about thirty pages remaining in the book, Malion's entries suddenly stopped. The page she was on only had one brief entry recorded. There was no date to mark when it was written.

Today I make it all end.

Munne frowned, her sense of dread nearing its peak. Elvarin was right, the journal did end abruptly. She had more questions than answers, and she wasn't sure if the ancestry tomes would provide any insight. Still, she had to try.

When she went to put the journal down, Munne realized her hand rested on one of the imprints on her arm. She set the journal on the stone floor and took a moment to wrap her arms around herself. The warmth from the imprints comforted her, and it helped ease her rapidly beating heart. In the back of her mind, she wondered how the shapeshifter had been able to touch her. Unless he was a god? She wasn't sure. Only the gods could perform such feats, as the priests said. But if he were a god, why wouldn't he have told her so?

Casting the thoughts away, she opened the first ancestry tome and skimmed through the pages, looking for any mention of Malion or Lithwyn. Almost all the pages were filled with feats and accomplishments of Huntaran I, her father's namesake. Under his rule, Lithalyon became a citadel for art and culture, the Paladins of the Gods were established, and the Daarian Council was formed between the Elviri and the other inhabitants of Daaria. Munne quickly jumped to the end of the book, trying to see if there was mention of any other *Se'vi*. There was none.

She set the book down and opened the second. In it were the feats and accomplishments of Huntruyn and Huntanan, the next two Elviri to sit on the Hunting Throne. There was no mention of Malion or Lithwyn in this book, either.

It wasn't until she got to the fourth book that she found mention of Malion and Lithwyn. As she flipped to the entry on Huntwyn, she saw Malion listed as the youngest of his three sons. Huntwyn had been the *Se'vi* to declare war on the Asaszi when they began raiding Promthus, and most of his entry detailed the success he found in war. His eldest son Huntryan succeeded him as *Se'vi*, and his second son Terephin became Chieftain of Elimere.

Malion served in the armed forces but was withdrawn when he became infected with disease while he marched in Promthus. When he returned to Elimere, he married Lithwyn, the niece of Andurin, current Lorelord. Shortly after their wedding, Malion and his wife died by his own hand. They bore no children.

Died by his own hand?

The next paragraph detailed the other lords and high-ranking generals under Huntwyn's rule. Munne's eyes returned to Malion's single paragraph. *Died by his own hand.*

The knot tightened in her stomach. *Tonight, I make it all end.* She knew what those words meant now. Malion had killed himself to get rid of the nightmares. But why had he killed Lithwyn? Had the nightmares driven him to such paranoia and fear that he would do so unknowingly?

Munne looked back at Malion's journal resting on the stone floor. Malion had mentioned his wife wanting "him" to leave in an earlier entry. Had she also seen the *Ardashi'ik*? Did she have the same nightmares as him? Is that what would become of her if the nightmares persisted?

Fear tugged at the knot in her stomach, and she thought she would be sick. She needed to get out of the archives and get some fresh air. With shaking hands, she returned Malion's journal to her satchel.

I need to ask Elvarin where he found this, so I can put it back. It clearly has no answers to my predicament. Munne gathered up the ancestry tomes and carried them back to their bookcase, placing them gently on the shelves. With great care, she calmly walked up the stairs back to the main level of the manor.

It was another cold and sunny day in the valley. Munne had thrown on a heavy coat before departing her room that morning. She wrapped her arms around herself, feeling the heat of the shapeshifter's mark through the fur and leather. The gardens beckoned to her, and she decided to take a walk through them to give herself time to think and be alone.

How much time do I have before the nightmares begin corrupting me? Will I start hurting those around me? When will I snap and decide to end it all, end my suffering, and—

"Lady Munne!" a voice called out to her from behind.

Munne stopped in her tracks right before the door to the gardens. She turned and saw Gilareana hurriedly walking toward her. Her friend wore the traditional winter dress of a noblewoman, and a high-collared dark blue silk gown underneath a long-sleeved gray coat. The gray fabric was thick with fur lining the inside of the sleeves. The coat was laced together across her chest, her hair braided and pulled across her left shoulder.

"Good morning, Gilareana," Munne greeted her friend with a quiet voice.

"May I walk with you through the gardens?" Gilareana asked with a smile on her face.

The question came as a surprise to Munne. It wasn't often that the two friends had a chance to catch up, and she certainly wasn't expecting it now given her current circumstances. "O-of course," she stuttered, leading the way into the gardens.

Will Gilareana be one of the ones I hurt, if the nightmares get worse? With a subtle twist of her chin, the thought was banished from her mind. *I won't be the cause of anyone else's suffering.*

Gilareana looped her arm through Munne's and placed a hand on her friend's forearm. The physical touch lightened Munne's mood, grounding her in reality. "I was hoping I'd find you today. I've heard many worrying things about you over the past couple of days from the other nobility," she whispered to Munne.

Munne's eyebrows rose in surprise. She remembered her earlier encounter with some of the noblewomen this morning, how they avoided her in the hallway. While she had no confirmation until now, she had a feeling something was amiss. "The others won't even offer me a greeting in the halls," she said. "What have you heard?"

Gilareana hummed, looking straight ahead, and led her away from the manor toward the center of the gardens. It was getting closer to the midday meal, so there wouldn't be as many people strolling around outside.

"Gil, please," Munne murmured, tugging Gilareana's arm.

"One moment," Gilareana whispered, tightening her grip on Munne's arm. From around the corner came a pair of Elviri women dressed in noble wear. Gilareana immediately gave them a charming smile and greeting. "Good morning!"

The two women smiled and nodded at Gilareana. Munne noticed they intentionally avoided looking in her direction. She waited until they were out of sight before she frowned. *Had the nobility looked at Malion this way when he came home from Promthus?*

Gilareana led Munne to a bench tucked away near the statue of Karonos. She sat down, gently pulling Munne down beside her, their arms still entwined. After glancing around to ensure their isolation, Gilareana finally turned to look at Munne.

"I'll get right to it," Gilareana murmured. "There are rumors going around that you aren't fit for your ascension." Munne's eyes widened. "With your outburst in front of the Hall of the Dead and your, hm, *early departure* from the war council, some of the nobilities are unsure if you're well enough to become *Se'vi* in the summer. They think that the war has changed you."

Munne's throat tightened. *The war with the Provira has indeed changed me, but it's the nightmares that are driving me to the point of insanity. If I wasn't losing sleep each night from being chased through some imaginary caves, I wouldn't have snapped the way I did. I'd have a better handle on my actions. But I can't tell her any of that—Gil doesn't understand the hardships of being a soldier.* "I-I've been handling so many different things..." Munne said softly.

"There are others who've been worrying for many years, long before the war started. They think it an ill omen that Huntaran only bore one child—a girl. And that girl hasn't begun courting, so the future of the line is uncertain. They think this means the end of the Hunting Throne." Gilareana spoke the words with a large amount of contempt.

A fire ignited inside of Munne. "Do they not remember that the leader of our gods is a woman? A woman who didn't take a husband? Or that women have been Chieftains since the Eldest Days?" Each question got louder and angrier.

Gilareana placed her hand on Munne's shoulder and gripped her tightly. "You don't need to remind me of our heritage," she snapped, meeting Munne's furious gaze. "But they look for any excuse to discredit you, even if it goes against the truth."

Munne held her steady gaze for a few tense moments before responding. "It doesn't matter what they think. The ascension of a new *Se'vi* isn't decided by anyone except the current *Se'vi*."

"But if they were to convince your father..." Gilareana trailed off, leaving the rest of her words unsaid. She removed her hand from Munne's shoulder and placed it on top of her other hand, which was still hooked around Munne's arm.

Munne looked back out to the gardens. She stared without focus, allowing the gardens to fill her mind. She heard the waterfalls rumbling in the distance. A gentle breeze blew through the hedges, and the shrubbery rustled. "Well, then I thank you for bringing this to my attention. I suppose I'll have to see what my father decides." The words left a bitter taste in her mouth.

"I think there may be a way to placate them, or at least some of the nobles," Gilareana said, lowering her voice again.

Munne didn't respond. Her gaze rested on one of the hedges where tiny white flowers wove in and around the sturdy shrubbery. Such resilience, even amidst the cold. Her vision started to blur, and she lost focus. Gilareana squeezed Munne's arm. Her attention was once again drawn to her friend, and she sharpened her focus. Undoubtedly her friend was frowning at her. She didn't need to turn to see it.

"If you were to start courting, it would ease many of their minds. Marriage would calm them further, but," Munne felt the glare her friend gave her, "I know your thoughts on that matter."

Munne scoffed and rolled her eyes. This was an argument they'd had several times before, which had created a schism in their friendship. Gilareana was a dutiful noble, and Munne just wanted to ride through the forest with her triple at her side. "I just don't feel that—"

"Laralos still fawns over you, just like when we were children," Gilareana cut in. "If you were to let him court you, you'd gain the favor of Elimaine's nobility."

"Kieron is supportive of me. I don't need anyone else's approval from there," Munne grumbled.

"Elimaine is the largest of our provinces. You'd be a fool to think that you only need his approval."

Munne was exasperated. "I didn't realize being *Se'vi* was a popularity contest."

"He will court you if you allow it, you know," Gilareana continued. "He's afraid to ask because you've been so distant as of late."

"There's a war going on!"

"And your soldiers come home to their loved ones after every march."

Munne faced away from her friend. She could feel the swell of emotions and thoughts bubbling up from deep within her mind. She knew Gilareana was right, and she knew Laralos would pursue her to the ends of the earth, but she felt very unsure about allowing him to court her. She and Laralos had drifted apart when she made the decision to join the armed forces, and he chose to join his parents in politics. During her early years of service there had been many times where passion threatened to overtake her, where she wanted nothing more than to run away with him and never look back. As she grew older, though, that passion dwindled. She couldn't remember the last time she thought of Laralos in that regard. She had come to depend and lean on her triple. Who else did she need in her life? Who else would understand what she had been through, and would be patient enough to handle the new fears and pains she had come to know?

An image of Cesa surfaced in her mind. *Perhaps he can offer me some guidance.*

"I'll give thought to your advice." Munne heard the words come from her lips, but she wasn't sure she had been the one to say them. "I depart in the morning for the Imalar Woods. I'll have time to come to a decision."

She heard Gilareana sigh. "If you were to announce your intention to begin courtship before your departure, it would help ease their minds while you are away."

"What if I just had you say something to them?" Munne asked.

"What?"

Munne shifted in her seat, so she was angled toward Gilareana. "After I've left, what if you announce to the court that I will allow suitors to court me?"

Gilareana tilted her head to the side as she considered the idea. "Perhaps that could work. Although it won't have as much of an impact if you say the words yourself."

Munne frowned. "You know I won't."

Gilareana returned the frown. "What, so you would leave me to tend to your suitors in your absence?" Munne only responded with a sheepish smile, which made Gilareana's frown curl into a grin. "I have enough of my own suitors to worry about. I can't take on yours as well."

"Oh, and why not?" Munne let out a playful whine. "You're much better at it than I am, and besides, you may meet someone *you* want to court."

The two friends laughed and got to their feet, returning to the manor. Munne glanced up to the ceiling, feeling the weight of the throne pushing down on her. Beyond the nightmares, she had an entire kingdom relying on her to be strong and make the right choices to ensure their survival. It was overwhelming, and she wanted nothing more than to retreat to her room and shut the world out. But that wasn't an option for the future *Se'vi*. She needed to seriously consider what Gilareana had told her and choose her next steps carefully.

"Thank you for the walk through the gardens. I need to go find Cesa and discuss some matters with him," Munne said to her friend.

Gilareana smiled. "I hope we can do it again some time."

Munne hugged Gilareana and departed, heading into the city to find her mentor.

—◦—

There was a tavern a short distance from the Hall of the Dead that catered to soldiers and veterans. Munne herself had been to the tavern many times before to celebrate and mourn with her men. During Cesa's tenure as Warlord, he was frequently found there when he was in the valley. After relinquishing the position to Munne, he would often spend his afternoons in the tavern with old friends.

The tavern was named Rael's Last Watch, an homage to the god Azrael. Despite its somber name, the tavern was painted in lively blues and whites, and often hosted musicians. As Munne passed through the heavy wooden doors, a few soldiers whooped and cheered in greeting. She grinned and waved at them. It felt good to know that her men still cherished her, even if the nobles were beginning to turn their backs on her.

She scanned the room and quickly caught sight of Cesa and Saendys sitting at a table against the wall. The two elderly Elviri had been friends for decades, and Saendys would often spend his time home with the previous Warlord. Above their table was a worn banner bearing the military sigil. There were only two mugs of beer on the table. Munne wondered if they had already eaten. As she approached them, they both turned and greeted her with the same cheer.

"Vere'cha! A sight for sore eyes!" Cesa grinned, raising his mug to her.

"What brings you to the Watch on a sunny day like this?" Saendys asked, raising his own mug as well.

Munne took a seat next to her former mentor. "I've come to make good on my offer for beer," she said to Saendys as he placed his mug on the table. "And perhaps seek some sage advice from Lord Cesa, if he's willing."

"Ah, I've already had my fill for now. I have some other business that needs tending to, but perhaps sometime soon?" Saendys said, brushing off the front of his tunic.

"Yes, sometime soon," Munne agreed.

"Excuse me, youngling," Cesa said politely, rising to his feet. "I must say goodbye to my friend." He came around the side of the table to stand in front of Saendys. "Safe travels." The two embraced, and Saendys walked toward the exit. Cesa watched him go, and then sat on the opposite side of the table.

"Hello, *sa'vani*," Munne said with a smile on her face. A serving girl came by with a mug full of ale and set it down in front of Munne. She raised it up and drank.

"Hello, Vere'cha," Cesa responded, returning the smile. "So, you've come seeking advice? Perhaps you should've visited me before the council yesterday, then."

His words twisted in her like a dagger, but she knew she had earned it. Though Cesa radiated warmth, she saw traces of disappointment in his lingering gaze. He spoke the truth, though. Perhaps she had made a mistake hiding the nightmares from him. Or at the very least, she should've sought him out for wisdom regarding her political situation. "I don't know what will happen this year." Her voice was quiet.

As Cesa looked at Munne, his smile faded. After a few moments of silence, he asked, "What do you mean?"

Munne broke eye contact and looked down at the table. Her grip on the mug tightened. "With my ascension."

He was silent for a few more moments before responding. "You will ascend and become *Se'vi*."

"I don't have the support of the nobility," she responded, the words bitter.

"The support of the nobility won't keep you from rising up and doing good things for your people," Cesa said thoughtfully.

"I've never wanted to be involved in politicking," Munne grumbled, taking a sip from her mug.

"Then don't get involved in politicking."

"Becoming *Se'vi* means getting involved in politics!" Munne looked back up at her mentor. She regretted her tone of voice as soon as the words left her mouth. She sighed and softened her voice before speaking again. "Simply being Huntaran's daughter means I'm involved in politics."

Cesa was silent again as he regarded her. The serving girl hadn't come back around to their table. Munne idly wondered if she would, or if she would stay away to avoid the tension.

"Being born into the Hunting Throne line means bearing the burden of supporting and leading our people. That is done through courage and resilience. You have compassion, and you seek to do what's right for your people. This is all you need to become *Se'vi*."

Munne frowned, her shoulders slumping. "The other nobles will fight me every step of the way."

"Act on your compassion, and they will realize your good virtue," Cesa replied.

They sat in silence again, and Munne contemplated her response. "Why did you pick me to succeed you and not someone else?"

She did omit one thought from her words, though. She had always wondered why Cesa hadn't chosen Araloth instead. She didn't come from a noble background, but she had more than proven herself during her tenure. Araloth always kept a level head, providing a much-needed balance to Munne's brash behavior.

Cesa shifted in his chair, taking a sip of ale. "One of Sariel's scribes used to assure me that you'd follow in your father's footsteps and choose being a scribe as your lifepath. You were quite the studious child." He waved his hand in the air and chuckled. "I remember the books you'd sneak into the dormitory. You would read about Ceyo, and her trials and tribulations. The battles she faced, both in war and in politics. After briefly meeting you during your lifepath rotation, I was sure the scribes would be right, that you would choose to become one of them, or perhaps a Paladin. And yet you chose to join the military."

Munne had her head propped up with one hand, the other wrapped around her mug. She allowed herself to stare blankly at the table. "I chose the military because that's where I would be able to help people. Where it matters."

Cesa locked eyes with her and she regained focus. He offered her a smile. "That is why I chose you."

Munne allowed herself to take in the moment and let it resonate within her. *Cesa thinks highly of me and respects me, even though we don't always get along. It humbling to know this wise old man trusts me with the fate of the Elviri, even when my courage wavers.*

"Who will become Warlord when I ascend?" Munne asked.

"That's for you to decide," Cesa told her, leaning back in his chair.

She looked away and frowned, letting herself get absorbed by her own question. "I've never thought about it before."

"And yet you've put in time to question why I chose you as my successor." Munne redirected her frown back at Cesa, and he laughed. "Araloth still has many good years left in her. It wouldn't be the first time a *Se'vi* and a Warlord were part of the same triple. Or you could spend time away from the capital, meet with some of the other generals, and decide if one of them is a better fit."

The frown slipped away from Munne's face, and she found herself nodding along with Cesa's words. When he finished, she opened her mouth to speak again. "Will you help me with the process?" For a moment, she felt like a young child, her voice quiet and meek.

"Of course, youngling. Once you return from the Imalar Woods."

If I go to the Imalar Woods. The thought surprised her. *Am I truly still considering abandoning the path my father set before me, in favor of this mad journey to Kherizhan? Should I... tell Cesa about the nightmares? The shapeshifter?*

"*Sa'vani*, do you know anything about my ancestor Malion?"

Cesa turned his head to the side and looked past her, brow furrowed. "I can't recall that name. Whose son was he?"

"Huntwyn, during the early years of the Second Sun."

"Ah, yes. Huntwyn and his heir Huntryan fought in the last of the Elviri-Asaszi wars. Malion was the third son, yes? The one whose mind was addled by some Asaszi plague?"

Munne shifted uncomfortably in her seat. "Yes."

Cesa looked back at her, tapping his fingers against his chin. "What did you want to know about him?"

She opened her mouth and shrugged. "I've just been reading again. I thought his death curious."

"It's a shame the Asaszi corrupted his mind. His death was a sour note in Huntwyn's legacy, but he avenged his son."

"Indeed." *Would Cesa believe that Malion's plague was actually the* Ardashi'ik? *Can I really risk telling Cesa about the nightmares now, when I'm on the verge of departing?*

She ultimately decided to stay silent and enjoy the midday meal with her mentor.

CHAPTER XVI: RAY

"Ray," a soft, quiet voice called out to her.

A warm, firm hand grasped her shoulder and shook her gently. She opened one eye to look at who woke her and saw Naro's face crouched next to hers. As her senses awakened, she felt the weight of Ajak in the bed next to her. She heard the soft snoring of Aldrin from across the room. Naro held a candle in his other hand that illuminated his face, the candlelight dancing in his blue and green eyes. All traces of anger were gone from his features.

"Good morning, sir," Ray mumbled, sleep hanging on her every word.

"Come to the other room," Naro whispered and stood. He didn't make a sound as he left the bedroom, the flame disappearing.

She sat up in bed, and rubbed her eyes. *What time is it? How long have we slept? I'll find out soon enough, I suppose.* Ray stood up and stretched her arms up, feeling parts of her spine crack. She still wore the barmaid's dress from the night before. She wondered if there were other clothes in the bunker.

Naro sat at the desk in his room. The bed was made up. His robe had been draped across the back of his chair, but otherwise he was still in the same outfit as the night before. The sleeves of his silk shirt were pushed up to his elbows. Had he even slept? There were a few lit candles in the room, illuminating his desk and the papers on it. He set his pen down and turned to face Ray, leaning back in his chair.

"How did you sleep?" he murmured, steepling his fingers over his chest.

"Fine I suppose," she responded and looked around the room. It was plainly decorated, very unlike his room at the safehouse. Besides the papers on the desk, she couldn't see anything else that could easily be identified as Naro's or the Walkers'.

251

"Thank you for playing your part in last night's dinner party. I'm sure you have questions." He stretched his hands out, gesturing for her to ask away.

It was her opportunity to ask all those bottled-up questions from the previous day, about the tunnel, the princess, the dinner party. But only one thing passed her lips. "Ajak thinks you're queueing me up to be a lieutenant," she said, the title feeling strange on her tongue.

"Ajak is very astute." Naro's response was enough of an answer for her. Her stomach twisted.

"I've only ever been the eyes," Ray mumbled, wrapping her arms around her midsection. "I-I don't know anything about leading others, or the other gangs."

Naro chuckled. "Your change in station wouldn't come without training. I take care of my own, do I not?"

Ray met his gaze and nodded.

He stood and approached Ray, placing his hands on her shoulders and squeezing gently. "This plot with the princess is just the beginning for you. More importantly, it forges a bond between you and Ajak. I need my lieutenants to trust each other, now more than ever."

Her thoughts drifted to the previous night when Sabyl slapped Aldrin. The two always had their differences, and often wouldn't work together on anything. Ray knew that Sabyl was cold, but Aldrin... he was never around often enough for her to form an opinion on him.

"Why me, though? Me in particular?"

Naro looked past Ray toward the door. Several silent, awkward seconds passed before he returned his gaze to her, his voice barely audible. "Because you have an important role to play in the future of this city."

Her brow furrowed, and she started to respond, but he placed a finger against her lips.

"You've seen the magic. The magic has shown me you. All that's left is for us to play our parts." He took a couple of steps back, his hands dropping to his sides. "I'll be waking Sabyl and Aldrin soon to send them off on new priorities. I'll send for you and Ajak after that. We'll discuss more details about the princess over breakfast."

Ray nodded, knowing the dismissal without needing further clarification. She turned and left Naro's room, returning to the bedroom where the others were sleeping. She crawled into bed beside Ajak and stared up at the ceiling.

Naro's talk of magic unnerved her. *"You've seen the magic. The magic has shown me you." Wish that I could go back to blissful ignorance. Back to childhood, perhaps.* She closed her eyes and imagined she was a child, being held and comforted as she fell asleep. But instead of her mother's arms wrapped around her, it was Naro's.

Eventually she fell back into an uneasy slumber.

Naro came back into the bedroom much later in the morning—Ray assumed it was morning—to get Aldrin and Sabyl up. She awoke to the dull *thud* of his footsteps as he crossed to the beds the other two were sleeping in.

"Get up. It's time to go." Naro's voice was firm yet gentle. It was enough for both lieutenants to hear, though. They stirred in their beds and sat up, rubbing the sleep from their eyes. Naro left the room as quietly as he came.

Ajak stirred in bed beside her. He rolled onto his back and stretched his legs. She felt him shiver. He must have felt her presence beside him because he leaned in toward her shoulder and side. "We going already?" he mumbled, half asleep.

"No, they are," Ray whispered back to him.

He merely grunted in response and rested his head on her shoulder. Without thinking she reached up to stroke his hair. *If only... no, don't go there.*

Sabyl was up and out the door in minutes. Aldrin, however, took his time standing, stretching, and even making the bed before he sauntered out of the room holding his head high. Something about his gait bothered Ray. *Surely Aldrin knows better than to provoke Naro right now when he's so clearly tense about the other gangs in the city. Is Aldrin aware of the plot to kidnap the princess? Naro must have told his lieutenants.* The recent memory of him asking her not to tell Sabyl about the false wall in the warehouse shouldered its way to the front of her thoughts. Perhaps Aldrin and Sabyl weren't aware.

What other secrets is Naro keeping from his trusted lieutenants?

She sighed, tilting her head back and resuming her staring at the ceiling.

Naro returned for Ajak and Ray not too long after the sounds of Sabyl and Aldrin climbing the ladder faded away. "Join me for breakfast," His honeyed voice called from the threshold.

"Yes, sir," Ray responded without a thought.

Beside her, Ajak stirred once again. "Yessir." He managed to speak with a decent amount of clarity.

She climbed out of bed, giving him room to stretch and get up. Light poured into the room from the main chamber beyond where Naro had lit several candles. There was a plain dresser leaning against one of the walls. She hoped there were some clothes in there that fit her, and that she'd have the time to change after breakfast. She knew better than to keep Naro waiting.

She exited the room with Ajak not too far behind her. Inside the main chamber of the bunker, Naro had set up a table and chairs with bread, smoked meats, and cheeses arranged on a platter. He had also put out a pitcher of water and some mugs.

"There's nothing sweet, I'm afraid, but this will have to do," Naro apologized, gesturing for them to join him at the table.

Ray moved some slices of meats and cheeses onto her plate. She hadn't eaten since the meal at the café the morning before, so she was famished. Not an unfamiliar feeling for a rogue on the streets, so she took advantage of the food placed before her. She wolfed down her first plate and filled it again with more food.

"Good morning, boss," Ajak said quietly, reaching for the loaf of bread.

"Good morning," Naro responded, looking between the two of them. He waited as they ate and drank.

Once the initial hunger abated, a bundle of nerves started to form and tighten in Ray's stomach. She nibbled on a piece of smoked beef, her eyes locked on her plate.

"Yesterday was a hitch in our plans," Naro said, choosing his words carefully. "But it is no matter. We're still moving forward with our plan, and we're going to move faster than anticipated."

Ajak shifted uncomfortably in his chair. "How fast, boss?"

Naro picked up his mug and gazed at it thoughtfully. "Three days hence."

Ray's throat tightened, and Ajak sputtered around a mouthful of bread. *So soon? Am I even ready for this?*

Naro looked at the two of them, his brow furrowed. "I'll take care of communicating this to our partners. You two need to stay here and lay low until I come back for you. I'll also need to give you more information than I initially planned because it's less likely that I'll be able to accompany you on the last leg of your journey."

Ray threw an alarmed glance at Ajak. He was as still as death in his chair.

"Before I take my leave, I'll give you the final piece. Ajak, you knew we would be going north after escaping the castle. It's time the two of you knew why." Naro adjusted himself in his chair, taking a drink from his mug. Ray caught his eye as he set it down. She had a sinking feeling that she knew what that reason was. "The princess is inhabited by a Doshara. A ghost from the past, set on wreaking havoc in the city if left unattended."

Ajak frowned and tried to interject. "How'd the—"

"It doesn't matter how it got in. What matters is we're getting it out. We're going to save the city." Naro glanced at Ray, and she swore he winked before looking back at Ajak. "We're going north because there are people who can help us get rid of the Doshara and return the princess to her own self. After that, we can ransom her back to the king."

Ajak let out a low whistle.

The plan seemed sound, but something ate at the back of Ray's mind. Something was off. "Where exactly are we taking her?" she asked.

"Na'roc of North. I was planning to join you on this part of the journey, but I have a feeling that I'll be preoccupied with other business in the city."

Na'roc of North. The frozen tundra past the northern shores of the Hourglass Lakes. Long ago, a king built a wall to separate Promthus from that land in an effort to keep the Proma safe. Ray grew up hearing bedtime stories of fierce cat-like people who killed and ate any who dared cross over that wall. *If the cold don't get ya, they will,* her mother had whispered. Were these the people who could get rid of the Doshara?

Prince Robyn, the second born son of the king, had crossed the Wall almost two years ago. He had never returned, so the people assumed he had died in Na'roc of North. Ray couldn't stop her mind from wandering down a rather insane path. *Could the prince still be alive? Does Naro know something about his disappearance? It can't be a coincidence that he wants to take the princess to the same place where the prince had disappeared.*

Naro spoke again, pulling her out of her thoughts. He was looking at Ajak. "You know we have a designated landing site on the northern shore. The boatman knows as well. You will have all the supplies you need to get to your destination. I'll ensure a map is available to you as well since I won't be joining you."

"What about our return to Auora?" Ray blurted out.

Naro turned his gaze to her and gave a gentle smile. He seemed proud of her question. "The Enthai will ensure your safe return to the city."

"Pardon the question, boss, but the Enthai aren't known to have friendly relations with anyone south of the Wall. How can you guarantee our survival?" Ajak muttered, tearing off another piece of bread.

"So long as you bear the mark of the Walkers, no harm will come to you," Naro responded, but his answer gave Ray no comfort. It only raised new questions. Judging by how Ajak shifted uncomfortably in his chair, he felt the same way. Naro didn't miss their reactions and leaned back in his chair with visible hurt on his face. "Friends, I understand your confusion, but this isn't the hour to lose hope in our plan. You must trust that I wouldn't put you in danger."

Ray couldn't control the shiver that raced down her spine. *That's exactly where he's putting us, though. The castle is one thing, one giant, horrible thing. But going north?*

The moment the thought crossed her mind, guilt flooded her senses. She tried taking a sip of water, but the knot in her throat wouldn't let her. Three days ago, her biggest fear had been the city guard and the deadly athra strain. She thought that the plot to kidnap the princess would invoke fear and dread within her heart, but the only thing she was afraid of was Na'roc of North, and all the different ways she could meet her death in that frozen hell.

"This is suspicious, boss," Ajak said after a few moments, setting his mug and bread down.

"This is years in the making. Believe in me when I tell you that the Enthai will take care of you and ensure your safe return to Auora. I have done my part to ensure that leg of the trip is safe." Naro's voice was filled with resolve. Ray found herself desperately clinging to it, trying to inspire the same feeling within herself. "Do your part and get the princess out of the castle without incident. Your safety falls entirely on your shoulders within those walls."

She looked to Ajak to see if she could read his face and understand what was going through his mind. A flicker of fear crossed his eyes, but he maintained his calm.

Naro continued. "You know this dance. You know these people. Blend in, speak sparingly, and get out without being caught."

As a pair of eyes, she knew that role well. She had never infiltrated a place like the castle before, but she knew Ajak had broken into various homes and businesses in the Sky District before. He would watch after her and ensure she did everything correctly. She had to believe that. She had to focus on the plan and not let herself get overwhelmed by what came after.

Ajak inhaled sharply and nodded. "Yes, sir. What're our orders?"

Naro's lips curled into a warm glowing smile. "Stay here. Lay low. I'll return for you in three days with everything you need."

Ray looked around the bunker, and her worry must have been obvious.

"Later today I'll have food and drink delivered above," Naro added. "Listen for their voices. They'll be instructed to announce their delivery, leave the items on the table above, and then leave." He rose to his feet. Ajak and Ray followed suit. "Stay low, stay quiet."

Ajak and Ray bowed their heads.

Naro looked over them for a moment before stepping away from the table. He ducked into his room to gather up a few belongings, and then headed for the ladder. Ajak sat back down and returned to his breakfast.

Ray stepped around her chair and wandered around the main chamber of the bunker. No decorations, no identifying markers. Besides the table and chairs, there were a few countertops nearby, as well as a couple of storage racks with crates and sacks on them. Sconces burned low all around the room, bathing it in an orange glow. There was a small bookcase near the second bedroom door with a handful of unorganized books on its shelves.

The third door, unopened, caught her attention. She crossed to it and discovered that it led to a washing room where they could bathe and take care of other business. Several barrels lined the edges of the room with scented candles stacked on top. Instead of a tub there was a small basin on a pedestal. *Makes sense. Not enough room for a tub, nor is there a good place to draw water. I'll come back once I finish looking around. Been a while since I scrubbed myself down.*

She returned to the bookcase and picked a few of the books up, looking over their covers and spines. Her mother had taught her the basics of reading when she was a child, but it was Naro who introduced her to literature and history. She didn't often come across many books that interested her, but there were two or three on the bookcase that she felt she could read. *Histories of Two Islands,* a book detailing the rise of Auora and its castle over the years. *The Woodwalker,* a piece of fiction about a Proma living alone within the Imalarii Woods. There were others she wasn't particularly interested in but knew that there was a very real possibility that she would end up reading them anyway while staying in the bunker.

"Three days." Ajak spoke quietly.

"Three days." Ray echoed.

<hr />

Later in the day, sometime in the late afternoon Ray assumed, there was a voice upstairs from a courier announcing their delivery of a crate of food. Ajak emerged from the second bedroom and hovered by the ladder, listening closely for the sound of a door closing before climbing up to retrieve the goods.

Ray had cleaned herself as best as she could in the washing room, and then spent the better part of the day reading the history book about Auora. She hadn't gotten very far into it. It was much denser than she anticipated, beginning over ten thousand years ago with the start of the Second Sun. She was currently reading about the year 1429 when a plague swept across Promthus and wiped out several villages on the southern shores of the lakes. That led to the Elviri declaring war against the Asaszi and sweeping across the land to defend the Proma.

"Lots of smoked meat, but there's some fruit in here, too," Ajak mumbled as he descended the ladder.

Ray set her book down and crossed over to help him with the crate. It was heavier than she expected, so she quickly turned to set it down on the table they ate at earlier. Ajak stood behind her, peering into the crate as she plucked things out of it. They had lit several candles throughout the bunker so there was enough light to see without straining their eyes.

Sure enough, there was a lot of smoked meat and fish. More than enough for her and Ajak to eat while cooped up. There were also a couple of loaves of bread, several apples and oranges, two glass jars of milk, a bottle of wine, and some waterskins. Naro had ensured they wouldn't starve while in hiding.

"Awful nice of the boss to give us some wine," Ajak snickered, grabbing it and inspecting the branding. "Frostleaf Vineyard, no less. He really likes us. Should help pass the time in this hellhole."

Ray rolled her eyes and took one of the oranges to peel. "Have at it, then."

"Only if you join me." Ajak tossed her a sly grin.

She looked between him and her orange. She had never really cared to drink beer or wine, but right now it promised a good way to pass the time with a good companion. She set the orange down on the table. "Fine but keep your hands to yourself."

Ajak held his hands up in the air. "A gentleman's promise."

Ray crossed her arms. "You wish you were a gentleman," she said.

He laughed in response and uncorked the bottle. "Fine, then. Rogue's promise."

They moved to the second bedroom and sat down on different beds.

Ajak took the first drink from the bottle and then handed it over to Ray. "Pretty sweet... you should like it."

She raised the bottle to her lips and took a small sip. The wine tasted like blueberries. Very tart blueberries, but with a mild underlying sweetness. She grimaced as she swallowed but found the taste to be rather pleasant. Her throat warmed. "This is nice."

"Probably shouldn't drink the whole thing in one sitting, though. Still have a few days to go," he murmured. He folded his hands and twiddled his thumbs.

Ray nodded, looking over the bottle. The glass was a dark green color, with a piece of parchment wrapped around the middle. The vineyard's name was written in fancy penmanship. She wished she had the artistic talent to do that. Maybe once the job was over, she would take the time to work on her penmanship.

"Don't hog it all." Ajak leaned over toward her, his hand extended.

Ray passed the bottle off to him and then drew her knees up to her chest. "I hate this dress," she grumbled, fisting the hem of the dress. Although her skin was clean, the dress felt grimy.

"I saw some extra clothes in the dresser earlier. Some of them might fit."

"Thanks," Ray mumbled.

She got up and walked over to the dresser, pulling the top drawer open. Inside was a hodgepodge of shirts that ranged from too small to too large. She managed to dig out a beige shirt with a ruffled collar that seemed comfortable enough. The fabric was soft to the touch. She continued her hunt through the other drawers to find some kind of pants or leggings. She planned on keeping the boots she wore since they were very comfortable.

Ray didn't bother trying to hide her body as she changed clothes. Ajak was too distracted with the bottle of wine, or so she told herself.

"You have any scars yet?" Ajak asked quietly.

She turned to give him an inquisitive look, adjusting the ruffled shirt around her chest.

He averted his eyes and took another drink from the bottle. "Maybe it's just the territory the boss has me running in. Got some scars from the city guard. Had a couple of nasty run-ins with the Iron Hawks, too." He raised his arm and pulled his sleeve back to show her a jagged line running from his elbow to his armpit. "Their steel's every bit as good as they say."

Ray frowned and sat down across from him on his bed. She took the wine bottle from him. "How often are you getting into scraps like that?" she asked.

Ajak flashed her a grin, but she saw it for what it was—an attempt to play it off. "It's not so bad. And ever since he put me on this, I haven't seen much of the streets. Aldrin's crew really deals with the brunt of it."

"What's he do? Naro and Sabyl are usually all about information, or nabbing trinkets, but I heard Wyatt say Aldrin's got him sitting in taverns trying to find someone."

"Him and his crew watch the safehouses and patrol the streets mostly. Naro's got a few people that report to him directly, but most of the muscle reports to Aldrin. He might have Wyatt meeting up with traders or something like that."

"Huh, okay," she mumbled, her thoughts drifting elsewhere. *That doesn't line up with what Wyatt and Dol were talking about the other day, though. What is Aldrin up to?* It bothered her that she wasn't as familiar with what Aldrin did for the Walkers. Perhaps that was intentional, but whether from Naro or Aldrin, she wasn't certain. *Shouldn't I know this, if I'm to become a lieutenant one day? What kind of jobs and responsibilities would Naro expect me to take charge of? Ajak will probably follow in Sabyl's footsteps, although I'm sure Sabyl would remain a lieutenant until she retired or died, neither of which would happen for many years if Sabyl had her way. Perhaps the structure within the Walkers was going to change?*

Ray didn't even understand the full picture of what the Walkers did today, so she couldn't speculate about their future. She racked her brain for other potential tasks, other groups of people she might be able to give orders to. Memories of Naro watching after her as a child kept passing before her mind's eye. *Perhaps I can work with the kids we always manage to recruit? That might not be so bad.*

Ajak nabbed the wine from her grasp and left the bedroom. She watched him go, wondering if she missed something he said or if he was angry with her.

"It was an orange you were messing with, right?" he called out from the other room.

"Y-yeah," she managed to respond.

He returned to the bedroom with an orange in his hand. "Here. Something to fiddle with while you're daydreaming."

Her eyes lingered on his face, looking for any traces of annoyance or anger. She found none. Maybe he had been doing his own daydreaming.

"What are you gonna do?" she asked, adjusting her posture so she was sitting straighter.

"I dunno. Walk in circles, maybe. Or bang my head against a wall until I pass out." He shrugged and left the room.

She looked down at the orange and began to peel off its skin.

———◦———

The next day—or what she assumed was a new day after she slept—was much the same. Ajak paced around and she read her book. Every so often he'd stop his pacing to rifle through their provisions, but he never took anything from the table. Ray worried about what was going through his head, but she didn't want to risk upsetting him. *Better he paces than be angry with me while we're stuck down here,* she reasoned.

Ray and Ajak took the time to eat their rations together. That day they ate two meals of salted trout and sliced apples. After the second meal, they spent an hour passing the wine bottle between them, taking only the smallest sips to preserve the wine for the next day. They had plenty of water to share between them, so this was more for enjoyment than anything else. *Whatever enjoyment can be had from tiny sips of wine.*

Ray looked over to Ajak and frowned. A sullen look passed over his eyes, his brown eyes staring at the floor. She summoned her courage and asked, "Why don't you do something else, besides walking in circles?"

"What else am I supposed to do?" She gestured to the bookcase. Ajak scoffed. "Not my thing."

She frowned. "Don't you know how to read? I thought Naro had taught everyone—"

"I know how," he said sharply. "It's just not my thing."

"Fair enough." She took another sip of the wine and then passed the bottle back to Ajak.

He took the bottle and got to his feet, disappearing into the bedroom again.

With a sigh, Ray cleaned up her spot at the table and returned to her book. She had covered a couple of centuries of history that day. Not much had happened after the Elviri reclaimed Promthus and destroyed the Asaszi. The Proma suffered heavily from the war, but they rebuilt their homesteads and villages and continued their lives. Although the Proma had plenty of history with the Asaszi, it was all legend and myth for Ray. The Asaszi had been gone for thousands of years. No Proma alive held any fear for the archaic snake people who had dwelled in the rainforests to the south. The only boogeymen mothers spoke of were the Enthai in Na'roc of North and the Provira.

Eventually she could no longer keep her eyes open. She returned to the bedroom and kicked off her boots.

"Drink with me?" Ajak murmured with a slight slur. He was lounging on one of the beds, one leg kicked out. Though he tried to play it off as a casual request, she could hear the plea underneath—the request to do something she wasn't entirely sure she was prepared to do.

A small flame ignited deep inside her. *We could get caught or killed any day now*, that tiny part of her whispered. *Better to know and love him than shut him out. Do I want to die without having loved someone?* The flame spread throughout her midsection, and she very much wanted to get up and sit beside him, perhaps crawl into his lap, and share the bottle of wine with him.

But Naro could come back at any moment, interrupting us. Or we could walk free tomorrow, all plans to kidnap the princess abandoned. If I sleep with him tonight and we survive, can I accept him going back to his old ways? Or will my heart break from the jealousy?

"Too tired to," Ray finally forced out, trying to ignore the ache in her abdomen and how disappointed she felt in herself.

He grunted and pulled both of his legs up to his chest, taking a swig from the bottle. She resisted the urge to reach out and comfort him, and instead climbed into one of the other beds and pulled the blanket up to her chin.

Ajak finished off the bottle of wine that night and fell asleep without saying another word to Ray. She eventually nodded off into an uneasy sleep. In her dreams she found herself in the hidden stairwell beyond Naro's wardrobe, the blue flames flickering eerily around her. No matter how far up or down the stairs she climbed, she never found an exit.

⸺●○●⸺

On the third day, Ray asked Ajak about the castle over breakfast, eager to put the previous night behind them. "What's going to happen when we're inside?"

Ajak leaned back in his chair, rubbing his hand against the growing stubble on his chin. He must have felt the same way, because he started talking as if nothing had transpired. "We'll be going in as kitchen help. The inside man was supposed to find a way to get rid of the other staff, so he'd have a reason to bring us in. Poison, bad food, something like that. Boss must be taking care of that."

Ray frowned but said nothing. *We can't murder the others because then it would be easy to pin the kidnapping on the inside man. Good. I don't want their deaths on my conscience.* The thought did little to ease the knot in her stomach, though.

He took a bite of bread before continuing. "We'll take the princess her dinner. It'll be laced with the brew the boss made. That'll all be easy enough, even with guards escorting us around. The real tricky part happens after we leave her chambers. We have to find a way to stay in the castle and get back to her chambers without alerting the guards, and then get out. The boss'll probably need to get new information from his insider after that scuff-up in the Sky District. There's probably going to be more guards hovering around the princess."

They both ate in silence for a few moments. Ray mulled over several different questions and thoughts in her head, not quite sure how to address her fears. *Would we be carrying any weapons? What am I thinking, of course we will. I just hope we won't need to use them. But there's only two ways off the castle island—by boat or by bridge. Ajak already mentioned a sailor before, so we must find a way to get her to the water undetected. Could we go out a window?*

Her voice was very quiet when she finally asked, "Ajak, will I need to... Am I expected to hurt, or... *kill* anyone?"

Ajak met her gaze, his face solemn. "Not if I can help it," he replied with a gentle tone. The flame from the previous night rekindled and she quickly looked away, feeling a blush spread across her cheeks.

After their meal, they sat together on the same bed and idled away the rest of the morning and the early afternoon. Ray swapped the history book out in favor of *The Woodwalker*. She found herself desperately wanting to get lost in the Imalarii Woods, far away from the city.

Ajak slept, or at least appeared to sleep. His eyes were closed, and he leaned back against the headboard, his legs tangled together with hers. She would periodically lift her gaze from the book and watch his chest rise and fall.

After a time, Ajak became the only thing she could think about. She did trust him. His company had been rather pleasant over the past few days. Perhaps once this was all over, she could come to love him and want him the way he wanted her to. She couldn't deny that she wanted that anymore. She wondered what kind of a person he would be after this mission was over. Would he change his ways after infiltrating the castle with her, having to put his life in her hands? Although the thought gave her some measure of hope, the dread and fear of such a task overwhelmed all other thoughts.

Sleep had started to claim Ray when she heard someone moving upstairs. She grabbed Ajak's forearm and lay perfectly still, eyes focused on the open doorway to the other room.

Ajak woke immediately.

"Upstairs," Ray whispered.

He stood and crept to the threshold, grabbing his dagger from his discarded jacket. Pressing his body against the wall, he looked around the corner. Ray followed suit, retrieving one of her own daggers from nearby.

They waited with bated breath as they heard the wall slowly sliding open.

Is it Naro? Or one of the other lieutenants? Or has someone else found our hideout?

A figure in black descended the ladder with surprising speed and stealth. They tore off the hood of their cloak to reveal Naro's dark blue hair and bronze face. Ray swore she saw a look of relief cross his face before he approached the table in the other room. He removed a bag from his back and set it down on the counter, beckoning the two of them to join him.

Ray hurried to Naro's side, tossing her dagger onto one of the beds. She heard Ajak's footsteps behind her.

Naro wasted no time giving orders. "We move now. Your clothes are in this bag, along with a small phial of the princess's remedy. You are to report to the castle kitchens immediately. A man named Claud will be waiting for you at the bridge to escort you across."

So, this was it. The time had finally come. A knot grew in her stomach in mere seconds. She started to reach for the bag, but Ajak's voice gave her pause.

"You're never dressed like that, boss," he said.

Her eyes darted back to Naro. Dressed head to toe in black. His clothes were nondescript. The attire of a thief in the night. *Where would he be infiltrating tonight? Or is he on the run, too?*

Her blood ran cold.

"Never mind me. Focus on the mission and *do not fail.*"

Naro and Ajak stared each other down for what felt like a lifetime. "Yes, sir," Ajak finally muttered, bowing his head.

Naro cast a quick glance at Ray as he turned to leave. A sea of emotions danced across his face. The one that stood out to her was fear. As she tried processing that emotion—*Naro* having that emotion—he vanished back up the ladder.

Ajak nudged her, and they picked through the pack to gather their clothes. There were two sets of clothes for them—uniforms for the kitchens and dark clothing to change into after serving the princess her dinner. Ray put on both sets of clothing so there'd be nothing for her to carry once they left the safehouse. The top layer was a loose gray dress with an apron wrapped around the waist. Underneath she wore dark leather leggings and a black cloth shirt. Naro had also included a black headwrap which she tucked into the hem of her leggings. The extra layers would bring some level of comfort out on the cold streets.

Ajak opted to leave his second set of clothing in the pack and filled the rest of it with food from their supplies. He changed into his kitchen attire—gray tunic and pants—and then shrugged the pack onto his shoulder.

"Boss didn't leave us any weapons, so we'll have to sneak some knives once we're in the kitchen," Ajak said as they headed for the ladder.

Ray frowned but said nothing. Carrying knives was something she had always done, and she knew the basics of how to use them. The idea of having to use them inside the castle made her uneasy. It was one thing to defend herself on the street from other thugs, but against knights?

She stayed close to Ajak as they left the safehouse, ensuring to close the hatch and wall. Outside the suns were slipping below the horizon. The cold autumn air felt refreshing on her face and hands after being cooped up for so long. She breathed in deeply, savoring the smells of smoke, lake water, and ovens preparing meals. Even the unsavory smells of sewage and dirt were better than the stagnant air of the underground flat.

People filled the streets as they went on their way home, or out to a tavern. They blended in without any issue and passed through the Market District. The bridge to the castle was in the Market District on the western edge of the island. Guards were always stationed at the ramp in two small towers flanking either side of it. Naro said that someone named Claud would be waiting for them. *Is it normal for kitchen staff to be crossing over to the castle so late in the day? Will the guards try to stop us?*

She silenced her thoughts, pushing her anxiety as far down inside of her as she could. It wasn't the time to be distracted with fear. She had to stay focused, both for her sake and Ajak's.

A blond man wearing a similar outfit to Ajak idly chatted to one of the guards by the bridge. When he noticed the two of them approaching, he called out to them and waved. "Good evening! Glad to see you made it on time. First shifts are always daunting."

Ray forced a smile and waved back. "It's an honor to work in the castle," she said once they were a little closer.

"Well come on, no sense in dawdling about. The bridge is the easy part of getting to the kitchens." Claud turned back to the guard and bowed cordially. "'Til next time, my friend!"

The guard murmured a goodbye and returned to their post, facing the city. Ajak, Ray, and Claud strolled right by the guards and onto the bridge. The absurdity of the moment filled her head with a pleasant sense of irony. She latched onto that feeling as the city's noise faded behind them and the castle loomed ahead.

Claud wasn't wrong. Once they were across the bridge, it was a maze getting to the kitchens. It didn't help that Ray felt stricken by a sense of awe as they traversed the castle's interior. Beautiful woven tapestries hung on every wall, as well as painted shields and polished weapons. A warmth resonated within her. It was her heritage, even if she was just a lowly street rat. She looked at the might and strength of all the kings of Promthus. It was with those weapons that her ancestors' kings fought back the Asaszi, the Enthai, and all other dangers that threatened their people.

The kitchens were only one floor below the main level, but there were many twists and turns through several corridors before they arrived. Several people moved about at frantic speed, and yet they spoke calmly to one another and handled all their tasks with ease.

Claud immediately wandered off toward a tall, thin woman holding a large wooden spoon in her hand. She seemed to be a supervisor over the other kitchen workers. "Roona, these are the two new ones I was talking about."

"We could have used them earlier this afternoon." Roona scolded, folding her arms in front of her chest. "But now is better than never. Show them to Thom and then get back to the spit."

"Of course, Roona." Claud did some sort of half-bow before turning back to face Ajak and Ray. He pushed them off toward a flock of young men and women who were gathered around a couple of empty tables. "Thom! Fresh meat!"

Without another word, Claud was gone. One of the young men turned to look at them and beckoned them over. "Right. Names?"

"Lorie and Adam," Ray chirped.

"Lorie and Adam." Thom nodded and looked back at the others. "Lorie and Adam are going to be the new servers for Princess Niamnh. No more doubling up." A few of the other servers murmured enthusiastically. "Jayne, you'll be their lead for the week. Need to make sure they know the layout of the castle."

Two boys snickered. A stout woman near the back of the crowd raised her hand to smack them on the backs of their heads. They stifled their laughs and scurried away.

"Everyone else, you're back to your normal routes. Meals will start coming out in ten minutes. Get your trays prepped." Thom finished giving orders and then left to attend to another matter elsewhere in the kitchens.

The stout woman approached Ajak and Ray, looking them up and down. "I doubt they gave you the necessary background on *what* it is you'll be delivering to the princess," she said.

Ray threw a concerned look at Ajak, who merely shrugged and replied, "Food, I would assume."

The woman, Jayne, waved her hand in the air. "Bah, tonight is a light night, so it'll ease you into the job. The princess doesn't eat like any of the rest of us. Come, follow me." She reached behind them to grab a bowl from a set of shelves.

The three of them hurried through the kitchen and into another room with a large table in the center, a cow carcass laid across it, and a man with a butcher's knife hacking away at it. The metallic smell of gore hit Ray in force and she had to throw her hand over her nose and mouth. It was like the warehouse she found with the staged athra scene. *How can they work like this? I've seen animal butchery before, but this is worse.*

"You got the bits carved out yet?" Jayne called out to the butcher, wrinkling her nose up.

He turned to look at her and then pointed toward a pile of organs next to the carcass. "I think she'll like these ones. Better than how we've been serving her."

Jayne pushed the organs into the bowl and then turned back toward the exit. "Come, we need to assemble the tray now."

Jayne had Ajak grab a gold-tinted glass bowl from a separate set of shelves near the exit. These were the royal serving dishes, Jayne explained. "And this particular dish is something new we're trying out. Cow liver." She arranged the liver in the glass bowl, in what Ray could only assume was an effort to make it look presentable.

"We don't cook the liver for the princess first?" Ajak asked warily.

Jayne looked up at him with a grimace. "The princess is sick. She can only eat raw flesh from animals, nothing cooked. Else she gets ill. It's not for the faint of heart."

Is this because of the Doshara inside of her? It has to be. What else could reduce a person to such animalistic tendencies? Ray grabbed the hem of her apron and squeezed tightly, trying to calm her stomach.

"Remember the oaths you swore when you agreed to take this job. The castle's secrets belong to the *castle*. If word of the princess's ailment gets out, it'll be your corpses feeding the fish," Jayne said, the threat very clear in her tone.

Oaths we never made because we didn't get these jobs honestly. Not that I'd tell anyone this secret. Her grip on the apron loosened a little.

"I'm going to clean up. Lorie, you'll carry the tray when it's time. Wait here. Put one of those glass goblets on the tray, too. Adam, come with me and I'll show you where we fill the water pitchers. Grab one of the glass pitchers behind you."

Ajak pulled down both his pitcher and Ray's goblet, handing it off to her and following Jayne to another section of the kitchens.

Ray placed the goblet in the top right corner of the tray. As she waited for Ajak and Jayne to return, she studied her surroundings and the tray in front of her. It would be easy enough to pour the draught into the water when Jayne wasn't looking, even with guards stationed throughout the castle. The bigger concern was how they would get out of the castle with the princess later in the evening. She had to pay careful attention to the hallways and stairwells when Jayne escorted them to the princess's tower later.

"We have a few minutes before we must get moving. Do either of you have any questions so far?" Jayne asked as she and Ajak returned to the table, her hands cleaned of blood. Ajak no longer had his pack slung across his back.

"How often does the princess receive her meals?" Ajak inquired.

"Just the one, every evening," Jayne answered.

Ray tried to come up with questions she may have if she had legitimately been brought on to work in the kitchens. "Does she always take water, or does she take wine as well?"

"She will sometimes take wine, although she still prefers water."

Ray looked down at the raw liver in the glass bowl. "Will the princess need a fork and knife?" she asked.

"Pardon?"

Ray looked back up at Jayne and frowned. "For her meal." *Something to make her feel normal.*

Jayne was silent for a moment, and then nodded. "I'll go retrieve some. Wait here."

As she hurried away, Ajak and Ray exchanged quiet whispers. "Where did the pack go?" Ray asked.

"Jayne showed me where the staff keeps their personal belongings while on shift," Ajak told her.

"Did you pull anything out of it?"

"Aye." His eyes darted toward the water pitcher, which had been filled.

Ray bowed her head ever so slightly and said no more. Jayne returned not too long after with a fork and knife, which she placed on the tray in a delicate manner.

"Come, it's time we get moving. Both of you, be very careful. These glasses have been in this castle since before your grandparents were born." Jayne lifted her skirts and took off, leaving Ajak and Ray to hurry after her while balancing the tray and pitcher. "Princess Niamnh's chambers are at the base of the southwestern tower," she added over her shoulder as they climbed a stairwell back to the floor they came in from.

They crossed through the main hall and entered another corridor, climbing a set of stairs up two floors and then navigating through another corridor. Ray made note of any memorable tapestry or other item on display. They passed several guards on patrol. She also made note of what weapons the guards had and what their armor looked like. The knife on the dinner tray was not very large, but Ray could pick out certain weak spots in the armor where she could do a decent amount of damage. Not that she wanted to, but she had to be prepared.

"We are still working out the exact instructions for serving dinner to the princess in this fashion," Jayne spoke as they climbed a tall spiral staircase. "Previously the princess would receive her meals in a room down the hall from her chambers. It's easier to clean up that way. With these smaller portions, though, her maids think that it will be alright to serve in her chambers."

"Should we become familiar with the other room? In case we have to go there in the future?" Ray asked.

"After, yes. The door to her chambers is up ahead. See the knight stationed outside?"

Sure enough, at the end of the hallway ahead of them was a man dressed neck to toe in plate armor. A crown was emblazoned on the chest plate. His right hand rested on the pommel of his sheathed longsword, and he cradled a helmet in his left arm against his hip. The knight's hair was black as night, pulled back out of his face. His neutral expression didn't change as the three of them approached.

"Sir Britten." Jayne stopped and curtseyed. "These two are the new servers for the princess's evening meals."

He took a good, long look at Ajak, and then turned his gaze to Ray. He had plain gray eyes. The faintest stubble covered his cheeks and chin. He must have been around Ajak's age, in his mid-twenties.

"Good evening," he said warily, stepping to his left. He reached behind him with his right hand and opened the door, pushing it inward. "The princess isn't back yet, but you can leave the food and drink in the main chamber."

Ray's grip on the tray tightened. *Where else would the princess be? Is she not normally confined to her chambers because of the Doshara? But this knight had said it so calmly, as if this was a normal occurrence. And Jayne said she ate every night. No need to start panicking just yet.* But her grip did not loosen.

Jayne nodded and entered the room, Ajak and Ray following closely behind. She looked down at her tray, trying her best to look as meek and unthreatening as possible.

The room was large and warm. Against one of the walls was a fireplace, which a maid was stoking. When she heard the door open, she half turned to look at the newcomers.

"Good evening, Jayne," the maid called over her shoulder. "I've already prepared the princess's table for her meal."

On the other side of the room was a small round table with two chairs. A golden satin tablecloth was draped over the top with a small vase of flowers in the middle. Ajak and Ray took their cue to set the water pitcher and tray down on the table. Ray took extra care in transferring the glass bowl and goblet from the tray to the table.

"Where should we put the tray?" Ray asked Jayne quietly.

"You can place it on that other table over there," the maid replied before Jayne had the chance. The table in question was a very narrow piece near the door to the hallway.

Ray nodded and set the tray down.

"Do we need to wait for the princess to return?" Ajak asked calmly.

Ray knew he was concerned, though, and that he was trying to ensure their plan was successfully executed.

"We don't serve the princess the same way we would the other members of the royal family," Jayne explained, her tone gentle. "She doesn't want that level of attention. You may pour the first glass of water, and if she requires more, then Wendola will serve her. We must get back to the kitchens."

"What about the dishes? When do we retrieve those?" Ray asked, trying her hardest to sound calm with only a hint of curiosity.

"We will come back in two or three hours to retrieve them."

Ray nodded. Two or three hours, then. They would need to determine an escape route during that time.

CHAPTER XVII:
MUNNE

ELIMERE: DAY 16, MONTH 11, YEAR 13,239

Much of the previous day was a blur. Munne recalled returning to her suite after the midday meal to assist her maids with preparations for her travels. Namyr and Laenis had gathered up most of her belongings and packed them away, sending them down to the stables to be loaded onto the pack mule. It would be neither a diplomatic nor bloody mission, so she wouldn't need dress robes or armor—only riding coats and casual attire. The effort was more taxing on her body than she anticipated, and when she laid down to rest for the night, she fell asleep quickly.

The sleep didn't last, though, and she awoke in the middle of the night again with beads of sweat on her temples.

When she awoke for the second time the next morning, the imprints were gone from her skin. She touched her arms where they had been, craving the warmth they had brought her. With reluctance, she got out of bed. Her triple would be joining her for breakfast, and she would announce her plan to abandon her father's plan and instead go to Kherizhan. She wondered how they would respond. Her stomach clenched at the thought.

As Munne took a seat at her dining table, Namyr entered her suite with Mayrien and Araloth trailing behind her. Munne met the maid's gaze and nodded. Namyr curtseyed and took her leave.

"Ah, good morning, friends. Please, take a seat," Munne said cheerfully, forcing away the ill feeling in her stomach. She gestured to the chairs around the table. They pulled a chair out and took a seat. "We need to discuss our next journey out of the valley."

Araloth nodded, and Mayrien flashed Munne an inquiring look.

"To the Imalar Woods? Are our orders not clear?" Araloth asked slowly, trying to understand the meaning behind this summons. Usually, they discussed tactics and travels at the Meeting Spire, or the barracks, or one of the other buildings the army used in Elimere—never in private chambers. Especially if the orders were as simple as Huntaran's had been: muster the necessary troops and depart within the week.

"I have a plan, and I require your assistance with it, as always." Munne lowered her voice, pulling her chair closer to the table.

"What would that be?" Araloth asked, resting her elbows on the table and folding her hands. Neither she nor Mayrien touched the food on the table.

Munne looked between them before speaking again. "I have decided that I won't be making the journey to the Imalar Woods and will instead be going somewhere else." She was as calm as if she were discussing the meal on the table in front of them.

Both Elviri stared at her as if she was crazy, but neither said a word. It wasn't the first outlandish plan or suggestion Munne had come up with, but it may have been the most dangerous since it would be crossing her father's orders. She appreciated that her friends were at least willing to hear her out before criticizing her decisions. It did little to ease the twisting in her stomach.

"I have found something very promising that may lead me to answers about the nightmares I've been having," she said quietly. "I don't plan on leaving the Imalarii defenseless. I would have you gather the necessary troops from the valley and send them to the Imalar Woods within the week, just as my father ordered. You will then meet me at Auora and accompany me on the journey I have chosen to take instead."

As soon as Munne finished speaking, Mayrien practically leaped out of her chair and began pacing the room. Araloth rested her forehead against her folded hands. Munne looked between the two of them, waiting for their response. A flash of panic hit her.

They think me mad.

"Vere'cha, you know I'd follow you to the ends of the world," Araloth said. "And I understand not wanting to go, but... Is this truly the right decision?" The older Elviri looked up at Munne, weariness in her eyes.

"Araloth, I swear to you, I wouldn't make this decision lightly," Munne responded, already imagining the consequences to this action. *Father will strip me of my title, perhaps even my inheritance. Will he try to conceive another heir? Or will he force me to marry and conceive one instead?*

"I know this, and yet I'm still concerned with it." Araloth rose from her chair but stayed by the table. "I don't support an open rebellion against the *Se'vi*."

"This isn't an open rebellion," Munne told her, leaning back in her chair. She had to muster all her strength to meet Araloth's gaze.

Araloth barreled through Munne's words and kept going. "You plan to defy the orders of the *Se'vi* and take off on a personal mission that very well could be taken care of if you sought the aid of a mindwalker."

"Mindwalkers can't help me with this." Munne hoped her voice sounded resolute. She felt anything but. Between politicking and matters of succession, she had spent much of her day yesterday fighting off thoughts about Malion and his demise.

By his own hand. Munne had to remain strong if she was going to tell them.

"What makes you think that?" Araloth snarled. "Have you even tried visiting them? They help the rest of us when we come home from the battlefield."

Araloth took two steps toward Munne, and she was suddenly overwhelmed by the older Elviri's presence. The two had fought before, countless times, but she could hear the accusations and bitterness in Araloth's voice. *You think yourself better than the rest of your troops?* Munne wanted to shrink back into her chair. She dug her fingers into the armrests, her nails chipping the wood.

"Araloth, give her space," Mayrien said. Munne heard her approach, but Araloth dominated her field of view so she couldn't see anything else.

"You lead us into battle, against a foe that knows no mercy, and yet you—"

Munne leapt to her feet, crossing what little space there was between her and Araloth. Her face twisted into a frown and her nose nearly rammed into Araloth's, the elder Elviri just barely taller than her. "I've scoured the archives, I've communed with the gods, and no one can explain what these nightmares mean. I'm not haunted by the battlefield, I'm haunted by something ancient and dark, and it wasn't until I found this damned journal that I had any idea what's wrong with me."

Munne could hear her heart beating rapidly, and the waterfalls off in the distance. Araloth's mouth hung open, words dying on her lips. She still bore an expression of frustration, but it fell away. The squeaking of leather indicated that Araloth was relaxing her hands, which had been balled into fists. A hand reached out and touched Munne on the shoulder, and she couldn't help but jump from the contact.

"What was in the journal, Vere'cha?" Mayrien asked quietly.

Died by his own hand.

Munne inhaled deeply and took a step back from Araloth. She could see the dining room again and Mayrien standing to the side. The light seemed to darken as she cast her gaze down to the table. She refused to endure the nightmares alone as Malion had. Perhaps that would give her more time before it consumed her.

I will make it end.

"Malion had nightmares of the *Ardashi'ik*, and it drove him mad. He sought aid from the Proma, from his own people... All to no avail." Munne looked up again at her friends, meeting their eyes. "When he returned home from the war, he was cast out from the army for endangering the other soldiers. I don't know what he did to them, he... there was no mention of it anywhere." She shook her head. "He killed himself to make the nightmares stop."

More silence. She thought she caught a glimpse of a moving shadow out of the corner of her eye. *Always watching.* She swallowed with difficulty. A lump had formed in her throat.

"Where would you have us go?" Mayrien's voice was soft. Munne clung to that, willing the shadows away.

The next words were painful because she knew how controversial it would be to say them aloud. She almost winced preemptively, but the memory of the small coin with the blue flame prompted her to continue. "There are... *rumors*... of the mountains in the southeast."

Araloth's expression twisted back into another snarl, but Mayrien's hand on her shoulder stilled her anger. Mayrien looked back at Munne, concern written on her face. "Vere'cha, you know those are just rumors. Nothing more."

It wasn't often that Munne lied to her friends, nor was it often that she could develop a lie so quickly under pressure. "There was mention of it in the journal," Munne blurted out, hoping that her confident tone would hide the truth. *What other trinkets lie hidden in Kherizhan?*

Both of her friends' expressions softened. It took several moments before either spoke.

"I didn't mean to raise my voice," Araloth finally mumbled.

Munne stood and stepped away from the table. "I understand I'm asking something absurd of you, both of you," Munne glanced at Mayrien before continuing. "But if there's a chance something in those mountains can cure me of these nightmares, I must take that risk. I don't want to succumb to the same fate as my ancestor."

Mayrien looked at Munne and saluted, crossing her left arm across her chest and patting it against her collarbone. "I'll do this for you, Vere'cha."

Munne returned the salute, relief washing over her. The two younger women turned to look at Araloth, who sighed and raised her arm across her chest as well.

"I'm sworn to you, Vere'cha, and it's my duty to protect you as you would protect me." Araloth cited the vows they had taken when their triple first formed in Elimaine. "But know this, young one. This is treason, and I'm only following you to ensure that the line of the Hunting Throne continues."

Emotions swelled in her chest. She had looked up to Araloth when she first joined the army. Araloth hadn't come from a military background, and yet she climbed the ranks and trained herself in all disciplines, so she could better serve her people. It was a great comfort that her friend was willing to stand by her side, even if she did so with great hesitation.

"Thank you, Araloth," Munne murmured, a grin spreading across her face. She placed her hand on Araloth's shoulder and squeezed gently. "I won't keep you any longer. Meet me in Auora once you have sent troops to the Imalarii. You'll find me at the Pike and Pint."

The two Elviri nodded and took their leave. After they left, Munne sat back down at her table and pulled some rolls and fruit onto her plate. She had to force down the food because her stomach was twisting about. She knew she had a long journey in store and would need all the energy she could get.

Munne sent Namyr and Laenis to find the servants in charge of packing the carriages. They would carry her trunk of riding and traveling gear down to the stables in preparation for her departure.

She hoped that the most difficult part of her journey would be disobeying her father's orders and lying about it, but something inside of her made her doubt it. She pushed those thoughts out of her mind and departed for the stables. *I hope I'm making the right decision to go to Kherizhan.*

The traveling party would be leaving from the stables near the guest houses. Huntaran had requested that Munne's mare, Alathyl, be brought to those stables so that she may depart with her companions. The steed had been outfitted with a riding saddle, as well as two bags containing Munne's traveling gear. She brought Malion's journal with her and placed it in one of the saddlebags. She wasn't sure if she would need the journal, but something compelled her to bring it.

The three Barauder were perched on the backs of their horses, each with a grim expression on their face. It was a bizarre sight, seeing a Barauder on a horse. Munne had never seen them ride any mount, and something about their stature and looks of discomfort told her it wasn't how they normally traveled.

Did they come to Elimere on these steeds, or had they purchased them from one of the towns in Promthus?

Rhorek and the other three Proma paced around restlessly, ready to depart. He was just as unhappy with Huntaran's decision about the Provira as Munne was, but he had held his tongue. Perhaps after they left Elimere, he would reveal his true feelings on the matter. Munne wondered if she would be privy to that conversation.

Huntaran stood near the stables, dressed in regal attire. His robes were made from dark blue silk, and his hair had been braided for the occasion. As Munne mounted her steed, he walked over to meet her.

"Daughter, I hope you slept well," Huntaran greeted her, dipping his head in a polite bow. "The skies are clear to the north. It seems that your journey out of the valley will be smooth."

The weather was indeed pleasant today. Snow hadn't yet begun to fall. The southern ridge of the Telatorr Mountains was less finicky than its northern kin. Munne and her companions would hopefully reach Ferilin without much delay. Her stomach tensed up and she caught herself reaching for her satchel where Malion's journal was. She tore her hand away, hoping she was discreet with her movements and that her father hadn't noticed.

"Yes, we should reach Ferilin before the end of the week," Munne responded. After a moment's pause, she continued. "Araloth and Mayrien are gathering the necessary troops and will meet us in the Imalar Woods."

Huntaran nodded, seemingly pleased with her report. He didn't press her for more details, which she found odd. He turned his gaze from the skies to Munne, and he lowered his voice. "I want to try to make amends with you before your departure. I didn't anticipate our outburst at the war council."

So that's why he isn't pressing for more information about my triple. Munne averted her eyes to look anywhere but at her father. She held her tongue, waiting for him to continue.

"I know that you only want what's best for our people, but you've spent so much time at war, I fear that is the only solution you know." Huntaran paused, perhaps thinking of a different way to approach this.

Munne's stomach twisted in anger. War was the only solution the *Provira* knew. Their discovery of some long-forgotten Asaszi usurper would only fuel their hatred for the Elviri and Proma. Her father should have known this; he was a scribe for hundreds of years before he ascended to *Se'vi*. She chose to stay silent.

"I'm hoping that your time with the Imalarii will help stay your hand and show you that there are other solutions than bloodshed and death," Huntaran murmured. "You will need to know this when it comes time for your ascension in the summer."

Her chest tightened. She felt the sudden need to make space between her and her father. "Thank you, *Se'vi*. I must attend to my traveling companions." Munne nodded curtly and urged her mare forward, moving toward the

Barauder and Proma. She inhaled deeply, trying to cut through the tension inside of her. Huntaran didn't follow her, and for that she was thankful.

"Companions, are we ready to depart?" Munne asked the others, her voice loud and unwavering. The Barauder all nodded, and the Proma mumbled their own agreements.

"Lead onward, Lady Vere'cha." Rhorek gestured for Munne to take the lead, and so she did. She would lead until they reached the foot of the mountains, and then Rhorek and his men would take over as they crossed into Promthus and made for the city-island of Auora.

To anyone else aware of Munne's journey, it would appear as if she was following her father's orders. Crossing the Hourglass Lakes was the quickest way to the Imalar Woods, and it made sense that she would wait in Auora for her triple and summoned troops before continuing her journey. It was also a convenient place to meet up with the caravan leader in secret, away from prying eyes.

As the party left the stables, Munne only looked forward. She didn't meet the eyes of her father, or any of the other guests who had come to see her off. The streets were filled with everyday bustle. Her father hadn't ordered the streets to be closed because he hadn't wanted to draw attention to who was departing the valley. Some passers-by looked at Munne and her companions, but no one stopped to question where she was going with their allies.

The main gate to the valley stood before them. On either side of the road were stables. Munne felt a pair of eyes watching her from the right. When she turned to look, she caught the gaze of the caravan leader and his mismatching eyes. He was sitting on the back of his horse, a faint smile on his lips. He winked with his green eye before turning to look at his companions tending to two large wagons. A shiver ran down her spine, and she wondered what would become of her agreement with the caravan leader.

Leaves crunched underfoot, and a crisp fall breeze rustled the bare branches of the surrounding trees. Munne's ears were filled with the sound of hooves hitting the ground below. It was unwise to gallop through the woods at that time of year, so the company had to take their time on the path. Those who had built the roads long ago took care to leave as much space between the road and the cliffs as possible, but in some parts of the mountains, if one were to so much as look over their shoulder, they would see the dips and valleys below with ease. Munne had traveled these roads all her life, so she was accustomed to hugging the cliffside whenever possible. She had been partnered with her horse Alathyl for nearly ten years, and the mare was by far one of her favorites. The mare was very good at minding where she stepped, and Munne trusted the horse to lead the way when she herself was unsure of the terrain.

Their current path took them out of the valley Elimere was nestled in and up the side of Mount Karrus. As they climbed the mountain, clouds filled the sky and snow began to fall around them. The ground became covered, and the sounds of hooves became muffled. Without the buffer of sound, thoughts began to flood Munne's head again.

Will Father tell the nobility where I'm going? I'm sure he will, to show that I'm capable of keeping the peace and fortifying defenses. She grimaced at the thought. Her mind drifted to Gilareana. *Will she tell Laralos that I'll allow him to court me? She surely will, and he'll try to write to me... and none of the letters will make it.* Munne's grimace deepened.

Trying to distract herself, Munne looked behind her and noticed her companions were following in her exact steps, so as not to come across any hidden holes or rocks on the ground. Munne met eyes with the eldest of the Barauder, Lagazi, and nodded. Lagazi returned the nod with a stiff neck. The Barauder were most certainly out of their element in the mountains, far from the three great lakes in the east. Their blue and green skin marked them as easy targets amidst the snowy peaks of the Telatorr Mountains.

Do their gills ache in the cold? What are their native lands, Balach Yor, like in the winter? Is there snow like there is here? She willed herself to focus on the swamplands. *I hope I can visit there one day during a time of peace.*

The party was silent, except for the occasional whisper between the Proma. They held the rear of the pack and watched out for any dangers on the path.

"What d'you think our new orders will be once we get back to Auora?" one of the Proma whispered to the others. Casting a glance over her shoulder,

Munne saw the man was the youngest of the three, with less wrinkles and gray hairs than his companions. Wisps of brown hair stuck out from under his hat.

"King Nelle won't have us sitting on our arses, unlike the others," the oldest of the Proma grumbled. He huddled around his horse's neck, trying to conserve warmth.

Munne couldn't help but smile. They either were unaware of what she could hear, or they didn't care. *Either way, I'm glad to know I'm not the only one yearning to fight the Provira.*

"Enough. We'll discuss new orders once we're back in the city!" Rhorek barked, turning sharply in his saddle so he faced his men. The Proma were silent after that.

As the suns peaked and began to sink into the sky, the air around them grew cold. Munne knew it would be time to step off the trail and make camp for the night very soon. They had climbed the side of Mount Karrus and had nearly reached the pass that would lead them down the other side into a valley that connected to Mount Belyn. They were approaching one of the few places to rest on the trail—the Stone Pillar Overhang.

Munne turned again to look at her companions. "We're close to where we'll make camp for the night."

They all nodded and mumbled about how eager they were for the warmth of the campfire. It was cold in the mountains. Munne shivered, also looking forward to the warmth of the campfire.

The suns were setting in earnest when Munne led them off the trail toward a rocky overhang. Builders of ages past had decided it would be a designated resting place in the mountains, and so they built columns to hold up the rocks, creating a covered shelter for travelers. Munne dismounted from Alathyl and led the horse under the overhang. Her companions followed suit. Having stayed at the resting place in the past, Munne walked over to the cache of logs and twigs and pulled out enough to start a fire. She returned to the center of the shelter, kicking away at the thin layer of snow. She knelt and began assembling her fire pit.

Two of the Proma approached the pack mule they had brought along and started putting together tents for everyone. The third was tending to the horses. Rhorek approached Munne and kneeled beside her, watching her work.

"It's gotten much colder since we arrived in Elimere," he said.

"Yes, winter has begun in earnest," Munne responded, urging her small spark to grow into a large flame. "If the gods are kind, we will reach the edge of the Telatorr Mountains before the larger snowstorms arrive."

Rhorek grunted in agreement. He had only visited Elimere a handful of times since he became a military advisor to King Nelle. It had always been during the summer, as Munne recalled.

"Is this your first true winter, Rhorek?" Munne inquired, leaning back as the flame grew larger still. The residual heat from the fire warmed her face and she was comfortable for the time being.

"I've been to the Wall many times, but I can't recall passing through the Telatorr Mountains during the winter." Rhorek pulled off his gloves and held his hands to the fire.

The Wall was a massive ancient structure that spanned the northeastern border between Promthus and Na'roc of North. Construction of the Wall occurred around the year 5,000, but neither the Proma nor the Elviri had any written records on its origin. The Proma were quick to station soldiers there, as it served as a perfect line of defense—or offense—from the frozen tundra to the north. Munne suspected winter at the Wall was comparable to winter in the Telatorr Mountains. Perhaps one day she would travel there and find out.

The three Barauder came to sit by the fire, all leaning forward to capture some of its warmth. The other Proma joined shortly after, bringing supplies for an evening meal.

"And you, traveling companions? Have you experienced true winter before?" Munne asked the Barauder.

"I have visited your valley in the cold before," Lagazi said with a small cauldron cradled in her lap. "S'raak has accompanied me. This is the first cold for Druuk." Druuk, the male Barauder, sat closest to the fire, his knees pulled to his chest. S'raak, the younger of the two females, was muddling some leaves in a small bowl. All three were sporting heavy cloaks and furs, much more clothing than Munne was wearing.

"It isn't cold like this in Balach Yor," S'raak grumbled, pouring the muddled leaves into Lagazi's cauldron. She picked up a waterskin and added some of the liquid, and then Lagazi placed the cauldron into the fire.

"Is there snow?" the youngest Proma, Mathis, asked, looking up from his own small cauldron. Inside was the makings of a stew using rations they'd brought from Elimere.

Lagazi shook her head. "There's no snow. Only rainfall that Our Father brings."

That intrigued Mathis. He looked off into the distance, perhaps contemplating a land without snow. He returned to tending his stew.

Munne got to her feet and brushed the snow off her. "The horses will need water. Let me go fetch one of the buckets. Excuse me."

She walked away toward the firewood cache. Nearby was a stack of stone buckets to hold water. She grabbed one and wandered off to fill it with snow. The suns had almost gone down at this point. Munne glanced around at the trees, their long shadows stretching across the ground. She closed her eyes and breathed in deeply. The rustle of the wind danced between the naked tree branches. No creature stirred in the mountains.

As the wind faded, she was enveloped in calming silence. When Munne opened her eyes, she saw dark caverns and the looming shadow of a terrible beast. She stepped back to open her mouth and scream, but the crunch of her boot in the fresh snow brought her back to the mortal plane. She blinked and in front of her were bare trees, falling snowflakes, and her breath on the wind. She blinked a few more times, taking in quick, shallow breaths, and bent down to fill the bucket with snow.

As Munne returned to the shelter with a bucket full of snow, she saw that all the tents had been raised, and a few more cooking pots had been placed around the fire.

Rhorek turned to her and rose to his feet. "Lady Vere'cha, allow me." He crossed the space between them and took the bucket from her hands, returning to the fire to put it down. "My men and I will tend to the horses. Please, sit."

Munne met Rhorek's eyes, and he offered her a smile. She nodded and moved to sit by the fire. The smell of cooking meat stirred something inside of Munne, and she felt the gnaw of hunger.

"Have the Elviri ever considered constructing buildings for rest places such as these?" Salvis asked, looking up from his stew pot.

"For us, to sleep under the stars brings us closer to our gods," she answered, pulling her knees to her chest. A shiver coursed through her body. "But it's rather cold in these mountains, so perhaps it would be best to construct something."

Salvis chuckled and returned to the pot. Their evening meal consisted of a meaty stew of sausage and potatoes for Munne and the Proma, and an herbal stew for the Barauder. They traded stories of winter traditions and festivities. Munne told them about the two winter traditions the Elviri celebrated, and how the celebration of *Ema'nala Ena'deth* would happen while she was away in the Imalar Woods.

"I'll still have my daily meditations, though I will be missing the feasts and gatherings," Munne said, cradling a stone bowl in her hands. It was still warm from the meat and potatoes.

"Your company of soldiers should arrive before the end of the year, and then you will be able to celebrate with them!" Mathis said cheerfully. "I pray that the Protector will be kind this year and allow me time to see my wife and children for the turning of the new year."

A twinge of guilt nestled into Munne's stomach at the thought of her troops arriving in Auora in a few weeks' time. *It'd be nice to celebrate with them, but I must go to Kherizhan. At least I'll have Araloth and Mayrien by my side.* "Do you hail from Auora?" Munne asked.

"We have a home on the island, yes, but Fara took the children to Trent for the winter to be with her parents."

The conversation continued to be light and pleasant. When her company retired to their tents, Munne got to her feet and headed toward the firewood cache. She grabbed a few more logs and added them to the campfire before climbing into her own tent.

She sat on her bedroll and went about the process of removing her riding boots and armor. The tent flap faced the campfire, and she could feel the fire's warmth. She also felt the cold seeping through the opposite side of the tent. Munne crawled into her bedroll and pulled it tightly around her body. She rolled onto her side and stared at the leather.

I pray that Araloth and Mayrien honor their word and meet me in Auora in a few weeks, and not tell Father about my plan. My current company is pleasant enough, but I'll be at ease when my triple catches up to me. She drifted off to sleep thinking of her dear friends.

Warmth surrounded Munne on all sides. When she opened her eyes, she was in Elimere again, standing on her balcony in her silk slip. The valley was warm, and there wasn't a flurry of snow in sight. The town below her was quiet underneath the starlit sky. Street lanterns burned low, and there were no people walking about. Banners were hung from the street lanterns with patterns of scrolls and stars on them—symbols of *Tessalothe*, a celebration that occurred in the middle of the summer celebrating the history of the Elviri. It wasn't an unusual sight, but she could tell that she was in a dream.

She looked to the sky and saw the constellations of the midsummer sky shining dimly. Munne closed her eyes and savored the warm air on her skin. It would be several months before she would feel it in the real world once more.

She turned and entered her bedroom, intrigued to see what else was happening in the dream world. There was no fire lit in the hearth, and the blankets on her bed were made of cotton. All signs of summertime. The doors to the balcony would stay open during the summer months to let in the cool breeze from the waterfalls.

I'll take this opportunity to roam the halls of Father's manor and see what else I can find. As she left her suite, she noticed there were no other people in the halls. *Not surprising, considering this is a dream. It's actually rather peaceful. What about in the city proper?*

As she left the manor, the scene before her changed. The valley was no longer in the midst of a summer celebration. It was now covered in snow. She wrapped her arms around herself and walked onward, confused by the sudden shift in time. Munne noticed that the warmth from earlier came from her hands. It felt as if someone had taken each of her hands to a small flame, and then wrapped her hands around it. It didn't feel like any fire Munne had encountered before, and yet she found herself comforted by it. She tightened her hold around her body, urging the warmth to spread.

On the streets, the snow came up to Munne's ankles. She shivered as her bare feet sunk into the heavy drifts. Buildings were coated in frost and flurry. Glass windows were shattered, and no lights came from within. She had never seen the valley so ill-maintained. What had happened?

As she continued down the abandoned streets, she realized where her feet were taking her—the Hall of the Dead. The building loomed over her, a silent behemoth on the horizon. The doors were thrown open, and the inside was pitch black. The dark stone stood out amongst the white snow.

Where are the caretakers and priests?

A thin layer of snow rested atop the stairs. As Munne climbed the steps, she glanced down at her footprints. Despite being surrounded by the cold, she didn't feel a thing. She looked back up at the hall and realized she still couldn't see through the open doors. What awaited her beyond?

Munne stood before the massive doors, her head tilted back to take in the dark stone and wood. As snow fell from the sky, she noticed that it stopped just before the threshold. Snow had not touched the hall.

"What are you hiding?" Munne asked aloud, lowering her hands to her sides.

A gust of wind blew past her from the hall. It hissed in her ear, and she tilted her head to the side to hear it better, but it was already gone. Something was inside. It called out to her with wordless invitation, beckoning for her to enter the hall and step into the shadows. She took a deep breath, her hands tightening into fists, and took a step toward the doors.

Munne opened her eyes and saw leather above her. Her brow furrowed, and she raised her hands to feel around her body. She wore a heavy tunic and pants, not her silk slip, and she was wrapped in a thick bedroll.

She was in the mountains, not in the valley.

She sat up and listened to her surroundings, hearing the faint snoring of one of the Proma nearby outside of her tent. The campfire crackled, and she still felt its warmth through her tent flaps. She barely heard whispering voices over the fire. Munne identified the whisperers as two of the Barauder, S'raak and Lagazi. Druuk must have still been in his tent. Heavy footsteps came from behind her tent.

"We should wake the others soon... It will be a long day of travel for us as is." Rhorek's voice followed the footsteps. He approached the campfire. Munne listened to him stop, exchange a few more words with the Barauder seated around the fire about the morning meal, and then walk toward the other tents his men slept in. "Trendin, Mathis, wake up. We depart soon."

The snoring stopped, and the two men stirred from within their tents. Rhorek walked off, perhaps in the direction of the horses. Munne couldn't tell. She noticed that none of her companions mentioned waking her up. She pulled on her boots and armor and started to climb out of her tent.

As she parted the flaps and got to her feet, the cold immediately seeped into her bones. *Wasn't I just feeling the warmth from the fire? Where did this cold come from?* She crouched back down and put her hands on her bedroll. The interior of the tent wasn't as warm as it had been. *Am I imagining things?* Without thinking, she placed a hand on her forearm and felt the warmth return. *Oh, of course.*

"Good morning, Lady Vere'cha," Rhorek called from across the clearing. She looked up to him and saw him with the horses, along with his third man Salvis. Druuk climbed out of his own tent from behind Lagazi and S'raak and jumped in place a few times, trying to warm his limbs.

"Good morning," Munne replied, mustering enough energy to smile at them. She looked around the clearing and to the sky, noticing that snow hadn't begun to fall. "Perhaps the gods will be kind, and we'll reach the valley between the mountains this evening."

"Aye, and hopefully that will get us to Ferilin by the next evening where we can sleep in warm beds for a night," Trendin mumbled, rubbing the sleep from his eyes. The other Proma chuckled at his words while the Barauder simply watched them break down their tents.

Munne turned to her own tent and knelt to pull her bedroll out, ready to continue their journey onward. It seemed that Rhorek and the Barauder had agreed to break their fast on the road, rather than around the campfire. This would save them time during their journey.

As Munne moved to break down her own tent, she realized that she hadn't had any nightmares during the night. The thought made her pause. *Did I catch a lucky break in the cycle? I wonder if the beast will be there to greet me tonight, or if I'll see another empty cityscape again. That was... different.* An involuntary shiver ran down her spine, and she returned to the task at hand. There was plenty of time between now and the next sunset, and she was in no rush to get there, whatever was in store for her.

"We'll need to be careful descending the mountains, though. Just because the snow isn't falling doesn't mean the path is clear," Munne told the Proma, bringing her tied-up bundles to the pack mule. Salvis helped her secure her pack, and then Munne walked over to Alathyl. The mare snorted and butted her head against Munne's hand as she approached. Munne stroked her mane and scratched behind one of her ears. "Good morning, dear friend. Are you ready to ride?"

"I fed and watered the horses earlier while waiting for everyone else to rise," Salvis said to her, appearing by Munne's side.

"Thank you, Salvis," Munne nodded and offered a friendly smile.

Soon enough all their belongings were packed, and they were off. Munne took the lead once again with the Barauder following her closely, and the Proma bringing up the rear of the pack. Most of the morning was spent traveling across Mount Karrus, and in the early afternoon they began their descent into the valley between Mount Karrus and Mount Belyn. Snow crunched underneath their horses' hooves. Munne kept a watchful eye on the path, making sure they always stayed between the stone markers. The roads had been reinforced over the years with stone to ensure safe travel, but beyond the markers, the ground was susceptible to all the burrowing creatures that made the mountains their home. It was a gamble to walk outside the path because the ground could crumble out from underneath travelers at a moment's notice.

The party broke their fast and ate their midday meals atop their horses. Munne picked at a bag of dried fruits and nuts, sharing some of the larger slices of fruit with Alathyl. The Proma passed around pieces of dried meat. She noticed that the Barauder didn't partake in the meat, just as they hadn't the night before for dinner. It didn't seem like they had any trail rations. She slowed Alathyl down so that she was closer to Lagazi.

"Pardon my question, but do your people not eat meat?" Mathis asked, his voice polite.

Lagazi grunted and looked up at the Proma. "The Barauder only eat what Our Father and Mothers provide. Fish from the lakes, and plants from the lands surrounding them."

Mathis nodded thoughtfully.

"If you'd like, I'll share my rations with you," Munne offered, holding out her bag of fruit and nuts for Lagazi to inspect.

Lagazi held up her hand and shook her head. "You honor me, Lady Vere'cha, but we don't require any rations. The stew we ate last night will be enough until this evening's meal."

Munne returned the bag back to her side and tied it to her saddle. "A most useful traveling meal."

"Indeed." Lagazi let out a hearty laugh. "The herbs from Balach Yor aren't like any other in all of Daaria."

"I know the scribes of Elimere would love to come study the wildlife and plants around the lakes... if the Barauder would host them," Munne said cautiously, knowing her words may irritate the green-skinned woman. The Barauder were a reclusive race, and Munne doubted that even though Lagazi was willing to join the war against the Provira, she wasn't yet ready to open her borders to others.

The Barauder tensed. "Perhaps after the wars, Lady Vere'cha," Lagazi responded, nodding curtly.

Munne took that as the end of the conversation, and she urged Alathyl to the front of the pack. She let her mind wander as she looked at the horizon. There was a gap between Mount Belyn and one of the lesser peaks where she could see over the northern part of Promthus, the farmlands belonging to the Proma. In the middle of the farmlands were the Hourglass Lakes on which

Auora stood. From their height, Munne could see the lakes on the edge of the horizon but couldn't make out the island or keep. Beyond the lakes, far to the south was Moonyswyn, the heavily forested land of the Provira. She wondered if she and the caravan would travel through Moonyswyn once they reunited in Auora, or if the caravan leader knew of another route to Kherizhan. She would find out in due time, she supposed.

She couldn't yet see Ferilin. She would be able to after they climbed the western side of Mount Belyn and began their descent on the other side. It was a sizable city, slightly larger than Elimere. It served as one of three mainland Proma hubs and hosted a formidable trading outpost for the Elviri. It was possible she would run into others of her kind, perhaps soldiers who were deployed to the southern border of Promthus. It would be good to speak with some of them and see how things have gone since she first returned home. Although it had only been about a week's time, much could have happened since she was last in Promthus. She could also use this as an opportunity to bolster her alibi and discuss her plans to travel east to the Imalar Woods.

It'd be better if I didn't come across the caravan in Ferilin. I need to put as much time and distance between Father and myself as possible before it's revealed that I didn't make it to the Imalar Woods. I also don't need any of my men seeing the caravan and reporting it to Father—otherwise he may assume I was kidnapped.

As the suns descended on the horizon, Munne looked to the sky and noticed dark clouds rolling in. "There's a storm approaching," she called out over her shoulder to her companions.

"How soon before we make camp?" Rhorek called from the rear of the pack.

She glanced back at the trail in front of her, and tried to remember when they would come across the next resting area. They had passed one no more than an hour ago, so they would come across the next one in another hour. Would the next place provide shelter from the oncoming storm? She willed herself to recall the resting areas on the eastern slope of Mount Karrus. They had passed the Ice Creek Camp earlier, a clearing nestled on the edge of one of the larger creeks that flowed down Mount Karrus. That camp could accommodate smaller groups, five or less travelers, and had three lean-tos built against the cliffside. The next campsite was Three Rock Clearing down in the valley. It was a spacious clearing with three standing stones in the middle, typically used by larger parties like her warbands. There wasn't much shelter at that camp, but wasn't there another one before the valley?

She remembered there was a small cave about halfway between their location and the valley. It would be a snug fit with everyone and the horses inside, but at least they would all be dry.

"There's a cave just before the valley that we can rest at." She hoped the storms would hold off until they got to the cave and that it would pass quickly so that they could continue their journey the next day.

The cave was naturally formed out of the side of the mountain, up a small slope from the path. Builders of ages past had done little work on it, aside from adding a small pathway leading to it. The inside was dry enough, and snow had only just begun to fall by the time they stopped for the evening. Munne climbed off Alathyl and led the mare into the cave, a lantern in hand. It was empty and large enough for the traveling party and their horses. Munne relayed as much to her companions, and they went about settling in for the night. Two of the Proma built a fire near the center of the cave while the other six companions built their tents and tended to the horses. Snow began to pile at the mouth of the cave, but fortunately didn't blow much farther in. The fire was safe from the winds as well.

The group sat around the fire with their evening meals. The Barauder had made another pot of herbal stew, while the rest of the party ate dried meats and berries. The aromatics from the herbal stew made Munne's mouth water and she craved a plate of roasted vegetables from the kitchens back home. Berries would have to do until they got to Ferilin.

Mathis squirmed on the ground, fidgeting with a piece of dried meat. "Lord Rhorek, Lady Vere'cha, forgive the question, I didn't know when to ask it, but," he stammered, "but who were the Provira referring to in their letter? Isyth?"

Munne's blood ran cold as she met eyes with Rhorek. It was a natural reaction, the hairs on her arms raising at the mere mention of that name. She had been raised to fear that name. Her ancestors had gone to war to banish all traces of that name from history. To eradicate the creatures who spoke that name. She opened her mouth to respond but found the words dying in her throat.

"Proma boy, do you know what the Asaszi are?" Lagazi asked.

Mathis had a look of shame on his face as he shook his head. Munne felt a twinge of sympathy for the man, but it did nothing to quell the uneasiness inside of her. He wouldn't understand what that name meant. He hadn't known what would happen when he said it. He wouldn't understand why she had to force out all the words she was about to speak.

"They are foul serpent-like creatures we banished to Moonyswyn thousands of years ago," Munne said, taking great care to choose her words before continuing. "That name you speak, that's the name of their god. The Elviri have worked to eradicate all traces of them and their god. If the Provira are so bold as to use that name now, that means they have found something that we didn't destroy. Some book, perhaps, or a mural. It matters not. What does matter is that we find whatever it is and destroy it, along with the Provira."

"It would be wise to not speak that name again, Proma boy," Lagazi muttered, rising to her feet.

She gave Munne a sympathetic nod as she crossed to her bedroll and laid down, the other two Barauder not far behind her. The uneasiness faded away. Munne was thankful for Lagazi's words.

Night fell and darkness quickly set in. Munne sat near the fire with one knee pulled to her chest and watched the shadows dance on the cavern walls while her traveling companions retired to their bedrolls. They hadn't bothered setting up a watch while they traveled through the mountains, because there was no risk of being attacked so far north. All the fighting was happening in Promthus.

We are getting close to Promthus, though, and it's not like I'll be able to sleep tonight anyway. Maybe I should stay up and keep watch, at least for a few hours. Then maybe I'll get some rest. She would find out soon enough, but first she would enjoy the dance of the shadows and keep an ear out for anything moving about in the snow.

CHAPTER XVIII:
SETH

The setting suns filled the stained-glass windows and cast warm puddles of light on the wooden floors. Faint music could be heard outside the library. From below, the chattering of other folk grew as they closed their books and left for the evening festivities. A low grumble spread through his stomach, reminding him that he hadn't eaten since the night before. Seth had been so consumed with searching for more answers to the chain of scribbles that he'd forgotten to eat today, and very nearly forgot about the festival that evening.

A blush spread across his cheeks as thoughts about Lisanthir's invitation resurfaced in his mind, and what the night would have in store for them. *"I'll come back shortly after sundown to walk you to the plaza."*

Seth glanced at one of the library windows before looking back at the books before him. There were several tomes spread across the table that had begun to feel like a second home. His studies had brought him to the end of the Eldest Days and the early years of the Second Sun, during the last great siege of the Asaszi. There were descriptions of a nightmarish creature known as the *Ardashi'ik* that the Asaszi used to dominate the Elviri in open battle. He had never heard of this term before, nor could he recall any specific champion or beast that matched the description from his childhood.

Could this *Ardashi'ik* be the *Tserys*? The Asaszi had rallied behind the *Tserys*, and he had been their strength. *But the Asaszi never described him as a beast. I don't recall the Asaszi describing the* Tserys's *physique at all, outside of calling him the "golden king". Maybe he had golden scales? And besides all of that, there's several entries in these books where the Elviri describe the serpentine characteristics of the Asaszi. So, what is this* Ardashi'ik?

He scooped up a couple of the books and debated sliding them into his bag. Could he take these back to the inn to read them? He wasn't sure if he would be returning to the library that evening, and he didn't want to lose track of the books. Depending on how the festival went...

He reached into his bag and pulled out the crystal decanter. The liquid within was dwindling. There was *maybe* enough in there for one more day in Lithalyon if he was careful about going to bed early enough.

I doubt I'll get back to the inn early tonight... I'll have to leave tomorrow morning, then. I won't be coming back to the library.

He removed the stopper and took the smallest of sips, wincing as the liquid hit the back of his throat. It would have to do. Replacing the stopper, he slid the decanter back into his bag. Without another thought, he shoved the two books into his bag as well. He stood up, wiggling his toes for good measure. Seth left the study nook, heading toward the stairs. Rows of books rushed by him as he quickened his pace. He didn't want to keep Lisanthir waiting. Several other patrons were packing up their belongings and heading to the front doors, all seemingly going to the town center for the festival.

Without the beautiful decorations to distract him, he struggled to wrap his mind around a festival dedicated to the first frost of winter. The fact that the Elviri openly celebrated such a dark turn in the weather was strange. The Asaszi would simply hiss and stock up on firewood. They didn't celebrate the changing seasons, and by extension, the Provira didn't either. Meanwhile, the Elviri apparently welcomed the freezing cold with food, drink, and dancing.

Would Lisanthir want to dance with me?

His stomach seized and he immediately cursed himself for even thinking of such a thing. He couldn't dance. He never learned from his parents, or the Asaszi, or anyone else back in Yiradia. *And if I did dance with Lisanthir, I may never leave Lithalyon.* The warmth drained from his face as the reality of his situation settled in. *I've been a fool for acclimating to this place so quickly. I let myself get swept up in the city's beauty, the grandness of the library, the kindness of Lisanthir... I must leave tomorrow, and I can only dream that I'll return one day. But then again, hasn't this entire journey been a dream from the beginning?*

Lisanthir was waiting near the front desk, in the middle of a conversation with another one of the library workers. He leaned over the counter, a strand of his hair falling across his face. His braids were more elaborate than before, with silver beads threaded throughout. He was garbed in an emerald green robe—the same shade as his eyes. Wrapping around the sleeves and down his chest were silver swirls sewn into the fabric. A matching silver sash was tied around his waist, holding the robe together. Underneath he wore dark gray clothing with boots to match.

The sight of the Elviri brought warmth back to Seth's face, his dark thoughts slipping away. He couldn't help but smile as soon as he saw Lisanthir, no longer bothering to try to hide it. *If this is my last night here, then so be it. I'll return to Yiradia with memories I can cherish for the rest of my life.*

Lisanthir looked up, their eyes meeting, and he returned the smile. He said something quietly to the other librarian, and then straightened himself out.

"Are you ready to go?" Lisanthir asked with a mischievous look in his eyes.

"Absolutely," Seth replied.

Outside the city had undergone a transformation. Garland hung from the lampposts, complemented with silver silks and blue flowers. The scent of freshly baked goods and roasted meats filled the air, and Seth was reminded again of just how hungry he was. Music and cheer came from whole city. The streets were crowded with partygoers. Children lead their parents with a great sense of urgency. Couples walked arm-in-arm, murmuring excitedly to one another. Most of the Elviri around them wore robes like Lisanthir's in shades of blues, greens, and silvers. Many had silks and lace woven into the robes, some more intricate than others. Seth's simple brown shirt and pants felt drab in comparison.

As they walked toward the road, Lisanthir gently took Seth's hand and led him farther down the road than. They weren't going to the central plaza but away from it.

"Where are we going?" Seth asked, not even processing what was going on. A chill breeze brushed by them. Lisanthir's hand felt warm in his. Not as warm as the fire inside of him.

"If you're leaving soon, you should see Lithalyon in all of its splendor, underneath Aelrindel." Lisanthir nodded toward the massive tree, a grin spreading across his face. "Don't worry. There will be another plaza very similar to the central one there. Plenty of food and drink as well."

Seth had no response. He let Lisanthir lead him onward, his eyes focused on the tree, Aelrindel, as it grew larger. The road led to another elegantly decorated plaza. This one was smaller than the central plaza, but it was surrounded by some of the most stunning buildings he had ever seen. Murals were painted on the sides of several buildings, depicting the Elviri pantheon and lush scenes of nature. Red leaves littered the ground, a stark contrast to the blue and silver decorations and stalls. Many of the other patrons here were dressed in even more elaborate robes and dresses, looking like royalty. Seth felt very insignificant by comparison, even more than at the previous plaza. He never imagined himself being in the presence of people this elegant and refined.

Lisanthir tugged gently on his hand. "Drinks?"

His vision once again focused on the handsome Elviri in front of him. Lisanthir, in his fancy clothes, with beautiful beads in his hair... "Yes please." Seth responded, a little louder than anticipated.

They made their way to the edge of the plaza where several stalls had been set up to distribute hot food and drink. Behind the stall they stopped at, Seth recognized one of the tavern workers from the previous night.

"Alda! Two mugs, if you please," Lisanthir called out. His hand slid free of Seth's as he approached the stall. Alda and Lisanthir exchanged money, and soon a mug of warm liquid was pushed into Seth's hands. "Alda's uncle has been working on this brew for the past three months. It's a blend of mulled wine, ground spices, and fresh fruit. Give it a try." Lisanthir watched as Seth raised the mug to his lips and took a sip. The flavor was incredible, unlike anything he had drank before. He couldn't help but smile as he drank again, enjoying the way the sweet fruit and tart spices mingled on his tongue. It was a nice contrast to the chilly autumn day.

Lisanthir laughed and drank from his own mug before leading them on. Crisp leaves fell from Aelrindel above them, swirling around all the partygoers. A thin layer already lined the edges of the pavilion. It was almost like the tree was contributing its own offerings to the festival.

As they moved through the crowds, the sound of laughter and chatter overwhelmed Seth's ears. He had to strain to hear Lisanthir when he turned around to ask if he wanted to sit down for a few moments. He nodded an agreement and found his hand once more being held by Lisanthir as he was led toward the edge of the festivities. One of the tables had a few seats to spare, so they sat down and turned back to look at everyone else.

"It's a shame the Twin Chieftains had to depart for Elimere. They outdid themselves with preparations this year," Lisanthir said in between sips of his drink.

"Do they normally join in the festivities?" *I don't think Osza or Father would be caught dead mingling with the commonfolk, much less throwing a celebration like this...*

Lisanthir chuckled. "Caedwyn and Faelwyn are normally the first to dance, and they stop at each farmer's stall to purchase something."

Seth raised his mug to his lips again. *How foolish the Provira are for hating such a welcoming group of people. What really happened to drive the Elviri to the point of banishing my kin?*

Lisanthir turned to Seth to grab his shoulder and point at a raised platform in the distance where an elegant Elviri woman was joining the gathered musicians. "Look, Ferathiel is joining them!"

Similar exclamations rose up among the crowd. Lisanthir set his mug on the table and nearly jumped to his feet, his hand trailing down to Seth's and grasping it firmly. A trail of fire burned through Seth's arm, and his head spun. Before he could process what was going on, Lisanthir led him into the crowd as the music started up again, this time with the distinct addition of a melodious stringed instrument.

When Lisanthir turned to face Seth, his breath caught in his throat. Lisanthir's eyes were lit up with pure joy, his cheeks flushed, and his lips parted in a breathless smile. His other hand found Seth's, and he took him into an upbeat dance. Seth hadn't even realized he had left his mug of wine and bag behind.

"What are we doing!?" Seth cried out with a laugh. "I've no idea how to do this!"

Lisanthir laughed in return, a noise Seth held onto and replayed in his head. "Just trust me!"

Seth realized that Lisanthir didn't even have to ask, he already did.

Although there were others dancing—too many for Seth to count—the pavilion was large enough for all the twirling pairs. Leaves spun around their feet. With each spin, the garland seemed to glisten in the setting suns.

Branches from Aelrindel swayed in the wind, as if joining in for a dance of its own. Seth could hardly believe the moment he was in, caught up in the same dance as countless others, in such a beautiful city. He allowed himself to think, just for one night, that it was where he belonged.

With Lisanthir.

The song hit a crescendo and then ended. Cheers erupted from the crowd, and Seth joined in. He would have clapped, but his hands were still firmly in Lisanthir's. And that was where they remained for the next three dances as well.

———◦○◦———

By the time there was a lull in the music, the two had worked up a thirst. With a simple look and nod, Lisanthir led Seth back to their table where they collected their mugs and Seth's bag before returning to Alda's stand for more. Many other Elviri had done the same, so there was no time for small talk with Lisanthir's friend. After topping off their mugs, they drifted around the pavilion in comfortable silence. When they reached the road leading toward Aelrindel, most of Seth's drink was gone and he felt like he was positively glowing. Lisanthir mumbled something to him, and he couldn't help but laugh. It flowed freely through him, and he felt it from head to toe.

The trunk of the great tree loomed in front of them, pathways twisting around and under the equally great roots. They were at the highest point in Lithalyon, looking down at the rest of the city. Its winding paths and stone buildings looked like a maze, one that Seth wanted to lose himself in. Behind them was the wall separating them from the forest. Even further away, nestled deep within the forest, were the pyramids, the dark place that Seth had ran away from.

A sliver of fear sliced through his head, clearing away the fuzzy warmth that had grown there. He immediately tried to push it away. He would not think about that place tonight. Tonight, he was Lisanthir's, and he belonged here where it was warm, and music could be heard from the city below, and the leaves in the great tree glowed in the suns' fading light. He took another long drink for good measure. The fuzzy warmth returned.

"This is one of my favorite spots in the whole city," Lisanthir said quietly, looking out at Lithalyon. "Especially at sunset. Seeing the blend of streetlights and sunlight. And Aelrindel towering above everything else. Just stunning." He sat down on the ground, placing his mug next to him.

Seth looked at the city for a long moment before deciding to sit down next to Lisanthir. It was a little more difficult than he expected—the mulled wine was much stronger than what he drank the night before—but he managed it without making a fool of himself. He set his cup down on his other side but cradled the bag in his lap. It never even crossed his mind earlier that he had left it sitting on a table. He had no reason to fear someone looking into it or taking it. But now that they were away from the festivities, he clung to it like an anchor. He felt himself growing unsteady, and he didn't know what would happen if he let go.

Lisanthir chuckled and shook his head. "I came up here the first night I spent in Lithalyon, during my lifepath rotation. Looking out at the city, I knew this was where I was meant to be. It's been three years since I chose to work in the library, and this sight still takes my breath away."

The city truly was beautiful. Down below, several areas were filled with people, like the pavilion they had left. Music floated in the air. Although he couldn't make out the individual decorations, he could tell that it looked different for the festival. It was incredible how the Elviri came together to celebrate, and how immense their celebrations were. Seth clutched his bag tighter, curling around it. Up on this hill he felt so small. Small, but warm.

"Calydrian," Lisanthir murmured, his voice close to Seth's ear. He thought he could feel his breath on his cheek but very quickly dismissed that thought. There was no way he was that close to him.

Seth straightened his back a little and turned his head toward Lisanthir and was surprised to see him leaning in so close. His lips were parted, his cheeks flushed and bright red. His eyes, a beautiful green, met his own, then lowered to his lips. Then the space in between them was gone, and he felt Lisanthir's lips brush against his, soft and hesitant at first, then more firmly. Inside of him the fire burned brighter than before, and he was afraid that his skin would crack open, and the flames would consume them both.

He tried to rationalize what was happening and *how* it was happening, but by the time his mind caught up with him, Lisanthir pulled away. The Elviri's cheeks were a deep scarlet, and Seth just wanted to cradle his face in his hands—

"Lisanthir," he said, trying to keep his voice even.

The Elviri looked up at him, and it was his turn to kiss him, but this time without any hesitation. They stayed together for several moments, savoring the feeling and taste of one another. When they broke apart, both were smiling and breathing through parted lips.

Lisanthir let out a breathless laugh. "Well, that... I... I'm happy I met you, Calydrian."

Calydrian.

Not *Seth.*

Something deep within Seth climbed its way up, trying to get out. He struggled to breathe as his heart pumped faster. *This isn't you. You're nothing but a fraud.* Seth recognized the panic but was too late to control it. His vision blurred as Lisanthir's expression changed to something Seth had not seen before. *You need to run.*

Seth looked down at his bag, and then at his feet. Could he still feel his toes? He tried to wiggle them, to feel that they were still there and under his control, but in the heat of the moment he couldn't tell if they were wiggling or not. His breathing shortened. He needed to get somewhere private and drink the rest of the phial, and then...

Was there enough liquid left for anything?

Go home, imposter.

He needed to get out of Lithalyon and run. He prayed he could make it before the effects wore off and his legs no longer worked. Seth scrambled to his feet, avoiding looking at Lisanthir—he couldn't bear to now. He turned to leave and felt his foot brush the mug on the ground. It fell over, spilling wine across the dirt and leaves.

"Calydrian, where are you—?"

"I'm sorry," Seth managed to mumble before fleeing.

CHAPTER XIX: MUNNE

FERILIN: DAY 20, MONTH 11, YEAR 13,239

Munne and her companions arrived in Ferilin nearly two days later than anticipated due to the storm in the valley. Snow fell all night and well into the next morning, delaying their travels. They were finally able to depart from the cave two days after they lit their first campfire in it. They faced no other ill weather as they descended from the Telatorr Mountains and into Promthus.

Hopefully Araloth and Mayrien don't get caught in a snowstorm like that, or the caravan, for that matter.

Munne didn't have any nightmares during their journey through the mountains. Instead, she had four nights of comforting dreams filled with festivals from her youth. The Annual Hunt after her fiftieth birthday when her father formally declared her his heir. Her first *Henayth'mar* after she joined the military and forged bonds with Mayrien and Araloth. But she couldn't shake the feeling that someone was watching her from the edge of the crowds. She had tried finding the person, but every time she thought she had found them, the figure disappeared into the crowds. Each morning, she awoke feeling much warmer than she should have been. The morning of their arrival in Promthus, Munne happened to look at her wrists and saw the same faint outline of handprints that she saw back in Elimere.

Is the shapeshifter the person stalking me in my dreams, or is it the caravan leader? Or is it the Ardashi'ik?

It was midday when the party passed through the heavily guarded gates of Ferilin. Rhorek wanted to spend the rest of the day in the city rather than press on to Auora, and Munne was more than happy to agree. They could have easily continued onward to the city-island and arrived just after sundown, putting Munne closer to her meeting with the caravan leader at the Pike and Pint. She was instead thankful for the opportunity to try to use the time to speak to any Elviri she could in Ferilin, to solidify the image of her journey to the Imalar Woods, and to give her triple time to catch up to her. The less time she spent in Auora, the better.

The party left their horses at the northern stables, just inside the walls of the city. At the behest of Rhorek, the party then made haste to the town hall to announce their presence to Ferilin's mayor, Gilman Ervaitt. Munne thought it was a ploy to get the mayor to offer them lodging in his own home. She had very rarely interacted directly with him in her past travels through Ferilin. She had always slept in one of the inns or at the Elviri outpost when she had stayed here before and had no issue doing so again. Rhorek and his men were nobles from the city of Auora, though, and probably missed the luxuries of home.

The town hall was a rather plain structure, home to Gilman and his family. It stood two stories tall and was made from wood and stone in traditional Proma fashion. The front door opened to a foyer with a large staircase in the middle of the room, and numerous doorways led to other rooms in the hall. Munne's eyes wandered, taking in the building in its entirety. There was a receiving room to the left of the front door, with several chairs and benches placed in front of a desk. On the other side of the foyer was a dining hall with a large fireplace. Tapestries hung on the walls, depicting what she assumed was the history of Ferilin and Gilman's family.

"Greetings, Lord Rhorek!" a hearty male voice called from the staircase.

Munne turned her attention to the man descending the stairs. Gilman was an older Proma, his hair beginning to turn gray. He wore a plain set of brown pants and a jacket to match. His cheeks were rosy red, and he had a smile on his face that reached his gray eyes.

Rhorek approached Gilman and the two men clasped hands together and embraced as old friends would. "Good afternoon, Gilman. I have a few more companions with me on the trip back to Auora, three emissaries from Balach Yor and Lady Vere'cha from Elimere. It'd be greatly appreciated if we could share your hearth and ale tonight."

Gilman let out a chuckle and nodded his head, waving a greeting to the rest of the travelers. "Of course, friend. Any companions of yours are companions of mine. Welcome, all! I'll let my wife know that we'll be having company this evening, and I'll send one of my serving girls to the market to gather food for tonight's meal."

"You are kind with your hospitality, Gilman," Rhorek said. "Where might my companions and I make our beds for the evening?"

"Ah yes, of course. One moment." Gilman turned to the rear of the house and called out. "Meria!"

A young girl wearing a dark blue dress came from behind the staircase. Her hair was yellow like wheat, and her eyes matched Gilman's own dark gray. "Yes, Father?" Meria asked, curtseying before the room.

Gilman crossed the room and stood beside her, wrapping his arm around her shoulders. "Meria, my child, please show our guests to the rooms they'll be staying in tonight." He removed his hand and beckoned toward the staircase.

Meria nodded and led the group up the stairs and down the hall on the right. There were four doors at this end of the hall, which Munne assumed all led to guest rooms. Meria swept her hand out across the hall. "We have four rooms for you to stay in. Please, make yourselves comfortable. I will send water and wine up for you in a few moments. If you need anything else, please let me know."

Salvis and Mathis headed for the second door on the right while Trendin went for the second door on the left. Lagazi led the Barauder into the first room on the left—she was the most comfortable of the three with foreign customs. Munne could tell that Druuk was uncomfortable being inside of the Proma home while S'raak seemed a little less on edge. They passed through the threshold with wary eyes, casting glances all around as if they thought the room would swallow them whole at any moment. Rhorek offered a bow to Meria and thanked her for her hospitality before following Trendin into the second room.

That left Munne with the first room on the right. She pushed the door open and was pleasantly surprised to see a hearth and two large feather beds with folded quilts placed on top of both. A small table stood near the hearth with a stone basin and a few candles placed on top, and a chamber pot rested on the floor nearby. There were a couple of chairs near the table. The room seemed comfortable enough, and would no doubt be nicer than any inn she would have stayed at. The four Proma would certainly be happy to be sleeping in real beds tonight.

Munne wanted to go to the market and see if she could purchase an apple, or perhaps a small bag of oats to feed Alathyl as a treat. Her mare had done so well with their traveling thus far, and Munne wanted to ensure that she knew she was appreciated. She tucked her coin purse into her coat and left the room.

Some of her companions were also leaving their rooms to go wander around Ferilin.

"My sister's husband's family owns a farm not too far from here. I wonder if they've got a stall open in the marketplace," Mathis said to Salvis as they stepped out into the hallway.

"What do they grow on their farm?"

"Apples and pears mostly. They might have some preserves from the earlier harvest."

Rhorek departed from his room as well, returning downstairs to speak with Gilman some more. The three Barauder were content to stay in their rooms, it seemed. Munne followed Salvis and Mathis out of the hall, but then headed in the opposite direction from them once out on the street.

The town hall stood in the center of Ferilin with shops and homes spread all around it. Between the homes and the outer walls were several fields with crops growing. Outside the walls were more farms and the Elviri outpost. The outpost itself was established as a place where the Elviri soldiers that passed through Ferilin could sleep. As time went on, the Proma opened their gates, and the Elviri started sleeping in the inns within Ferilin. Now the outpost served mostly as a formal location for soldiers to gather for meals, meetings, or marching. Munne planned on going to the outpost at some point in the evening to see if anyone she knew was there.

But first, she needed to purchase that treat for Alathyl. She followed one road until she came upon a small collection of booths where farmers were selling the last of their autumn crops. A few stalls had apples and pears on display, along with baked goods and preserves. Others were selling gourds. Another booth was manned by a young woman and her two fair-haired children, selling a variety of wheat, flour, and some loaves of bread. As Munne approached her booth, the woman smiled and smoothed out her skirt.

"Greetings to you, fair Elviri. Do you see anything that you would like to purchase?" The woman swept her arm across the display.

Munne looked thoughtfully over the selection, trying to decide between a braided loaf of bread and a bag of oats.

The younger of the children jumped up when he saw Munne and pointed at her ears. "Dav, look! Her ears!" Munne couldn't help but grin.

The older child slapped the younger one's hand out of the air. "It's rude to point."

"Daven, Corbyn, hush. You're both being rude to our guest," the woman whispered shrilly as she turned to her children.

"Do they not see Elviri that often?" Munne asked, looking up at the young woman.

A blush crept across the woman's face as she looked back at Munne. "My youngest just started comin' with me to the market. He hasn't seen much of anything yet."

Munne offered her a comforting smile, and then pointed to the braided loaf. "I'd like one loaf, please."

The woman composed herself and nodded. "Of course! Just a few copper pieces if you please."

Munne pulled out her coin purse and dug around until she grabbed what she needed. She exchanged coins for the bread, and then smiled down at the children. "Be good for your mother."

The younger one, Corbyn, grinned from ear to ear and tugged on his older brother's arm.

Munne headed toward the stables at the northern gate where Alathyl was staying, tucking her coin purse back into her tunic. Ferilin had grown steadily over the years, starting out as a single farmstead belonging to Gilman's ancestors close to the beginning of the Second Sun. A handful of other families flocked to the successful farmstead and began their own farms, and it grew from there. The Elviri outpost was created when Munne's father was a small child, and the city walls around Ferilin were constructed soon after that.

Munne could tell which buildings were older than the others, although the Proma did a fairly good job at making the newer ones match.

Entering the stable, Munne offered bits of the braided loaf to Alathyl, who accepted them gratefully. As the mare ate, Munne stroked her neck. The soft breathing and whinnies from the other horses gave Munne a small sense of comfort. If she closed her eyes, she could almost pretend she was back in the stables in the valley.

After feeding Alathyl her treat, Munne headed for the outpost. *Are the same men stationed here, or has new blood come to Ferilin since I was here last month?*

The outpost itself was enclosed with its own walls, though not nearly as tall as Ferilin's. It had been built using wood and stone from the area around Ferilin, which was far different from the wood and stone used in Elimere or Elimaine. The wood was closer to yellow, and the stone was a reddish-brown color. Inside the outpost were a handful of buildings—barracks, dining hall, commander's station, and supplies. Most of the Elviri who passed through Ferilin opted to stay in the town, which meant that the outpost didn't keep as many provisions as it had in the past.

The outpost had a rotating leadership between two triples of Elviri. Each came to the outpost to serve for six months before returning to Elimaine to be with their families. With the end of the year rapidly approaching, the leadership would be rotating soon. If she could find the current commanders and speak with them before she left for Auora, she could tell them of her travels to the Imalar Woods. No doubt they would spread word of that back at home, so her father would eventually hear of her carrying out her duties. He would be pleased.

How long it would take for word to travel back that I didn't follow Father's orders?

One of the three commanders was inside the commander's station, hovering over a table in the middle of the room. He wore dark pants and a white shirt, his black hair pulled back and out of his face.

Munne knocked on the door as she entered. "Greetings, Commander Ethelmar."

The Elviri straightened himself and turned around, a look of surprise on his face. "Warlord, I didn't expect your return so soon," he said, taking in her full appearance. "Has the *Se'vi* decided to march?"

Munne raised her hand and shook her head. "No, I'm not here on another campaign. He's still considering his options in the war to come."

"Forgive me for being so direct, but..." He glanced at the table, then at the floor, before meeting Munne's eyes again. "What else would draw you out of the valley, with Huntaran's descension so soon?"

Munne felt a squeeze in her stomach, one that had become all too familiar in recent days. She urged herself to relax, and then spoke. "The *Se'vi* has successfully made arrangements with the Imalarii to trade weapons for border defenses."

Hope flickered across Ethelmar's face at the promise of new equipment before he quickly regained composure. The weapons would indeed be nice to have. "I see."

Munne looked around the room. She tried to gather her thoughts, turn them into the correct words. There were maps strewn about the room, hanging from the walls, draped across chairs, resting on flat surfaces. So many plans.

"I'll be traveling to the Imalar Woods to discuss how many of our men are needed on the border, as well as strategic locations to place those men," she said.

Ethelmar nodded. He was a man of thoughtful few words, unlike the other members of his triple. Munne was appreciative that he was the one she was speaking to. If he had any questions for her, any reason to doubt her, he would take his time asking. She could take her time responding.

Instead, he posed one simple question. "Will you be needing anything from the outpost while you are here?"

"No, I don't believe so. I'll be departing in the morning, so I won't be in Ferilin for long."

Ethelmar nodded again, shifting restlessly on his feet. "Then I wish you safe travels, Warlord."

"Thank you, Commander." Munne offered him a smile that he tentatively returned. She looked around the room once more, wondering when she would see another Elviri outpost again, and then turned for the door.

When Munne returned to the mayor's home, the suns were beginning to set. Smoke rose from the stone chimneys and the scent of roasted meat filled the air. She was thankful for the mayor's hospitality after several nights of trail rations and campfire meals. Even the three Barauder seemed to enjoy the hot food, or at least the roasted vegetables and baked bread.

The dining room walls were painted in dark golds and reds with two stone fireplaces on the wall opposite the door. The traveling party sat packed around the dining table, along with the mayor, his wife, and three children. Rhorek's three men were closest to the family, with Munne and the three Barauder taking up the other end of the table. Gilman and Rhorek were seated at the heads of the table. Servants moved around the table, carrying plates of meats, vegetables, and breads. Another servant carried a jug of wine, filling everyone's glasses. Munne wondered if this spread was a common occurrence, or if Gilman was trying to impress them with his wealth.

The food was delicious, and she grew tired as she finished her own plate. Perhaps sleep would come easy tonight, and she would have another night without nightmares. At the very least she would be resting in a real bed, and not a bedroll.

I'm just happy to be sleeping in a bed again, after traveling through the mountains. I don't care much for this display of wealth, but the food is good. Hopefully Gilman's townsfolk will enjoy their own hot meals tonight.

"Thank you again for your hospitality," Rhorek said, raising his glass of wine to Gilman. Rhorek's men nodded and voiced their agreement.

A smile spread across Gilman's rosy face, enjoying a sip of wine. "You are most welcome, Rhorek. My family and I are honored that you chose to spend the night in our humble home."

Munne's eyes flickered to Gilman's wife Lysa and children. Lysa had a polite smile on her face as she neatly tucked into the plate of food before her. She would occasionally look at her guests but only her fellow Proma. She glanced at Munne once or twice, always showing that polite smile, but she didn't cast any glances at the Barauder. The children—Meria and two sandy-haired boys—kept their eyes fixed on their plates. Gilman was a natural at politicking. Munne wondered if he would take the time to teach it to his children.

The meal was rather quiet after that, which Munne was thankful for. She could only stomach so much flattery. She supposed she would need to get acclimated to it, though, if Huntaran still allowed her to inherit the Hunting Throne. Meetings with diplomats were to be expected, and the conversation wouldn't always be of war.

If only problems could be dealt with like a knife slicing through a good steak.

After a polite round of thanks, Munne and her companions climbed the stairs to their rooms, leaving Rhorek at the table with Gilman and his family. As Munne pushed the door to her room open, she noticed the hearth had a small, steady fire going in it. One of Gilman's servants must have visited while she had been away in town. Her trunk had been brought up to the room as well and rested in front of one of the beds. She hoisted it up onto the bed and opened it, taking out a pair of deerskin leggings and a long-sleeved white shirt from the trunk. She didn't bring her silk slip with her when traveling—she never felt comfortable wearing such little clothing outside the comfort of her suite. After securing the lock on the door, she took her clothes off and cleaned herself using the stone basin.

In the warm glow of the fire, the second bed looked very inviting. She slipped into her leggings and shirt, then crossed over and pulled back the quilt, the fabric soft in her hands. She climbed into the bed and pulled the quilt up to her chest, laying her head down on one of the pillows. The fire crackled. Munne watched the shadows dance on the walls and ceiling before sleep took her.

When Munne opened her eyes, she was in a forest clearing. *Ceyo's cabin.* Although she was reluctant to admit it, the sight brought her a small degree of comfort.

It's not the tunnels, at least.

She looked around at her surroundings. There were no leaves on the ground. Shapeless trees circled the clearing, towering over her. The sky was dark, and she couldn't see the moon or any stars. The edges of the clearing seemed distant, and she had trouble making out where one tree stopped and the next began. Everything seemed blurry, distant. She knew it was the same place as the time she met the shapeshifter. She was immediately on edge, wondering who or what was waiting for her just beyond the trees. She kept a careful watch for the caravan leader's mismatching eyes, in case he appeared in her dreams once more. Perhaps she could try communicating with him?

"Good evening," a voice said from behind her. Quiet, masculine, warm.

The shapeshifter.

Munne's skin prickled and she turned around. Behind her was the same man in plain black garb from before. He stood with his hands behind his back, and he had a faint outline of a smile on his lips.

Munne let out a quiet scoff and took a step back from the man. "Good evening, *shapeshifter.*"

He tilted his head to the side and laughed quietly. "I'm glad that you're on more amicable terms with me tonight."

"I have yet to decide if I'll be *amicable,*" Munne muttered, placing her hands on her hips. Fabric brushed against her skin, eliciting an involuntary shiver. She looked down and saw she was wearing a white bastian with a leather belt cinched around her waist. Underneath that was a pair of leather leggings and boots. Different clothing from what she fell asleep in. Different clothing from her last visit to this clearing.

"It seemed to fit for the season," the man said. When Munne glanced up, she realized he was looking her over as well. She scowled and squeezed her hands into fists at her sides, turning on her heel and quickly walking away from him.

She stopped only a handful of steps away, realizing what he said. "What do you mean?"

"These seemed like better clothes than the vest and pants." His voice was gentle. "From the last time we saw each other."

Munne turned back to him. He was still standing in the same spot, his hands behind his back. "You... This is your doing?" She threw her hand in the air, gesturing to their surroundings.

The man nodded, taking a step toward her. She slid one foot behind her and turned her torso into a defensive stance, left shoulder leading with her right hand close to her hip and ready to strike out if need be. He didn't take the next step but raised his hands to her, open with surrender. "I thought that if I brought you somewhere that you trust, you would be more receptive to what I have to say."

Munne stood still for a moment, lost in thought. The shapeshifter could manipulate her dreams. Was this truly a dream, or was she somewhere else? She distinctly remembered climbing into a feather bed in Ferilin. What else was this shapeshifter capable of?

"You left the imprints on my arms."

He nodded, lowering his hands. "I hope they kept the other dreams away."

Munne understood what he meant by the *other* dreams, and she nodded.

He smiled, and his eyes seemed to light up. For a moment, Munne could have sworn they were green. She blinked and they were brown again. "Good. That's good. It was the best I could manage with what little strength I had."

"How can you do these things? Are you one of the Pantheon?" Munne asked.

The man shook his head. "No, I'm not as holy as them. I'm… something else."

Her stomach twisted again. *Something else?* "But how can you do these things? Magic doesn't exist in Daaria."

"But it did," he murmured, folding his hands together again. "And still does, if you know where to find it."

Munne shifted her weight between her feet, feeling uneasy. She didn't like that response. She didn't understand that response. She wasn't sure if she would get a better answer, though. "Why are you doing these *things*? Why is it so important that I listen to what you have to say?"

"Because it's important that you travel to Kherizhan," he responded, the lightness gone from his voice. He spoke quietly, as if afraid someone might overhear him.

"And if I decide not to?" Munne bluffed, straightening her back.

He closed his eyes and was silent for a moment. The air around him vibrated, and a bright light surrounded his form. Munne narrowed her eyes and raised a hand to block most of the light, trying to watch as he… *shifted*. His body stretched upward, growing taller. His hair darkened and wrapped around his face, turning into a hood. His tunic tugged downward and became a long black robe. His hands turned black as gloves materialized around them. As the light faded, Munne could no longer see his face under the hood.

"I know you have already left the valley," he said, his voice raspier, more foreign than before. It piqued her interest. "But I don't know where you intend to go. I hope you have chosen to travel to the southeast."

"What's in Kherizhan that will help me? How do I know this is the best path for me?" Munne retorted. He sighed, his breath slipping past his lips like an agitated hiss. She found it amusing that he was showing signs of frustration. *I've been frustrated with you for much longer*, she thought.

"You must trust me," he told her.

Her mouth twisted into a snarl, and she quickly crossed the space between them, her boots stomping on the ground. "You say I need to trust you, but what have you done to earn it? You say you know what's plaguing my dreams, yet you talk in riddles. You hide your true face. You use magic to try to placate me. Why would I ever trust someone like you?" she demanded, filling the space in front of him, getting in his face.

The shapeshifter was silent. Now that she was face-to-face with him, she could barely make out the outline of his face underneath his hood. His eyes seemed to glow softly, and she saw that they were a pale milky green without any trace of a pupil. She wasn't sure she had seen eyes like his before. It caught her off-guard, and her frown wavered. He parted his lips, and she felt his breath on her face as he slowly exhaled. The heat made her cheeks flush. It renewed her frustration, and she raised her hands to shove him back.

His own gloved hands shot out as her palms nearly touched his chest. The sleeves of her bastian had slipped back toward her elbows, so his hands wrapped around her skin. It felt like her wrists were on fire. She jumped back and tried to tug her hands away, but he held onto her tightly, using his strength to keep her in place.

"Because we need each other if we're going to stop the *Ardashi'ik* Ardulphyx from returning to Daaria," he growled, his eyes brightening.

Heat radiated off him and spread throughout her body. A massive weight dropped in her stomach and her mouth ran dry. Fear consumed her. "Th-the *Ardashi'ik* was defeated in the Eldest Days, just a myth now, something parents tell their chil—"

"The *Ardashi'ik* is a monster from the Eldest Days that couldn't be stopped, only hindered," he insisted. "But he can be stopped now. He can become a myth and nothing more. You just have to trust me."

Munne wished she could see his face, so she knew how he was looking at her. All she could see was the fire in his pale green eyes. "How?"

The grip on her wrists loosened, and he let go of her. She put several feet between them, cradling her arms. She looked at her skin and saw red imprints of his hands.

"Look upon me, then, so that you can begin to trust me."

Munne shifted her gaze up to the shapeshifter. He raised his hands and lowered his hood to reveal his face. Bright red hair fell to his shoulders and surrounded his pale face like flames. Two dark brown horns rose from his head, curving back along the shape of his head. As she took his appearance in, she realized his skin had a sickly green tint to it. He had a long, curved nose, sharp cheekbones and a strong jawline. He was different from any other creature she had seen before.

Is this his true form? Judging by the way he squirmed uncomfortably and shifted his weight between his feet, she thought it was. *What strange beauty.* She realized he was frowning.

"Strange indeed," he muttered.

Will he always be able to intrude on my thoughts? "Do you have a name, shapeshifter?" Munne asked. She wondered which question he would answer.

"It's too complicated for any..." he trailed off, looking rather displeased. "Anyone not of my kind."

"I would still hear it," she responded quietly.

He let out a *hmph* and arched an eyebrow. "*Elyxphyrthalyondrall.*"

Munne hesitated for a moment. *Complicated indeed.* "What would you have me call you?"

The shapeshifter thought for a moment. "Ely."

"Ely," she repeated, and Ely nodded. "Ely. Do you already know my name?"

"I know your name as your mother and father named you, and I know the name you will carry throughout history," he answered ominously.

It was Munne's turn to contemplate her response. "I would have you call me Munne."

Ely nodded again. "As you wish, Munne. What else would you have from me before you decide to trust me?"

Munne's lips curled down. "Trust takes time. I still don't understand what you are. Or where you come from. Or how you can do the things that you do." *Or how he knows the things he knows.* She idly rubbed her wrist and felt something tugging at the knot in her stomach. "I would have you explain what's going on, so that I understand everything."

"There are only so many hours in the night, and you still need time to rest," Ely said.

"Can you not speak to me during the day?" Munne asked.

"That isn't one of the *things* I can do," he responded dryly.

"Then I would have you visit me again tomorrow night," she said with a firm voice, hoping it was enough to compel him to listen.

Ely nodded slowly. "I can return tomorrow night."

"In your true form." He didn't respond. "I can't trust you if you aren't completely honest with me."

"You ask for many things, Munne," Ely murmured. "I will do my best to be accommodating."

"Thank you."

"I need to let you sleep. We will speak again soon." As he spoke, everything around her blurred and dissolved into darkness. The last thing she saw was his pale green eyes fading away.

CHAPTER XX: SETH

Nar galloped through the forest with reckless abandon and Seth had no time to think about dodging branches or roots. He had to trust Nar to do what he was born to do. He had to focus on getting back to the pyramid. Back home. Could he even consider that place a home after the events of the past several days?

The precious last drops of the miracle elixir were gone. He had drunk the rest as he left the gates of Lithalyon to ensure he'd get to Yiradia safely. He cursed himself, and moments later felt the itch and sting of a small branch whipping him across the cheek. *A fitting punishment*, he thought bitterly. *Or perhaps it's not fitting enough?* He couldn't begin to imagine the punishment Amias would put him through if he found out where he had gone.

Would any punishment be sufficient to make up for the pain in Lisanthir's voice?

"Calydrian, where are you—?"

Seth had managed to avoid looking the Elviri in the eye before he fled, but he could imagine the hurt in his eyes. His lips curled downward into a frown. His cheeks still flushed after their shared kiss.

Calydrian.

Lisanthir didn't even know his real name. He only knew a fiction that Seth created in his desperate attempt to escape the prison in the pyramid. How cruel he had been, using Lisanthir like that.

If I had been using him, would I hurt this much after abandoning him?

Nothing made sense, and sharp pains spread throughout his body. From outward injury or emotional pain, he couldn't distinguish the two anymore. The forest blurred before Seth as he tried to wipe away the tears from his eyes.

He eventually gave up and gave complete control over to Nar, closing his eyes tightly.

Maybe it wouldn't be so bad for Nar to trip and kill us both.

A couple of hours passed, and Nar was steadily trotting through the forest. Seth knew he was entering the rainforest of Moonyswyn—the trees grew taller and closer together, and the canopy above thickened, blocking the moonlight out entirely. East was the only direction he knew to travel. Once he was back in the rainforest proper, he hoped to find traces of roads and paths that would lead him back to the pyramid. Anrak hadn't given him any directions for the return trip to Yiradia, so all he could do was keep moving and hope.

Seth's eyes were swollen and dry. He had cried until there was nothing left in him to give. His lungs burned. He felt blood drying all over his body from where he had been scratched by passing branches or twigs.

His mind had wandered back to his flight from Lithalyon. He had passed through the gates with little resistance. In fact, none of the guards had bothered to stop him and ask where he was going. To his credit, he didn't gallop out of the city at full speed. Seth had managed to collect himself enough to walk out of the gate and travel the road west until he was no longer in sight. Then he veered into the forest and turned around completely to spur Nar into a full gallop. Perhaps the festival had distracted the guards, and they weren't concerned with anyone leaving the city? Or was the city so untouched by the war that they didn't feel the need to question everyone who moved in or out of the city walls?

It didn't matter to Seth.

Soon he would be back in Yiradia, crippled once more. It would be as if this venture had never happened. He would harden his heart to this foolish excursion and all that occurred within it. Even Lisanthir. Seth wondered how long it would take the Elviri to forget him. The thought brought a sharp pain to his heart, worse than any injury he had received that day. He winced and felt himself crying—or would have been if any tears would spill from his eyes.

More than anything he was tired. He wanted nothing more than to crawl into bed and never emerge again.

A shrill screech cut through his thoughts. Seth instinctively jerked away from the direction of the noise, but Nar stubbornly corrected their course. The horse paid no mind to the creatures of the forest. As Seth tried to collect himself, a deep snarl came from behind them.

I've never heard anything like that before. What kind of beast is out here with us? Could it be one of those spotted cats I've read about? Sometimes hunters returned to Yiradia with their spotted pelts. Whatever the beast was, Seth hoped that Nar would carry him far away from it and avoid its attention.

The forest was pitch black, and Seth could no longer see the sky beneath the canopy. He had no means of telling time, but he was sure Yiradia wasn't too far away. With it being the dead of night, he wouldn't be able to see the pyramid in all its glory tonight.

Or ever again, he thought bitterly. *I'll be trapped on the upper floor until I die. Even if Szatisi can recreate the elixir, Father will never let me out of his sight again.*

Nar began to slow down, panting heavily. Seth patted the horse on the neck out of sympathy.

Seth's entire body felt like it was on fire. He could still feel his legs, for whatever that was worth. Although he supposed he would need them to get back into the pyramid without rousing any suspicion. Not for the first time, he wondered if it would just be better for Amias to kill him and be done with it. Except he wouldn't just "be done with it", would he? Finally, he could no longer keep his eyelids open, and he fell into a fitful sleep clutching tightly to Nar's mane.

<hr>

Seth woke up outside of the stables near Yiradia, unsure of how much time had passed. It was still dark outside, so he must have been out for one or two hours at most. Nar was snorting and pawing at the ground. Pain shot up Seth's back and he was wide awake again, twisting from side to side in the saddle.

"Is that Nar?" Marus called out, emerging from his home. The man rubbed at his eyes with one hand, a lantern in the other.

"Yes." Seth forced the word from his mouth. His throat was dry, and his voice cracked. He sounded just as miserable as he felt.

Marus grunted, reaching out for Nar's reins. With great effort, Seth swung one leg over Nar's back and began his descent. His feet hit the ground and burst into pain. The feeling of hundreds of needles stabbing his feet and legs nearly overwhelmed him, and he stumbled into Marus's side.

"You're the one who went to Lithalyon, aye? Did you rush to get back here?" the stablemaster asked, taking hold of Seth's shoulder, and gently pushing him away. He held him out at arm's length and gave him a once over. Seth used this anchor to steady himself and he was thankful for the large man.

"I just let Nar do what he wanted," Seth croaked.

Marus huffed and smiled, turning to look at the horse. "Stupid beast. Come on, let's rest."

Nar snorted in agreement. Marus let go of Seth and began leading the horse into the stables. Without his anchor, Seth stumbled sideways, the weight of his satchel dragging him down. He managed to stabilize himself after a moment, then pulled the hood of his cape over his head to mask his identity as he entered the ruined city. He hadn't been worried about Marus recognizing him, but anyone who worked in the pyramid might.

Walking down the decaying streets was torture, both physically and emotionally. Every building he passed was in a varying state of ruin. Provira and Asaszi alike lived here, but they fought a losing battle against nature. They didn't embrace it like the Elviri did in Lithalyon. For all the boasting the Asaszi did, Yiradia did not look like the beginning of a new empire. It looked like the ruins of one long-lost.

It felt like needles were piercing Seth's feet every time he took a step. His legs and back were sore. In an odd shift of emotions, he decided to savor this pain. After all, the decanter was empty, and he was back in Yiradia. In the morning, he would no longer have the use of his legs. He would enjoy the feeling of his legs and feet, even if that feeling made him want to scream. Despite this change of spirit, it didn't make the journey any easier. A fleeting thought crossed his mind that he may need to climb back into his room, but he quickly dismissed it. He would rather be caught by the guards than try climbing up the side of the pyramid in his condition.

Two people stood guard at the entrance to the pyramid. As he approached, Seth tried to figure out what he would say to them, but he miscalculated how long it would take to approach them. They asked him to stop before he even had an inkling of what to say.

"Who are you, and why do you approach the pyramid?" the guard on the left asked. Both brandished swords and torches and stood in a defensive position.

It took Seth a moment, but the words came to him. He pulled out one of his journals from his satchel and held it up. "*Pyredan* Octavia. Where is she? I have a report for her."

The guards looked at each other, and then back to Seth. Clearly both were suspicious of him, but his specific mention of Octavia made them pause.

"It's late. You can deliver the report in the morning," the guard on the right growled. He took a step toward Seth and raised his torch, trying to get a better look at his face.

"And delay the delivery of pertinent information about Lithalyon's defenses? I think not!" Seth snapped. His stomach churned mentioning the Elviri city, but he needed to get inside *now.*

The guard on the left hesitated, and then stepped to the side. They turned to the other guard and gestured for him to do the same, and then spoke to Seth. "Our apologies. She is more than likely resting in her chambers."

Seth nodded and proceeded into the pyramid before the guards could change their minds or get a better look at him. He tried to carry himself with purpose, despite the screeching pain shooting up his legs. He clutched the journal in his hands, ready to use it again if anyone tried to question him. Several guards walked through the halls, but no one tried to stop him.

As he climbed higher and higher into the pyramid, he felt his limbs becoming heavy. His eyelids threatened to shut even as he forced himself to walk faster. As he reached the floor his chambers were on, his stomach twisted into a huge knot.

What about the guards outside his door? Seth had to go see Octavia first before he could crawl into his bed. The two of them could devise a way to get past the guards and inside his room.

He pivoted and began walking toward her chambers, which weren't too far away from his own. Outside her door stood two more guards, also equipped with swords. Before either could speak, Seth raised the book in his hand and said loudly, "I have an urgent report for *Pyredan* Octavia about Lithalyon. I need to speak with her."

Both guards stared him down, neither moving from their positions. Seth's legs began to shake, but he couldn't tell if it was from Szatisi's cure wearing off or his own nerves getting the better of him. After what felt like an eternity, one of the guards turned and knocked on Octavia's door. A few moments later, Octavia opened the door. She was still dressed in her day clothes, and she had dark circles under her eyes. She appeared wide awake, though, and glanced at the two guards before looking Seth. Her lips parted, but otherwise she made no indication that she recognized him.

"You're here with your report?" she asked him. He nodded and said nothing. She pursed her lips and then nodded. "Very good. Walk with me and give me the details. I was just about to go check on my brother."

Octavia pulled the door shut behind her and took off at a brisk pace. Seth had no choice but to keep up. The two guards relaxed, returning to their post on either side of her door.

They made the quick trek to his chambers without a word exchanged between them. As they were about to turn the corner to his chambers, Octavia stopped and held her hand out to slow him.

"I need to check on my brother, soldier." Octavia made eye contact as she spoke. She pointed toward a dark alcove nearby with a large plant standing in front of a window. "Meet me on the promenade and we will discuss your report."

Without another word, she turned the corner toward his chambers. Seth hoped he understood her cues correctly, and slid into the alcove, trying to hide as much of himself behind the plant as possible.

"Go fetch something to eat for my brother," Octavia commanded the stewards with a firm voice. It wasn't often that he heard that voice of his sister, the military commander. It was easy for him to forget that his twin lived in a completely different world from himself. "Soup of some kind. There should still be some from earlier today. Heat it up and bring it in. He should be ready for visitors."

Ready for visitors?

There was no response, but a steward came around the corner dressed head to toe in black silks and robes. Seth found himself thankful that he didn't have to look upon an Asaszi face tonight. He didn't think he could stomach it after the past couple of days.

"Ensure that a pot of passionflower tea is brewed as well. It seems to be helping him sleep," Octavia said, and soon the other steward came around the corner as well.

Seth heard the door to his chambers being opened but not closed. After a few moments, Octavia appeared and beckoned for him to follow her. They slipped into his room, and she shut the door behind them. He stopped in the middle of the dark chamber and let himself acclimate to his surroundings. The massive stone nest of silks and pillows. The gray wardrobe and dressers. The wooden bookcase. He blinked and realized he felt nothing coming back into this room.

"Seth, I—"

He turned around to look at Octavia. His eyes had begun to adjust to the darkness, but he could only vaguely make out her silhouette. She moved closer and pulled him into a tight hug. She went back and forth between resting her head on his shoulder and touching his cheek with her forehead. He maneuvered his arms so he could return the hug.

"I'm glad to see you again," she whispered, her face pressed into his shoulder.

"I've missed you too, Tav," Seth murmured in response. "The past couple of days have been..."

Octavia pulled herself away from him and held him at arms' length. "I have to catch you up, but you need to get into bed. Now."

Seth gave her a confused look, but she began tugging at his cloak.

"The stewards can't catch you standing up," she said sharply.

Oh, right. He sat down on the bed, placed the satchel next to him, and tugged his boots off. "Can you get me a different shirt and pants?" he asked his sister.

She nodded and moved over to the wardrobe. His sister tossed around different clothes while he stripped out of what he was wearing. Holding the shirt and pants in his hands, he realized just how much of a beating he took on the ride back. The clothes were soaked in sweat and had small holes and tears all over. No wonder he didn't face too much trouble getting here. He must have looked like a legitimate scout, wounds and all. The clothes would need to be thrown out or burned.

Octavia threw a silk shirt and pair of pants over her shoulder, giving him as much privacy as she could. Seth pulled on the clothes as quickly as possible and then burrowed into the blankets, taking care to bring the satchel with him. He couldn't risk anyone finding the books he had brought back with him.

"Okay, I'm in bed," he mumbled, shuffling and adjusting his pillows. The silks felt cold against his skin, and he shivered. Deep underneath the silken nest, he could feel the solid slab of stone. He missed the soft bed in Lithalyon.

Octavia turned around and rushed over to the side of the bed. She fiddled with something he couldn't see, but suddenly she had a small flame burning on the table beside his bed. A few moments later she had a few candles burning.

"Sorry for rushing you," she whispered as she turned back to look at him. "I'm not sure how long it will take them to brew the tea and get back here."

"That's alright," Seth responded.

The twins sat in silence again, each taking stock of the other. Octavia looked tired, and the bags under her eyes were only deepened with the candles' flames. Her day clothes—a jade green tunic with elaborate embroidery and a pair of leather pants—were disheveled. Her hair had been hastily pulled up and as a result loose strands framed her face. He was sure she was noticing similar bad things about his own appearance. The forest hadn't been kind to him.

Her mouth curved downward. "Were you found out?"

Seth shook his head. "No, what makes you think that?"

"Your face looks horrible. Did you run into every tree between here and Lithalyon, then?" Octavia asked, the ghost of a smile dancing across her face.

Seth couldn't help but guffaw at that. "It definitely felt like it."

There was a knock at the door. They both turned to look as Octavia commanded, "Enter."

One of the stewards had returned with a tea tray, complete with a steaming tea pot, a cup, and a small container of sugar. Octavia gestured to the bedside table where the steward gently set the tray down. Seth tried to hide as much of himself in Octavia's shadows, so the steward couldn't see his face as clearly. While he was unsure what tales Octavia had spun to cover for his adventure, he was sure it didn't involve scratches on his face.

"Thank you. You may return to your post."

The steward nodded and left the room, pulling the door shut behind them. Octavia leaned over and poured a cup of tea. Seth watched her, trying to gauge exactly what had happened in the past few days. He didn't know where to begin regarding his own travels. She added a touch of sugar to the cup and stirred it. The scent of passionflower wafted past his nose, and his stomach did a massive kick and flip. Hunger and anxiety never mixed well, but hopefully the tea would help him. Octavia offered him the cup, and he accepted gratefully. He inhaled deeply and closed his eyes, savoring the sweet aroma. The cup was warm in his hands, almost too warm.

He opened his eyes and focused on the tea, his voice barely above a whisper. "What's happened since I've been gone?"

Octavia shifted on the bed as if trying to get comfortable. She rubbed the back of her neck and let out a nervous laugh. "Well, for starters, they all think you're in here because you're sick. And in trouble."

Seth couldn't stop himself from smiling. There were many layers of irony behind that statement, and he was too tired to sift through them all. He could appreciate his sister's laugh, though, and knew how silly it sounded to say it out loud. He decided to further the joke. "What did I do this time?"

Octavia didn't respond right away. He raised the cup of tea to his lips and attempted to take a sip. Still blistering, but not bad enough that he couldn't swallow. The sweetened herbal remedy tasted good. He frowned for a moment then turned to look at his sister, whose expression mirrored his own. He relaxed his features and waited for her to speak.

"You're supposed to be in here contemplating your upcoming ascension, and why you should do it. They think your fever is the gods fighting for your soul," Octavia mumbled, looking down at the bed. She fidgeted with the edge of the silks.

"Tav…" The frown returned to his face. Amias's plan for his ascension had completely slipped his mind while he was away from the pyramid. And now this added mess about a fever and the gods? Thoughts swirled around violently in his head. *Which gods? The* Tserys? He had to stifle a laugh. *Let the Asaszi's gods fight for my soul. But did Octavia create these lies on her own?* He was touched that his sister would cover for him, but what were her motivations in picking the excuses she had? *Did she have any other choice?*

There was another knock at the door. Octavia cleared her throat and called for them to enter. It was the second steward carrying a tray with two large bowls. Steam rose from them both, and Seth could smell salty broth and meat. His stomach growled.

Octavia rose to her feet and took the tray from the steward. "You may leave now." Her voice was quiet yet firm.

The steward nodded and left. Once the door was closed, Octavia turned and set the tray down on the bed. There wasn't enough room for both it and the tea tray on the nightstand. She shuffled dishes around, so the teapot and sugar bowl were on one end with enough space on the other end for one of the soup bowls. Octavia picked up the soup tray and set it gently across Seth's lap. She then returned to her seat on the bed, picked up one of the soup bowls, and began eating.

Seth took another sip from his cup, letting the tea sit in his mouth for a moment before swallowing. He set the cup down on the soup tray, and then picked up the spoon to eat. It wasn't as delicious as the food in Lithalyon, which left him craving the exotic fruits and meats of the Elviri. But the soup was warm and filling, if not a little bland, and that's what he needed right now.

The two ate in silence for several moments. Seth found himself continuously bringing the spoon to his lips while Octavia spent more time stirring the soup than eating it. She was troubled, but Seth wasn't sure how to help. He couldn't even sort through his own thoughts properly.

"Szatisi knows the potion went missing," Octavia said suddenly. "But not what happened to it."

His stomach did another flip. It suddenly became very difficult to raise his spoon. "Does she suspect anyone?" *Does she suspect me?*

"She's been asking the other *pyredans*, but none of them have any clue. There are whispers of dissension in the lower ranks, but no one has come forward and said anything." Octavia let out a sigh and paused. She raised her spoon to her lips, slurped, swallowed, and continued. "She keeps asking me about it. I don't think she suspects I took it, but she thinks I know more than I say."

"Octavia, I—"

"I don't regret stealing it from her," Octavia said, leaving no room for him to argue. "Every day I'm thankful that your legs are healed now, and that you can walk again."

It was Seth's turn to avert his gaze and feel his cheeks flush with shame. "I'm not healed. Not completely."

He looked back at his sister, a look of shock spread across her face. "What do you mean?"

"It didn't fix me. Not permanently." His words were bitter and his grip on the spoon tightened. Octavia gasped. "That potion wears off after six or so hours. And now it's all gone. It's almost like a cruel joke..." He trailed off, tears suddenly welling in his eyes. A lump formed in his throat, and he couldn't push it down.

"So, when you wake up..."

"Back to my chair," Seth spat.

Who knew if Szatisi could even recreate this cursed potion. He wanted to go to sleep and forget about the world. His whole body felt heavier and slower as the exhaustion finally hit him. He let go of the soup spoon, the muscles in his hand loosening. The joint between his thumb and finger was sore. At least he could feel his hands. By morning the pain in his legs would be gone, and he had no idea if he would ever feel anything like it again. He cursed the Asaszi. He cursed his father.

"Mother's missed you," Octavia said quietly.

Seth straightened up, shifting his eyes from his bowl of soup to his sister. "Did you tell her where I went?"

"No, I couldn't risk that. She thinks you're sick, just like everyone else."

"Wouldn't she have visited my room? How does she not—"

"I told her you were contagious, and that you said you didn't want your sickness to spread to her, too."

His eyes dropped back to his soup. Part of him was upset Octavia hadn't told their mother about his escape. He wanted to tell her all about the city and the library. *Should I continue to lie to her, or should I tell her what really happened these past few days?*

"Do you... want to talk about the city?" Octavia's voice cut through his thoughts.

Ah, yes, the mission. Seth shifted around in bed until he was laying on his back, staring at the canopy. The soup tray was still across his lap. "What do you want to know?" he replied, a hint of bitterness still present in his voice.

"Were you able to get inside without a problem?" She paused for a moment, but he didn't feel like answering right away. "Where did you stay? Were you comfortable?"

So, she's truly on Amias's side. I thought I could trust her, but she's just using me for her own personal gain. I won't be fooled by her questions. She doesn't care how comfortable I was; she only wants to know the city layout, the guards' habits, and how fortified the city is. She can pry that information from another scout. I am not a slave to Amias.

He stopped, thinking about what he was about to say. If there was any shred of decency within his sister, she would take the hint.

"Comfortable enough. The inn was pleasant. They let me in because of my ears." Octavia stiffened. Seth felt her shift in stance. *Good. Let her be uncomfortable.* He refused to say another word. He just wanted the world to melt away.

"I'm glad to know you encountered little trouble on your journey." Her voice was stoic, and her face was a mask. He knew he had struck a nerve, although he had no clue what was going through her head right now. "I'll let you get some rest. Father will be home tomorrow. I'm sure he'll want to see you at his welcoming feast." She stood up and removed the soup tray from his lap. Without waiting for a response, she blew out the candles and left his room.

For several minutes, Seth just stared at the canopy, no longer fighting the tears in his eyes. They freely rolled down his cheeks and stained the pillows. Returning home had been a mistake, but what else could he have done? He didn't want Lisanthir to know who or what he was. The potion would have run out and he would have become crippled again, and in such a foreign and hostile place. Except it wasn't hostile, was it? The Elviri had been welcoming, even if he spoke and acted strangely.

With great effort, he turned onto his side, wincing from the pain in his limbs. His satchel was next to him, half buried under the silks. At least he had the texts from the library. But what if he couldn't figure out the riddles left behind? He supposed that was a problem for tomorrow. He needed to keep them hidden from everyone else. Octavia had seen one of the journals, but hopefully she wouldn't inquire about it. For all she knew, it was something he had taken with him on the journey. He *had* brought a journal with him, hadn't he?

I'm alone in this cold place, and tomorrow I'll once again be trapped in this cage. His thoughts turned back to the festival and the dances he had shared with Lisanthir. *For a few brief days I had escaped and flown free.*

CHAPTER XXI:
MUNNE

When Munne awoke the next morning, she felt as if she was on fire. She opened her eyes to the sight of a smoldering fire in the stone hearth, the suns' first light reaching into the foreign room. Ferilin. She wasn't in the valley any longer. She drew in a deep breath and closed her eyes again.

In the darkness surrounding her, she only saw those pale green orbs framed by bright flaming hair. Something twisted inside of her, and she opened her eyes again. She pulled her hands out from underneath the blanket and held them above her face, her sleeves falling toward her elbows. Just as she had suspected, there were handprints on her wrists from where he had touched her. That creature with the absurdly long, complicated name.

Ely.

Munne sat up, looking around the room once more. Everything was exactly as she left it the night before, with her trunk sitting on top of the other bed and her boots on the ground. She threw the quilt back and stood, suddenly eager to saddle Alathyl and be gone from Ferilin.

They would be arriving in Auora today, and she expected she would be staying there for a few days. It would be expected of her to request an audience with the Proma king to discuss the war with him and his council. She didn't know when to expect the caravan or her triple, but she knew she wouldn't be able to leave the city until she had met with them both.

After she threw on her riding clothes, she descended the stairs and saw Rhorek sitting in the dining room with Gilman. They were in the same spots as the previous night, and if it weren't for the change of clothes, Munne would have thought they would have stayed there all night. They spoke in low voices which abruptly cut off when Gilman saw Munne.

"Good morning, my lady!" Gilman called out, waving a hand in her direction. "My servants are preparing a morning meal for you to indulge in before continuing to Auora."

Rhorek turned in his seat to look back at her, a neutral expression slipping onto his face. She wondered what they had been discussing. She chose not to inquire.

"Your hospitality is appreciated," Munne responded, and a polite smile spread across her face. She began to turn back to the staircase. "I can take my belongings to the stables while—"

"That won't be necessary, my lady," Gilman interjected, his voice louder than before. "My servants will take care of that as well."

He was awfully keen to show off his power. Munne nodded and turned back to the dining room. She chose to take the seat to Rhorek's left, smoothing down the front of her riding coat. When she looked back at the table, a servant was hovering near the doorway, pitcher in hand. Munne nodded to the servant, and they crossed over to the table, pouring water into the mug in front of her. Just as quickly as they appeared, they were gone. Munne raised the mug to her lips and took a sip.

After a few moments of silence, Rhorek and Gilman began a new discussion about the surrounding farms. Having recently finished their last harvests for the year, it would be time to preserve as many fruits and vegetables as they could and fill up their silos with wheat. The Elviri in Elimaine had faced similar work in recent months. Elifyn would still be able to plant and harvest crops with their warmer southern weather.

During their conversation, the rest of the party slowly trickled into the dining hall. Each had their mug filled with water or wine. The conversation shifted into discussion of traveling to Auora, the weather on the lake, and the goings-on in the city.

"Always colder on the island," Salvis mumbled before drinking a swig of wine.

"Aye, but the barracks always keep their fires lit," Mathis told him.

Servants once again filled the room as food was brought in. It wasn't the most impressive spread, but there was smoked fish, berries, and a warm savory porridge. Munne enjoyed the porridge—it had an egg cracked over the top. The meal was finished a lot quicker than the previous night's dinner, and soon the companions rose to their feet to make their way to the stables. Gilman thanked them profusely for their visit and wished them well on the next leg of their journey. It took Rhorek a few tries to get Gilman to allow them to leave the manor, which Munne found greatly amusing. The mayor wanted nothing more than to chat with an old friend by the fire.

The group left out of the same northern gate they entered through. There were four or five armed guards standing on either side of the gate. Munne had noticed their increased presence on the way in, but now she considered why that was. *There are more enemies to the south than the north, so why are they stationing so many men at the northern gate? Perhaps that was one of the things Rhorek and Gilman discussed. I'll ask Rhorek about it once we're out of Ferilin.*

<hr />

Their path took them along the edge of the Hourglass Lakes. Munne saw Auora in the distance—a massive spiral of buildings upon buildings, all nestled on top of an island in the middle of the lake. She had visited Auora several times before, but the sight of the city and the bridges leading to it always took her breath away. When she studied in the archives, she had read about the first Proma settlers on the island, and how their first city was burned down by dissenters within their ranks. From the ashes came the fabled Protector, and with him plans to rebuild the city with stone. And build they did. It was an impressive feat to build a vertical city on an island.

The journey only lasted a handful of hours. By the time the bridge to Auora was within sight, the suns had reached their peak in the sky. A massive gate stood in front of the bridge, flanked by two stone towers, and surrounded by a modest number of other buildings. A wall encircled the outpost, providing added security. There was an increased number of men on the walls and outside the gate, just like there were in Ferilin. Munne's brow knitted in confusion. *Did something happen during our journey?*

"Halt! Who goes there?" a voice called out as Munne's group approached the gate in the outer wall.

Rhorek rode his horse close to the gate and looked up, removing his riding hood. "Sir Rhorek Gondamire, and these are my traveling companions. We're returning from our journey to Elimere."

There was shouting from behind the wall, and the gate began to open. "Greetings, Sir Rhorek. Welcome home."

Rhorek led Munne and the others through the gate. On the other side, one of the soldiers stopped them in their path. "Sir Rhorek, it's joyous news that you have returned. I'm afraid much has happened since your departure." The man glanced at the rest of the group, shifting restlessly on his feet.

"Mayor Ervaitt informed me of the king's orders for increased presence at the gates," Rhorek responded, obviously withholding information he didn't want to share with everyone else.

Have the Provira found a way around Ferilin? Is Auora in danger? Why didn't Rhorek tell any of us what Gilman told him? Munne watched his interaction carefully with the soldier.

"Sir, it might be best if we, um," The soldier looked back at one of the buildings and nodded his head a little bit. "Sir, before I can let you onto the bridge..."

"Sir Rhorek, what's going on?" Lagazi raised her voice from the rear of the group. All eyes immediately shifted to her. Munne watched panic fly across the soldier's face before he regained composure.

"Sir, I need to know who it is you're traveling with, and why they have come to the city," the soldier said quietly. Munne wasn't sure if Lagazi could hear, but she certainly could. *Perhaps I should've packed some of my dress robes, so this foolish Proma would recognize me. Even without knowing who I am, surely with Rhorek and his three generals traveling with us, it doesn't matter who the rest of us are.*

Munne started forward on her horse, but Rhorek held a hand out to her to hold her back. "What is the meaning of this?" Rhorek asked the soldier, his voice matching the same low volume.

"It's on the orders of the king," the soldier answered and made painful eye contact with Rhorek, who simply held his gaze. After an uncomfortable moment of silence, the soldier spoke again. "Sir, it's Princess Niamnh... She's been missing for three days."

Panic set in among her Proma traveling companions. Munne's eyes widened, but she held her tongue. That was grave news, indeed.

"I'm traveling with ambassadors from the Black Lakes, as well as the Warlord of the Elviri. You will let us pass, so that I may return to my king and aid him in this dire hour," Rhorek said. His voice was filled with an intensity that Munne admired.

The soldier exchanged glances with the other men around him. After a tense moment, he stepped to the side and motioned for his men to do the same, allowing Munne's group to continue toward the island city. Rhorek took the lead, the others falling into line behind him. Munne bridged the gap between the Proma and the Barauder. She cast a glance over her shoulder at Lagazi, hoping to convey that they would discuss the encounter in more detail once they were in the city. Lagazi's lips tightened, but the Barauder didn't ask any questions.

The journey across the western bridge would take nearly an hour to get to the city-island. No one spoke. A gentle breeze blew past them from the surface of the lake. Ships sailed around them, some idling in the waters to fish, others swiftly making their way to the city docks. Despite the colder weather setting in, the lake was alive with activity.

This must be some evil plot of the Provira, no doubt. They must have managed to infiltrate the castle and whisk away the princess, but to where? To what end? A shiver ran down Munne's spine, the hairs on the back of her neck standing on end. *I must offer my aid to the king and put any other plans of travel on hold. Father would understand, if he knew.* She pursed her lips together and frowned. *But what about the nightmares? What if they get worse while I'm in the city, and I lash out as Malion lashed out at his wife? Can I afford to stay and help?*

A gull cried out overhead. Munne looked to the sky where the two suns looked down upon Daaria. Her stomach clenched at the thought of her immediate future, and what choices she would have to make on the floating city island.

CHAPTER XXII: RAY

Time passed slowly in the castle. After delivering the princess's "dinner", Jayne took them down the hall to the other room, which was little more than a prison cell if Ray was being completely honest. The room was bare and had bloodstains on the floor and walls.

How long has the princess been infected with the Doshara? What goes through her mind when she's in this room, eating butchered, uncooked animals? The thought made Ray's stomach churn.

Jayne's face was pale as she described the princess's previous evening ritual. Even though she spoke with a level tone, fear oozed from her every word. "Depending on the princess's hunger, we sometimes have to bring larger... *portions*... into the chamber."

The staff was afraid of the princess, Ray realized. As they should be, if she correctly remembered the mythos of the Doshara. It was nothing short of a miracle if the princess was still of sound mind and wasn't trying to kill or devour anyone around her. That must have been why Naro specially prepared their concoction, so that neither the princess nor the Doshara would try to kill them during the kidnapping.

They returned to the kitchens, Jayne continuing to explain castle life all the while. "With the change in the princess's dining, you'll be expected to arrive at the castle every day an hour before sundown. Your earnings will be distributed at the end of your shift."

She showed Ray and Ajak around the kitchen and introduced them to other kitchen and serving staff members. She also offered them a couple of pastries leftover from the younger princess's afternoon tea. They were some of the tastiest pastries Ray had ever eaten.

"What are these made from?" Ray asked Jayne around a mouthful of pastry and filling.

"The filling is a mixture of silverberries from Elimaine and pears from Ferilin. It was a favorite of Queen Annalah before her passing, and Princess Celia seems to have inherited her mother's sweet tooth." Jayne touched her fingertips to her lips, then her heart, then her forehead.

Queen Annalah had been a favorite of the people. Ray remembered her mother speaking kindly of the queen, more so than any of the other royal family members. The entire city had mourned when she passed away.

"I have some other business to attend to. Since it's your first day, if you want to get acclimated to the castle you can wander around for a little bit. Please be prompt with returning here in two hours, and we'll go retrieve the dishes from the princess's room." Without waiting for their responses, Jayne left them to speak to one of the other kitchen staff.

"One moment," Ajak murmured, then scurried away to one of the tables where a woman was furiously rolling out dough.

Ray watched him ask the woman a question, make small talk and a quick joke, and place his fingers briefly on the countertop before returning to her.

"Flour. Let's go walking," he whispered and didn't elaborate further beyond that.

Ray nodded and wandered over to the same baking area. She tapped the woman on the shoulder, then placed her hand on the countertop, careful to cover the tips of her fingers in flour. "Adam said you're the genius behind those pear and silverberry tarts?"

"Aye. Jayne let you try one?" the woman asked, a smile on her face.

"She did. It was absolutely wonderful." Ray returned the smile. "I'll be keeping an eye out for any extras that come back to the kitchens."

She left the woman to her work and returned to Ajak's side. They exchanged the briefest of nods and then left the kitchen. They went their separate ways outside, Ajak to the right and Ray to the left.

She retraced their steps to the foyer of the castle, taking care to leave a trail of white fingerprints along the way. She took care to only drag one fingertip at a time, alternating between her four fingers and her thumb so she had enough flour to last. It was highly unlikely they would return this way, but it was an important route to remember. There were four guards stationed in the foyer, with more certainly patrolling the bridge itself. As Ray moved throughout the foyer, she feigned interest in all the tapestries hanging on the walls. Each symbolized an important moment in Proma history, such as the first inhabitants of the islands, the first king, and the building of the castle. Some of them she didn't recognize.

She hoped the guards weren't suspicious of her behavior. They were the same crew that saw her on the way in. *Is it normal for servants to wander the halls in between tasks? Jayne said we could, so hopefully that's the case.* She risked glancing in their direction only to notice they weren't paying her any mind. Her shoulders dropped in relief.

She had other places to explore. She left the foyer and tried to find an exterior wall of the castle, so she could look down to see if there were any ramps or exits to the shore. There was a window facing the city not too far from the foyer that she was able to look out. Looking out and down, nothing protruded from the castle. The stonework was smooth down to the ground. She would have to find another window.

Ray made her way back down to the kitchens and looked around. Perhaps Ajak would have found a way out. It had only been about thirty minutes, so she had plenty of time to continue looking around. She decided to follow the flour trail that Ajak had left behind.

"You're new, aren't you?" one of the guards called to her as she meandered down a hallway.

Ray nearly jumped out of her skin. "I-is it that obvious?" she responded coyly.

"We were told there'd be new kitchen staff today." He took his helmet off to reveal a middle-aged man with warm brown eyes and a kind smile. "Where are you trying to get to?"

This is a rather fortunate turn of events, she thought. She spoke again, keeping up her demure appearance. "I'm trying to keep it all straight, but there's so much to see here."

"Aye, that there is. Come on, I'll show you around."

The guard led her through various twists and turns, descending further into the foundations of the castle. He pointed out the larder rooms close to the kitchen, as well as the path down to the castle chapel.

Where did the servants draw their water from? "Oh, that reminds me of something I forgot to ask Jayne." Ray wailed, smacking her forehead.

"I can try to help," the guard reassured her.

"You're too kind! And it's probably time that I head back to the kitchens anyway... but where do the servants get their water?"

"I can show you on the way back. There's a lift that connects to a cave down below." The guard placed his hand on her back and led her toward the kitchens.

Sure enough, two doors down from the kitchen was a small room with a large well in the middle. A pulley system had been installed to raise up a rather large bucket from down below. Ray leaned over the edge of the well to look down and was pleasantly surprised. The bucket was large enough to fit one person, and the well opened into a cavern with a stream running through it.

"Where's the water come from?" she asked over her shoulder. From what she could tell, no one was down there. *Could this be our way out?*

"That stream was dug out by architects a long, long time ago," the guard explained. "Probably a lot easier pulling up the bucket than going down to the beach and back."

Ray hummed in agreement. "Thank you for showing me this! I'm sure I'll be in here often."

"Of course. I should get back to my post. Goodnight and good luck." The guard smiled at her and left the room.

She didn't linger much longer after that. She made sure to drag a fingertip along the wall next to the door to leave her mark. The kitchens were still bustling when she slipped back in. Ajak still hadn't returned, and Jayne was nowhere to be found. She frowned and drifted over to an empty countertop and leaned against it, watching the hustle and bustle around her.

Could this have been me, if I hadn't joined the Walkers? Ray tried imagining herself working in these kitchens, day after day. Wearing the same drab dress and apron, handling the same glasses and silverware. *I'd be bored to tears, I think. No, I belong on the streets where everything's constantly changing. This isn't me.*

She was forced back into reality. She needed more flour, and she needed to ensure she had a weapon of some kind on her, even if Ajak said he would take care of any conflicts that arose. It wouldn't be fair for her to let him fight their battles alone. There was the knife that they brought up to the princess...

Would that work? Should I try to get something while I'm still in the kitchens, in case we run into any problems on the way back up to the princess's chambers? She glanced around to see what kind of tools were nearby, and who was paying attention to their surroundings. Most of the utensils in the kitchen were spoons, rolling pins, and the occasional fork.

Damnit, where are the knives?

She walked around the kitchens, taking care not to get in anyone's way. Flour still covered the one countertop where the pastry girl had stopped to chat with one of the other chefs. Ensuring no one was watching her, Ray grabbed a handful of flour then clasped her hands behind her back. She returned to her perch near the exit, looking out for Jayne and Ajak.

"Made it back in time, I see," Jayne said, navigating through the workspaces to get to Ray. "Right then, let's go."

Ray's brow furrowed. She was about to speak up and ask if they should wait for Ajak to return, but his voice stopped her.

"Yes, ma'am," Ajak responded from behind Ray. She tossed him a questioning glance over her shoulder before following Jayne out of the kitchens.

As they navigated their way back up to the princess's chamber, Ray held her hand out to Ajak to coat his fingers in flour again. They took turns reaching out to touch the walls, tapestries, and tables with their flour-covered fingers. In one of the spiral staircases, Ray felt Ajak press something gently against her back. Jayne was too busy climbing the stairs to look behind her, so Ray grabbed the item—a sheathed dagger by the feel of it—and tucked it into her apron.

Where did he get this? She shrugged the thought away. There was no time to get concerned with the details.

"Odd," Jayne said as they approached the princess's door.

There were no guards posted outside. The hallway was empty besides the three of them.

"Should we still go inside?" Ray asked quietly.

"Sir Trys should be here. Perhaps he took the princess for a walk," Jayne muttered to herself and frowned. Then she spoke up to the others. "Yes, we should still gather up the dishes. Come on." The woman opened the door and cautiously took a step inside.

Ajak placed a hand on Ray's shoulder. She turned to look at him, and the gleam in his eyes was unmistakable. It was time.

But what are we going to do?

She looked back to Jayne and followed her into the room, Ajak bringing up the rear. Jayne was crossing the room to the table where the glass dishes had been stacked up on a tray. The princess had eaten. *But has she drank from the goblet? More importantly, where did she go?*

Behind Ray came the almost imperceptible sound of the door closing. Her years of experience had honed her senses. First thing, they had to deal with Jayne. She was larger than either of them, but she didn't appear to be in as good of shape as they were. They could incapacitate her. Ray had very little experience with that, but she knew she had to do it if they were to be successful. Besides, she didn't want to *kill* the woman if she could help it. The weight of the dagger pulled on her apron. She wouldn't use it. Not yet.

Jayne had made it to the dishes and was reaching to pick up the tray. Ray sprinted forward, slapping one hand across the woman's nose and mouth, and wrapping the other around her midsection. She pulled the woman back with all her strength, staggering backward into the center of the room. Jayne tried to scream, but the noise was muffled underneath Ray's hand.

Ray clamped down as hard as she could, pinching the woman's nostrils together and hoping that there truly was no one else in the princess's chambers. Jayne thrashed around in Ray's grasp. Ray held on as tight as she could, but the woman was trying to leverage her weight to her advantage. Ajak's hand pressed down on top of Ray's as he positioned himself on the other side of the woman and pressed himself against her to keep her still. It didn't take long for Jayne to fall unconscious. Ajak and Ray laid the woman down on the floor.

"What now?" Ray whispered, not daring to speak any louder.

"We hide her, then we hide and wait for the princess to get back," Ajak replied in a low voice.

"What's the exit strategy?"

"Dress her like a servant and drag her along toward the bottom. I found a way out but it's a long trek. You?"

"There's a well by the kitchens. Bucket's big enough for one person at a time."

"That'll have to do. Shorter distance to the water, shorter distance to our boat."

A low moan came from one of the doors beyond them. From further in the princess's chambers.

Ray's spine quivered. "What was—?"

"Find somewhere to put Jayne. I'll check it out." Ajak gave the order, and Ray fell into line. Now was not the time to question the plan.

From the main room there were two other doors beside the entrance. The moaning had come from the door opposite the entrance. Ajak slunk toward it, pulling a dagger from the back of his pants. Ray moved to the other door, which was on the wall to the left of the entrance. She pressed an ear against it and listened for a moment. Satisfied by the sound of silence, she opened it and took in her surroundings. It was a bathing chamber with a large stone tub in the center of the room. No other doors. A large privacy screen leaned against one of the walls across from a beautiful wooden dresser on the opposite side.

We could put Jayne into the tub and then bar the door shut. That could potentially buy us some time. It would all depend on how often the guards changed shifts outside the princess's room.

Ray returned to the main chamber. Ajak had his ear pressed against the other door, dagger in hand. She hissed quietly and beckoned him over.

"Bathing tub. Let's put her in there," she muttered.

He nodded silently, then sheathed the dagger and moved to grab Jayne's arms. Ray took hold of her legs, and together they shambled over to the bathing chamber and managed to get the large woman inside the tub. The two of them managed to shimmy Jayne out of most of her clothes. They closed the door, and Ray was about to tell Ajak about barring the door when he grabbed her wrist and walked back over to the other door.

"I think it's Princess Niamnh in there with the knight Jayne mentioned, having a bit of fun," Ajak breathed.

In any other circumstance that would have been quite a scandal. Ray couldn't help but wonder, though, if they were about to kill a knight to get away with the princess. That would be much more scandalous.

"I'll take care of the knight. Get the princess out of bed."

Ray nodded. A thousand thoughts raced through her head, and she wished she could ask them all, but there was no time. There was no time to wonder if Princess Niamnh had, in fact, drunk from the goblet. Or if her knight had done the same, and what his reaction would have been to the drug. Or what would happen if the knight was able to reach for his sword before Ajak got to him.

Or if Ajak was about to kill a man in front of her.

Suddenly the door was open, and Ajak was sprinting to the bed, dagger raised in the air. Beside the bed was a flickering candle, casting shadows on the wall of two people tangled in blankets and each other. The knight's armor had been discarded on the floor beside the bed, along with the princess's gown. The mingled moans of the princess and the knight were bewitching and... *wrong*. The princess sounded as if she was experiencing both pleasure and pain, not from the thrusts of the knight but something else.

Ray followed behind Ajak, watching as he struck the back of the knight's head with the hilt of his dagger. The knight slumped forward, and the princess let out a pained and confused wail. Ajak grabbed the knight's shoulders and dragged him out of the bed, off the princess. He wasn't trying to kill him. It felt like a weight was being lifted off Ray's shoulders.

"Ssstop, wh-what are you—" Princess Niamnh slurred and tried to scream.

Ray had moved into place at the right time, though, and managed to wrap Jayne's apron around the princess's mouth to muffle her screaming. She grabbed the princess's arm and pulled her out of the bed. The princess tried to fight back, but her movements were very sluggish.

She *had* drunk from the goblet!

That strengthened Ray's resolve, and she pulled harder, dragging the princess to her feet and across the room. She glanced over her shoulder to see what Ajak was doing but only caught a glimpse of him throwing himself over the knight. Was the man still conscious after Ajak hit him? Skin slapped against skin as Ajak punched the knight several times before he fell to the ground, unconscious.

Princess Niamnh's naked skin felt warm and feverish under her touch. Ray's cheeks flushed as she wondered if it was because of the sex or the poison. She pushed the thought from her mind. Underneath her hand, the princess had stopped trying to scream. Ray could tell that she was struggling to stand, and she was struggling to hold the princess up. She leaned against one of the walls, breathing heavily. She needed Ajak's help to get her dressed in Jayne's clothes.

He appeared behind her, reaching to take Princess Niamnh under the arms so he could hold her up. "You got the clothes?"

Ray grunted in response and slipped away from the princess. She grabbed Jayne's dress and threw it over the princess's head, sliding her arms through the sleeves and adjusting the skirts around her legs. The dress could easily fit two more of the princess inside, so she used the apron to tighten it up as best she could. She stepped back and took in the appearance of the princess. They would have to do something about her hair.

Ray noticed for the first time that the princess had stark white hair against pristine bronze skin. Anyone who saw her would know who she was, regardless of what else she was wearing.

We must cover up her hair.

She took off her own apron and wrapped it around the princess's head. Her hands shook as the princess struggled to keep her eyes open.

"She doesn't look so good," Ray mumbled.

Ajak gritted his teeth. "Keep going."

"Are you sure we can get downstairs with her like this? Won't we get stopped?" Ray asked.

"Don't do this, Ray. Not now," he warned.

She pressed her lips together and did her best to make the apron look like a head wrap.

That's when she noticed Ajak's hands were red. They were lucky Jayne's dress was black, otherwise it would have been obvious that his hands were covered with—

"Ajak, your hands..."

"We need to *go*."

Ray started to protest again, but Ajak pushed Princess Niamnh into her arms. Ray struggled to shift the princess around so she could wrap one arm around her waist, holding her upright.

"I'll wash. But we have to go *now*." He darted into the bathing chamber. Was there a pot of water in there? Ray couldn't remember. She couldn't stop to remember.

Ray took one step forward, her legs suddenly shaking. She inhaled deeply and pushed onward. She had to leave the room and get to the well by the kitchens.

One step in front of the other.

No one was out in the hallway. Ray took another deep breath and started toward the stairs.

The princess's breathing was erratic, and she struggled to keep her eyes open. She didn't say a word. The sleeper they had slipped into her drink should have knocked her out. Was it the Doshara that was keeping her awake? Naro had said the blueleaf they added was to subdue the Doshara. Perhaps it was only strong enough to keep her semiconscious at this point.

One step in front of the other.

Ajak caught up to them on the stairs. He touched Ray's hand and took the princess from her. Although the physical burden was lifted from her arms, she still felt the weight of the situation on her shoulders. It pushed down on her, crushing her underneath the sheer intensity and absurdity of it all.

We're kidnapping Princess Niamnh.

"Keep moving," Ajak hissed through clenched teeth. He had shuffled the princess around to a more natural appearance. Her head lolled against his chest, his arm wrapped around her shoulders. A fleeting thought of them looking like a husband tending to his sick wife crossed Ray's mind. It was gone before she even had time to dwell on it.

Another step, and then another.

They retraced their way down to the kitchens without running into any guards. *Is fortune really on our side tonight?*

"She doesn't look too good," someone murmured not too far behind them.

Ray's blood turned to ice. *Who said that? Could they tell this is the princess?* She forced herself to keep her mouth shut and her eyes forward, trying so very hard not to look scared.

Ajak chuckled and responded. "Aye, I think she ate something bad. We're just taking her to get some air."

Ray turned and offered a half smile. It was a guard. It felt like her face was going to crack from the pressure.

"We'll take care of her," she managed to choke out. *Did that sound normal enough?* Her skin prickled and boiled. The guard passed them without a second glance.

"Could you get the door for me, Lorie?" Ajak asked.

Lorie?

Lorie.

Ray stopped abruptly and turned to the door on their left. A small white smudge denoted it as the well room. She reached for the door handle, her hands shaking so violently she honestly thought she might miss the handle entirely. She managed to open it and took a shaky step inside, giving room for Ajak to follow her in with the princess.

The well room had two lit sconces that flickered and bathed it in yellow light. The stone circle and pulley system in the middle loomed ominously before them. The bucket wasn't at the top. Someone must have left it at the bottom of the well.

"Pull the damn thing up," Ajak grumbled, closing the door with his foot, and leaning against it. Princess Niamnh's head rolled to the side. Her eyes were closed. Had she finally drifted off to sleep?

Ray hurried over to the pulley system and began raising the bucket from down below.

One hand over the other.

"Wh-where is the boat going to be?" she sputtered.

"North end of the island," Ajak answered calmly.

"Where are we?" Her voice sounded small and childish. She should know their relative location on the island. She had been tracking that earlier. She should know—

"Closer to the southern end. Hopefully the cave has a north exit."

She latched onto Ajak's soothing voice and focused on pulling the bucket up.

One hand over the other. One shaking hand over the other.

She wished it was Naro telling her what to do.

The bucket lifted over the top of the well. She straightened up and looked at it in shock. She had done that. And now it was time to go *down* it.

"Who first?" she asked.

"You first. Make sure the coast is clear. Tug on the rope and I'll send the princess down after you."

Her stomach clenched. If she was going down first, she would have to deal with whoever was down there. *She* would have to make the decision to take a life or knock them unconscious. She was so small, though... could she even do it?

Ray blinked.

Ajak was by her side, placing his hand around the small of her back and holding onto the edge of the bucket.

Princess Niamnh sat up against the door, hunched over and leaning slightly to the left.

"Come on, Ray. We're almost out."

She climbed into the bucket with as much care and grace as she could muster. She managed to quell the shaking in her legs, but her fingers trembled as she grasped the edge of the bucket. She could crouch down in it so only the top of her head was sticking out.

"Do you have your dagger?" Ajak murmured.

She patted around her hips until she found it, nestled between the hem of her pants and her waist.

"Y-yes."

"Okay, good. I'm lowering you down now." He leaned over and kissed the top of her head. "I'll be down after you in just a few moments, okay?"

"O-okay."

He began lowering her down into the cave. The well room had been warm with a draft, but as she descended into the cave below, the air chilled. The winter evening seeped into her skin through the layers of clothes. She prayed to the Protector that no one would be down below.

The bucket continued to descend. She listened for other noises beyond the creaking of the rope and the whisper of a breeze. She listened for footsteps, voices, or armor.

She heard nothing.

The bucket touched the top of the stream, the water pushing back against her weight. She raised her head high enough to look at her surroundings. The cave was made of sleek stone. The only thing manmade was the well she just descended from, the wooden walkways along the stream, and the torches that lit them. The bucket had touched down within arm's reach of one of the walkways. She reached out to grab at it and pull the bucket slightly to the side so she could climb out. If anyone had been down here, they would have shouted, screamed, or attacked her.

She turned in a circle to take in everything else. To her left the walkways continued in a straight line. To her right the walkway went around a bend a short distance away. They would need to go to the left. She reached back out to the bucket and tugged on the rope. It began to rise into the well chamber.

It felt like hours as the bucket lifted and descended again. Princess Niamnh was curled up inside, mumbling something under her breath. It took Ray a couple of tries to pull the girl out of the bucket and onto the walkway, but she managed. She tugged on the rope again to let Ajak know it was his turn. How would he get down, though, without someone to lower him? Perhaps he would cut the rope and drop into the stream. Was it deep enough for a drop like that, or would he hurt himself in the fall? What if he fell out of the bucket?

She watched the well opening with bated breath, the princess leaning heavily against her. It was Ajak's turn. He had to come down here and help her get to the boat. They had to do it together.

Several moments passed and she knew something had gone wrong. Over the gentle lapping of water against wood, she could hear a scuffle come from the well room high above.

She saw what came down the well, but her mind refused to accept it. A dark blur fell from above, much too small to be a wooden bucket. It wasn't until she heard the splash of the stream and felt the water droplets hit her face that she was forced to think and react.

347

Ajak's body had hit the water, and he floated facedown, blood pooling around him.

Ray was unable to tear her eyes away from him as he floated along the stream, unmoving. *He has to get out of the water. We have to run.* Part of her knew that he wouldn't be climbing out of the water, though, and that she had to move *now*.

"They're escaping through the well!" a voice roared from the well chamber above, shattering Ray's trance.

Every muscle in her body tensed and sprang into action. She grabbed Princess Niamnh's arm and dragged her down the walkway to the left, straight ahead. The movement jolted the princess awake if only slightly, and she managed to throw one foot in front of the other without falling over.

Ray saw a cave mouth in the distance. Fortune was still on her side. She just needed to get out of the cave and find the boat. There would be a man waiting at the boat to take them to the other side of the lake. She just needed to keep putting one foot in front of the other, and not let go of the princess.

One foot in front of the other.

Beyond the cave mouth was the darkness of night. A few torches lined the walkway as it curved to the right, hugging the side of the island.

She could only hear her footsteps and the princess's, and the gentle lapping of water against the walls of the stream. There were no screams, no battle cries. The guards had not made their way down into the cave yet. She still had time.

One foot in front of the other.

As they cleared the cave and turned to the right, she saw a dinghy haphazardly moored along the walkway. A single man stood by it, straightening up as he saw Ray running toward him, dragging the princess behind her.

"Sshh, quiet, quiet!" he hissed, raising his hands.

Ray forced herself to slow down to a walk. Her legs felt like they were on fire. She had to *move*. If she walked, she would get caught. She had to sprint to the boat, throw the princess in, and take up the paddles—

"Who are you with?" the man asked with a low voice.

"The Walkers. Are you the boatman Naro hired?" Ray responded, all thought of caution and personas blown to the wind. She had to escape.

"Aye. Name's Wendelgar. I was told there would be three of you." He frowned.

Ray shook her head. "J-just the two. We have to go now. They know she's missing." She wanted to throw the princess into the boat and run back for Ajak, or hope that when she looked behind her, he'd be swimming or running towards her.

Stop. You saw him. You saw what happened to him. You can't ruin the mission, not now.

Wendelgar grunted and helped Ray lift the princess into the boat. He untied the rope that bound the dinghy to the walkway and pushed off. He jumped in and took a seat on the end closest to the island, picking up the oars and began rowing. Ray sat in the other seat, wrapping her arms around herself, and shivering violently. The princess was splayed out on the floorboards between them.

They just needed to get to the northern shore of the lake.

"Pick up some oars and help me get this over to those other ships. We need to blend in," Wendelgar said gruffly, nodding his head toward the second pair of oars at Ray's feet.

She picked them up and helped row the dinghy toward the fleet of ships to the north. Those ships were either docked or waiting to dock at the city of Auora. They could blend in with those ships and navigate their way through to the other side. They'd be safe.

The princess groaned. *How long is the sleeper supposed to last?*

It felt like hours as they rowed their way between ships. The city was quiet. No one was out on the docks tonight. The gang lords had listened to Naro it seemed.

"We can turn north from here," Wendelgar said quietly as they passed the last row of ships and entered the open water again. The water was calm. The sound of it gently lapping against the dinghy brought Ray some small measure of comfort.

"Thank you," she murmured.

"It's just business," Wendelgar responded with a mischievous glint in his eye, offering her a smile.

His grin cracked and shattered, blood dribbling from his lips. An arrow pierced through his back and out his chest. A scream tried to rip its way out of her throat, but she suppressed it.

Have the guards caught up to us? Are they going to kill me like they killed Ajak?

As Wendelgar's body slumped forward, she followed her gut instinct and ducked down, pulling the princess down as well. She covered the lower half of princess's body with her own, her face pressed against the servant's skirts. She could smell the flour, sweat, and sex baked into the fabric. And now the stench of fresh metallic blood from Wendelgar's cooling body. His face was pressed against the princess's chest.

The scents were too much to bear. Tears poured from Ray's eyes and a sob ripped itself out of her throat. *I'm going to die out here, just like Wendelgar. Just like Ajak.* She cried harder for her fallen companion. "Stop it, *stop it*," she hissed to herself.

To the archer it would look like no one else was in the boat. Ray forced herself to breathe normally and quietly. She needed to hear her surroundings. She had to listen.

The water splashed gently against the boat. The princess murmured something unintelligible underneath the weight of Wendelgar. The city was quiet. She didn't hear anything else. No other arrows cutting through the air, cutting through skin. Nothing pierced the boat. Everything else remained whole.

Who shot Wendelgar?

She parted her lips and breathed. The fabric of the princess's skirts stuck to her bottom lip, moistening with every breath.

I'm alive.

The boat continued to float onward in the direction they had been rowing. North. She sent out a silent prayer of thanks.

She had to continue her mission. Naro was depending on her.

CHAPTER XXIII: SETH

Seth didn't feel any better the next morning. His entire body was sore, no thanks to the stone platform he was laying on. He frowned and tried to wiggle his toes, only for the inevitable disappointment when he couldn't feel anything. He reached a hand down toward his thighs and tried poking and pushing at the skin both above and below his knees. Above, he felt, but below, not at all. He let out a loud groan and threw his head into the pillow. Not better at all.

If only I'd woken up in Lithalyon, in that soft bed at the inn...

Dim light spilled into his room from the window. It was a misty morning, and clouds covered the suns. He opened one eye and stared out at gray skies. He groaned again quietly and shifted an arm to cover his eyes. He smacked his hand against something hard.

"Ow..." he grumbled, moving his head so he could look at what he hit. It was his satchel that contained the books from the library.

Instantly he was awake and moved to sit up. He pulled one of the books from the satchel and opened it. Unfortunately, there wasn't enough light in the room for him to read the text. It would probably be best to just light a candle here, but part of him yearned to take the books into his mother's library and read them there. It just felt like the better place to do it. But what would his mother say if she saw what he was reading? A part of him wanted to show her. Maybe she could help him figure out the mysterious riddles.

He glanced around the room, his gaze settling on his wheeled chair. It stood at the end of his bed within arm's reach. Bitter feelings swelled within him, but he needed to use the chair. It was the only way to get to his mother's library, regardless of whether he was going to show the books to his mother or not. He sighed and crawled toward the other end of the bed, his legs useless underneath him.

The satchel.

Before he could forget, he reached back and grabbed the satchel, dragging it with him to the end of the bed. He would need to hide it underneath a blanket or robe if he was going to sneak it by the stewards, or anyone for that matter. It was a chilly enough day that he could get away with draping a blanket over his lap, which was all too convenient for his plans. At least one thing was going his way.

Most winters in Moonyswyn were mild, but today was *cold*. His muscles tightened and ached, and he seriously reconsidered his course of action. The silken nest would be warmer and more comfortable than the wheelchair.

I need to see Mother, though.

With great effort, Seth pulled himself into his chair and rolled it around the room so he could gather up a change of clothes. The air nipped at his skin and goosebumps raised on his skin. The blanket would serve more than one purpose, it seemed. He grabbed a dark green tunic with long sleeves and began the long, arduous process of shimmying the robe over his body and around his hips and thighs. Humiliation filled his thoughts, his cheeks flushing. Even though he was accustomed to this, it didn't feel good, especially after the past few days. Putting on a pair of pants and boots took less time, but the pang of embarrassment grew until all Seth felt was anger and frustration toward himself, his father, and the world.

He maneuvered back over to the bed and snatched both the satchel and one of the heavier blankets. The decanter was still nestled inside the bag. With a sigh, he withdrew the glass container and inspected it in the dim morning light. The only traces of the healing elixir were a few droplets that pooled at the bottom, easily mistaken for water or tea.

Time to get rid of this thing.

The cup of tea and soup bowl caught his attention. For a moment his anger subsided, and he thought of his sister who had ensured he had something warm to eat and drink last night—made sure he returned safely to his room. Octavia cared for him in her own way, and he cared for her, too, despite everything that had happened. Maybe one day...

Silencing that line of thinking, Seth put the decanter on the tray. He set the satchel down in his lap, and then hastily draped the blanket on top, smoothing it out so there was no evident bulge from what was underneath. It was time to visit his mother's library and see what he could find out from these books.

And perhaps tell her about the library in Lithalyon. Then we can both daydream about its splendor.

Outside stood two stewards, one covered from head to toe, and one showing off their face covered in shimmering gray scales.

"Good morning Ssseth," the Asaszi rasped, bowing their head toward him. "It isss very good to sssee you have recovered."

"Thank you," he managed to say without his voice wavering, which was a truly impressive feat considering it felt like there was an endless void in his stomach. "I would like to visit my mother and see how she is doing."

The Asaszi nodded and turned to the other steward. Before they had a chance to step behind him and push his chair along, Seth grabbed the wheels and moved forward. The stewards had no choice but to fall in line behind him as he made his way down the hall. Once more he had two shadows, much to his displeasure. He yearned to disappear into a crowd and become no one again.

The clouds had parted. As Seth and his stewards made their way to the library, more light poured into the pyramid. Candles still burned in the candelabras in the hall from the previous night. The door to the library was ajar. *Mother must already be inside searching for some entertainment for the day.* That little sense of normalcy calmed his nerves. He made his way inside as the stewards took up their posts on either side of the doorway.

His mother wasn't sitting by the window today. She must have picked a spot further inside, perhaps near a table with a lamp. Several tall rows of bookcases filled the center of the room, and he had to roll past three of them before he spotted his mother tucked away at the end of the bookcases on an oversized pillow. In her hands was a large volume, and she was roughly three-quarters of the way through it. On the table next to her was a lit candle, burning quite low.

How long has she been here? "Good morning, Mother," Seth said.

His mother raised her head and looked toward him. Underneath her eyes were dark circles. She smiled and responded, but her cheerful cadence didn't seem to match her eyes. "Hello, my sweet," As she took in his appearance, her smile wavered. "Oh, you look terrible! What happened to you?"

His cheeks burned hot, hotter where the scratches and cuts were healing. "I-I'm fine. Did you spend the night here?" he asked, guiding his chair toward her.

She adjusted her posture, reaching out and grabbing one of his hands, squeezing gently. "I suppose I did. It's quite captivating, reading about the rainforest. But darling, what happened?"

Evelyn raised her other hand to his face, her fingertips gently grazing one of the larger cuts on his cheek. Their eyes met, and he immediately looked away. His stomach clenched, and his mind raced.

She deserves to know. Perhaps she can help. But I'll be putting her in danger.

"Did you fall from—?"

"I've been gone."

His mother let out a small gasp, but otherwise was silent. After a moment, he raised his chin to meet her gaze again, ready to recoil out of shame. A look of concern was plastered on her face, but she didn't look angry. He forced himself to relax. He could tell that she was going to wait for him to continue speaking.

"Szatisi, she's been working on a cure for..." He briefly glanced down at his legs, then cleared his throat before continuing. "Well, it works. I was able to acquire it three days ago, and I used it to leave the pyramid and go to Lithalyon."

His mother's eyes widened, and she lunged across the space between them to slap her hand over his mouth, silencing him. "This must be a joke," she whispered.

He gently pried her hand away from his mouth. "It's not. I've been to the Elviri city. I walked their streets, drank in their taverns, and visited their library."

Her look of shock faded into one of cautious curiosity at the mention of the library. Before he could convince himself otherwise, he pulled the satchel out from underneath the blanket and handed it to her.

"It was even more grand than you described. There were multiple wings, multiple floors, filled with books on every subject. It was incredible, I wish you could have been there. And I-I brought some books home with me. That seemed interesting. That have things in them we need to talk about."

His mother furrowed her brow and opened the satchel, pulling out two of the books from within. One was a book on the Elviri's understanding of the Asaszi culture at the end of the Eldest Days. The second was about the last of the Elviri-Asaszi wars.

"Seth, this is extremely dangerous." His mother's voice lowered with caution. "If anyone were to find these books, or if Szatisi hears... We must get rid of them. You can't speak of this to anyone."

Seth shook his head and took the satchel back, pulling out the third book. *Langlir.* He opened it to page fifty-four and handed it to his mother.

His mother took the book, her face twisting into a look of confused fear. Evelyn looked at the handwriting on the page and recoiled. She gripped the book tightly and kept reading for a few moments more. Seth knew she had finished reading the notes and was trying to process it all.

"I don't know what this means. But it's not good," Seth mumbled.

"It's my mother's handwriting," she whispered.

What? Seth recoiled, gripping the satchel tightly. *She's never spoken of her own mother before. Who was she? How did she know Father? What happened to her?*

She stood up, forcing him to roll his chair back to give her space. The other books fell onto the floor beside her. "We need to get rid of these as soon as possible. Burn them if we must. Your father must *never* know about this."

Never had he heard such deep levels of dread and panic in his mother's voice, or anyone else's for that matter. It chilled him to the bone, and a part of him knew she was right. *If Amias found these books, he would hunt down the person who brought them back here, submit them to endless torture and experiments.* A chill ran down his spine and he shivered.

Seth rolled his chair backward into the main area of the library. His mother stooped down to pick up the fallen books and thrust them into the satchel. She leaned over and blew out the candle on the table. "But, Mother, she mentioned her research. Maybe she knew of a way to stop the experiments, to prove that Father's a danger to us all," he said as loudly as he dared, knowing the stewards weren't too far away.

"Speak no more of this." Her tone was unyielding.

"But those notes, the warnings about—"

"My mother was a historian. A genius." Evelyn glanced around the room, ensuring the door closed and the stewards were out of sight. His mother crouched next to his chair, clutching the satchel tightly to her chest. She leaned in close, her voice barely audible. "And your father loathed her. Despised her for hoarding her knowledge and never sharing it with him. So, if she thought he was *wrong*, then we must be thankful that she's dead and her research is gone, hopefully somewhere your father will never find it. That is all we can do."

Seth's blood ran cold and his hands tightened up into fists. *This can't be the end of it. But what else can I do? Especially with Mother taking the books from me, and planning to destroy them?*

"We must be thankful," his mother had said.

"Do not speak of your escape to anyone. We must pretend it never happened, and that you never read those notes." Evelyn stood and smoothed out her skirts with one hand. "Now come, escort your mother back to her chambers and share a meal with her. And let's see what we can do about those scratches," she said cheerily, but the light didn't reach her eyes.

She slung the satchel strap over one shoulder and headed toward the door. Seth felt as if he had no choice but to follow her. His mind was still reeling from what his mother told him, and he felt lost. His hands worked the wheels of his chair on their own. Even the ache in his lower back seemed to dissipate before this new onslaught of misery. It was as if he was drowning in his own sorrow and guilt over the past several days. Had anything he'd done been worth it?

<hr />

The rest of the morning and afternoon passed uneventfully. Seth and his mother had picked at a spread of fruits and nuts, although neither ate much. For Seth it was because of his guilt and frustration. Resentment towards his mother built up to the point where he didn't want to talk even if she did. He was sure his mother hadn't eaten much because she was afraid. Little was said between them, and after the meal he returned to his room and crawled back into bed.

What's the point of telling her anything? Like she said, I must pretend like it never happened. Doesn't Mother want to put an end to Father's madness? Why would she destroy our one chance to do so? Maybe she's afraid he'd find us out. Grandmother's notes did mention she knew the answer to what he was looking for...

He stared at the red and green canopy, his lunch sitting uneasily in his stomach. With a scowl he threw an arm over his face.

I should've tried convincing her to leave instead—no! Stupid. There is no escape, not anymore.

He managed to fall back asleep for a couple of hours, and when he awoke again the suns were shining brightly outside. Light spilled into his room and made the stones glow. Had he been in a better mood, he might have found some beauty in the scene, but as is, he wanted to roll over and shut out the world.

In the early evening, there was a knock on his door. He groaned and pulled himself up into a sitting position and called out, "Enter!"

Octavia opened the door and entered the room. She was dressed in an ornamented green jacket and leather pants. Her hair was done into an elaborate knot. She looked as if she was dressed for a ceremony, or some kind of special event.

"Father has arrived," Octavia announced, her tone pleasant. She shut the door behind her and stood at the foot of the bed.

His stomach dropped. Of course, that's why she was dressed up. And he would be expected to dress up for dinner, too. He started pulling himself toward his chair so he could find something to wear. It was tense being in the same room as his sister. He could tell something was amiss, but he had no idea if it was a continuation of the past several days, or if Octavia had encountered a new problem. He wasn't sure she would share that information with him, and he wasn't sure that he wanted to know about it, so he stayed quiet.

"I can help," Octavia said gently, going to his wardrobe and sifting through his clothes.

She pulled out a jacket similar to her own, except it was dark blue instead of green. She handed it to him and then went back to digging. Seth accepted the jacket but did nothing. He waited for her to hand him a pair of pants and a plain tunic to wear under the jacket, and then he began changing. She walked over to the window and stared out at the forest, her hands behind her back.

After a few moments he was presentable enough, although he had a small cramp in his hip from moving the wrong way as he put his pants on. Usually, he was better about his posture, but time was of the essence, and he couldn't keep his father waiting.

"Alright, ready," he said.

Octavia turned back to him and crossed the room once more, opening the door, and gesturing for him to exit first. He obliged and rolled his chair out of the room with his sister right behind him.

In the hallway stood two stewards and a soldier dressed in full armor. It was odd seeing someone donning a helmet inside the pyramid, but perhaps his father wanted the guards in full uniform for his welcoming feast. Or maybe that particular soldier had offended Octavia, and she was subjecting him to some kind of punishment. He didn't know, nor did he care.

The strange group made their way toward the dining hall. It appeared as though they had arrived before Amias, which Seth considered a good thing. He would need time to move from his wheelchair to the stone dining chair. He doubted his sister would pull another stunt like the last dinner before he left. Best to just act like the past few days hadn't happened and draw as little attention to himself as possible.

Inside the dining hall, several servants placed dishes on the table and filled goblets with wine and water. The stewards peeled away from Seth's side and took their places at the edge of the room, standing silently and observing. Seth's mother had already taken her place on the left of where Amias would be seated. Neither he nor the Asaszi rulers were there yet. Seth couldn't see her full outfit, but it looked like his mother was dressed very extravagantly in an embroidered dress and jewelry. Octavia and Seth approached the opposite side of the table. His sister pulled one of the chairs out and then moved behind Seth's wheelchair, holding onto the back for stability.

Seth couldn't stop his lips from curling into a frown. *We really have gone down our separate paths,* he thought bitterly. He grimaced and pulled himself into the stone chair, straining his lower back and thighs. From behind them he heard the rustle and clinking of the armored soldier.

Octavia turned her head and hissed, "Against the wall, *soldier.*" She placed a strange enunciation on the title, and Seth couldn't tell why.

More rustling and clinking indicated that the soldier heeded her order, moving to stand farther away from the table. Seth had finished pulling himself onto the stone chair and was adjusting his jacket. Octavia pushed the wheelchair away, steering it next to the soldier. She took her place on Seth's left to act as a buffer between him and Amias. He looked across the table to his mother and tried to force a smile on his face. His mother returned the smile with ease, but he knew it was a mask.

"Hello, children," she said softly, looking between him and Octavia.

"Hello, Mother," Octavia responded in a similar tone. Seth glanced over at her and noticed that she too was hiding her true feelings. Interesting. He reached for his goblet of water and took a drink. Perhaps he should nurse a goblet of wine tonight instead.

The servants continued to bring dish after dish out to the table. It was a miracle that there was enough room on the table to hold it all, in addition to their own plates and bowls. The smell of the feast was intoxicating, and he felt his stomach growling. Directly in front of him were platters of roasted fish, smoked meats, and piles of steamed fruits and roots. Two servants brought a large platter of roast boar to the table. No expense was spared for the welcoming feast. Seth couldn't recall the last time they had a feast so extravagant.

"How was your day, Octavia? Seth spent his morning with me in the library." Seth strained to hear his mother's soft voice over the clamor of the servants.

Octavia stared into her goblet. "It was fine. I spent a lot of time in the training yard."

"Practicing with Arcyr'ys, or...?"

"Training new recruits," came Octavia's curt response. It led to a tense few moments between the family.

Normally she's more forthcoming with information about the troops. Did something happen while I was gone?

"Oh, new recruits! How wonderful," their mother finally responded. Seth felt how forced it was.

He reached for his wine goblet and drank. The bitter flavors assaulted his tongue, but he forced it down, nonetheless. It was nowhere near as sweet on the tongue as the Elviri wine had been. His heart ached at the memory of it.

Octavia made a polite noise of agreement and then drank from her goblet. The room grew silent once more. Their mother dropped her gaze to the all the food before them. She made no comments, however. *This will only get worse once Father arrives.* The thought of it made Seth drink again. He swallowed the wine and grimaced.

After a few more minutes of strained silence, the doors to the hall opened. An entourage of soldiers filed into the room, escorting Amias, Osza, Astohi, and Szatisi in. The soldiers took their places along the walls alongside Seth's stewards and Octavia's soldier. Octavia and their mother stood to greet them. Amias crossed to his seat at the end of the table closest to Octavia and their mother. Astohi stood behind the empty seat beside Seth's mother. Szatisi pulled Osza's seat back, giving the Asaszi queen room to sit down. Once Osza took her seat, the others around the table sat as well. Szatisi merely stood to the side of Osza's chair like a statue.

Seth's stomach churned at the sight of his father and the Asaszi, wishing he was anywhere but in this room.

Amias looked around the table with a hungry gleam in his eye. He always returned to Yiradia with that look. Judging by the faint smile on his face, Amias had been successful in Iszairi. That smile sent chills down Seth's spine. Progress had been made on whatever project he was working on, and he was eager to continue the work.

"How has my family been?" Amias asked, his voice barely above a whisper. His eyes settled on Octavia and Seth, and Seth had to fight the urge to panic and look away. He met his father's gaze and held it for what felt like hours.

Octavia's voice cut through his thoughts. "Excellent." Both Seth and Amias turned to look at her. For a moment, she seemed so sure of herself, but under the pressure of everyone's gaze she began to crumble. Seth saw the corners of her mouth start to turn downward, and one of her fingers twitched against her goblet.

Amias either didn't want his child to show any signs of weakness, or he didn't notice the signs to begin with. He continued, his voice louder now. "We made great progress in Iszairi. I believe we have solved a key component to opening the tomb. We should soon have a means of testing our theory."

Is the Tserys locked away in that tomb? And does Amias truly know how to open it, or is this another experiment that will end with someone else suffering for his mistakes?

Osza hissed in delight, and the sound made Seth's skin crawl.

"A toast!" Amias boomed, rising to his feet with his wine goblet held high in the air. Everyone else followed suit. Seth raised his own goblet out of fear of what would happen if he chose not to. "Very soon we will have power unimaginable to our foes and use it to strike them down. Soon we will indulge in feasts like this for every meal. To the *Tserys*!"

"To the *Tserys*!" everyone echoed, including Seth. They all drank deeply, although Seth wondered how many were toasting Amias and how many were trying to drink their problems away.

Everyone sat back down. Amias clapped his hands and the servants around the room began distributing the food amongst the guests. Soon Seth's plate was filled with meats, fish, vegetables, and fruit. He subtly looked back and forth between Amias and Osza to gauge when he could start eating. Although, with how his anxiety was twisting his stomach he wasn't sure how much he would be able to eat. Osza picked up a knife, indicating that Amias could pick up his own utensils. They both began to eat, which signaled that the others could do the same. For several minutes the only sounds in the room were the scraping and tapping of forks and knives on plates, goblets being moved, and quiet chewing and crunching.

Seth tried his best to appear interested in the food on his plate, but he struggled. Normally he would have enjoyed the roasted boar, but today it was difficult to chew and swallow. The combined smells of stewed fruits and roasted fish made him nauseous. Part of him wished he hadn't come back here, that he had stayed in Lithalyon.

I could've made it work. The Elviri would've accepted me, surely. He knew he was being foolish, though. His real identity would've been revealed, and he would've been taken prisoner, no doubt. *And poor Lisanthir... What would he think, knowing his Calydrian is actually a Provira half-blood? At least I wouldn't have had to see Father again.* Seth took solace in his cup of wine.

Seth's mother broke the silence. "Husband, does this mean we will be moving to Iszairi soon?"

Amias grunted and nodded. He took his time finishing his current bite and then swallowing a healthy swig of wine before responding. "Very soon. There is one last thing we are waiting on before we can relocate."

Seth hadn't visited the other pyramid since he was a child. Iszairi was even more ruinous than Yiradia, making travel hazardous, especially with his wheelchair. He didn't enjoy traveling to Iszairi, due to its proximity to Kherizhan. The barren mountains loomed over the other pyramid, casting a dark shadow over the rainforest below.

He paused to continue eating and drinking. It seemed to Seth that Amias was struggling to maintain his dignified persona when they had such a fanciful spread before them. Although Amias insisted that the family act like royalty, there were often times where their meals amounted to little more than cooked roots and the occasional boar. The Asaszi always had first claim to the rainforest's bounty. His father was caught between stuffing his face and maintaining an aura of regality.

Amias swallowed the last bite of fish and then cleared his throat. He had captured the attention of everyone around the table, and they were all waiting for him to elaborate on what that *one last thing* might be. He raised his gaze and met Osza's unblinking stare.

"News from Elimere. The Elviri have heard our call, and they have sent an emissary to treat with us." Amias couldn't keep the dark grin from returning to his face. "They should be arriving in Lithalyon in a matter of days. I plan on acting the moment I receive word that they are there."

The hairs on the back of Seth's neck stood on end. He remembered mention of this plan before he left but was surprised to hear the Elviri were taking up his father's offer to meet. *Don't they know not to trust Father?*

Although the Asaszi gave no outward indication of their feelings, Seth knew this was important news to them. Despite Amias's claim that it was "our" call, the message truly came from Osza.

"Have the Proma given their responsssse?" Osza asked.

"I have heard no word from the North," Amias responded, his voice suddenly cool. That wasn't what Osza wanted to hear.

Silence spread across the room. Osza blinked slowly, then turned to her mate. The two stared at each other for what felt like several minutes before they turned back to Amias.

"I will ensssure the troops are prepared for that day," Astohi hissed, glancing between Amias and Octavia.

Octavia looked at Astohi with deep reverence. *She must feel so honored to be acknowledged by the king consort,* Seth thought. He reached out for his wine goblet but did not bring it to his lips. Something shattered in his head, like glass falling to the floor. Everything suddenly became *sharper,* and he heard his labored breathing, his heart pounding in his ears. His mouth went dry. *They're planning on raiding Lithalyon.* A wave of dread crashed over him, drowning out his surroundings. *Lisanthir. How far are they going to go when they reach Lithalyon?*

For the first time since departing the Elviri city, he was glad he left when he did. His stomach churned as he thought about what would have happened if the Asaszi had raided the city while he had been there. No one would have recognized him. It's entirely possible that he would have been slaughtered without a thought.

Will Lisanthir be safe? A large knot wedged itself in Seth's throat, and he found it difficult to breathe. He needed air. He needed water. *I need to know that Lisanthir will be safe.*

But he would never know.

Seth wanted to lash out and scream. He wanted to demand that they avoid doing any harm to the tall, black-haired Elviri with glimmering green eyes.

"I'm happy I met you, Calydrian."

Guilt threatened to consume him whole. Even though he wouldn't be marching with Astohi and the soldiers, he felt like he had condemned Lisanthir to death. His heart ached.

363

"Lord Amiasss, after the feassst I would like to meet with you." Szatisi's raspy voice slithered into Seth's mind and banished away the mental fog.

He was back at the dinner table again, his fingers touching the stem of his wine goblet. There was a slight tremor in his pinky and ring finger. To mask it, he grabbed the cup with a tight fist and raised it to his lips, forcing down a small gulp of wine.

"There are... important mattersss to dissscussss," the high priestess said, her eyes darting between Octavia, Amias, and Osza.

Amias looked at the priestess from over the rim of his own goblet. He savored his sip and then placed the goblet back on the table. "Of course, High Priestess. We will adjourn to my study."

The rest of the meal carried on in silence, but Seth hardly noticed. His own thoughts were screaming inside his head. Lisanthir was in danger. Szatisi knew *something* and would be telling Amias what she knew. Octavia was also clearly hiding something. His stomach ached from all the paranoia.

He managed to choke down some of the more mild-tasting vegetables and two more cups of wine. His cheeks and throat had warmed considerably, and he had a difficult time focusing his eyes on anything in front of him. Seth hunched over his plate to minimize the distance the food had to go before it made it into his mouth. The wine goblet sat to his left, on level with his chin so that all he had to do was tip it a little to take a drink.

A raucous scraping filled the air as everyone around the table stood. Seth strained to raise his eyes from his plate, watching with hazy vision as Osza and Astohi exited the room with their escort. After, Amias crossed the room and left with Szatisi. That left Seth's mother and Octavia standing, and himself, inebriated and nearly folded over onto the table. He heard quiet murmurs but couldn't quite make out the words.

Suddenly his wheeled chair was beside him, and Octavia leaned over to pick Seth up and move him. He tried to relax his body to make it easier for her, but he felt the tension in her muscles as she strained to lift him.

"You'll be doing this as his steward," Octavia grumbled to someone standing nearby.

Seth squinted, his eyes landing on the soldier with the helmet. *Is this one going to become a steward? Bah. I don't care.*

He must have made a noise out loud because both his mother and sister were turned toward him with curious expressions.

Octavia looked to the stewards hovering against the wall and said, "Come, let us take my brother back to his chamber."

Now properly seated in his wheeled chair, one of the stewards pulled it back and began navigating it toward the exit of the room. Seth didn't recall much else about the evening, only that even being drunk he could still feel his anxiety eating away at his stomach.

Lisanthir's in danger and there's nothing I can do to save him. His imagination got the better of him and he was overwhelmed with images of Asaszi and Provira forces overrunning Lithalyon. Aelrindel on fire. *Those poor people. What if I had told them who I was? Could I have prevented all of this?* He felt like he needed to retch. Perhaps he already had. He could no longer tell, being in a state somewhere between consciousness and unconsciousness.

The door to his room opened with a loud groan and it startled Seth awake. He sat up, his heart beating rapidly. His vision swirled for a moment as he oriented himself. Two stewards entered covered from head to toe and began shuffling around his room, gathering clothes he'd need for the day. Seth inwardly grumbled and hauled himself to the edge of the bed. Although it didn't happen frequently, Seth wasn't unaccustomed to the stewards waking him in this manner. It was his father's doing, and it meant he had something he wanted to show everyone right away. It was only in these circumstances that the stewards would enter his room and dress him to get to the experiment chamber quickly. To be late to a showing would mean punishment.

The two stewards lifted Seth up and changed him out of his bedclothes into a modest blue robe and pants. As they finished dressing him, a third covered steward came in, their steps a little uncertain and nowhere near the pace of the other two. The two stewards handed Seth over to the third as if he were a limp doll. He gritted his teeth as his sore muscles awoke and started screaming under the stewards' touch.

The third steward was surprisingly gentle when they took him into their arms. They eased him into his wheelchair, their hands lingering on his sides for a few moments before standing up straight. Seth had never felt that kind of warm touch from anyone besides his mother and sister.

And Lisanthir.

A knot swelled up in his throat and he forced himself to blink away the tears that suddenly appeared in his eyes. The gentle steward went behind his chair and pushed it along. There was no time to waste, after all. Amias had summoned them.

It seemed like the entire pyramid was in the experiment chamber that morning—and on the floor, much to Seth's surprise. Normally the audience would have been standing on the balconies. He spared a glance upward and noticed it was mainly guards stationed along the balcony. *Odd. Why are there so many guards here today? Amias's announcements are never paired with forces like this.* The residents of the pyramid, Asaszi and Provira upper class, murmured quietly to one another. They all faced a platform in the center of the room, the same one that Octavia had been mutilated on. Seth's stomach churned.

His stewards escorted him to the front of the crowd, just a few steps away from the platform. Amias stood on top of it, flanked by two of his guards. Seth searched his father's face for any clues as to what was going on, but Amias was as neutral as the stones of the pyramid. Seth turned and saw Astohi and Osza sitting on another platform, surrounded by their own guards as well.

A hand gently grabbed Seth's shoulder, and he spun around. His mother stood beside him with Octavia. The three of them shared looks of comfort and confusion, although they said nothing to each other. They had no time to.

Szatisi joined Amias on the platform. Amias gave the cue to his guards to begin beating on their shields, and they were joined by the other guards in the room. The sound was deafening, and everyone became very still and quiet.

"My kinsmen," Amias said with resounding authority, "it pains me to greet you all this way, when we are on the cusp of victory." His eyes scanned the room before him.

What's he searching for?

As Amias's gaze passed over Seth, he felt as if a layer of his skin was peeled back. He couldn't suppress the shiver running down his spine. His mother's hand tightened her grip on his shoulder. He had nearly forgotten she was standing beside him.

"It has been brought to my attention that blasphemy has spread amongst us." Amias waved a hand at Szatisi before continuing. "Our most esteemed High Priestess has informed me of a robbery of her sanctified chambers. A potion, meant for restoring my son's legs, was stolen."

Quiet murmurs and gasps rippled throughout the room. Amias's piercing gaze once more landed on Seth, and he wanted nothing more than to melt into the floor. Szatisi found out, and she had told Amias. Seth wondered what cruel fate his father had devised for him. As he met his father's gaze he wished only for a quick, sudden end.

"My boy may never walk again," Amias continued, looking back out over the crowd. Seth didn't dare hope that he was wrong, that Amias was still in the dark over what had happened. "As if this offense against my family wasn't bad enough, it has been revealed that Elviri propaganda has infiltrated my wife's library."

He found the books?

Panic set in, but he couldn't allow himself to show it. He forced himself to slowly look over at his mother, her hand ironclad on his shoulder. She revealed nothing on her face, but the pain in his shoulder was enough of an indicator that she was just as frightened as he was.

"It would seem that someone is trying to sabotage my family and try to rob us of our glory." Amias's voice boomed through the chamber. "This will *not* be tolerated. Not after everything I have done to ensure the *survival*, the... the *victory* that is at hand." Seth noticed Amias's shoulders beginning to slump. His demeanor felt off. Wrong.

He was lapsing.

The room was no longer safe. Seth looked around at the soldiers along the balconies. Some had crossbows, which he hadn't seen before. He also noticed that some spellsingers had appeared amidst their ranks. He could just barely make out the movement of their mouths. Something bad was about to happen. *Surely Amias isn't about to harm this entire room of people? He's cruel, but not* that *cruel.*

"I will give… one chance… for this traitorous bastard to step forward," Amias rasped, his face twisted into a nasty snarl. "And if he isn't revealed to me, I will find him by force."

He raised his hands to the balconies just as the spellsingers raised their own voices. Their songs burrowed deep into Seth's head and heart, twisting everything until it felt wrong. The weight of his hands on his armrests was wrong. His head tilted wrongly to the side. Breathing was *wrong.*

Amias was going to kill them all.

Seth parted his lips, his heart pounding furiously, but no sound came out. Not with those horrid sorcerers singing. His mouth went dry. His heart was in his throat, his temples. He could vaguely make out other people beginning to panic and notice how wrong everything was. No one made a sound.

Perhaps I should just confess?

Perhaps Amias wouldn't take out his full fury and wrath upon me.

Would Amias forgive his only son?

"It was me, Amias."

Seth hadn't even noticed that his mother was no longer digging her nails into his shoulder, nor that she had left his side.

Now she stood at the foot of the platform, looking up at Amias. The crazed man lowered his hands and looked down at his wife, tilting his head ever so slightly. Seth thought he saw him mouth his mother's name, but he couldn't be certain.

"I took the potion. And the books are mine."

Seth managed to tear his eyes away from his mother, turning to look at Octavia. Upon her face was a look of sheer horror. She wasn't even trying to mask it.

Surely Amias wouldn't harm his own wife?

Octavia's eyes met Seth's.

"Guards," came Amias's quiet command from the platform.

The two flanking guards descended on Seth's mother without a second thought. They hauled her onto the platform, each with an iron grip on her upper arms. She didn't struggle. Amias approached his wife, reaching out to gently touch her cheek.

Seth's heart was in his throat, his hands gripping his chair so tightly that his knuckles were white.

"I suppose it was only a matter of time before you turned out like your bitch mother," Amias crooned, pushing her face away from his. He turned to face the Asaszi priestess. "Szatisi, I give you this sacrifice in the name of the *Tserys*."

Seth's eyes were wide with fear. The Asaszi bowed her head and gracefully crossed the platform to his mother. She reached out and forced Evelyn's head to the side, and then unhinged her jaw and bit into her neck. Evelyn let out a bloodcurdling screech and fell silent as Szatisi ripped half of her throat out. Deafening silence fell across the room, no one daring to speak or breathe. Szatisi cradled the mangled piece of flesh in her hands, coating them with blood before approaching Amias with an outstretched hand. He bowed his head and closed his eyes as she gently dragged her fingers from his forehead to his chin, painting a grotesque mask on his face. Szatisi leaned her head back and let out a garbled wail that chilled Seth down to the bone.

Amias stood up straight and opened his eyes once more. For a moment it looked as if his irises were black.

ACKNOWLEDGEMENTS

This book has been over 15 years in the making, and there's no shortage of people I want to thank for helping me see this project over the finish line. First and foremost, thank you to my partner Tyler for sticking with me for the past ten years and keeping me grounded while I daydream about my fantasy worlds. I don't think I would have been able to finish this book without his support. Another big thank-you goes to my editor, Katie. She helped me sculpt my work so that my story shines through in all its glory. Thank you to Mel, who gave me all the best advice a new author could use. Thank you, too, to my parents for giving me both personal and professional support in writing and publishing this book. I also want to thank my kinmates from Lord of the Rings Online, both old and new. So many members of Honor's Blood have shaped this book and given their voices to these characters and helped with proofreading this book. Most importantly, though, thank *you*, the reader, for picking up this book and supporting a new author find their voice and bring their creations to life.

About the Author

Jay Olsen-Thrift holds many titles: Project Manager, Raid Leader, Business Wizard, and Content Creator.

I have been building worlds and telling stories since I was a child. I write across many mediums: novels, short stories, screenplays, and stage plays. I have a bachelor's degree in software engineering with a minor in professional writing. I earned my master's degree in business administration in May 2024. When I'm not working or writing, I can be found online leading raids in Lord of the Rings Online or tending to my farm in Stardew Valley.

Made in the USA
Middletown, DE
11 September 2024